D1076748

Dear Reader,

Wow! It's time to savor another Westmoreland. I actually felt the heat between Micah and Kalina while writing their story.

Feeling the Heat is a story of misunderstanding and betrayal. Kalina thinks Micah is the one man who broke her heart. A man she could never love again. Micah believes if Kalina really knew him she would know he could never cause her pain. So he is determined that she get to know the real Micah Westmoreland. He also intends to prove that when a Westmoreland wants something—or someone—he will stop at nothing to get it, and Micah Westmoreland wants Kalina Daniels back in his life.

Relax and enjoy Micah and Kalina's story. And with every Brenda Jackson book it is suggested that you have a cold drink ready. Be prepared to feel the heat!

Happy reading!

Brenda Jackson

FEELING THE HEAT

BY
BRENDA JACKSON

Published in Great Britain 2012
by Mills & Boon, an imprint of Harlequin (UK) Limited,
Eton House, 18-24 Paradise Road, Richmond, Surrey TW9 1SR

ISBN: 978 0 263 89205 5
ebook ISBN: 978 1 408 97776 7

51-0812

Harlequin (UK) policy is to use papers that are natural, renewable and recyclable products and made from wood grown in sustainable forests. The logging and manufacturing processes conform to the legal environmental regulations of the country of origin.

Printed and bound in Spain
by Blackprint CPI, Barcelona

Brenda Jackson is a die "heart" romantic who married her childhood sweetheart and still proudly wears the "going steady" ring he gave her when she was fifteen. Because she believes in the power of love, Brenda's stories always have happy endings. In her real-life love story, Brenda and her husband of thirty-eight years live in Jacksonville, Florida, and have two sons.

A New York Times bestselling author of more than seventy-five romance titles, Brenda is a recent retiree who now divides her time between family, writing and traveling with Gerald. You may write Brenda at PO Box 28267, Jacksonville, Florida 32226, USA, by e-mail at WriterBJackson@aol.com or visit her website at www.brendajackson.net.

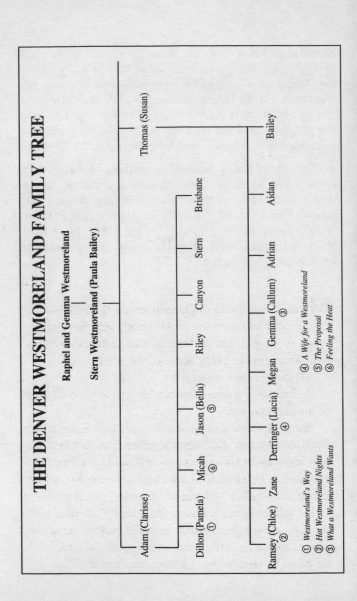

THE DENVER WESTMORELAND FAMILY TREE

Raphel and Gemma Westmoreland

Stern Westmoreland (Paula Bailey)

Thomas (Susan)

Adam (Clarisse)

Dillon (Pamela) ①

Micah ⑥   Jason (Bella) ⑤   Riley   Canyon   Stern   Brisbane

Ramsey (Chloe) ②   Zane   Derringer (Lucia) ④   Megan   Gemma (Callum) ③   Adrian   Aidan   Bailey

① Westmoreland's Way
② Hot Westmoreland Nights
③ What a Westmoreland Wants

④ A Wife for a Westmoreland
⑤ The Proposal
⑥ Feeling the Heat

One

Micah Westmoreland glanced across the ballroom at the woman just arriving and immediately felt a tightening in his gut. Kalina Daniels was undeniably beautiful, sensuous in every sense of the word.

He desperately wanted her.

A shadow of a smile touched his lips as he took a sip of his champagne.

But if he knew Kalina, and he *did* know Kalina, she despised him and still hadn't forgiven him for what had torn them apart two years ago. It would be a freezing-cold day in hell before she let him get near her, which meant sharing her bed again was out of the question.

He inhaled deeply and could swear that even with the distance separating them he could pick up her scent, a memory he couldn't seem to let go of. Nor could he let go of the memories of the time they'd shared together while in Australia. And there had been many. Even now, it didn't take much to recall the whisper of her breath on him just seconds before her mouth—

"Haven't you learned your lesson yet, Micah?"

He frowned and shot the man standing across from him a narrowed look. Evidently his best friend, Beau Smallwood, was also aware of Kalina's entry, and Beau, more than anyone, knew their history.

Micah took a sip of his drink and sat back on his heels. "Should I have?"

Beau merely smiled. "Yes, if you haven't, then you should. Need I remind you that I was there that night when Kalina ended up telling you to go to hell and not to talk to her ever again?"

Micah flinched, remembering that night, as well. Beau was right. After Kalina had overheard what she'd assumed to be the truth, she'd told him to kiss off in several languages. She was fluent in so damn many. The words might have sounded foreign, but the meaning had been crystal clear. She didn't want to see him again. Ever. With the way she'd reacted, she could have made that point to a deaf person.

"No, you don't need to remind me of anything." He wondered what she would say when she saw him tonight. Had she actually thought he wouldn't come? After all, this ceremony was to honor all medical personnel who worked for the federal government. As epidemiologists working for the Centers for Disease Control, they both fell within that category.

Knowing how her mind worked, he suspected she probably figured he wouldn't come. That he would be reluctant to face her. She thought the worst about him and had believed what her father had told her. Initially, her believing such a thing had pissed him off—until he'd accepted that given the set of circumstances, not to mention how well her father had played them both for fools, there was no way she could not believe it.

A part of him wished he could claim that she should have known him better, but even now he couldn't make that assertion. From the beginning, he'd made it perfectly clear to her, as he'd done with all women, that he wasn't interested in a serious relationship. Since Kalina was as into her career as he'd been into his, his suggestion of a no-strings affair hadn't bothered her at all and she'd agreed to the affair knowing it wasn't long-term.

At the time, he'd had no way of knowing that she would eventually get under his skin in a way that, even now, he found hard to accept. He hadn't been prepared for the serious turn their affair had taken until it had been too late. By then her father had already deliberately lied to save his own skin.

"Well, she hasn't seen you yet, and I prefer not being around when she does. I do remember Kalina's hostility toward you even if you don't," Beau said, snagging a glass of champagne from the tray of a passing waiter. "And with that said, I'm out of here." He then quickly walked to the other side of the room.

Micah watched Beau's retreating back before turning his attention to his glass, staring down at the bubbly liquid. Moments later, he sighed in frustration and glanced up in time to see Kalina cross the room. He couldn't help noticing he wasn't the only man watching her. That didn't surprise him.

One thing he could say, no matter what function she attended, whether it was in the finest restaurant in England or in a little hole in the wall in South Africa, she carried herself with grace, dignity and style. That kind of presence wasn't a necessity for her profession. But she made it one.

It had been clear to him the first time he'd met her— that night three years ago when her father, General Neil Daniels, had introduced them at a military function here in D.C.—that he and Kalina shared an intense attraction that had foretold a heated connection. What had surprised him was that she had captivated him without even trying.

She hadn't made things easy for him. In fact, to his way of thinking, she'd deliberately made things downright difficult. He'd figured he could handle just about anything. But when he'd later run into her in Sydney, she'd almost proven him wrong.

They'd been miles away from home, working together while trying to keep a deadly virus from spreading. He hadn't been ready to settle down. While he didn't consider himself a player in the same vein as some of his brothers and cousins, women had shifted in and out of his life with frequency once they saw he had no intention of putting a ring on anyone's finger. And he enjoyed traveling and seeing the world. He had a huge spread back in Denver just waiting for the day he was ready to retire, but he didn't see that happening for many years to come. His career as an epidemiologist was important to him.

But those two months he'd been involved with Kalina he had actually thought about settling down on his one hundred acres and doing nothing but enjoying a life with her. At one point, such thoughts would have scared the hell out of him, but with Kalina, he'd accepted that they couldn't be helped. Spending time with a woman like her would make any man think about tying his life with one woman and not sowing any more wild oats.

When he'd met the Daniels family, he'd known immediately that the father was controlling and the daughter was determined not to be controlled. Kalina was a woman who liked her independence. Wanted it. And she was determined to demand it—whether her father went along with it or not.

In a way, Micah understood. After all, he had come from a big family and although he didn't have any sisters, he did have three younger female cousins. Megan and Gemma hadn't been so bad. They'd made good decisions and stayed out of trouble while growing up. But the youngest female Westmoreland, Bailey, had been out of control while following around her younger hellion brothers, the twins Aidan and Adrian, as well as Micah's baby brother, Bane. The four of them had done a number of dumb things while in their teens, earning a not-so-nice reputation in Denver. That had been years ago. Now, thank God, the twins and Bailey were in college and Bane had graduated from the naval academy and was pursuing his dream of becoming a SEAL.

His thoughts shifted back to Kalina. She was a woman who refused to be pampered, although her father was determined to pamper her anyway. Micah could understand a man wanting to look out for his daughter, wanting to protect her. But sometimes a parent could go too far.

When General Daniels had approached Micah about doing something to keep Kalina out of China, he hadn't gone along with the man. What had happened between him and Kalina had happened on its own and hadn't been motivated by any request of her father's, although she now thought otherwise. Their affair had been one of those things that just happened. They had been attracted to each other from the first. So why she would assume he'd had ulterior motives to seek an affair was beyond him.

Kalina was smart, intelligent and beautiful. She possessed the most exquisite pair of whiskey-colored eyes, which made her honey-brown skin appear radiant. And the lights in the room seemed to highlight her shoulder-length brown hair and show its luxuriance. The overall picture she presented would make any male unashamedly aware of his sexuality. As he took another sip of his drink and glanced across the room, he thought she looked just as gorgeous as she had on their last date together, when they had returned to the States. It had been here in this very city, where they'd met, when their life together had ended after she discovered what she thought was the truth. To this day, he doubted he would ever forgive her father for distorting the facts and setting him up the way he had.

Micah sighed deeply and took the last sip of his drink, emptying his glass completely. It was time to step out of the shadows and right into the line of fire. And he hoped like hell that he survived it.

Micah was here.

The smile on Kalina's face froze as a shiver of awareness coursed through her and a piercing throb hit her right between the legs. She wasn't surprised at her body's familiar reaction where he was concerned, just annoyed. The man had that sort of effect on her and even after all this time the wow factor hadn't diminished.

It was hard to believe it had been two years since she had found out the truth, that their affair in Australia had been orchestrated by her father to keep her out of Beijing. Finding out had hurt—it still did—but what Micah had done had only reinforced her belief that men couldn't be trusted. Not her father, not Micah, not any of them.

And especially not the man standing in front of her with the glib tongue, weaving tales of his adventures in the Middle East and beyond. If Major Brian Rose thought he was impressing her, he was wrong. As a military brat, no one had traveled the globe as much as she had. But he was handsome enough, and looked so darn dashing in his formal military attire, he was keeping her a little bit interested.

Of course, she knew that wherever Micah was standing he would look even more breathtaking than Major Rose. The women in attendance had probably all held their breath when he'd walked into the room. As far as she was concerned, there wasn't any man alive who could hold a candle to him, in or out of clothes. That conclusion reminded her of when they'd met, almost three years ago, at a D.C. event similar to this one.

Her father had been honored that night as a commissioned officer. She'd had her own reason to celebrate in the nation's capital. She had finally finished medical school and accepted an assignment to work as a civilian for the federal government's infectious-disease research team.

It hadn't taken her long to hear the whispers about the drop-dead-gorgeous and handsome-as-sin Dr.

Micah Westmoreland, who had graduated from Harvard Medical School before coming to work for the government as an infectious-disease specialist. But nothing could have prepared her for coming face-to-face with him.

She had been rendered speechless. Gathering the absolute last of her feminine dignity, she had picked up her jaw, which had fallen to the floor, and regained her common sense by the time her father had finished the introductions.

When Micah had acknowledged her presence, in a voice that had been too sexy to belong to a real man, she'd known she was a goner. And when he had taken her smaller hand in his in a handshake, it had been the most sensuous gesture she'd ever experienced. His touch alone had sent shivers up and down her spine and put her entire body in a tailspin. She had found it simply embarrassing to know any man could get her so aroused, and without even putting forth much effort.

"So, Dr. Daniels, where is your next assignment taking you?"

She was jerked out of her thoughts by the major's question. Was that mockery she'd heard in his voice? She was well aware of the rumor floating around that her father pretty much used his position to control her destinations and would do anything within his power to keep her out of harm's way. That meant she would never be able to go anyplace where there was some real action.

She'd been trying to get to Afghanistan for two years and her request was always denied, saying she was needed elsewhere. Although her father swore up and down he had nothing to do with it, she knew better.

Losing her mother had been hard on him, and he was determined not to lose his only child, as well. Hadn't he proven just how far he would go when he'd gotten Micah to have that affair with her just to keep her out of Beijing during the bird-flu epidemic?

"I haven't been given an assignment yet. In fact, I've decided to take some time off, an entire month, starting tomorrow."

The man's smile widened. "Really, now, isn't that a coincidence. I've decided to take some time off, too, but I have only fourteen days. Anywhere in particular that you're going? Maybe we can go there together."

The man definitely didn't believe in wasting time, Kalina thought. She was just about to tell the major, in no uncertain terms, that they wouldn't be spending any time together, not even if her life depended on it, when Brian glanced beyond her shoulder and frowned. Suddenly, her heart kicked up several beats. She didn't have to imagine why. Other men saw Micah as a threat to their playerhood since women usually drooled when he was around. She had drooled the first time *she'd* seen him.

Kalina refused to turn around, but couldn't stop her body's response when Micah stepped into her line of vision, all but capsizing it like a turbulent wave on a blast of sensual air.

"Good evening, Major Rose," he said with a hard edge to his voice, one that Kalina immediately picked up on. The two men exchanged strained greetings, and she watched how Micah eyed Major Rose with cool appraisal before turning his full attention to her. The hard lines on his face softened when he asked, "And how have you been, Kalina?"

She doubted that he really cared. She wasn't surprised he was at this function, but she *was* surprised he had deliberately sought her out, and there was no doubt in her mind he'd done so. Any other man who'd done what he had done would be avoiding her like the plague. But not Dr. Micah Westmoreland. The man had courage of steel, but in this case he had just used it foolishly. He was depending on her cultured upbringing to stop her from making a scene, and he was right about her. She had too much pride and dignity to cause a commotion tonight, although she'd gone off on him the last time they had seen each other. She still intended to let him know exactly how she felt by cutting him to the core, letting it be obvious that he was the last person she wanted to be around.

"I'm fine, and now if you gentlemen will excuse me, I'll continue to make my rounds. I just arrived, and there are a number of others I want to say hello to."

She needed to get away from Micah, and quick. He looked stunning in his tux, which was probably why so many women in the room were straining their necks to get a glimpse of him. Even her legs were shaky from being this close to him. She suddenly felt hot, and the cold champagne she'd taken a sip of wasn't relieving the slow burn gathering in her throat.

"I plan to mingle, myself," Micah said, reaching out and taking her arm. "I might as well join you since there's a matter we need to discuss."

She fought the urge to glare up at him and tell him they had nothing to discuss. She didn't want to snatch her arm away from him because they were already getting attention, probably from those who'd heard what happened between them two years ago. Unfortunately, the gossip mill was alive and well, especially when it came to Micah Westmoreland. She had heard about him long before she'd met him. It wasn't that he'd been the type of man who'd gone around hitting on women. The problem was that women just tended to place him on their wish list.

"Fine, let's talk," she said, deciding that if Micah thought he was up to such a thing with her, then she was ready.

Fighting her intense desire to smack that grin right off his face, she glanced over at Major Rose and smiled apologetically. "If you will excuse me, it seems Dr. Westmoreland and I have a few things to discuss. And I haven't decided just where I'll be going on vacation, but I'll let you know. I think it would be fun if you were to join me." She ignored the feel of Micah's hand tightening on her arm.

Major Rose nodded and gave her a rakish look. "Wonderful. I will await word on your plans, Kalina."

Before she could respond, Micah's hand tightened on her arm even more as he led her away.

"Don't count on Major Rose joining you anywhere," Micah all but growled, leaning close to Kalina's ear while leading her across the ballroom floor toward an exit. He had checked earlier and the French doors opened onto the outside garden. It was massive and far away from the ball, so no one could hear the dressing-down he was certain Kalina was about to give him.

She glared at him. "And don't count on him doing otherwise. You don't own me, Micah. Last I looked, there's nothing of yours on my body."

"Then look again, sweetheart. Everything of mine

is written all over that body of yours. I branded you. Nothing has changed."

They came to a stop in front of what was the hotel's replica of the White House's prized rose garden. He was glad no one was around. No prying eyes or over-eager ears. The last time she'd had her say he hadn't managed to get in a single word for dodging all the insults and accusations she'd been throwing at him. That wouldn't be the case this time. He had a lot to say and he intended for her to hear all of it.

"Nothing's changed? How dare you impose your presence on me after what you did," she snarled, transforming from a sophisticated lady to a roaring lioness. He liked seeing her shed all that formality and cultural adeptness and get downright nasty. He especially liked that alteration in the bedroom.

He crossed his arms over his chest. "And what exactly did I do, other than to spend two months of what I consider the best time of my life with you, Kalina?"

He watched her stiffen her spine when she said, "And I'm supposed to believe that? Are you going to stand here and lie to my face, Micah? Deny that you weren't in cahoots with my father to keep me away from Beijing, using any means necessary? I wasn't needed in Sydney."

"I don't deny that I fully agreed with your father that Beijing was the last place you needed to be, but I never agreed to keep you out of China."

He could tell she didn't want to hear the truth. She'd heard it all before but still refused to listen. Or to believe it. "And it wasn't that you weren't needed in Sydney," he added, remembering how they'd been sent there to combat the possible outbreak of a deadly virus.

"You and I worked hard to keep the bird-flu epidemic from spreading to Australia, so it wasn't just sex, sex and more sex for us, Kalina. We worked our asses off, or have you forgotten?"

He knew his statement threw her for a second, made her remember. Yes, they might have shared a bed every night for those two months, but their daytime hours weren't all fun and games. No one except certain members of the Australian government had been aware that their presence in the country had been for anything other than pleasure.

And regardless of what she'd thought, she had been needed there. He had needed her. They had worked well together and had combated a contagious disease. He had already spent a year in Beijing and had needed to leave when his time was up. Depression had started to set in with the sight of people dying right before his eyes, mostly children. It had been so frustrating to work nonstop trying unsuccessfully to find a cure before things could get worse.

Kalina had wanted to go to Beijing and get right in the thick of things. He could just imagine how she would have operated. She was not only a great epidemiologist, she was also a compassionate one, especially when there was any type of outbreak. He could see her getting attached to the people—especially the children—to the point where she would have put their well-being before her own.

That, and that alone, was the reason he had agreed with her father, but at no time had he plotted to have an affair with her to keep her in Sydney. He was well aware that all her hostility was because she believed otherwise. And for two years he had let her think the worst, mainly because she had refused to listen to anything he had to say. It was apparent now that she was still refusing to listen.

"Have you finished talking, Micah?"

Her question brought his attention back to the present. "No, not by a long shot. But I can't say it all tonight. I need to see you tomorrow. I know you'll be in town for the next couple of days and so will I. Let's do lunch. Even better, let's spend that time together to clear things up between us."

"Clear things up between us?" Kalina sneered in an angry whisper as red-hot fury tore through her. She was convinced that Micah had lost his ever-loving mind. Did he honestly think she would want to spend a single minute in his presence? Even being here now with him was stretching her to the limit. Where was a good glass of champagne when she wanted it? Nothing would make her happier right now than to toss a whole freakin' glass full in his face.

"I think I need to explain a few things to you, Micah. There's really nothing to clear up. Evidently you think I'm a woman that a man can treat any kind of way. Well, I have news for you. I won't take it. I don't need you any more than you need me. I don't appreciate the way you and Dad manipulated things to satisfy your need to exert some kind of power over me. And I—"

"Power? Do you think that's what I was trying to do, Kalina? Exert some kind of *power* over you? Just what kind of person do you honestly think I am?"

She ignored the tinge of disappointment she heard in his voice. It was probably just an act anyway. At the end of those two months, she'd discovered just what a great actor Micah could be. When she'd found out the truth, she had dubbed him the great pretender.

Kalina lifted her chin and straightened her spine. "I think you are just like all the other men my father tried throwing at me. He says jump and you all say how high. I thought you were different and was proven wrong. You see Dad as some sort of military hero, a legend, and whatever he says is gospel. And although Micah is a book in the Bible, last time I checked, my father's name was not. I am twenty-seven and old enough to make my own decisions about what I want to do and where I want to go. And neither you nor my father have anything to say about it. Furthermore—"

The next thing she knew, she was swept off her feet and into Micah's arms. His mouth came down hard, snatching air from her lungs and whatever words she was about to say from her lips.

She struggled against him, but only for a minute. That was all the time it took for those blasted memories of how good he tasted and just how well he kissed to come crashing over her, destroying her last shred of resistance. And then she settled down and gave in to what she knew had to be pleasure of the most intense kind.

God, he had missed this, Micah thought, pulling Kalina closer into his embrace while plundering her mouth with an intensity he felt in every part of his body. She had started shooting off her mouth, accusing him of things he hadn't done. Suddenly, he'd been filled with an overwhelming urge to kiss her mouth shut. So he had.

And with the kiss came memories of how things

had been between them their last time together, before anger had set in and destroyed their happiness. Had it really been two years since he'd tasted this, the most delectable tongue any woman could possess? And the body pressed against his was like none other. A perfect fit. The way she was returning the kiss was telling him she had missed this intimate connection as much as he had.

Her accusations bothered him immensely because there was no truth to what she'd said. He, of all people, was not—and never would be—a yes-man to her father, or to anyone. Her allegations showed just how little she knew him, and he intended to remedy that. But for now, he just wanted to enjoy this.

He deepened the kiss and felt the simmer sear his flesh, heat his skin and sizzle through to his bones. Then there was that surge of desire that flashed through his veins and set off a rumble of need in his chest. He'd found this kind of effect from mouth-to-mouth contact with a woman only happened with Kalina. She was building an ache within him, one only she had the ability to soothe.

Over the past two years he'd thought he was immune to this and to her, but the moment she had walked into the ballroom tonight, he'd known that Kalina was in his blood in a way no other woman could or would ever be. Even now, his heart was knocking against his ribs and he was inwardly chanting her name.

Lulled by the gentle breeze as well as the sweetness of her mouth, he wrapped his arms around her waist as something akin to molten liquid flowed over his senses. Damn, he was feeling the heat, and it was causing his pulse to quicken and his body to become aroused in a way it hadn't in years. Two years, to be exact.

And now he wanted to make up for lost time. How could she think he had pretended the passion that always flowed through his veins whenever he held her, kissed her or made love to her? He couldn't help tunneling his fingers through her hair. He'd noticed she was wearing it differently and liked the style on her. But there was very little about Kalina Daniels that he didn't like. All of which he found hard to resist.

He deepened the kiss even more when it was obvious she was just as taken, just as aroused and just as needy as he was. She could deny some things, but she couldn't deny this. Oh, she was mad at him and that was apparent. But it was also evident that all her anger had transformed to passion so thick that the need to make love to her was clawing at him, deep.

Conversation between an approaching couple had Kalina quickly pulling out of his arms. All it took was one look in her eyes beneath the softly lit lanterns to see the kiss had fired her up.

He leaned in, bringing his lips close to hers. "You are wrong about me, Kal. I never sold out to your father. I'm my own man. No one tells me what to do. If you believe otherwise, then you don't really know me."

He saw something flicker in her eyes. He also felt the tension surrounding them, the charged atmosphere, the electrified tingle making its way up his spine. Now more than ever, he was fully aware of her. Her scent. Her looks.

She was breathtaking in the sexy, one-shoulder, black cocktail dress that hugged her curves better than any race car could hug the curves at Indy. There was a sensuality about her that would make any man's pulse rise. Other men had been leery of approaching her that night in D.C. when he'd first flirted with her. After all, she was General Daniels's daughter and it was a known fact the man had placed her on a pedestal. But unlike the other men, Micah wasn't military under her father's command. He was civilian personnel who didn't have to take orders from the general.

She surprised him out of his thoughts when she leaned forward. He reached out for her only to have his hands knocked out of the way. The eyes staring at him were again flaring in anger. "I'm only going to say this once more, Micah. Stay away from me. I don't want to have anything else to do with you," she hissed, her breath fanning across his lips.

He sighed heavily. "Obviously you weren't listening, Kalina. I didn't have an affair with you because your father ordered me to. I was with you because I wanted to be. And you're going to have a hard time convincing me that you can still be upset with me after having shared a kiss like that."

"Think what you want. It doesn't matter anymore, Micah."

He intended to make it matter. "Spend tomorrow with me. Give it some thought."

"There's nothing to think about. Go use someone else."

Anger flashed through him. "I didn't use you." And then in a low husky tone, he added, "You meant a lot to me, Kalina."

Kalina swallowed. There was a time when she would have given anything to hear him say that. Even now, she wished that she could believe him, but she could not forget the look of guilt on his face when she'd stumbled across him discussing her with her father. She had stood in the shadows and listened. It hadn't been hard to put two and two together. She had fled from the party, caught a cab and returned to the hotel where she quickly packed her stuff and checked out.

Her father had been the first one she'd confronted, and he'd told her everything. How he had talked Micah into doing whatever it took to keep her in Sydney and away from Beijing. Her father claimed he'd done it for her own good, but he hadn't thought Micah would go so far as to seduce her. An affair hadn't been in their plan.

"You don't believe you meant something to me," he said again when she stood there and said nothing.

She lifted her chin. "No, I don't believe you. How can I think I meant anything to you other than a good time in bed when you explicitly told me in the very beginning that what we were sharing was a no-strings affair? And other than in the bedroom, you'd never let me get close to you. There's so much about you I don't know. Like your family, for instance. So how can you expect me to believe that I meant anything to you, Micah?"

Then, without saying another word, she turned and walked back toward the ballroom. She hoped that would be the end of it. Micah had hurt her once, and she would not let him do so again.

Two

By the time Micah got to his hotel room he was madder than hell. He slammed the door behind him. When he had returned to the ballroom, Kalina was nowhere to be found. Considering his present mood, that had been a good thing.

Now he moved across the room to toss his car keys on a table while grinding his teeth together. If she thought she'd seen the last of him then he had news for her. She was sadly mistaken. There was no way he would let her wash him off. No way and no how.

That kiss they'd shared had pretty much sealed things, whether she admitted it or not. He had not only felt her passion, he'd tasted it. She was still upset with him, but that hadn't stopped them from arousing each other. After the kiss, there had been fire in her eyes. However, the fire hadn't just come from her anger.

He stopped at a window and looked out, breathing heavily from the anger consuming him. Even at this hour the nation's capital was busy, if the number of cars on the road was anything to go by. But he didn't want to think about what anyone else was doing at the moment.

Micah rubbed his hand down his face. Okay, so Kalina had told the truth about him not letting her get too close. Thanks to an affair he'd had while in college, he'd been cautious. As a student, he'd fallen in love with a woman only to find out she'd been sleeping with one of her professors to get a better grade. The crazy thing about the situation was that she'd honestly thought he should understand and forgive her for what she'd done. He hadn't and had made up in his mind not to let another woman get close again. He hadn't shared himself emotionally with another woman since then.

But during his affair with Kalina, he had begun to let his guard down. How could she not know when their relationship had begun to change from a strictly no-strings affair to something more? Granted, there hadn't been any time for candlelight dinners, strolls in the park, flowers and such, but he had shared more with her than he had with any other woman...in the bedroom.

He drew in a deep breath and had to ask himself, "But what about outside the bedroom, man? Did you give her reason to think of anything beyond that?" He knew the answer immediately.

No, he hadn't. And she was right, he hadn't told her anything about his family and he knew why. He'd taken his college lover, Patrice, home and introduced her to the family as the woman he would one day marry. The woman who would one day have his children. She had gotten close to them. They had liked her and in the end she had betrayed them as much as she had betrayed him.

He lifted his head to stare up at the ceiling. Now he could see all his mistakes, and the first of many was letting two years go by without seeking out Kalina. He'd been well aware of what her father had told her. But he'd assumed she would eventually think things through and realize her dad hadn't been completely truthful with her. Instead, she had believed the worst. Mainly because she truly hadn't known Micah.

His BlackBerry suddenly went off. He pulled it out of his pocket and saw it was a call from home. His oldest brother, Dillon. There was only a two-year difference in their ages, and they'd always been close. Any other time he would have been excited about receiving a call from home, but not now and not tonight. However, Dillon was family, so Micah answered the call.

"Hello?"

"We haven't heard from you in a while, and I thought I would check in," Dillon said.

Micah leaned back against the wall. Because Dillon was the oldest, he had pretty much taken over things when their parents, aunt and uncle had died in a plane crash. There had been fifteen Westmorelands—nine of them under the age of sixteen—and Dillon had vowed to keep everyone together. And he had.

Micah had been in his second year of college and hadn't been around to give Dillon a hand. But Ramsey, their cousin, who was just months younger than Dillon, had pitched in to help manage things.

"I'm fine," Micah heard himself saying when in all

honesty he was anything but. He drew in a deep breath and said, "I saw Kalina tonight."

Although Dillon had never met Kalina he knew who she was. One night while home, Micah had told Dillon all about her and what had happened to tear them apart. Dillon had suggested that he contact Kalina and straighten things out, as well as admit how he felt about her. But a stubborn streak wouldn't let Micah do so. Now he wished he would have acted on his brother's advice.

"And how is she?"

Micah rubbed another hand down his face. "She still hates my guts, if that's what you want to know. Go ahead and say I told you so."

"I wouldn't do that."

No, he wouldn't. That wasn't Dillon's style, although saying so would have been justified.

"So what are you going to do, Micah?"

Micah figured the only reason Dillon was asking was because his brother knew how much Kalina meant to him…even if *she* didn't know it. And her not knowing was no one's fault but his.

"Not sure what I'm going to do because no matter what I say, she won't believe me. A part of me just wants to say forget it, I don't need the hassle, but I can't, Dil. I just can't walk away from her."

"Then don't. You've never been a quitter. The Micah Westmoreland I know goes after what he wants and has never let anyone or anything stand in his way. But if you don't want her enough to fight for her and make her see the truth, then I don't know what to tell you."

Then, as if the subject of Kalina was a closed one, Dillon promptly began talking about something else. He told Micah how their sister-in-law, Bella, was coming along in her pregnancy, and that the doctors had verified twins, both girls.

"They're the first on our side," he said. Their parents had had all boys. Seven of them.

"I know, and everyone is excited and ready for her to be born," Dillon replied. "But I don't think anyone is as ready as Jason," he said of their brother and the expectant father.

The rest of the conversation was spent with Dillon bringing Micah up to date on what was going down on the home front. His brother Jason had settled into wedded bliss and so had his cousin Derringer. Micah shook his head. He could see Jason with a wife, but for the life of him, considering how Derringer used to play the field and enjoy it immensely, the thought of him settled down with one woman was still taking some getting used to. Dillon also mentioned that Ramsey and Chloe's son would be born in a few months.

"Do you think you'll be able to be here for li'l Callum's christening?"

Micah shook his head. Now, that was another one it was hard to believe had settled down. His cousin Gemma had a husband. She used to be a real pistol where men were concerned, but it seemed that Callum Austell had changed all that. She was now living in Australia with him and their two-month-old son.

"I plan to be there," Micah heard himself saying. "In a few weeks, I'll have thirty days to kill. I leave for Bajadad the day after tomorrow and I will be there for two weeks. I'll fly home from there." Bajadad was a small and beautiful city in northern India near the Himalayan foothills.

"It will be good seeing you again."

Micah couldn't help chuckling. "You make it sound like I haven't been home in years, Dil. I was just there seven months ago for Jason's wedding reception."

"I know, but anytime you come home and we can get everyone together is good."

Micah nodded. He would agree to that, and for Gemma's baby's christening, all the Westmorelands would be there, including their cousins from Atlanta, Texas and Montana.

Moments later, Micah ended his phone conversation with Dillon. He headed for the bedroom to undress and take a shower. The question Dillon asked him rang through his head. What was he going to do about Kalina?

Just like that, he remembered the proposition she'd made to Major Rose. And as he'd told her, he had no intention of letting the man go anywhere with her.

And just how are you going to stop her? His mind taunted. *She doesn't want to have anything to do with you. Thanks to her daddy's lie, you lost her. Get over it.*

He drew in a deep breath, knowing that was the kicker. He couldn't get over it. Dillon was right. Micah was not a quitter, and it was about time he made Kalina aware of that very fact.

Micah was pulled from his thoughts when his cell phone rang again. Pulling it from his pants pocket, he saw it was an official call from the Department of Health and Human Services. "Yes, Major Harris?"

"Dr. Westmoreland, first I want to apologize for calling you so late. And secondly, I'm calling to report changes in the assignment to India."

"And what are the changes, Major?"

"You will leave tomorrow instead of Monday. And Dr. Moore's wife went into labor earlier today so he has to be pulled off the team. We're going to have to send in a replacement."

Micah headed the U.S. epidemic response team consisting of over thirty epidemiologists, so calling to let him know of any changes was the norm. "That's fine."

He was about to thank her for calling and hang up when she said, "Now I need to call Dr. Daniels. Unfortunately, her vacation has to be canceled so she can take Dr. Moore's place."

Micah's pulse rate shot up and there was a deep thumping in his chest, close to his heart. "What did you say?" he asked, to make sure he'd heard her correctly.

"I said Dr. Daniels will be Dr. Moore's replacement since she's next in line on the on-call list. Unfortunately, her vacation was supposed to start tomorrow."

"What a pity," he said, not really feeling such sympathy. What others would see as Kalina's misfortune, he saw as his blessing. This change couldn't be any better if he'd planned it himself, and he intended to make sure Kalina's canceled vacation worked to his advantage.

Of course, when she found out she would automatically think the worst. She would assume the schedule change was his idea and that he was responsible for ruining her vacation. But it wouldn't be the first time she'd falsely accused him of something.

"Good night, Dr. Westmoreland."

He couldn't help smiling, feeling as if he had a new lease on life. "Good night, Major Harris."

He clicked off the phone thinking someone upstairs

had to like him, and he definitely appreciated it. Now he would have to come up with a plan to make sure he didn't screw things up with Kalina this time.

Kalina paced her hotel room. *What was she going to do about Micah?*

She came to a stop long enough to touch her lips. She'd known letting him kiss her had been a bad move, but she hadn't been able to resist the feel of his mouth on hers. She should have been prepared for it. She'd seen the telltale signs in his eyes. He hadn't taken her off to a secluded place to talk about the weather. She'd been prepared for them to face off, have it out. And they'd done that. Then they'd ended up kissing each other senseless.

As much as she would like to do so, she couldn't place the blame solely at his feet. She had gone after his mouth just as greedily as he'd gone after hers. A rush of heat had consumed her the moment he'd stuck his tongue inside her mouth. So, okay, they were still attracted to each other. No big deal.

Kalina frowned. It *was* a big deal, especially when, even now, whirling sensations had taken over her stomach. She knew with absolute certainty that she didn't want to be attracted to Micah Westmoreland. She didn't want to have anything to do with him, period.

She glanced over at the clock and saw it was just past midnight. She was still wearing her cocktail dress, since she hadn't changed out of her clothes. She had begun pacing the moment she'd returned to her hotel room. Why was she letting him do this to her? And why was he lying, claiming he had not been in cahoots with her father when she knew differently?

Moving to the sofa, she sat down, still not ready to get undressed, because once she got in bed all she would do was dream about Micah. She leaned back in her seat, remembering the first time they'd worked together. She had arrived in Sydney, and he had been the one to pick her up from the airport. They had met a year earlier and their attraction to each other had been hot and instantaneous. It had taken less than five minutes in his presence that day to see that the heat hadn't waned any.

She would give them both credit for trying to ignore it. After all, they'd had an important job to do. And they'd made it through the first week, managing to keep their hands off each other. But the beginning of the next week had been the end of that. It had happened when they'd worked late one night, sorting out samples, dissecting birds, trying to make sure the bird flu didn't spread to the continent of Australia.

Technically, he had been her boss, since he headed the government's epidemic response team. But he'd never exerted the power of that position over her or anyone. He had treated everyone as a vital and important part of the team. Micah was a born leader and everyone easily gave him the respect he deserved.

And on that particular night, she'd given him something else. He had walked her to her hotel room, and she had invited him in. It hadn't been a smart move, but she had gotten tired of playing games. Tired of lusting after him and trying to keep her distance. They were adults and that night she'd figured they deserved to finally let go and do what adults did when they had the hots for each other.

Until that night, she'd thought the whole sex act was

overrated. Micah had proven her wrong so many times that first night that she still got a tingling sensation just remembering it. She'd assumed it was a one night-stand, but that hadn't been the case. He had invited her out to dinner the following night and provided her with the terms of a no-strings affair, if she was interested. She had been more than interested. She was dedicated to her career and hadn't wanted to get involved in a serious relationship any more than he did.

That night they had reached a mutual agreement, and from then on they'd been exclusively involved during the two months they'd remained in Sydney. She was so content with their affair that when her earlier request for an assignment to Beijing had been denied, it really hadn't bothered her.

That contentment had lasted until she'd returned to the States and discovered the truth. Not only had her father manipulated her orders, but he'd solicited Micah's help in doing whatever he had to do to make sure she was kept happy in Sydney. She had been the one left looking like a complete fool, and she doubted she would forgive either of them for what they'd done.

Thinking she'd had enough of strolling down memory lane where the hurt was too much to bear, Kalina got up from the sofa and was headed toward the bedroom to change and finally attempt to sleep, when her cell phone rang. She picked it up off the table and saw it was Major Sally Harris, the administrative coordinator responsible for Kalina's assignments. She wondered why the woman would be calling her so late at night.

Kalina flipped on the phone. "Yes, Major Harris?"

"Dr. Daniels, I regret calling you so late and I want to apologize, because I have to deliver bad news."

Kalina frowned. "And what bad news is that?"

"Dr. Moore's wife went into labor earlier today so he has to be pulled off the epidemic response team headed out for Bajadad. I know your vacation was to start tomorrow, but we need your assistance in India."

Kalina drew in a deep breath. Although she hadn't made any definite vacation plans, she had looked forward to taking time off. "How long will I be needed in Bajadad?"

"For two weeks, beginning tomorrow, and then you can resume your vacation."

She nodded. There was no need to ask if there was someone else they could call since she knew the answer to that already. The epidemic response team had thinned out over the past few years with a war going on. And since the enemy liked to engage in chemical warfare, a number of epidemiologists had been sent to work in Afghanistan and Iraq.

"Dr. Daniels?"

Resigned, she said. "Yes, of course." Not that she had a choice in the matter. She was civilian, but orders from her boss were still meant to be followed, and she couldn't rightly get mad at Jess Moore because his wife was having a baby. "I'll be ready to head out tomorrow."

"Thanks. I'll send your information to your email address," Major Harris said.

"That will be fine."

"And Dr. Westmoreland has been notified of the change in personnel."

Kalina almost dropped the phone. "Dr. Westmoreland?"

"Yes?"

She frowned. "Why was he notified?"

"Because he's the one heading up the team."

Kalina's head began spinning. No one would be so cruel as to make her work with Micah again. She drew in a deep breath when a suspicion flowed through her mind. "Was Dr. Westmoreland the one to suggest that I replace Dr. Moore?"

"No, the reason you were called is that you're the next doctor on the on-call list."

Lucky me. Kalina shook her head, feeling anything but lucky. The thought of spending two weeks around Micah had her fuming inside. And regardless of what Major Harris said, it was hard to believe it was merely a coincidence that she was next on the call list. Micah was well liked and she knew all about his numerous connections and contacts. If she found out he had something to do with this change then…

"Dr. Daniels?"

"Yes?"

"Is there anything else you'd like to know?"

"No, there's nothing else."

"Thank you, Dr. Daniels, and good night."

"Good night, Major Harris."

Kalina hung up the phone knowing she couldn't let her feelings for Micah interfere with her work. She had a job to do, and she intended to do it. She would just keep her distance from him. She went into the bedroom and began tugging off her clothes as she became lost in a mix of disturbing thoughts.

The first thing she would do would be to set ground rules between her and Micah. If he saw this as a golden opportunity to get back in her bed then he was sadly mistaken. She was not the type of woman to forgive easily. Just as she'd told him earlier tonight, there was nothing else they had to say to each other regarding what happened between them two years ago. It was over and done with.

But if that kiss was anything to go by, she would need to be on guard around him at all times. Because their relationship might be over and done with, but the attraction between them was still alive and well.

Three

Micah saw the fire in Kalina's eyes from ten feet away. She glared as she moved toward him, chin up and spine stiff. She meant business. He slid a hand into the pocket of his jeans, thinking that he was glad it was Sunday and there were few people around. It seemed they were about to have it out once again.

This morning, upon awakening, he had decided the best way to handle her was to let her assume he wasn't handling her at all, to make her think that he had accepted her decision about how things would be between them. And when he felt the time was right, he would seize every opportunity he could get and let her know in no uncertain terms that her decision hadn't been his.

His gaze swept over her now. She was dressed for travel, with her hair pulled back in a ponytail and a pair of comfortable shoes on her feet. She looked good in her jeans and tank top and lightweight jacket. But then, she looked better than any woman he knew, in clothes or out of them.

He continued to stare at her while remembering her body stretched out beneath his when he'd made love to her. Even now, he could recall how it felt to skim his hands down the front of her body, tangle his fingers in her womanly essence while kissing her with a degree of passion he hadn't been aware of until her.

His heart began racing, and he could feel the zipper of his pants getting tight. He withdrew his hands from his pockets. The last thing he needed was for her to take note of his aroused state, so he turned and entered the private office he used whenever he was in D.C. on business. Besides, he figured the best place to have the encounter he knew was coming was behind closed doors.

By the time she had entered the office, all but slamming the door behind her, he was standing behind the desk.

He met her gaze, and felt the anger she wasn't trying to hide. As much as he wanted to cross the room and pull her into his arms and kiss her, convince her how wrong she was about him, common sense dictated he stay put. He intended to do what he hadn't done two years ago. Give her the chance to get to know him. He was convinced if she'd truly known him, she would not have been so quick to believe the worst about him.

"Dr. Daniels, I take it you're ready to fly out to Bajadad."

Her gaze narrowed. "And you want me to believe you had nothing to do with those orders, Micah?"

He crossed his arms over his chest and met her stare head-on. "At this point, Kalina, you can believe whatever you like. For me to deny it wouldn't matter since you wouldn't believe me anyway."

"And why should I?" she snapped.

"Because I have no reason to lie," he said simply. "Have you ever considered the possibility that I could be telling the truth? Just in case you need to hear it from me—just like I had nothing to do with your father's plan to keep you out of Beijing, your orders to go to Bajadad were not my idea. Although I embrace the schedule change wholeheartedly. You're a good doctor, and I can't think of anyone I want more on my team. We're dealing with a suspicious virus. Five people have died already and the government suspects it might be part of something we need to nip in the bud as soon as possible. However, we won't know what we're dealing with until we get there."

He watched as her whole demeanor changed in the wake of the information he had just provided. Her stiffened spine relaxed and her features became alert. No matter what, she was a professional, and as he'd said, she was good at what she did.

"What's the point of entry?" she asked, moving to stand in front of the desk.

"So far, only by ingestion. It's been suspected that something was put in the water supply. If that's true, it will be up to us to find out what it is."

She nodded, and he knew she completely understood. The government's position was that if the enemy had developed some kind of deadly chemical then the United States needed to know about it. It was important to determine early on what they were up against and how they could protect U.S. military personnel.

"And how was it detected, Micah?" she was calm

and relaxed as she questioned him. He moved to sit on the edge of his desk. Not far from where she stood. He wondered if she'd taken note of their proximity.

He wished she wasn't wearing his favorite perfume and that he didn't remember just how dark her eyes would become in the heat of passion. Kalina Daniels was an innately sensuous woman. There was no doubt about it.

"Five otherwise healthy adults over the age of fifty were found dead within the same week with no obvious signs of trauma," he heard himself saying. "However, their tongues had enlarged to twice the normal size. Other than that, there was nothing else, not even evidence of a foreign substance in their bloodstream."

He saw the look in her eyes while she was digesting what he'd said. Most terrorist groups experimented on a small number of people before unleashing anything in full force, just to make sure their chemical warfare weapon was effective. It was too early to make an assumption about what they would be facing, but the researcher who was already there waiting on them had stated his suspicions. Before 9/11 chemical weapons were considered a poor man's atomic bomb. However, because of their ability to reach millions of people in so many different ways, these weapons were now considered the worst and most highly effective of all forms of warfare.

"Have you ever been to Bajadad?" she asked him.

He met her gaze. "Yes, several years ago, right after the first democratic elections were held. It was my first assignment after leaving college and coming to work for the federal government. We were sent there on a peace-finding mission when members of the king's household had become ill. Some suspected foul play. However, it didn't take us long to determine it hadn't been all that serious, just a contaminated sack of wheat that should never have been used."

He could tell by the look in her eyes that she'd become intrigued. That's how it had always been with her. She would ask a lot of questions to quench that curiosity of hers. She thought he'd lived an adventurous life as an epidemiologist, while, thanks to her father, she'd been deliberately kept on the sidelines.

In a way, he was surprised she was going to Bajadad. Either the old man had finally learned his lesson or he was getting lax in keeping up with his daughter's whereabouts. He knew her father had worked behind the scenes, wielding power, influencing his contacts, to make sure Kalina had assignments only in the States or in first-world countries. He'd discovered, after the fact, that her time in Sydney had been orchestrated to keep her out of Beijing without giving her a reason to get suspicious.

Micah stood and decided to shift topics. He met Kalina's gaze when he said, "I think we need to talk about last night."

He watched her spine stiffen as she once again shifted into a defensive mode. "No, we don't."

"Yes, we do Kalina. We're going out on a mission together, and I think it's going to be important that we're comfortable around each other and put our personal differences aside. I'd be the first to admit I've made a lot of mistakes where you're concerned, and I regret making them. Now you believe the worst of me and nothing I can say or do will change that."

He paused a moment, knowing he had to chose his

words carefully. "You don't have to worry about me mixing business with pleasure, because I refuse to become involved with a woman who doesn't trust me. So there can never be anything between us again."

There, he'd said it. He tasted the lie on his tongue, but knew his reasons for his concocted statement were justified. He had no intention of giving her up. Ever. But she had to learn to trust him. And he would do whatever he had to do to make that happen.

Although she tried to shelter her reaction, he'd seen how his words had jolted her body. There was no doubt in his mind she had felt the depth of what he'd said. A part of him wanted to believe that deep down she still cared for him.

She lifted her chin in a stubborn frown. "Good. I'm glad we got that out of the way and that we understand each other."

He glanced down at his watch. "Our flight leaves in a few hours. I would offer you a ride to the airport, but I'm catching a ride with someone myself."

She tilted her head back and looked at him. "No problem. I reserved a rental car."

Kalina looked at her own watch and slipped the straps of her purse onto her shoulders. "I need to be going."

"I'll walk out with you," he said, falling into step beside her. He had no problem offering her a ride if she needed one, but he hadn't wanted to appear too anxious to be in her company. "We're looking at a twelve-hour flight. I'd advise you to eat well before we fly out. The food we're going to be served on the plane won't be the best."

She chuckled and the sound did something to him. It felt good to be walking beside her. "Don't think I don't know about military-airplane food. I'm going to stop and grab me a sandwich from Po'Boys," she said.

He knew she regretted mentioning the restaurant when he glanced over and saw the blush on her face. Chances were, like him, she was remembering the last time they'd gone there together. It had been their first night back in the States after Australia. He might not recall what all they'd eaten that night, but he did remember everything they'd done in the hotel room afterward.

"Whatever you get, eat enough for the both of us," he said, breaking the silence between them.

She glanced over at him. "I will."

They were now outside, standing on the top steps of the Centers for Disease Control. "Well, I guess I'll be seeing you on the flight. Take care until then, Kal."

Then, without looking back, he moved to the car that pulled up to the curb at that very moment. He smiled, thinking the timing was perfect when he saw who was driving the car.

He glanced up at the sky. He had a feeling someone up there was definitely on his side. His cousin, Senator Reggie Westmoreland, had called him that morning, inviting him to lunch. Reggie, his wife, Olivia, and their one-year-old twin sons made Washington their home for part of the year. It was Olivia and not Reggie who'd come to pick him up to take him to their house in Georgetown. She was a beautiful woman, and he could just imagine the thoughts going through Kalina's mind right now.

* * *

Kalina stood and watched Micah stroll down the steps toward the waiting car. He looked good in a chambray shirt that showed the width of his broad shoulders and jeans that hugged his masculine thighs, making her appreciate what a fine specimen of a man he was.

He worked out regularly and it showed. No matter from what angle you saw him—front, back or side— one looked just as good as the other. And from the side-glances of several women who were climbing the steps and passing by him as he moved down, she was reminded again that she wasn't the only one who appreciated that fact.

Oh, why did he have to call her Kal? It was the nickname he'd given her during their affair. No one else called her that. Her father detested nicknames and always referred to her by her first and middle name. To her dad she was Kalina Marie.

She tried not to show any emotion as she watched a woman get out of the car, smiling brightly while moving toward Micah. She was almost in his face by the time his foot touched the last step, and he gave the woman a huge hug and a warm smile as if he was happy to see her, as well.

No wonder he's so quick to write you off, she thought in exasperated disgust, hating that seeing Micah with another woman bothered her. *He's already involved with someone else. Well, what did you expect? It's been two years. Just because you haven't been in a serious relationship since then doesn't mean he hasn't. And besides, you're the one who called things off. Accused him of being in league with your father...*

Kalina shook her head as the car, with Micah in it,

pulled off. Why was she trying to rehash anything? She knew the truth, and no matter how strenuously Micah claimed otherwise, she believed her father. Yes, he was controlling, but he loved her. He had no reason to lie. He had confessed his part and had admitted to his involvement in Micah's part, as well. So why couldn't Micah just come clean and fess up? And why had she felt a bout of jealousy when he'd hugged that woman? Why did she care that the woman was jaw-droppingly beautiful, simply gorgeous with not a hair on her head out of place?

Tightening her hand on her purse, Kalina walked down the steps toward the parking lot. She had to get a grip on more than her purse. She needed to be in complete control of her senses while dealing with Micah.

"Sorry to impose, but I think this is the only seat left on the plane," Micah said as he slid into the empty seat next to Kalina.

Her eyes had been closed as she waited for takeoff, but she immediately opened them, looking at him strangely before lifting up slightly to glance around, as if to make sure he was telling the truth.

He smiled as he buckled his seat belt. "You need to stop doing that, you know."

She arched an eyebrow. "Doing what?"

"Acting like everything coming out of my mouth is a lie."

She shrugged what he knew were beautiful shoulders. "Well, once you tell one lie, people have a tendency not to believe you in the future. Sort of like the boy who cried wolf." She then closed her eyes again as if to dismiss him.

He didn't plan to let her response be the end of it. "What's going to happen when you find out you've been wrong about me?"

She opened her eyes and glanced over at him, looking as if the thought of her being wrong was not even a possibility. "Not that I think that will happen, but if it does then I'll owe you an apology."

"And when it does happen I might just be reluctant to accept your apology." He then leaned back in his seat and closed his eyes, this time dismissing her and leaving her with something to chew on.

The flight attendant prevented further conversation between them when she came on the intercom to provide flight rules and regulations. He kept his eyes closed. Kalina's insistence that he would conspire with her father grated on a raw nerve each and every time she said it.

Moments later, he felt the movement of the plane glide down the runway before tilting as it eased into the clouds. Over the years, he'd gotten used to air travel, but that didn't mean he particularly liked it. All he had to do was recall that he had lost four vital members of his family in a plane crash. And he couldn't help remembering that tragic and deep-felt loss each and every time he boarded a plane, even after all these years.

"She's pretty."

He opened his eyes and glanced over at Kalina. "Who is?"

"That woman who picked you up from the CDC today."

He nodded. "Thanks. I happen to think she's pretty, too," he said honestly. In fact, he thought all his cousins and brothers had married beautiful women. Not only were they beautiful, they were smart, intelligent and strong.

"Have the two of you been seeing each other long?"

It would be real simple to tell her that Olivia was a relative, but he decided to let her think whatever she wanted. "No, and we really aren't seeing each other now. We're just friends," he said.

"Close friends?"

He closed his eyes again. "Yes." He had been tempted to keep his eyes open just to see her expression, but knew closing them would make his nonchalance more effective.

"How long have the two of you known each other?"

He knew she was trying to figure out if Olivia had come before or after her. "Close to five years now."

"Oh."

So far everything he'd said had been the truth. He just wasn't elaborating. It was his choice and his right. Besides, he was giving her something to think about.

Deciding she'd asked enough questions about Olivia, he said, "You might want to rest awhile. We have a long flight ahead of us."

And he intended on sharing every single hour of it with her. It wasn't a coincidence that the last seat on the military jet had been next to her and that he'd taken it. There hadn't been any assigned seats on this flight. Passengers could sit anywhere, and, with the help of the flight attendant, he'd made sure they had sat everywhere but next to Kalina. The woman just happened to know that *New York Times* bestselling author Rock Mason, aka Stone Westmoreland, was Micah's cousin. The woman was a huge fan and the promise of an autographed copy of Stone's next action thriller had gone a long way.

Micah kept his eyes closed but could still inhale Kalina's scent. He could envision her that morning, dabbing cologne all over her body, a body he'd had intimate knowledge of for two wonderful months. He was convinced he knew where every mole was located, and he was well acquainted with that star-shaped scar near her hip bone that had come as a result of her taking a tumble off a skateboard at the age of twelve.

He drew in a deep breath, taking in her scent one more time for good measure. For now, he needed to pretend he was ignoring her. Sitting here lusting after Kalina wasn't doing him any good and was just weakening his resolve to keep her at a distance while he let her get to know him. He couldn't let that happen. But he couldn't help it when he opened his eyes, turned to her and said, "Oh, by the way, Kalina. You still have the cutest dimples." He then turned to face straight ahead before closing his eyes once again.

Satisfied he might have soothed her somewhat, he stretched his long legs out in front of him, at least as far as they could go, and tilted his seat back. He might as well get as comfortable as he could for the long flight.

He'd been given a good hand to play and he planned on making the kind of win that the gambler in the family, his cousin Ian, would be proud of. The stakes were high, but Micah intended to be victorious.

So Micah had known the woman during their affair. Did that mean he'd taken back up with her after their time together had ended? Kalina wondered. He said he and the woman were only friends, but she'd known men to claim only friendship even while sleeping with a woman every night. Men tended not to place the same importance on an affair as women did. She, of all people, should know that.

And how dare he compliment her on her dimples at a time like this and in the mood she was in. She had to work with him, but she was convinced she didn't even like him anymore. Yet in all fairness, she shouldn't be surprised by the comment about her dimples. He'd told her numerous times that her dimples were the first thing he'd noticed about her. They were permanent fixtures on her face, whether she smiled or not.

And then there was the way he'd looked at her when he'd said it. Out of the clear blue sky, he had turned those gorgeous bedroom-brown eyes on her and remarked on her dimples. Her stomach had clenched. It had been so unexpected it had sent her world tilting for a minute. And before she'd recovered, he'd turned back around and closed his eyes.

Now he was reclining comfortably beside her. All man. All sexy. All Westmoreland. And seemingly all bored...at least with her. She had a good mind to wake him up and engage in some conversation just for the hell of it, but then she thought better of it. Micah Westmoreland was a complex man and just thinking about how complex he could be had tension building at her temples.

She couldn't help thinking about all the things she didn't know about him. For some reason, he'd never shared much about himself or his family. She knew he had several brothers, but that fact was something she'd discovered by accident and not because he'd told her about them. She'd just so happened to overhear a conversation between him and his good friend Dr. Beau Smallwood. And she did know his parents had died in a plane crash when he was in college. He'd only told her that because she'd asked.

Her life with her military father was basically an open book. After her mother had died of cervical cancer when Kalina was ten, her father had pretty much clung to her like a vine. The only time they were separated was when he'd been called for active duty or another assignment where she wasn't allowed. Those were the days she spent on her grandparents' farm in Alabama. Joe and Claudia Daniels had passed away years ago, but Kalina still had fond memories of the time she'd spent with them.

Kalina glanced over at Micah again. It felt strange casually sitting next to a man who'd been inside her body...numerous times. A man whose tongue had licked her in places that made her blush to think about. Someone who had taken her probably in every position known to the average man and in some he'd probably created himself. He was the type of man a woman fantasized about. A shiver raced through her body just thinking about being naked with him.

Up to now, she had come to terms with the fact that she'd be working with Micah again, especially after what he'd said in his office earlier that morning. He didn't want to become involved with her, just as she didn't want to become involved with him. So why was she tempted to reach out and trace the line of his chin with her fingers or use the tip of her tongue to glisten his lips?

Oh, by the way, you still have the cutest dimples. If those words had been meant to get next to her, they had. And she wished they hadn't. She didn't want to remember anything about the last time they were together or what sharing those two months with him had meant to her.

And she especially did not want to remember what the man had meant to her.

Having no interest in the movie currently being shown and wanting to get her mind off the man next to her, she decided to follow Micah's lead. She tilted her seat back, closed her eyes and went to sleep.

Four

Micah awakened the next morning and stretched as he glanced around his bedroom. He'd been too tired when he'd arrived at the private villa last night to take note of his surroundings, but now he couldn't help smiling. He would definitely like it here. Kalina's room was right next door to his.

He slid out of bed and headed for the bathroom, thinking the sooner he got downstairs the better. The government had set up a lab for them in the basement of the villa and, according to the report he'd read, it would be fully equipped for their needs.

Twelve hours on a plane hadn't been an ideal way to spend time with Kalina, but he had managed to retain his cool. He'd even gone so far as to engage in friendly conversation about work. Otherwise, like him, she'd slept most of the time. Once he'd found her watching

some romantic movie. Another time she'd been reading a book on one of those eReaders.

A short while after waking, Micah had dressed and
was headed downstairs for breakfast. The other doctor
on the team had arrived last week and Micah was looking forward to seeing him again. Theodus Mitchell was
a doctor he'd teamed with before, who did excellent
work in the field of contagious diseases.

Micah opened his bedroom door and walked out into
the hallway the same time Kalina did. He smiled when
he saw her, although he could tell by her expression that
she wasn't happy to see him. "Kalina. Good morning."

"Good morning, Micah. You're going down for
breakfast?"

"Yes, what about you?" he asked, falling into step
beside her.

"Yes, although I'm not all that hungry," she said.

He definitely was, and it wasn't all food that had him
feeling hungry. She looked good. Well rested. Sexy as
hell in a pair of brown slacks and a green blouse. And
she'd gotten rid of the ponytail. She was wearing her
hair down to her shoulders. The style made her features
appear even more beautiful.

"Well, I'm starving," he said as they stepped onto
the elevator. "And I'm also anxious to get to the lab to
see what we're up against. Did you get a chance to read
the report?"

She nodded as the elevator door shut behind them.
"Yes, I read it before going to bed. I wasn't all that
sleepy."

They were the only ones in the elevator and suddenly memories flooded his brain. The last time they
had been in an elevator alone she had tempted him so

much that he had ended up taking her against a wall in one hell of a quickie. Thoughts of that time fired his blood.

Now, she had moved to stand at the far side of the elevator. She was staring into space, looking as if she didn't have a care in the world. He wanted to fire her blood the way she was firing his.

The elevator stopped on the first floor and as soon as the doors swooshed open, she was out. He couldn't help chuckling to himself as he followed her, thinking she was trying to put distance between them. Evidently, although she'd pretended otherwise, she had remembered their last time in an elevator together, as well.

A buffet breakfast was set up on the patio, and the moment he walked out onto the terrace, his glance was caught by the panoramic view of the Himalayas, looming high toward a beautiful April sky.

"Theo!"

"Kalina, good seeing you again."

He turned and watched Theo and Kalina embrace, not feeling the least threatened since everyone knew just how devoted Theo was to his beautiful wife, Renee, who was an international model. Inhaling the richness of the mountain air, Micah strolled toward the pair. The last time the three of them had teamed up together on an assignment had been in Sydney. Beau had also been part of their team.

Theo released Kalina and turned to Micah and smiled. "Micah, it's good seeing you, as well. It's like old times," Theo said with a hearty handshake.

Micah wondered if Theo assumed the affair with Kalina was still ongoing since he'd been there with them in Australia when it had started. "Yes, and from what I understand we're going to be busy for the next two weeks."

Theo nodded and a serious expression appeared on his face. "So far there haven't been any more deaths and that's a good thing."

Micah agreed. "The three of us can discuss it over breakfast."

Kalina sat beside Micah and tried to unravel her tangled thoughts. But there was nothing she could do with the heat that was rushing through her at that moment. There was no way she could put a lid on it. The desire flowing within her was too thick to confine. For some reason, even amidst the conversations going on— mostly between Micah and Theo—she couldn't stop her mind from drifting and grabbing hold of memories of what she and Micah had once shared.

"So what do you think, Kalina?"

She glanced over at Micah. Had he suspected her of daydreaming when she should have been paying attention? Both men had worked as epidemiologists for a lot longer than she had and had seen and done a lot more. She had enjoyed just sitting and listening to how they analyzed things, figuring she could learn a lot from them.

Micah, Theo and another epidemiologist by the name of Beau Smallwood had begun work for the federal government right out of medical school and were good friends; especially Beau and Micah who were the best of friends.

"I think, although we can't make assumptions until we have the data to support it, I agree that the deaths are suspicious."

Micah smiled, and she tried downplaying the effect that smile had on her. She had to remind herself that smile or no smile, he was someone who couldn't be trusted. Someone who had betrayed her.

"Well, then, I think we'd better head over to the lab to find out what we're up against,' Micah said, standing.

He reached for her tray and she pulled it back. "Thanks, but I can dispense with my own trash."

He nodded. "Suit yourself."

She stood and turned to walk off, but not before hearing Theo whisper to Micah, "Um, my friend, it sounds like there's trouble in paradise."

She was tempted to turn and alert Theo to the fact that "paradise" for them ended two years ago. Shaking off the anger she felt when she thought about that time in her life and the hurt she'd felt, she continued walking toward the trash can. She'd known at the start of her affair with Micah that it would be a short-term affair. He'd made certain she understood there were no strings, and she had.

But what she couldn't accept was knowing the entire thing had been orchestrated by her controlling father. The only reason she was here in India now was because the general was probably too busy with the war in Afghanistan to check up on her whereabouts. He probably felt pretty confident she was on vacation or assigned to some cushy job in the States. Although he claimed otherwise, she knew he was the reason she hadn't been given any hard-hitting assignments. If it hadn't been for Dr. Moore's baby, chances are she wouldn't be here now.

She was about to turn, when Micah came up beside

her to toss out his own trash. "Stop being so uptight with me, Kalina."

She glanced over at him and drew in a deep breath to keep from saying something that was totally rude. Instead, she met his gaze and said, "My being uptight, Micah, should be the least of your worries." She then walked off.

Micah watched her go, admiring the sway of her hips with every step she took. His feelings for Kalina were a lot more than sexual, but he was a man, and the woman had a body that any man would appreciate.

"I see she still doesn't know how you feel about her, Micah."

Micah glanced over and saw the humor in Theo's blue gaze. There was no reason to pretend he didn't know what the man was talking about. "No, she doesn't know."

"Then don't you think you ought to tell her?"

Micah chuckled. "With Kalina it won't be that easy. I need to show her rather than tell her because she doesn't believe anything I say."

"Ouch. Sounds like you have your work cut out for you then."

Micah nodded. "I do, but in the end it will be worth it."

Kalina was fully aware of the moment Micah entered the lab. With her eyes glued to the microscope, she hadn't looked up, but she knew without a doubt he was there and that he had looked her way. It was their first full day in Bajadad, and it had taken all her control to fight the attraction, the pull, the heat between them. She had played the part of the professional and

had, hopefully, pulled it off. At least she believed Theo
hadn't picked up on anything. He was too absorbed
in the findings of today's lab reports to notice the air
around them was charged.

But *she* had noticed. Not only had she picked up on
the strong chemistry flowing between her and Micah,
she had also picked up on his tough resistance. He
would try to resist her as much as she would try to
resist him, and she saw that as a good thing.

Even if they hadn't been involved two years ago,
there was no way they would not be attracted to each
other. He was a man and she was a woman, so quite
naturally there would be a moment of awareness between them. Some things just couldn't be helped. But
hopefully, by tomorrow, that awareness would have
passed and they would be able to get down to the business they were sent here to carry out.

What if it didn't pass?

A funny feeling settled in her stomach at the thought
of that happening. But all it took was the reminder of
how he had betrayed her in the worst possible way to
keep any attraction between them from igniting into
full-blown passion.

However, she felt the need to remind herself that
her best efforts hadn't drummed up any opposition to
him when they'd been alone in the lab earlier that day.
He had stood close while she'd gone over the reports,
and she'd inhaled his scent while all kinds of conflicting emotions rammed through her. And every time
she glanced up into his too-handsome face and stared
into his turn-you-on brown eyes she could barely think
straight.

Okay, she was faced with a challenge, but it wouldn't

be the first time nor did she figure it would be the last. She'd never been a person who was quick to jump into bed with a man just for the sake of doing so, and she had surprised herself with how quickly she had agreed to an affair with Micah two years ago. She had dated in college and had slept with a couple of the guys. The sex between them hadn't been anything to write home about. She had eventually reached the conclusion that she and sex didn't work well together, which had always been just fine and dandy to her. So when she'd felt the sparks fly between her and Micah in a way she'd never felt before, she'd believed the attraction was something worth exploring.

Kalina nibbled on her bottom lip, thinking that was then, this was now. She had learned her lesson regarding Micah. They shared a chemistry that hadn't faded with time. If he thought she had the cutest dimples then she could say the same about his lips. She could imagine her tongue gliding over them for a taste, and it wouldn't be a quick one.

She shook her head. Her thoughts were really getting out of hand, and it was time to rein them back in. Today had been a busy day, filled with numerous activities and a conference call with Washington that had lasted a couple of hours. More than once, she had glanced up from her notes to find Micah staring at her. And each time their gazes connected, a wild swirl of desire would try overtaking her senses.

"Have you found anything unusual, Kalina?"

Micah's deep, husky voice broke into her thoughts, reminding her he had entered the room. Not that she'd totally forgotten. She lifted her gaze from the microscope and wished she hadn't. He looked yummy enough to eat. Literally.

He had come to stand beside her. Glancing up at him, she saw the intense concentration in his eyes seemed hot, near blazing. It only made her more aware of the deep physical chemistry radiating between them, which she was trying to ignore but finding almost impossible to do.

"I think you need to take a look at this," she said, moving aside so he could look through her microscope.

He moved in place and she studied him for a minute while he sat on the stool, absorbed in analyzing what she'd wanted him to see. Moments later, he glanced back up at her. "Granulated particles?"

"Yes, that's what they appear to be, and barely noticeable. I plan on separating them to see if I can pinpoint what they are. There's a possibility the substance entering the bloodstream wasn't a liquid like we first assumed."

He nodded, agreeing with her assumption. "Let me know what you find out."

"I will." God, she needed her head examined, but she couldn't shift her gaze away from his lips. Those oh-so-cute lips were making deep-seated feelings stir inside her and take center stage. His lips moved, and it was then she realized he had said something.

"Sorry, did you say something?" she asked, trying to regain her common sense, which seemed to have taken a tumble by the wayside.

"Yes, I said I dreamed about you last night."

She stared at him. Where had that come from? How on earth had they shifted from talking about the findings under her microscope to him having a dream about her?

"And in my dream, I touched you all over. I tasted you all over."

Her heart thudded painfully in her chest. His words left her momentarily speechless and breathless. And it didn't help matters that the tone he'd used was deep, husky and as masculine as any male voice could be. Instead of grating on her nerves, it was grating on other parts of her body. Stroking them into a sensual fever.

She drew in a deep breath and said, "I thought you were going to stay in your place, Micah."

He smiled that sexy, rich smile of his, and she felt something hot and achy take her over. Little pangs of sexual desire, and the need she'd tried ignoring for two years, expanded in full force.

"I *am* staying in my place, Kalina. But do you know what place I love most of all?"

Something told her not to ask but she did anyway. "What?"

"Deep inside you."

She wasn't sure how she remained standing. She was on wobbly legs with a heart rate that was higher than normal. She compressed her lips, shoving to the back of her mind all the things she'd like to do to his mouth. "You have no right to say something like that," she said, shaking off his words as if they were some unpleasant memory.

A crooked smile appeared on his face. "I have every right, especially since you've practically spoiled me for any other woman."

Yeah, right. Did he think she didn't remember the woman who'd picked him up yesterday at the CDC?

"And what happened to your decision not to become involved with a woman who didn't trust you?"

He chuckled. "Nothing happened. I merely mentioned to you that I dreamed about you last night. No harm's done. No real involvement there."

She frowned. He was teasing her, and she didn't like it. A man didn't tell a woman he'd dreamed about her without there being a hint of his desire for an involvement. What kind of game was Micah playing?

"Theo has already made plans for dinner. What about you?"

She answered without thinking. "No, I haven't made any plans."

"Good, then have dinner with me."

She stared at him. He was smooth, but not smooth enough. "We agreed not to become involved."

He chuckled. "Eating is not an involvement, Kalina. It's a way to feed the urges of one's body."

She didn't say anything, but she knew too well about bodily urges. Food wasn't what her body was craving.

"Having dinner with me is not a prerequisite for an affair. It's where two friends, past lovers, colleagues... however you want to describe our relationship...sit down and eat. I know this nice café not far from here. It's one I used to frequent when I was here the last time. I'd like to take you there."

Don't go, an inner voice warned. *All it will take is for you to sit across from him at a table and watch him eat.* The man had a way of moving his mouth that was so downright sensual it was a crying shame. It had taken all she had just to get through breakfast this morning.

"I don't think going out to dinner with you is a good idea," she finally said.

"And why not?"

"Mainly because you forgot to add the word *enemy* to the list to describe our relationship. I don't like you."

He simply grinned. "Well, I happen to like you a lot. And I don't consider us enemies. Besides, you're not the injured party here, I am. I'm an innocent man, falsely accused of something he didn't do."

She turned back to the microscope as she spoke. "I see things differently."

"I know you do, so why can't you go out to eat with me since nothing I say or do will change your mind? I merely invited you to dinner because I noticed you worked through lunch. But if you're afraid to be with me then I—"

"I'm not afraid to be with you."

"So you say," he said, turning to leave. Before reaching the door, he shot her a smile over his shoulder. "If you change your mind about dinner, I'll be leaving here around seven and you can meet me downstairs in the lobby."

Kalina watched him leave. She disliked him, so she wasn't sure why her hormones could respond to him the way they did. The depth of desire she felt around him was unreal. And dangerous. It only heightened the tension between them, and the thought that he wanted them to share dinner filled her with a heat she could very well do without.

The best thing for her to do was to stay in and order room service. That was the safest choice. But then, why should she be a coward? She, of all people, knew that Micah did not have a place in her life anymore. So, despite his mild flirtation—and that's what it was whether he admitted to it or not—she would not succumb. Nor would she lock herself in her room because she couldn't control her attraction to him. It was time that she learned to control her response to him. There would be other assignments when they would work together, and she needed to put their past involvement behind her once and for all.

She stood and checked her watch, deciding she would have dinner with Micah after all. But she would make sure that she was the one in control at all times.

Five

At precisely seven o'clock, Micah stepped out of the elevator hoping he hadn't overplayed his hand. When he glanced around the lobby and saw Kalina sitting on one of the sofas, he felt an incredible sense of relief. He had been prepared to dine alone if it had come to that, but he'd more than hoped that she was willing to dine with him.

He walked over to her. From the expression on her face, it was obvious she was apprehensive about them dining together, so he intended to make sure she enjoyed herself—even as he made sure she remembered what they'd once shared. A shiver of desire raced up his spine when she saw him and stood. She was wearing a dress that reminded him of what a nice pair of legs she had. And her curvy physique seemed made for that outfit.

He had gone over his strategy upstairs in case she joined him. He wouldn't make a big deal of her accompanying him. However, he would let her know he appreciated her being there.

He stopped when he reached her. "Kalina. You look nice tonight."

"Thanks. I think we need to get a couple of things straight."

He figured she would say that. "Let's wait until we get to the restaurant. Then you can let go all you want," he replied, taking her arm and placing it in the crux of his.

He felt her initial resistance before she relaxed. "Fine, but we will have that conversation. I don't have a problem joining you for dinner, but I don't want you getting any ideas."

Too late. He had gotten plenty already. He smiled. "You worry too much. There's no need for me to ask if you trust me because I know you don't. But can you cut me a little slack?"

Kalina held his gaze for a moment longer than he thought necessary, before she released an exasperated breath. "Does it matter to you that I don't particularly like you anymore?"

He took her hand in his to lead her out of the villa. "I'm sorry to hear that because I definitely like you. Always have. From the first."

She rolled her eyes. "So you say."

He chuckled. "So I know."

She pulled her hand from his when they stepped outside. The air was cool, and he thought it was a smart thing that she'd brought along a shawl. He could visualize her wrapped up in it and wearing nothing else.

She had done that once, and he could still remember her doing so. It had been a red one with fringes around the hem. He had shown up at the hotel where they were staying in Sydney with their take-out dinner, and she had emerged from the bedroom looking like a lush red morsel. She had ended up being his treat for the night.

"Micah?"

He glanced over when he realized she'd said something. "Yes?"

"Are we walking or taking a cab?"

"We'll take a cab and tell the driver not to hurry so we can enjoy the beautiful view. Unless, however, you prefer to walk. It's not far away, within walking distance."

"Makes no difference to me," she said, moving her gaze from his to glance around.

'In that case, we'll take the cab. I know how much you like a good ride."

Kalina's face flushed after she heard what Micah said. There was no way he could convince her he hadn't meant what she thought he'd meant. That innocent look on his face meant nothing. But then, he, of all people, knew how much she liked to be on top and he'd always accommodated her. She just loved the feel of being on top of a body so well built and fine it could make even an old woman weep in pleasure.

She decided that if he was waiting on a response to his comment, he would be disappointed because she didn't intend to give him one. She would say her piece at the restaurant.

"Here's our cab."

The bellman opened the door for her. Kalina slid in

the back and Micah eased in right behind her. The cab was small but not small enough where they needed to be all but sitting in each other's lap. "You have plenty of space over there," she said, pointing to Micah's side.

Without any argument he slid over, but then he turned and flashed those pearly-white teeth as he smiled at her. Her gaze narrowed. "Any reason you find me amusing?"

He shrugged. "I don't. But I do find you sexy as hell."

That was a compliment she didn't need and opened her mouth to tell him so, then closed it, deciding to leave well enough alone. He would be getting an earful soon enough.

When he continued to sit there and stare at her, she found it annoying and asked, "I thought you said you were going to enjoy the view."

"I am."

God, how had she forgotten how much he considered seduction an art form? Of course, he should know that using that charm on her was a wasted effort. "Can I ask you something, Micah?"

"Baby, you can ask me anything."

She hated to admit that his term of endearment caused a whirling sensation in her stomach. "Why are you doing this? Saying those things? I'm sure you're well aware it's a waste of your time."

"Is it?"

"Yes."

He didn't say anything for a moment and then, "To answer your question, the reason I'm doing this and saying all these things is that I'm hoping you'll remember."

She didn't have to ask what he wanted her to remember. She knew. Things had been good between them. Every night. Every morning. He'd been the best lover a woman could have and she had appreciated those nights spent in his arms. And speaking of those arms…they were hidden in a nice shirt that showed off the wide breadth of his shoulders. She knew those shoulders well and used to hold on to him while she rode him mercilessly. And then there were his hands. Beautiful. Strong. Capable of delivering mindless pleasure. And they were hands that would travel all over her body, touching her in places no man had touched her before and leaving a trail of heat in their wake.

Her gaze traveled upward past his throat to his mouth. It lingered there while recalling the ways he would use that mouth to make her scream. Oh, how she would scream while he took care of that wild, primal craving deep within her.

Gradually, her gaze left his mouth to move upward and stared into the depth of his bedroom-brown eyes. They were staring straight at her, pinning her in place and almost snatching the air from her lungs with their intensity. She wished she could dismiss that stare. Instead she was ensnarled by it in a way that increased her heart rate. An all-too-familiar ache settled right between her thighs. He was making her want something she hadn't had since he'd given it to her.

"Do you remember all the things we used to do behind closed doors, Kalina?"

Yes, she remembered and doubted she could ever forget. Sex between them had been good. The best. But it had all been a lie. That memory of his betrayal cut through her desire and forced a laugh from deep within her throat. "I've got to hand it to you, Micah. You're good."

He shrugged and then said in a low, husky tone, "You always said I was."

Yes, she had and it had been the truth. "Yes, but you're not good enough to get me into bed ever again. If you'll recall, I know the reason you slept with me." She was grateful for the glass partition that kept the cabby from hearing their conversation.

"I know the reason, as well. I wanted you. Pure and simple. From the moment you walked into that ballroom on your father's arm, I knew I wanted you. And being with you in Sydney afforded me the opportunity to have you. I wanted those legs wrapped around me, while I stroked you inside out. I wanted to bury my head between your thighs, to know the taste of you, and I wanted you to know the taste of me."

Her traitorous body began responding to his words. Myriad sensations were rolling around in her stomach. "It was all about sex, then," she said, trying to once again destroy the heated moment.

He nodded. "Yes, in the beginning. That's why I gave you my ground rules. But then…"

She shouldn't ask but couldn't help doing so. "But then what?" she asked breathlessly.

"And then the hunter got captured by the prey."

She opened her mouth and then closed it when the cabdriver told them via a speaker that they'd arrived. She glanced out the window. It was a beautiful restaurant—quaint and romantic.

He opened the door and reached for her hand. The reaction to his touch instantly swept through her. The man could make her ache without even trying.

"You're going to like the food here," he said, helping her out of the cab and not releasing her hand. She wanted to pull it from his grasp, but the feel of that one lone finger stroking her palm kept her hand where it was.

"I'm sure I will."

They walked side by side into the restaurant and she couldn't recall the last time they'd done so. It had felt good, downright giddy, being the center of Micah Westmoreland's attention and he had lavished it on her abundantly.

She didn't know what game Micah was playing tonight or what he was trying to prove. The only thing she did know was that by the time they left this restaurant he would know where she stood, and he would discover that she didn't intend to be a part of his game playing.

"The food here is delicious, Micah."

He smiled. "Thanks. I was hoping you would join me since I knew you would love everything they had on the menu. The last time I was here, this was my favorite place to eat."

He recalled the last time he'd been in Bajadad. He'd felt guilty about being so far away from home, so far away from his family, especially when the younger Westmorelands, who'd taken his parents' and aunt's and uncle's deaths hard, had rebelled like hell. Getting a call from Dillon to let him know their youngest brother, Bane, had gotten into trouble again had become a common occurrence.

"We need to talk, Micah."

He glanced across the table at Kalina and saw the firm set of her jaw. He'd figured she would have a lot to say, so he'd asked that they be given a private room in the back. It was a nice room with a nice view, but nothing was nicer than looking at the woman he was with.

He now knew he had played right into her father's hands just as much as she had. The general had been certain that Micah would be so pissed that Kalina didn't believe him that he wouldn't waste his time trying to convince her of the truth. He hadn't. He had allowed two years to pass while the lie she believed festered.

But now he was back, seeking her forgiveness. Not for what he had done but for what he hadn't done, which was to fight for her and to prove his innocence. Dillon had urged him to do that as soon as Kalina had confronted him, but Micah had been too stubborn, too hurt that she could so easily believe the worst about him. Now he wished he had fought for her.

"Okay, you can talk and I'll listen," he said, pushing his plate aside and taking a sip of his wine.

She frowned and blew out a breath. "I want you to stop with the game playing."

"And that's what you think I'm doing?"

"Yes."

He had news for her, what he was doing was fighting for his survival the only way he knew how. He intended to make her trust him. He would lower his guard and include her in his world, which is something he hadn't done since Patrice. He would seduce her back into a relationship and then prove she was wrong. He would do things differently this time and show her he wasn't the man she believed him to be.

"What if I told you that you're wrong?"

"Then what do you call what you're doing?" she asked in a frustrated tone.

"Pursuing the woman I want," he said simply.

"To get me in your bed?"

"Or any other way I can get you. It's not all sexual."

She gave a ladylike snort. "And you expect me to believe that?"

He chuckled. "No, not really. You've told me numerous times that you don't believe a word I say."

"Then why are you doing this? Why would you want to run behind a woman who doesn't want you?"

"But you *do* want me."

She shook her head. "No, I don't."

He smiled. "Yes, you do. Even though you dislike me for what you think I did, there's a part of you that wants me as much as I want you. Should I prove it?"

She narrowed her gaze. "You can't prove anything."

He preferred to disagree but decided not to argue with her. "All right."

She lifted her brow. "So you agree with what I said?"

"No, but I'm not going to sit here and argue with you about it."

She inclined her head. "We are not arguing about it, we are discussing it. Things can't continue this way."

"So what do you suggest?"

"That you cease the flirtation and sexual innuendoes. I don't need them."

Micah was well acquainted with what she needed. It was the same thing he needed. A night together. But sharing one night would just be a start. Once he got her back in his bed he intended to keep her there. Forever. He drew in a deep breath. The thought of forever with any other woman was enough to send him into a panic. But not with her.

He placed his napkin on the table as he glanced over at her. "Since you've brought them up, let's take a moment to talk about needs, shall we?"

She nodded. That meant she would at least listen, although he knew in the end she wouldn't agree to what he was about to suggest. "Although our relationship two years ago got off on a good start, it ended on a bad note. I'm not going to sit here and rehash all that happened, everything you've falsely accused me of. At first I was pretty pissed off that you would think so low of me. Then I realized the same thing you said a couple of nights ago at that party—you didn't know me. I never gave you the chance to know the real me. If you'd known the real *me* then you would not have believed the lie your father told you."

She didn't say anything, but he knew that didn't necessarily mean she was agreeing with him. In her eyes, he was guilty until proven innocent. "I want you to get to know the real me, Kalina."

She took a sip of her wine and held his gaze. "And how am I supposed to do that?"

At least she had asked. "You and I both have a thirty-day leave coming up as soon as we fly out of India. I'd like to invite you to go home with me."

Kalina sat up straight in her chair. "Go home with you?"

"Yes."

She stared at him across the lit candle in the middle of the table. "And where exactly is home?"

"Denver. Not in the city limits, though. My family and I own land in Colorado."

"Your family?"

"Yes, and I would love for you to meet them. I have fourteen brothers and cousins, total, that live in Denver. And then there are those cousins living in Atlanta, Montana and Texas."

This was the first time he'd mentioned anything about his family to her, except for the day he had briefly spoken of his parents when she'd asked. "What a diverse family." She didn't have any siblings or cousins. He was blessed to have so many.

He leaned back in his chair with his gaze directly on her. "So, will you come?"

"No." She hadn't even needed to think about it. There was no reason for her to spend her vacation time with Micah and his family. What would it accomplish?

As if he had read her mind, he said, "It would help mend things between us."

She narrowed her gaze. "Why would I want them mended?"

"Because you are a fair person, and I believe deep down you want to know the truth as much as I want you to. For whatever reason—and I have my suspicions as to what they are—your father lied about me. I need to redeem myself."

"No, you don't."

"Yes, I do, Kalina. Whether there's ever anything between us again matters to me. Like I told you before, I truly did enjoy the time we spent together, and I think if you put aside that stubborn pride of yours, you'll admit that you did, too."

He was right, she had. But the pain of his betrayal

was something she hadn't been able to get beyond. "What made you decide to invite me to your home, Micah?"

"I told you. I want you to get to know me."

She narrowed her gaze. "Could it be that you're also planning for us to sleep together again?"

His mouth eased into a smile, and he took another sip of his wine. "I won't lie to you. That thought had crossed my mind. But I have never forced myself on any woman and I don't ever plan to do so. I would love to share a bed with you, Kalina, but the purpose of this trip is for you to get to know me. And I also want you to meet my family."

She set down her glass. "Why do you want me to get to know your family now, Micah, when you didn't before?"

Kalina noted the serious expression that descended upon his features. Was she mistaken or had her question hit a raw nerve? Leaning back in her chair, she stared at him while waiting for an answer. Given that he'd invited her to his home to meet his family, she felt she deserved one.

He took another sip of wine and, for a moment, she thought he wasn't going to answer and then he said. "Her name was Patrice Nelson. I met her in my second year of college. I was nineteen at the time. We dated only a short while before I knew she was the one. I assumed she thought the same thing about me. We had been together a few months when a plane carrying my parents went down, killing everyone on board, including my father's brother and his wife."

She gasped, and a sharp pain hit her chest. She had known about his parents, but hadn't known other family members had been killed in that plane crash, as well. "You lost your parents and your aunt and uncle?"

"Yes. My father and his brother were close and so were my mother and my aunt. They did practically everything together, which was the reason they were on the same plane. They had gone away for the weekend. My parents had seven kids and my aunt and uncle had eight. That meant fifteen Westmorelands were left both motherless and fatherless. Nine of them were under the age of sixteen at the time."

"I'm sorry," she said, feeling a lump in her throat. She hadn't known him at the time, but she could still feel his pain. That had to have been an awful time for him.

"We all managed to stay together, though," he said, breaking into her thoughts.

"How?"

"The oldest of all the Westmorelands was my brother Dillon. He was twenty-one and had just graduated from the university and had been set to begin a professional basketball career. He gave it all up to come home. Dillon, and my cousin Ramsey, who was twenty, worked hard to keep us together, even when people were encouraging him to put the younger four in foster homes. He refused. Dil, with Ramsey's help, kept us all together."

In his voice, she could hear the admiration he had for his brother and cousin. She then recalled the woman in his life at the time. "And I'm sure this Patrice was there for you during that time, right?"

"Yes, so it seemed. I took a semester off to help with things at home since I'm the third oldest in the family, although there's only a month separating me from my cousin Zane."

He took a sip of wine and then said, "Patrice came to visit me several times while I was out that semester, and she got to know my family. Everyone liked her... at least everyone but one. My cousin Bailey, who was the youngest of the Westmorelands, was barely seven, and she didn't take a liking to Patrice for reasons we couldn't understand."

He didn't say anything for a moment, as if getting his thoughts together, then he continued, "I returned to school that January, arriving a couple of days earlier than planned. I went straight to Patrice's apartment and..."

Kalina lifted a brow. "And what?"

"And I walked in on her in bed with one of her professors."

Of all the things Kalina had assumed he would say, that definitely wasn't one of them. She stared at him, and he stared back. She could see it, there, plain, right in his features—the strained look that came from remembered pain. He had been hurt deeply by the woman's deception.

"What happened after that?" she asked, curious.

"I left and went to my own apartment, and she followed me there. She told me how sorry she was. She said that she felt she needed to be honest with me, as well as with herself, so she also admitted it hadn't been the first time she'd done it with one of her professors, nor would it be the last. She said she needed her degree, wanted to graduate top of her class and saw nothing wrong with what she was doing. She said that if I loved her I would understand."

Kalina's mouth dropped. *The nerve of the hussy assuming something like that!* "And did you understand?"

"No." He didn't say anything for a moment. "Her actions not only hurt me, but they hurt my family. They had liked her and had become used to her being with me whenever I came home. It probably wouldn't have been so bad if Dillon's and Ramsey's girls hadn't betrayed them around the same time. We didn't set a good example for the others as far as knowing how to pick decent and honest women."

He paused a moment and then said in a low, disappointed voice, "I vowed then never to get involved with a woman to the extent that I'd bring her home to my family. And I've kept that promise...until now."

Kalina took a sip of her drink and held Micah's gaze, not knowing what to say. Why was he breaking his vow now, for her? Did it matter that much to him that she got to know him better than she had in Sydney?

Granted, she realized he was right. Other than being familiar with how well he performed in bed, she didn't know the simplest things about him, like his favorite color, his political affiliation or his religious beliefs. Those things might not be important for a short-term affair, but they were essential for a long-term relationship.

But then they'd never committed to a relationship. They had been merely enjoying each other's company and companionship. She hadn't expected "forever" and frankly hadn't been looking for it, either. But that didn't mean the thought hadn't crossed her mind once or twice during their two-month affair.

And she was very much aware that the reason he wanted her to get to know him now still didn't have anything to do with "forever." He assumed if she got to know him then she would see that she'd been wrong to accuse him of manipulating her for her father.

The lump in her throat thickened. What if she was wrong about him and her father had lied? What if she had begun to mean something to Micah the way he claimed? She frowned, feeling a tension headache coming on when so many what-ifs flooded her brain. Her father had never lied to her before, but there was a first time for everything. Perhaps he hadn't outright lied, but she knew how manipulative he could be where she was concerned.

"You don't have to give me your answer tonight, Kal, but please think about it."

She broke eye contact with him to study her wineglass for a moment, twirling the dark liquid around. Then she lifted her gaze to meet his again and said, "Okay, I will think about it."

A smile touched his lips. "Good. That's all I'm asking." He then checked his watch. "Ready to leave?"

"Yes."

Moments later, as they stood outside while a cab was hailed for them, she couldn't help remembering everything Micah had told her. She couldn't imagine any woman being unfaithful to him, and she could tell from the sound of his voice while he'd relayed the story that the pain had gone deep. That had been well over ten years ago. Was he one of those men, like her father, who could and would love only one woman?

She was aware of how her mother's death had affected her father. Although she'd known him to have lady friends over the years, she also knew he hadn't gotten serious about any of them. Her mother, he said, would always have his heart. Kalina couldn't help wondering if this Patrice character still claimed Micah's heart.

When they were settled in the cab, she glanced over at him and said, "I'm sorry."

He lifted a brow. "For what?"

"Your loss. Your parents. Your uncle and aunt." She wouldn't apologize for Patrice because she didn't see her being out of the picture as a loss. Whether he realized it or not, finding out how deceitful his girlfriend was had been a blessing.

His gaze held hers intensely, unflinchingly, when he said, "I didn't share my history with you for your pity or sympathy."

She nodded. "I know." And she did know. He had taken the first steps in allowing her to get beyond that guard he'd put up. For some reason, she felt that he truly wanted her to get to know him. The real Micah Westmoreland. Was he truly any different from the one she already knew?

She had to decide just how much of him, if any, she wanted to get to know. He had invited her to spend time with him and his family in Denver, and she had to think hard if that was something she really wanted to do.

A few hours later, back in his room at the villa, Micah turned off the lamp beside his bed and stared up at the ceiling in darkness. He had enjoyed sharing dinner with Kalina, and doing so had brought back memories of the time they'd spent together in Sydney. Tonight, more than ever, he had been aware of her as a woman. A woman he wanted. A woman he desired. A woman he intended to have.

He'd never wanted to be attracted to Kalina, even in the beginning. Mainly because he'd known she would hold his interest too much and for way too long. But there hadn't been any hope for him. The chemistry had been too strong. The desire too thick. He had been attracted to her in a way he had never been attracted to another woman.

And tonight she had been a good listener. She had asked the questions he had expected her to ask and hadn't asked ones that were irrelevant. The private room they'd been given had been perfect for such a conversation. But even the intense subject matter did nothing to lessen the heat that stirred in the air, or waylay the desire that simmered between them.

Very few people knew the real reason he and Patrice had ended things. He'd only told Dillon, Ramsey and Zane, the cousin he was closest to. Micah was certain the others probably assumed they knew the reason, but he knew their assumptions wouldn't even come close.

Walking in and finding the woman he loved in bed with another man had been traumatic for him, especially given that he'd been going through a very distressing time in his life already. The sad thing was that there hadn't been any remorse because Patrice had felt justified in doing what she'd done. She just hadn't been able to comprehend that normal men and women didn't share their partners.

He shifted in bed and thought about Kalina. He had enjoyed her company tonight and believed she'd enjoyed his. He'd even felt an emotional connection to her, something he hadn't felt with a woman in years. He didn't need to close his eyes to remember the stricken look on her face two years ago when she'd overheard words that had implicated him. And no matter how much he had proclaimed his innocence, she hadn't believed him.

For two years, they had gone their separate ways. At first, he'd been so angry he hadn't given a damn. But at night he would lie in bed awake. Wanting her and missing her. It was then that he'd realized just how much Kalina had worked her way into his bloodstream, how deeply she'd become embedded under his skin. He had traveled to several countries over the past two years. He had worked a ton of hours. But nothing had been able to eradicate Kalina from his mind.

Now she was back in his life, and he intended to use this opportunity to right a wrong. If only she would agree to go home to Denver with him. He wouldn't question why it was so important to him for her to do so, but it was. And although he hadn't told her, he wouldn't accept no for an answer.

So what are you going to do if she turns you down, Westmoreland? Kidnap her?

Kidnapping Kalina didn't sound like a bad idea, but he knew he wouldn't operate on the wrong side of the law. He hoped that she gave his invitation some serious consideration so it didn't come to that.

It had been hard being so close to her and having to keep his hands to himself when he'd wanted them all over her, touching her in places he'd been privy to before. But as he'd told her, it was important that they get to know each other, something they hadn't taken the time to do in Sydney.

On the cab ride back, he'd even discovered she knew how to ride a horse and that her grandparents had been farmers in Alabama. Her grandparents had even raised, among other things, sheep. His cousin Ramsey, who was the sheep rancher in the Westmoreland family, would appreciate knowing that. And Micah couldn't wait to show Kalina his ranch. He hoped she liked it as much as he did. And...

He drew in a deep breath, forcing himself to slow down and put a lid on his excitement. He had to face the possibility that she would decide not to go to Denver. He refused to let that happen. The woman had no idea just how much he wanted her and he intended to do whatever he had to to have her.

If he had to turn up the heat to start breaking down her defenses then that's what he would do.

Six

The next day, Kalina's body tensed when she entered the lab and immediately remembered that she and Micah would be working alone together today. Theo was in another area analyzing the granules taken from the bodies of the five victims.

She eased the door closed behind her and stood leaning against it while she looked over at Micah. He was standing with his head tilted back as he studied the solution in the flask he was holding up to the light. She figured he wasn't aware she had entered, which was just as well for the time being.

His request from last night was still on her mind, and even after a good night's sleep, she hadn't made a decision about what she would do. She had weighed the pros and cons of accompanying him to Denver, but even that hadn't helped. It had been late when she had returned from dinner, but she'd tried reaching her father. The person she'd talked to at the Pentagon wouldn't even tell her his whereabouts, saying that, at the moment, the general's location was confidential. She had wanted to hear her father tell her again how Micah had played a role in keeping her out of China. A part of her resented the fact that Micah was back in her life, but another part of her felt she deserved to know the truth.

She wrapped her arms around herself, feeling a slight damp in the air. Everyone had awakened to find it raining that morning. And although the showers only lasted for all of ten minutes, it had been enough to drench the mountainside pretty darn good.

Micah's back was to her, and her gaze lowered to his backside, thinking it was one part of his body she'd always admired. He certainly had a nice-looking butt. She'd heard from Theo that Micah had gotten up before five this morning to go to the villa's gym to work out. She would have loved to have been a fly on the wall, to watch him flex those masculine biceps of his.

Her thoughts drifted to the night before. On the cab ride back to the villa he'd told her more about his brothers and cousins. She wasn't sure if he was feeding her curiosity or deliberately enticing her to want to meet them all for herself. And she would admit that she'd become intrigued. But was that enough to make her want to spend an entire month with him in Denver?

"Are you going to just stand there or get to work? There's plenty of it to be done."

She frowned, wondering if he had eyes in the back of his head, as he'd yet to turn around. "How did you know it was me?"

"Your scent gave you away, like it always does."

Since she usually wore the same cologne every day, she would let that one slide. She moved away from the door at the same time as he turned around, and she really wished he hadn't when he latched those dark, intense eyes onto her. Evidently, this was going to be one of her "drool over Micah" days. She'd had a number of them before. He was looking extremely handsome today. He probably looked the same yesterday, but today her hormones were out in full force, reminding her just how much of a woman she was and reminding her of all those sexual needs she had ignored for two years.

"Have most of the tissues been analyzed?" she asked, sliding onto her stool in front of a table that contained skin samples taken during autopsies of the five victims.

"No, I left that for you to do."

"No problem."

She glanced over at Micah, who was still studying the flask while jotting down notes. He was definitely engrossed in his work. Last night, he'd been engrossed in her. Was this the same man whose gaze had filled her with heated lust last night during the cab rides to the restaurant and back? The same man who'd sat across from her at dinner with a look that said he wanted to eat her alive? The same man whose flirtation and sexual innuendoes had stirred her with X-rated sensations? The same man who exuded a virility that said he was all man, totally and completely?

"Are you going to get some work done or sit there and waste time daydreaming?"

She scowled, not appreciating his comment. Evidently, he wasn't in a good mood. She wondered who had stolen his favorite toy. Now he was sitting on a stool at the counter and hadn't glanced up.

"For your information, I get paid for the work I do and not the time it takes me to do it."

She shook her head. And to think that this was the same man who'd wanted her to spend thirty days with him and his family. She'd have thought he would be going out of his way to be nice to her.

"In other words…"

"In other words, Dr. Westmoreland," she said, placing her palms on the table and leaning forward. "I can handle my business."

He looked up at her and his mouth twitched in a grin. "Yes, Dr. Daniels, I know for a fact that you most certainly can."

She narrowed her eyes when it became obvious he'd been doing nothing more than teasing her. "I was beginning to wonder about you, Micah."

"In what respect?" he asked.

"Your sanity."

"Ouch."

"Hey, you had that coming," she said, and couldn't help the smile that touched her lips.

"I wish I had something else coming about now. My sanity as well as my body could definitely use it."

Her eyebrows lifted. The look in his eyes, the heated lust she saw in their dark depths told her they were discussing something that had no place in the lab. Deciding it was time to change the subject, she said, "How are things going? Found anything unusual?"

He shook his head. "Other than what you found yesterday, no, I could find nothing else. Theo's dissecting those tissue particles now. Maybe he'll come across something else in the breakdown."

She blew out a breath, feeling a degree of frustration. Granted, it was just the second day, but still, she was anxious about those samples Theo was analyzing. So far there hadn't been any more deaths and that was a good thing. But, at the same time, if they couldn't discover the cause, there was a chance the same type of deaths could occur again.

She glanced over at Micah at the exact moment that he raised his head from his microscope. "Come and take a look at this."

There was something in his voice that made her curious. Without thinking, she quickly moved across the room. When he slid off his stool, she slid onto it. She looked down into his microscope and frowned. She then looked up at him, confused. "I don't see anything."

"Then maybe you aren't looking in the right place."

Kalina wasn't sure exactly what she was expecting, but it wasn't Micah reaching out and gently pulling her from the stool to wrap his arms around her. His manly scent consumed her and his touch sent fire racing all through her body. She drew in a steadying breath and tilted her head back to look up at him. And when he brought her closer to his hard frame, she felt every inch of him against her.

Although her pulse was drumming erratically in response, she said, "I don't want this, Micah." She knew it was a lie the moment she said it and, from the heat of his gaze, he knew it was a lie, as well.

"Then maybe I need to convince you otherwise," he said, seconds before lowering his mouth to hers.

She had intended to shove him away...honestly she

had, but the moment she parted her lips on an enraged sigh and he took the opportunity to slide his tongue in her mouth, she was a goner. Her stomach muscles quivered at the intensity and strength in the tongue that caught hold of hers and began sucking as if it had every right to do so. Sucking on her tongue as if it was the last female tongue on earth.

He was devouring her. Feasting on her. Driving her insane while tasting her with a sexual hunger she felt all the way to her toes. A strong concentration of that hunger settled in the juncture of her thighs.

And speaking of that spot, she felt his erection—right there—hard, rigid, pressing against her belly, making her remember a time when it had done more than nudge her, making her remember a time when it had actually slid inside her, between her legs, going all the way to the hilt, touching her womb. It had once triggered her inner muscles to give a possessive little squeeze, just seconds before they began milking his aroused body for everything they could get and forcing him to explode in an out-of-this-world orgasm. She remembered. She couldn't forget.

And then she began doing something she was driven to do because of the way he was making love to her mouth, as well as the memories overtaking her. Just like the last time he'd overstepped his boundaries in a kiss, she began kissing him back, taking the lead by escaping the captivity of his tongue and then capturing his tongue with hers. Ignoring the conflicting emotions swamping her, she kissed him in earnest, with a hunger only he could stir. She took possession of his mouth and he let her. He was allowing her to do whatever she wanted. Whatever pleased her. And when she heard a deep guttural moan, she wasn't sure if it had come from his throat or hers.

At the moment she really didn't care.

Micah deepened the kiss, deciding it was time for him to take over. Or else he would have Kalina stretched across the nearest table with her legs spread so fast neither of them would have a chance to think about the consequences. He doubted he would ever get tired of kissing her and was surprised this was just the second time their tongues had mingled since seeing each other again. But then, staying away from each other had been her decision, not his. If he had his way, their mouths would be locked together 24/7.

As usual, she fit perfectly in his arms, and she felt as if she belonged there. There was nothing like kissing a beautiful woman, especially one who could fill a man's head with steamy dreams at night and heated reality during the day. He found it simply amazing, the power a woman could wield over a man. Case in point, the power that this particular woman had over him.

It didn't matter when he kissed her, or how often, he always wanted more of her. There was nothing quite like having her mouth beneath his. And he liked playing the tongue game with her. He would insert his tongue into her mouth and deepen the kiss before withdrawing and then going back in. He could tell from her moans that she was enjoying the game as much as he was.

His aroused body was straining hard against his zipper, begging for release, pleading for that part of her it had gotten to know so well in Australia. Her feminine scent was in the air, feeding his mind and body with a heated lust that had blood rushing through his body.

A door slamming somewhere had them quickly pulling apart, and he watched as she licked her lips as if she could still taste him there. His guts clenched at the thought. He'd concluded from the first that she had a very sexy mouth, and from their initial kiss he'd discovered that not only was it sexy, it was damn tasty as sin. She took a step back and crossed her arms over her chest, pulling in quick breaths. "I can't believe you did that. What if someone had walked in on us?"

He shrugged while trying to catch his own breath. His mouth was filled with her taste, yet he wanted more. "Then I would have been pretty upset about the interruption," he said.

She glared. "We should be working."

He smiled smoothly. "We are. However, we are entitled to breaks." He leaned against the table. "I think you need to loosen up a little."

"And I think you need to get a grip. You've gotten your kiss, Micah. That's two now. If I were you, I wouldn't try for a third."

He had news for her, he would try for a third, fourth, fifth and plenty more beyond that. There was no way his mouth wouldn't be locking with hers again. She had sat back down on the stool and had picked up one of the vials as if to dismiss not only him but also what they'd just shared. He had no intention of letting her do that. "Why can't we kiss again? I'm sure there's plenty more where those two came from."

She lifted her gaze to his. "I beg to differ."

He chuckled. "Oh, I plan to have you begging, all right."

Her eyes narrowed, and he thought she looked absolutely adorable. Hot, saucy and totally delectable. "If you're trying to impress me then—"

"I'm not. I want you to get to know me and the one thing you'll discover about me is that I love the unexpected. I like being unpredictable, and when it comes to you, I happen to be addicted."

"Thanks for letting me know. I will take all that into consideration while deciding if I'm going home with you in a couple of weeks. You might as well know none of it works in your favor."

"I never took you for a coward."

She frowned. "Being a coward has nothing to do with it. It's using logical thinking and not giving in to whims. Maybe you should do the same."

He couldn't help the grin that spread across his lips. Lips that still carried her taste. "Oh, sweetheart, I *am* using logical thinking. If I got any more sensible I would have stripped you naked by now instead of just imagining doing it. In fact, I'm doing more than imagining it, I'm anticipating it happening. And when it does, I promise to make it worth every moan I get out of you."

Ignoring her full-fledged glare, he glanced at his watch. "I think I'll go grab some lunch. I've finished logging my findings on today's report, but if you need help with what you have to do then—"

"Thanks for the offer, but I can handle things myself."

"No problem. And just so we have a clear understanding… My invitation to go home with me to Denver has no bearing on my kissing you, touching you or wanting to make love to you. You have the last word."

She raised an eyebrow. "Do I really?"

"Absolutely. But I'd like to warn you not to say one thing while your body says another. I tend to listen more to body language."

"Thanks for the warning."

"And thanks for the kiss," he countered.

She frowned, and he smiled. If only she knew what he had in store for her... Hell, it was a good thing that she didn't know. His smile widened as he removed his lab jacket. "I'll be back later. Don't work too hard while I'm gone. You might want to start storing up your energy."

"Storing up my energy for what?"

He leaned in close, reached out, lightly stroked her cheek with his fingertips and whispered, "For when we make love again."

Seeing the immediate flash of fire in her gaze, he said, "Not that I plan on gloating, but when you find out the truth, that I've been falsely accused, I figure you'll want to be nice to me. And when you do, I'll be ready. I want you to be ready, as well. I can't wait to make love to you again, and I plan to make it worth the hell you've put me through, baby."

The heat in her gaze flared so hotly he had to struggle not to pull her back into his arms and go after that third kiss. He was definitely going to enjoy pushing her buttons.

As he moved to walk out of the lab, he thought that if that last kiss was anything to go by, he might as well start storing up some energy, as well. He turned back around before opening the door and his gaze traveled over her. He wanted her to feel the heat, feel his desire. He wanted her to want to make love to him as much as he wanted to make love to her.

She held his gaze with a defiant frown and said nothing. He smiled and gave her a wink before finally opening the door to leave.

"It's all his fault," Kalina muttered angrily as she tossed back her covers to ease out of bed. It had been almost a week since that kiss in the lab and she hadn't had a single good night's sleep since.

She was convinced he was deliberately trying to drive her loony. Although he hadn't taken any more liberties with her, he had his unique ways of making her privy to his lusty thoughts. His eye contact told her everything—regardless of whether it was his lazy perusal or his intense gaze—whenever she looked into his eyes there was no doubt about what was on his mind. More than once she'd looked up from her microscope to find those penetrating dark eyes trained directly on her.

It didn't take much to get her juices flowing, literally, and for the past week he'd been doing a pretty good job of it. She knew he enjoyed getting on her last nerve, and it seemed that particular nerve was a hot wire located right at the juncture of her thighs.

She had tried pouring her full concentration into her work. All the test results on the tissues had come back negative. Although they suspected that some deadly virus had killed those five people, as of yet the team hadn't been able to pinpoint a cause, or come up with conclusive data to support their hypothesis. The granules were still a mystery, and so far they had not been able to trace the source. The Indian government was determined not to make a big to-do about what they considered nothing and wouldn't let them test any others who'd gotten sick but had recovered. The team had reported their findings to Washington. The only thing left was to wrap things up. She knew that Micah was still concerned and had expressed as much in his report. A contagious virus was bad enough, but one that could not be traced was even worse.

Although it had been over a week since he'd issued his invitation, she still hadn't given Micah an answer regarding going with him to Denver. With only three days before they left India, he had to be wondering about her decision. Unfortunately, she still didn't have a clue how she would answer him. The smart thing would be to head for Florida for a month, especially since Micah hadn't made the past week easy for her. He deliberately tested her sanity every chance he got. And although he hadn't tried kissing her again, more than once he had intentionally gotten close to her, brushed against her for no reason at all or set up a situation where he was alone with her. Those were the times he would do nothing but stare at her with a heated gaze as potent as any caress.

Kalina drew in a deep breath, suddenly feeling hot and in need of cool air. After slipping into her robe, she crossed the room and pushed open the French doors to step out on the balcony. She appreciated the whisper of a breeze that swept across her face. The chill made her shiver but still didn't put out the fire raging inside her.

Over the past two years she'd gone each day without caring that she was denying her body's sexual needs. Now, being around Micah was reminding her of just what she'd gone without. Whenever she was around him, she was reminded of how it felt to have fingertips stroke her skin, hands touch her all over and arms pull her close to the warmth of a male body.

She missed the caress of a man's lips against hers, the graze of a male's knuckles across her breasts, the lick of a man's tongue and the soft stroke of masculine fingers between her legs.

There was nothing like the feel of a man's aroused body sliding inside, distended and engorged, ready to take her on one remarkable ride. Making her pleasure his own. And giving all of himself while she gave everything back to him.

Her breathing quickened and her pulse rate increased at what she could now admit she'd been missing. What she had given up. No other man had brought her abstinence more to the forefront of her thoughts than Micah. She felt hot, deliriously needy, and she stood there a moment in silence, fighting to get her bearings and control the turbulent, edgy desire thrumming through her.

Nothing like this had ever happened to her before. All it took was for her to close her eyes to recall how it felt for Micah's hands to glide over the curve of her backside, cup it in his large palms and bring her closer to his body and his throbbing erection.

The memories were scorching, hypnotic and almost more than she could handle. But she would handle them. She had no choice. She would not let Micah get the best of her. She had no qualms, however, about getting the best of him—in the area right below his belt.

She rubbed her hand down her face, not believing her thoughts. They had gotten downright racy lately, and she blamed Micah for it. She was just about to turn to go back inside when a movement below her balcony caught her attention. A man was out jogging and she couldn't help noticing what a fine specimen of a man he was.

The temperature outside had to be in the low thirties, yet he was wearing a T-shirt and a pair of shorts. In her opinion, he was pneumonia just waiting to happen. Who in their right mind would be out jogging at this hour of the night, half dressed?

She leaned against the railing and squinted her eyes in the moonlight. That's when she saw that the man who'd captured her attention was Micah. Evidently, she wasn't the only one who couldn't sleep. She found that interesting and couldn't help wondering if perhaps the same desire that was keeping her awake had him in its lusty clutches, as well.

Serves him right if it did. He had spent a lot of his time this week trying his best to tempt her into his bed, but apparently he was getting the backlash.

He was about to jog beneath her balcony, so she held her breath to keep him from detecting her presence. Except for the glow of the half moon, it was dark, and there was no reason for him to glance up…or so she reasoned. But it didn't stop him from doing so. In fact, as if he'd sensed she was there, he slowed to a stop and stared straight up at her, locking in on her gaze.

And he kept right on staring at her while her heart rate increased tenfold. Suddenly there was more than a breeze stirring the air around her, and it seemed as if her surroundings got extremely quiet. The only thing that was coming in clear was the sound of her irregular breathing.

She stared right back at him and saw that his gaze was devouring her in a way she felt clear beneath her robe. In fact, if she didn't know for certain she was wearing clothes, she would think that she was naked. Oh, why were the sensual lines of his lips so well-defined in the moonlight? Knowing she could be headed for serious trouble if their gazes continued to connect, she broke eye contact, only to be drawn back to his gaze seconds later.

He had to be cold, she thought, yet he was standing in that one spot, beneath her balcony, staring up at her. She licked her lips and felt his gaze shift to her mouth.

Then he spoke in a deep, husky voice, "Meet me in the staircase, Kalina."

His request flowed through her, touching her already aroused body in places it shouldn't have. Turbulent emotions swept through her, and from the look in his eyes it was obvious that he expected her to act on his demand. Should she? Could she? Why would she?

She was bright enough to know that he didn't want her to meet him so they could discuss the weather. Nor would they discuss their inability to pinpoint the origin of the deadly virus. There was no doubt in her mind as to why he wanted to meet her on the stairs, and she would be crazy, completely insane, to do what he asked.

Breaking eye contact with him, she moved away from the balcony's railing and slid open the French doors to go back inside. She moved toward her bed, tossed off her robe and was about to slide between the sheets, when she paused. Okay, she didn't like him anymore, but why was she denying herself a chance to have a good night's sleep? She had needs that hadn't been met in more than two years, and she knew for a fact that he was good at that sort of thing. She didn't love him, and he didn't love her. It would be all about needs and wants being satisfied, nothing more.

She drew in a deep breath, thinking she might be jumping the gun here. All he'd asked her to do was to meet him at the stairs. For all she knew, he might just want to talk. Or maybe he merely wanted to kiss her. She gave herself a mental shake, knowing a kiss would only be the start. Any man who looked at her the way Micah had looked at her a few moments ago had more than kissing on his mind.

Deciding to take the guesswork out of it, she reached for the blouse and skirt she'd taken off earlier and quickly put them on. She knew what she wanted, and Micah better not be playing games with her, because she wasn't in the mood.

Heaven help her, but she was only in the mood for one thing, and at the moment, she didn't care whether she liked him or not just as long as he eased that ache within her.

As she grabbed her room key off the nightstand and shoved it into the pocket of her skirt, she headed toward the door.

Micah paced the stairway, trying to be optimistic. Kalina would come. Although he knew it would be a long shot if she did, he refused to give up hope. He had read that look in her eyes. It had been the same one he knew was in his. She wanted him as much as he wanted her. He had been playing cat-and-mouse games with her all week, to the point where Theo had finally pulled him aside and told him to do something about his attitude problem. He'd almost laughed in his friend's face.

Nothing was wrong with his attitude; it was his body that had issues.

So here he was. Waiting. Hoping she wouldn't walk through the door just to tell him to go to hell. Well, he would have news for her. As far as he was concerned, he was already there. Going without a woman for two years hadn't been a picnic, but he hadn't wanted anyone except her and had denied himself because of it. It was unbelievable how a man's desire for one woman could rule his life, dictate his urges and serve as a thermostat for his constant craving. He was feeling the heat. It was flooding his insides and taking control of every part of his being.

Over the past several days, he'd thought about knocking on Kalina's door but had always talked himself out of it. He wouldn't have been so bold as to ask her to meet him on the staircase tonight if he hadn't seen that particular look in her eyes. He knew that look in a woman's eyes well enough: heated lust. He'd seen it in Kalina's eyes many times.

He turned when he heard footsteps. It was late. Most normal people were asleep. He should be asleep. Instead, he was up, wide awake, horny as hell and lusting after a woman. But not just any woman. He wanted Kalina. She still hadn't told him whether she'd made a decision about going home with him, and he hoped that no news was good news.

He heard the sound of the knob turning and his gaze stayed glued to the door. Most people used the elevator. He preferred the stairs when jogging, for the additional workout. He drew in a deep breath. Was it her? Had she really come after two years of separation and the misunderstanding that still existed between them?

The door slowly opened, and he gradually released his breath. It was Kalina, and at that moment, as his gaze held tight to hers, he couldn't stop looking at her. The more he looked at her, the more he wanted her. The more he needed to be with her.

Had to be with her.

But he needed her to want to be with him just as much. Deciding not to take her appearance here for granted, he slowly moved toward her, his steps unhurried yet precise. His breathing was coming out just as hard as the erection he felt pressing against his shorts.

Micah reached her and lifted his hand to push a lock of hair from her face. Knowing what she thought was the truth about him, he understood that it had taken a lot for her to come to him. He intended to make sure she didn't regret it.

He opened his mouth to say something, but she placed a finger to his lips. "Please don't say anything, Micah. Just do it. Take me now and take me hard."

Her words fired his blood, and his immediate thought was that, given the degree of his need, he would have no problem doing that. He tightened his hand on hers. "Come on, let's go up to my room."

She pulled back and shook her head. "No. Do it here. Now."

He met her gaze, stared deep into her eyes. "I wouldn't suggest that if I were you," he warned. "You just might get what you ask for."

"I'm hoping."

He heard the quiver in her voice and saw the degree of urgency in her expression. There was a momentous need within her that was hitting him right in the gut and stirring his own need. He drew in a deep breath.

There was no doubt in his mind that he was about to lose focus, but he also knew he was about to gain something more rewarding.

He then thought of something. *Damn, damn and triple damn.* "I don't have a condom on me."

His words didn't seem to faze her. She merely nodded and said, "I'm still on the pill and still in good health."

"I'm still in good health, as well," he said and thought there was no need to admit that he hadn't made love to another woman since her.

"Then do it, Micah."

He heard the urgency and need in her voice. "Whatever you want, baby."

Reaching behind her, he locked the entry door before lifting her off her feet to place her back against the wall. Raising her skirt, he spread her legs so they could wrap around him. His shaft began twitching, hardening even more as he lowered his zipper to release it. He skimmed his hands between Kalina's legs and smiled when he saw there were no panties he needed to dispense with. She was hot, and ready.

So was he.

He lowered his head to take her mouth, and at the same moment he aimed his erection straight for her center and began sliding in. Her hands on his shoulders were used to draw him closer into the fit of her.

She took in several deep breaths as he became more entrenched in her body. She felt tight, and her inner muscles clenched him. He broke off the kiss, closed his eyes and threw his head back as he clutched her hips and bottom in his hands and went deeper and deeper. There was nothing like having your manhood gripped, pulled and squeezed by feminine muscles intent on milking you dry.

His lips returned to hers in a deep, openmouthed kiss as he began thrusting hard inside her, tilting her body so he could hit her G-spot. He wanted to drive her wild, over the edge.

"Micah. Oh, Micah, don't stop. Please don't stop. I missed this."

She wasn't alone. He had missed this, as well. At that moment, something fierce and overpowering tore through him and like a jackhammer out of control, he thrust inside her hard, quick and deep. Being inside her this way was driving him over the edge, sending fire through his veins and rushing blood to all parts of his body, especially the part connected to her.

"Micah!"

Her orgasm triggered his as hard and hot desire raged through him. He plunged deeper into her body. The explosion mingled their juices as his release shot straight to her womb as if that's where it wanted to be, where it belonged. She shuddered uncontrollably, going over the edge. He followed her there.

Unable to resist, he used his free hand to push aside her blouse and bra and then latched his mouth to her nipple, sucking hard. At the same time, his body erupted into yet another orgasm and a second explosion rocketed him to heights he hadn't scaled in two years.

He now knew without a doubt what had been missing in his life. Kalina. Now more than ever he intended to make sure she never left him again.

Seven

Kalina slowly opened her eyes. Immediately, she knew that although she was in her room at the villa, she was not in bed alone. Her backside was spooned against hard masculine muscles with an engorged erection against the center of her back.

She drew in a deep breath as memories of the night before consumed her. Micah had a way of making her feel feminine and womanly each and every time he kissed her, touched her or made love to her. And he had made love to her several times during the night. It was as if they were both trying to make up for the two years they'd been apart.

Considering the unfinished business between them, she wasn't sure their insatiable passion had been a good thing. But last night she hadn't cared. Her needs had overridden her common sense. Instead of concentrating on what he had done to betray her, she had been focused on what he could do to her body. What he had done last night had taken the edge off, and she had needed it as much as she'd needed to breathe. He had gone above and beyond the call of duty and had satisfied her more than she had imagined possible. Now all she wanted to do was stay in bed, be lazy and luxuriate in the after-glow.

"Hey, babe. You awake?" Micah asked while sliding a bare leg over her naked body.

If she hadn't been awake, she was now, she thought when the feel of his erection on her back stiffened even more. She drew in a deep breath, not sure she was ready to converse with him yet. With the sensation of him pressing against her, however, she had a feeling con-versation was the last thing on Micah's mind.

"Kal?"

Knowing she had to answer him sometime, she slowly turned onto her back. "Yes, I'm awake."

He lifted up on his elbow to loom over her and smiled. "Good morning."

She opened her mouth to give him the same greet-ing, but that was as far as she got. He slid a hand up her hip just seconds before his lips swooped down and captured hers. The second his tongue entered her mouth she was a pathetic goner. No man kissed like Micah. He put everything he was into the kiss, and she could feel all kinds of sensations overtaking her and wrap-ping her in a sensual cocoon.

A part of her felt that maybe she should pull back. She didn't want to give him the wrong message, but another part of her was in a quandary as to what the wrong message could be, in light of what they'd shared the night before.

And as he kissed her, she remembered every moment of what they'd shared.

She recalled them making love on the stairwell twice before he'd carried her back to her room. Once inside, they had stripped off their clothes and showered together. They'd made out beneath the heated spray of water before lathering each other clean. He had dried her off, only to lick her all over and make her wet again.

Then they had made love in her bed several times. She had ridden him, and he had ridden her. Then they had ridden each other. The last thing she remembered was falling asleep totally exhausted in his arms.

It was Micah who finally pulled his mouth away, but not before using his tongue to lick her lips from corner to corner.

"You need to stop that," she said in a voice that lacked any real conviction.

"I will, when I'm finished with you," he said, nibbling at the corners of her mouth.

She knew that could very well be never. "You need to go to your room so I can get dressed for work, and you need to get dressed, too."

"Later."

And then he was kissing her again, more passionately than before. She tried to ignore the pleasure overtaking her, but she couldn't. So she became a willing recipient and took everything he was giving her. His kiss was so strong and potent that when he finally pulled his mouth away, she actually felt light-headed.

"I missed that," he murmured, close to her ear. "And I missed this, as well." He moved to slide his body over hers, lifted her hips and entered her in one smooth thrust.

He looked down at her and held her gaze in a breathless moment before moving his body in and out of her. "Being inside you feels so incredibly good, Kal," he whispered, and she thought a woman could get spoiled by this. She certainly had been spoiled during their time in Sydney. So much so that she had suffered through withdrawal for months afterward.

"Oh, baby, you're killing me," Micah growled out, increasing the intensity of his strokes. Kalina begged to differ. He was the one killing her. Her body was the one getting the workout of a lifetime. Blood was rushing through all parts of her, sending shock waves that escalated and touched her everywhere. Never had she been made love to so completely.

All further thought was forced from her mind when he hollered her name just seconds before his body bucked in a powerful orgasm. She felt the essence of his release shoot straight to her womb. The feel of it triggered a riot of sensations, which burst loose within her.

"Micah!"

"I'm here, baby. Let it go. Give yourself to me completely. Don't hold anything back."

She heard his words and tried closing her mind to them but found that she couldn't. She couldn't hold anything back, even if she tried. The strength of her need for him stunned her, but whether she wanted to admit it or not, she knew that what she and Micah were sharing was special. She wanted to believe it was meant just for them.

He continued to hold her, even when he eventually

shifted his body off hers. He'd gotten quiet, and she wondered what he was thinking. As if he'd read her thoughts, he reached out and cupped her chin in his hand then tilted her head so she could look at him and he could look at her.

She felt the heat of his gaze in every part of her body. He brushed a kiss across her lips. "Have dinner with me tonight."

She quickly recalled that dinner after a night of passion was how their last affair had begun. They had slept together one night after work and the next evening he'd taken her out to eat. After dinner, they'd gone back to her place and had been intimately involved for two glorious months.

"We've done that already, Micah."

At his confused look, she added. "Dinner and all that goes with it. Remember Sydney? Different place. Same technique."

He frowned. "Are you trying to say I'm boring you?"

She couldn't help smiling. "Do I look bored? Have I acted bored?"

He laughed. "No to both."

"All right, then. All I meant was that I recall a casual dinner was how things started between us the last time."

"You have to eat."

"Yes, but you don't have to be the one who's always there to feed me. I'm a big girl. I can take care of myself."

"Okay, then," he said, leaning in close to run the tip of his tongue around her earlobe. "What do you want from me?"

She chuckled. "What I got last night and this morning was pretty darn good. I have no complaints."

He lifted his head and frowned down at her. "Shouldn't you want more?"

"Are you prepared to give me more?" she countered.

He seemed to sober with her question. He held her gaze a moment then said, "I want you to get to know the real me, Kal. You never did decide if you're willing to go home with me or not."

Mainly because she'd tried putting the invitation out of her mind. She hadn't wanted to talk about it or even think about it. "I need more time."

"You have only two days left," he reminded her.

Yes, she knew. And she wasn't any closer to making a decision than she had been a week ago. Sleeping together had only complicated things. But she had no regrets. She had needed a sexual release.

She had needed him.

"Well, that's it," Micah told Kalina and Theo several hours later, at the end of the workday. "There haven't been any more reported deaths, and with the case of the few survivors, the Indian government won't let us get close enough to do an examination since we have no proof it's linked and the people did survive."

"The initial symptoms were the same. They could have survived for a number of reasons," Kalina said in frustration.

The only way to assure the U.S. military had a preventative mechanism in place if the virus popped up again was to come up with a vaccine. Micah and his team hadn't been able to do that. The chemicals that had been used were not traceable in the human body after death. And the only sign of abnormality they'd been able to find was the enlargement of the tongue. Other than that, all they had was an unexplained virus that presented as death by natural causes.

She, Theo and Micah knew there was nothing natural about it, but there was nothing they could do in this instance except report their findings to Washington and hope this type of "mysterious illness" didn't pop up again. Before the Indian government had pulled the plug on any further examinations of the survivors, Kalina had managed to obtain blood samples, which she had shipped off to Washington for further study.

"I'm flying out tonight," Theo said, standing. "I'm meeting Renee in Paris for one of her shows. Where are you two headed now?"

"I'm headed home to Denver," Micah said. He then glanced over at Kalina expectantly.

Without looking at Micah, she said. "I'm not sure where I'm going yet."

"Well, you two take care of yourselves. I'm going up to my room to pack. It's been a lot of fun, but I'm ready to leave."

Micah was ready to leave as well and looked forward to going home to chill for a while. He glanced over at Kalina, deciding he wouldn't ask her about her decision again. He'd made it pretty clear he wanted her to spend her time off with him.

He glanced over at her while she stood to gather up her belongings. He couldn't stop his gaze from warming with pleasure as he watched her. Kalina Daniels had the ability to turn him on without even trying. His response to her had set off warning bells inside his head in Sydney, and those same bells were going off now.

He hadn't taken heed then, and he wouldn't be taking heed now.

He wanted her. Yes, she had hurt him by believing the worst, but he was willing to overlook that hurt because he had been partially to blame. He hadn't given her the opportunity to really get to know him. Now, he was offering her that chance, but it was something she had to want to do. So far, she didn't appear to know if she wanted to make that effort.

"I'm glad I was able to draw that blood and have it shipped to Washington before the Indian government stepped in," he heard her say.

He nodded as he stood. "I'm glad, as well. Hopefully, they'll be able to find something we couldn't."

"I hope so."

He studied her for a moment. "So, what are your plans for the evening?" Because of what she'd said that morning, he didn't want to ask specifically about dinner.

She drew in a deep breath. "Not sure. I just might decide to stay in with a good book."

"All right."

He fought back the desire to suggest they stay in together. Regardless of what they'd shared last night and this morning, Kalina would have to invite him to share any more time with her. The decision had to be hers…but there was nothing wrong with making sure she made the right one.

"I'm renting a car and going for a drive later," he offered.

She glanced over at him. "Really? Where?"

"No place in particular. I just need to get away from the villa for a while." He felt that they both did. Although they would be leaving India in a couple of days, they had pretty much stayed on the premises during the entire investigation. "You're invited to come with me if you'd like."

He could tell by her expression that she wanted to but was hesitant to accept his invitation. He wouldn't push. "Well, I'll see you later."

He had almost made it to the door, when she called after him. "Micah, if you're sure you don't mind having company, I'll tag alone."

Inwardly, he released a sigh of relief. He slowly turned to her. "No, I wouldn't mind. I would love having you with me. And there's a club I plan to check out, so put on your dancing shoes." Then without saying anything else, he walked out of the room.

Dancing shoes?

She shook her head recalling Micah's suggestion as she moved around her room at the villa. She loved dancing, but she'd never known him to dance. At least he'd never danced with her during those two months they'd been together. Even the night they'd met, at the ball. Other guys had asked her to dance, but Micah had not.

Micah had a lean, muscular physique, and she could imagine his body moving around on anyone's dance floor. So far, that had been something she hadn't seen. But she had been more than satisfied with all his moves in the bedroom and couldn't have cared less if any of those moves ever made it to the dance floor.

She heard a knock at the door, and her breath caught. Even with the distance separating them, she could feel the impact of his presence. After making love that morning, he had left her room to go to his and dress. They had met downstairs for breakfast with Theo. Today had been their last day at the lab. Tomorrow was a free day to do whatever they wanted, and then on Friday they would be flying out.

Major Harris had already called twice, asking where she wanted to go after she returned to Washington, and Kalina still wasn't certain she wanted to join Micah in Denver.

She knew she'd have to decide soon.

She quickly moved toward the door and opened it. Micah's slow perusal of her outfit let her know she'd done the right thing in wearing this particular dress. She had purchased it sometime last year at a boutique in Atlanta while visiting a college friend.

"You look nice," he said, giving her an appreciative smile.

She let her gaze roam over him and chuckled. "So do you. Come in for a moment. You're a little early, and I haven't switched out purses."

"No problem. Take your time."

Micah followed her into a sitting area and took the wingback chair she offered. When she left the room, he glanced around at the pictures on the wall. They were different from the ones in his room. His cousin Gemma was an interior decorator, and while taking classes at the university, she had decorated most of her family members' homes for practice. He would be the first to admit she'd done a good job. No one had been disappointed. He had been home for a short visit while she'd decorated his place, and she had educated him about what to look for in a painting when judging if it would fit the decor.

He was sure these same paintings had been on the wall when he'd carried Kalina through here in his arms last night. But his mind had been so preoccupied with getting her to bed, he hadn't paid any attention.

"I'm ready. Sorry to make you wait."

He glanced around, smiled and came to his feet. "No problem."

For a moment, neither of them said anything, but just stood there and stared at each other. Then finally he said, "I'm not going to pretend last night and this morning didn't happen, Kal."

She nodded slowly. "I don't recall asking you to."

She was right, she hadn't. "Good, then I guess it's safe for me to do this, since I've been dying to all day."

He reached out, tugged her closer to him and lowered his mouth to hers.

The arms that encompassed Kalina in an embrace were warm and protective. And the hand that rubbed up and down her spine was gentle.

But nothing could compare to the mouth that was taking her over with slow, deep, measured strokes. Already, desire was racing through her, and she couldn't do anything but moan her pleasure. No other two tongues could mate like theirs could, and she enjoyed the feel of his tongue in her mouth.

He shifted his stance to bring them closer, and she felt his hard erection pressing into her. It wouldn't bother her in the least if he were to suggest they stay in for the evening.

Instead, he finally broke contact, but immediately placed a quick kiss on her lips. "I love your taste," he whispered hotly.

She smiled up at him. "And I love yours, too."

The grin he shot her was naughty. "I'm going to have to keep that in mind."

She chuckled as she saw the glint of mischief in his gaze. "Yes, you do that."

Kalina always thought she could handle just about anything or anyone, but an hour or so after they'd left her room, she wasn't sure. She was seeing a side of Micah she had never seen before. It had started with the drive around the countryside. There had been just enough daylight left to enjoy the beauty of the section of town they hadn't yet seen, especially the shops situated at the foot of the Himalayas.

They had dined at a restaurant in the shopping district, and the food had been delicious. Now they were at the nightclub the restaurant manager had recommended.

She was in Micah's arms on the dance floor. The music was slow, and he was holding her while their bodies moved together in perfect rhythm. She was vaguely aware of their surroundings. The inside of the club was dark and crowded. Evidently this was a popular hangout. The servers were moving at a hurried pace to fill mixed-drink orders. And the live band rotated periodically with a deejay.

"I like this place, Micah. Thanks for bringing me here."

"You're welcome."

"And this is our first dance," she added.

He glanced down at her, tightened his arms around her and smiled. "I hope it's not our last."

She hoped that, as well. She liked the feel of being held by him in a place other than the bedroom. It felt good. But she could tell he wanted her from the hard bulge pressing against her whenever their bodies moved together. She liked the feel of it. She liked knowing she was desired. She especially appreciated knowing she could do that to him—even here in a crowded night-club in the middle of a dance floor.

"Excalibur."

She glanced up at him. "Excuse me."

"My middle name is Excalibur."

She blinked, wondering why he was telling her that. "Oh, okay."

He chuckled. "You didn't know that, did you?"

She shrugged. "Was I supposed to?"

"I wish you had. I should have told you. We were involved for two months."

Yes, they had been involved, but their affair had been more about sex than conversation. He interrupted her thoughts by saying, "I know more about you than you know about me, Kalina."

She tilted her head to the side and looked at him. "You think so?"

"Yes."

"Well, then, tell me what you know," she said.

He tightened his arms around her waist as they swayed their bodies in time with the music. "You're twenty-seven. Your middle name is Marie. Your birth-day is June fifteenth. Your favorite color is red. You hate eating beets. Your mother's name was Yvonne, and she died of cancer when you were ten."

He grinned as if proud of himself. "So what does that tell you?"

She stared at him for a few moments as if collect-ing her thoughts and then said, "I did more pillow talk than you did."

He laughed at that. "Sort of. What it tells me is that you shared more of yourself with me than I did with you."

They had already concluded there were a lot of things they didn't know about each other. So, okay, he had a heads-up on her information. That was fine. What they'd shared for those two months was a bed and not much else.

"It should not have been just sex between us, Kalina. I can see that now."

Now, *that's* where she disagreed. Their affair was never intended to be about anything but sex. For those two months, they had gotten to know each other intimately but not intellectually, and that's the way they'd wanted it. "If what you say is true, Micah, nobody told me. I distinctively recall you laying down the rules for a no-strings affair. And I remember agreeing to those rules. Your career was your life, and so was mine."

Evidently, she'd given him something to think about, because he didn't say anything to that. The music stopped, and he led her back to their table. A server was there, ready to take their drink order. One thing she'd noticed, two years ago and today, was that Micah was always a gentleman. He was a man who held doors open for ladies, who stood when women entered the room and who pulled out chairs for his date…the way he was doing now. "Thanks."

"You're welcome."

She glanced across the table at him. "You have impeccable manners."

He chuckled. "I wouldn't go that far, but I do my best."

"Do your brothers and cousins all have good manners like you?"

He winked. "Come home to Denver with me and find out."

Kalina rolled her eyes in exasperation. "You won't give up, will you?"

"No. I think you owe me the chance to clear my name."

He didn't say anything for a moment, allowing the server to place their drinks in front of them. Then she took a sip of her wine and asked, "Is clearing your name important to you, Micah?"

Leaning back, he stared over at her before saying, "If you really knew me the way I want you to know me, you wouldn't be asking me that."

She didn't say anything for a while. A part of her wanted to believe him, to believe that he truly did want her to get to know him better, to believe that he hadn't done what her father had said. But what if she went home with him, got to know him and, in the end, still felt he was capable to doing what she had accused him of doing?

"Micah—"

"You owe me that, Kalina. I think I've been more than fair, considering I am innocent of everything you've accused me of. Some men wouldn't give a damn about what you believed, but I do. Like I said, you owe me the chance to prove your father lied."

She drew in a deep breath. Did she owe him? She didn't have much time to think about it. He reached across the table and captured her small hand in his bigger one. Just a touch from him did things to her, made her feel what she didn't want to feel.

"I hadn't wanted to make love to you again until we resolved things between us," he said in a low tone.

She gave a cynical laugh. "So now you're going to claim making love last night and this morning was my idea?"

"No. I wanted you, and I knew that you wanted me."

He was right, and there was no need to ask how he'd known that. She had wanted him, and she'd been fully aware that he had wanted her.

"Would it make you feel more comfortable about going home with me if I promise not to touch you while you're there?"

She narrowed her gaze. "No, because all you'll do is find ways to tempt me to the point where I'll end up being the one seeking you out. I'm well aware of those games you play, Micah."

He didn't deny it. "Okay, then. We are adults," he said. "With needs. But the purpose of you going to Denver with me is not to continue our sexual interactions. I want to make that clear up front."

He had made that clear more times than she cared to count. Her stomach knotted, and she wondered when she would finally admit that the real reason she was reluctant to go to Denver was that she might end up getting too attached to him, to his family, to her surroundings...

Her heart hammered at the mere thought of that happening. For years, especially after her grandparents' deaths, she had felt like a loner. She'd had her father—whenever he managed to stay in one place long enough to be with her. But their relationship wasn't like most parent-child relationships. She believed deep down that he loved her, but she also knew that he expressed that love by trying to control her. As long as she followed his orders like one of his soldiers, she remained in his good graces. But if she rebelled, there was hell to pay. The only reason he had apologized for his actions regarding her canceled trip to Beijing was that, for the first time in his life, he saw that he could make her angry enough that he could lose her. She had been just that upset with him, and he knew it. Although he had never admitted it, her father was just as much of a maverick as she was.

She glanced down at the table and saw that Micah was still holding her hand. It felt good. Too good. Too right. She thought about pulling her hand away, but decided to let it stay put since he seemed content holding it. Her breathing quickened when he began stroking her palm in a light caress. His touch was so stimulating it played on her nerve endings as if they were the strings of a well-tuned guitar.

She glanced up and met his gaze. He stopped stroking her skin and curved his hand over hers to entwine their fingers. "No matter what you believe, Kal, I would never intentionally hurt you."

She nodded and then he slowly withdrew his hand from hers. She instantly felt the loss of that contact.

He glanced around the club and then at the dance floor. The deejay was playing another slow song. "Come on, I want to hold you in my arms again," he said, reaching out and taking her hand one more time.

He led her to the dance floor, and she placed her head on his chest. He wrapped his arms around her, encompassing her in his embrace. His heart was beating fast against her cheek, and his erection pressed hard against her middle again. She smiled. Did he really think they could go to Denver together and not share a bed?

She chuckled. Now she was beginning to wonder if he really knew *her* that well.

He touched her chin and tipped her head back to meet his gaze. "You okay?"

She nodded, deciding not to tell him what she'd found so comical, especially since he was wearing such a serious expression on his face.

She saw something in the depths of his dark eyes that she didn't understand at first glance. But then she knew what she saw. It was a tenderness that was reaching out to her, making her feel both vulnerable and needed at the same time. At that moment she knew the truth.

"Kalina?"

The release of her name from his lips sent a shiver racing up her spine. Drawing in much-needed air, she said. "Yes, I'm fine. And I've reached a decision, Micah. I'm going to Denver with you."

Eight

"Welcome to Micah's Manor, Kalina,"

Micah stood aside as Kalina entered his home and looked around. He saw both awe and admiration reflected in her features. He hadn't told her what to expect and now he was glad that he hadn't. This was the first official visit to his place by any woman other than one of his relatives. What Kalina thought mattered to him.

In his great-grandfather's will, it had been declared that every Westmoreland heir would receive one hundred acres of land at the age of twenty-five. As the oldest, Dillon got the family homestead, which included the huge family house that sat on over three hundred acres.

Micah had already established a career as an epidemiologist and was living in Washington by the time his twenty-fifth birthday came around. For years, he'd kept the land undeveloped and whenever he came home he would crash at Dillon's place. But when Dillon got married and had a family of his own, Micah felt it was time to build his own house.

He had taken off six months to supervise the project. That had been the six months following the end of his affair with the very woman now standing in his living room. He had needed something to occupy his time, and his thoughts, and having this house built seemed the perfect project.

He could count on one finger the number of times he had actually spent the night here, since he rarely came home. The last time had been when he'd come to Denver for his brother Jason's wedding reception in August. It had been nice to stay at his own place, and the logistics had worked out fine since he, his siblings and cousins all had houses in proximity to each other.

"So, what do you think?" he asked, placing Kalina's luggage by the front door.

"This place is for one person?"

He couldn't help laughing. He knew why she was asking. Located at the south end of the rural area that the locals referred to as Westmoreland Country, Micah's Manor sat on Gemma Lake, the huge body of water his great-grandfather had named in honor of his wife when he'd settled here all those years ago. Micah's huge ranch-style house was three stories high with over six thousand square feet of living space.

"Yes. I admit I let Gemma talk me into getting carried away, but—"

"Gemma?"

"One of my cousins. She's an interior designer. To

take full advantage of the lake, she figured I needed the third floor, and as for the size, I figured when my time ended with the feds, I would want to settle down, marry and raise a family. It was easier to build that dream house now instead of adding on later."

"Good planning."

"I thought so at the time. I picked the plan I liked best, hired a builder and hung around for six months to make sure things got off to a good start," he added.

"Oh, I see."

He knew she really didn't. She had no idea that when he'd selected this particular floor plan he had envisioned her sharing it with him, even though the last thing she had uttered to him was that she hated his guts. For some reason, he hadn't been able to push away the fantasy that one day she would come here and see this place. He had even envisioned them making love in his bedroom while seeing the beauty of the lake. Having Kalina here now was a dream come true.

"I had to leave on assignment to Peru for a few months and when I returned, the house was nearly finished. I took more time off and was here when Gemma began decorating it."

"It is beautiful, Micah."

He was glad she liked it. "Thanks. I practically gave Gemma an open checkbook, and she did her thing. Of course, since it wasn't her money, she decided to splurge a little."

Kalina raised a dubious brow. "A little?"

He shrugged and grinned. "Okay, maybe a lot. Up until a year ago she used this place as a model home to showcase her work whenever she was trying to impress new clients. As you can see, her work speaks for itself."

Kalina glanced around. "Yes, it sure does. Your cousin is very gifted. Is she no longer in the business?"

"She's still in it."

"But she no longer needs your house as a model?" Kalina asked.

"No, mainly because she's living in Australia now that she and Callum are married. That's where he's from. They have a two-month-old son. You'll get to meet them some time next week. She's coming home for a visit."

He had given his family strict orders to stay away from his place to give him time to get settled in with his houseguest. Of course, everyone was anxious to meet the woman he'd brought home with him.

"This should be an interesting thirty days," she said, admiring a huge painting on the wall.

"Why do you say that?"

She shrugged. "Well, all those markers I saw getting here. Jason's Place. Zane's Hideout. Canyon's Bluff. Ramsey's Web. Derringer's Dungeon. Stern's Stronghold… Need I go on?"

He chuckled. "No, and you have my cousin Bailey to thank for that. We give her the honor of naming everyone's parcel of land, and she's come up with some doozies." He picked up her luggage. "Come on, I'll show you to your room. If you aren't in the mood to climb the stairs, I do have an elevator."

"No, the stairs are fine. Besides, it gives me the chance to work the kinks out of my body from our long flight."

She followed him to one of the guest rooms on the

third floor. They hadn't slept together since that one night he'd spent with her after they'd met on the staircase. Even after he'd taken her dancing, he had returned her to her room at the villa, planted a kiss on her cheek and left. The next day had been extremely busy with them packing up the lab's equipment and finalizing reports.

They had been too busy to spend time getting naked on silken sheets. But that hadn't meant the thought hadn't run through his mind a few times. Yesterday they'd taken the plane here, and sat beside each other for the flight. The twelve hours from India to Washington, and then the six hours from Washington to Denver had given him time to reflect on what he hoped she would get from her thirty days with him and his family.

"Wow!" Kalina walked into Micah's guest bedroom and couldn't do anything but stare, turn around and stare some more.

The room was done in chocolate, white and lime green. Everything—from the four-poster, white, queen-size bed, to the curtains and throw pillows—was perfectly matched. The walls of the room were painted white, which made the space look light and airy. Outside her huge window was a panoramic view of the lake she'd seen when they arrived. There was a private bath that was triple the size of the one she had in her home in Virginia. It had both a Jacuzzi tub and a walk-in shower.

She wasn't surprised Micah had given her one of his guest rooms to use. He wanted to shift their relationship from the physical to the mental. She just wasn't so sure she agreed with his logic. She could still get to know him while they shared a bed, and she didn't understand why he assumed differently. She watched him place the luggage by her bed. He said nothing as she continued to check out other interesting aspects of the room.

"I can see why Gemma used your house as a model home," Kalina said, coming to stand in front of him. "Your house should be featured in one of those magazines."

He chuckled. "It was. Last year. I have a copy downstairs. You can read the article if you like."

"All right."

"I'll leave you to rest up and relax. I plan on preparing dinner later."

She raised a surprised brow. "You can cook?"

He laughed. "Of course I can cook. And I'm pretty good at it, you'll see." He reached out and softly kissed her on the lips. "Now, get some rest."

He turned to leave, but she stopped him. "Where's your room?"

He smiled down at her as if he had an idea why she was asking. "It's on the second floor. I'll give you a tour of my bedroom anytime you want it."

She nodded, fully aware that a tour of his bedroom wasn't what she was really interested in. She wanted to try out his bed.

A few hours later, Kalina closed her eyes as she savored the food in her mouth. "Mmm, this is delicious," she said, slowly opening her eyes and glancing across the dinner table at Micah.

After indulging in a bath in the Jacuzzi, she had taken a nap, only to awaken hours later to the smell of something good cooking in the kitchen downstairs. She had slipped into a T-shirt and a pair of capris, and, not bothering to put shoes on, she had headed downstairs to find Micah at the stove. In his bare feet, shirtless, with jeans riding low on his hips, he'd looked the epitome of sexy as he moved around his spacious kitchen. She had watched him and had seen for herself just how at home he was while making a meal. She couldn't help admiring him. Some men couldn't even boil water.

He had told her he could cook, but she hadn't taken him at his word. Now, after tasting what he'd prepared, she was forced to believe him. *Almost*. She glanced around the kitchen.

"What are you looking for?" he asked her.

She looked back at him and smiled. "Your chef."

Micah chuckled. "You won't find one here. I did all this myself. I don't particularly like cooking, but I won't starve if I have to do it for myself."

No, he wouldn't starve. In fact, he had enough cooking skills to keep himself well fed. He had prepared meat loaf, rice and gravy, green beans and iced tea. He'd explained that he'd called ahead and had gotten his cousin Megan to go grocery shopping for him. She'd picked up everything he'd asked her to get and a few things he hadn't asked her for…like the three flavors of ice cream now in the freezer.

"Do you ever get lonely out here, Micah?"

He glanced across the table at her and laughed. "Are you kidding? I have relatives all around me. I try to catch up on my rest whenever I'm home, but they don't make it easy. Although I'm not here the majority of the time, I'm involved in the family business. I have a share in my brother's and cousins' horse-breeding business, in my cousin Ramsey's sheep business and I'm on the board of Blue Ridge Land Management." He then told her how his father and uncle had founded the company years ago and how his brother Dillon was now CEO.

Kalina immediately recognized the name of the company. It had made the Forbes Top 50 just this year. She could only sit and stare at him. She'd had no idea he was one of *those* Westmorelands.

Not that having a lot of money was everything, but it told her more about his character than he realized. He worked because he wanted to work, not because he had to. Yet he always worked just as hard as any member of his team—sometimes even harder. She couldn't help wondering how he'd chosen his field of work and why he was so committed and dedicated to it.

Over dinner he told her more about his family, his brothers and cousins, especially the escapades of the younger Westmorelands. Although she tried not to laugh, she found some of their antics downright comical and could only imagine how his cousins Dillon and Ramsey had survived it all while still managing to keep the family together.

"And you say there are fifteen of you?" she asked, pushing her plate away.

"Yes, of the Denver clan. Everyone is here except Gemma, who now lives in Sydney, and the few who are still away at college. Needless to say, the holidays are fun times for us when everyone comes home."

Getting up to take their plates to the sink, he asked, "Do you feel like going horseback riding later? I thought I'd give you a tour of the rest of the house and then we can ride around my property."

Excitement spread through her. "I'd like that."

He returned to the seat next to her. "But first I think we need to have a talk."

She lifted an eyebrow. "About what?"

"About whose bed you'll be sleeping in while you're here."

And before she could respond, he had swept her out of her chair and into his arms. He carried her from the kitchen into the living room where he settled down on the sofa with her in his lap.

Micah smiled at the confused look on Kalina's face. She brushed back a handful of hair and then pinned him with one of her famous glares. "I didn't know there was a question about where I'd be sleeping."

She wasn't fooling him one bit. "Isn't there? I put you in the guest room for a reason."

She waved off his words. "Then maybe we do need to talk about that foolishness regarding your no-sex policy again."

He'd figured she would want to discuss it, which was why he'd brought up the subject. "It will be less complicated if we don't share the same bed for a while."

"Until I really get to know you?"

"Yes."

"I disagree with your logic on taking that approach, especially since you want me. Do you deny it?"

How could he deny it when he had an erection he knew she could feel since she was practically sitting on it. "No, I don't deny it, but like I said when I invited you here, I want you to—"

"Get to know you," she muttered. "I heard you. More times than I care to. And I don't think us sharing a bed has anything to do with what we do outside the bedroom."

"Well, I do. Last time we had an affair it was strictly

sexual. Now I want to change the way you think about me, about us."

Now she really looked confused. "To what?"

He wished he could tell her the truth, that she was the woman he wanted above all others. That he wanted to marry her. He wanted her to have his babies. He wanted her to wear his name. But all the things he wanted meant nothing until she could trust him. They would never come into existence until she could believe he was not the man her father had made him out to be. This time around, Micah refused to allow sex to push those wants to the side.

"I want you to think of things other than sex when it comes to us, Kalina," he said.

She frowned. "Why?"

He could come clean and tell her how he felt about her, but he didn't think she would believe him, just as she still didn't believe he had not betrayed her two years ago. "Because we've been there before. Even you said that our relationship was starting with the same technique. I want you to feel that it's different this time."

He could tell she still didn't know where he was coming from, but the important thing was that *he* knew. A dawning awareness suddenly appeared on her features, but he had a feeling, even before she opened her mouth, that whatever she was thinking was all wrong.

"Okay, I think I get it," she said, nodding.

He was afraid to ask, but knew he had to. "And just what do you get?"

"You're one of the older Westmorelands and you feel you should set an example for the others." She nodded her head as if her assumption made perfect sense.

"Set an example for them in what way?" he asked.

"By presenting me as a friend and not a lover. You did say your cousin Bailey was young and impressionable."

He had to keep a straight face. He forced his eyes to stay focused even though he was tempted to roll them. Once she met Bailey she would see how absurd her assumption was. First of all, although she was twenty-three years old, Bailey probably didn't have much of a love life, thanks to all her older, overbearing and protective brothers and male cousins. And she had gone past being impressionable. Bailey could curse worse than any sailor when she put her mind to it. He and his brothers and cousins had already decided that the man who fell for Bailey would have to be admired...as well as pitied.

"The key word where Bailey is concerned is *was*. Trust me. I don't have to hide my affairs from anyone. Everyone around here is an adult and understands what grown-ups do."

"In that case, what other reason could you have for not wanting us to sleep together? Unless..."

He stared at her for several long moments, and when she didn't finish what she was about to say, he prompted her. "Unless what?"

She looked down at her hands in her lap. "Nothing."

He had a feeling that again, whatever was bothering her, she'd figured wrong. He reached out, lifted her chin up and brought his face closer to hers. "And I know good and well you aren't thinking what I think you're thinking, not when my desire for you is about to burst through my zipper. There's no way you can deny that you feel it."

She nodded slowly. "Yes, I can feel it," she said softly.

So could he, and he was aware, even more than he'd been before, of just how much he wanted her. Unfortunately, pointing out his body's reaction made her aware of how much he wanted her, as well.

She stuck her tongue out and slowly licked the corner of his lips. "Then why are you denying me what I want? Why are you denying yourself what you want?"

Good question. He had to think hard to recall the reason he was denying them both. He had a plan. A little sacrifice now would pay off plenty of dividends in the years to come. Remembering his goals wouldn't have been so hard if she hadn't decided at that very moment to play the vixen. She purposely twisted that little behind of hers in his lap, against his zipper, making him mindful of just how good his erection felt against her backside. And what the hell was she doing with her tongue, using the tip of it to lick his mouth? She was deliberately boggling his mind.

"Kalina?"

"Mmm?"

"Stop it," he said in a tone he knew was not really strong on persuasion. It wasn't helping matters that he'd once fantasized about them making love in this very room and on this very sofa.

"No, I don't want to stop and you can't make me," she said in that stubborn voice of hers.

Hell, okay, he silently agreed. *Maybe I can't make her stop.* And he figured that reasoning with her would be a waste of time....

At that moment she moved her tongue lower to lick the area around his jaw and he groaned.

"Oh, I so love the way you taste, Micah."

Those were the wrong words for her to say. Hearing them made him recall just how much he loved how she tasted, as well. He drew in a deep breath, hoping to find resistance. Instead, he inhaled her feminine scent, a telltale sign of how much she wanted him. He could just imagine the sweetness of her nectar.

He thought of everything…counting sheep, the pictures on the wall, the fact that he hadn't yet cleaned off the kitchen table…but nothing could clear his mind of her scent, or the way she was using her tongue. Now she had moved even lower to lick around his shoulder blades. Hell, why hadn't he put on a shirt?

"Baby, you've got to stop," he urged her in a strained voice.

She ignored him and kept right on doing what she was doing. He tried giving himself a mental shake and found it did not work. She was using her secret weapon, that blasted tongue of hers, to break him down. Hell, he would give anything for something—even a visit from one of his kin—to interrupt what she was doing, because he was losing the willpower to put a stop to it.

Hot, achy sensations swirled in his gut when she scooted off his lap. By the time he had figured out what she was about to do, it was too late. She had slid down his zipper and reached inside his jeans to get just what she wanted. He tightened his arms on her, planning to pull her up, but again he was too late. She lowered her head and took him into her mouth.

Kalina ignored the tug on her hair and kept her mouth firmly planted on Micah. By the time she was finished with him, he would think twice about resisting her, not giving her what she wanted or acting on foolish thoughts like them not sharing a bed now that she'd come all the way to Denver with him. He had a lot of nerve.

And he had a lot of this, she thought, fitting her mouth firmly on him, barely able to do so because he was so large. He was the only man she'd ever done this to. The first time she hadn't been sure she had done it correctly. But he had assured her that she had, and he'd also assured her he had enjoyed it immensely. So she might as well provide him with more enjoyment, maybe then he would start thinking the way she wanted him to. Or, for the moment, stop thinking at all.

"Damn, Kalina, please stop."

She heard his plea, but thought it didn't sound all that convincing, so she continued doing what she was doing, and pretty soon the tug on her hair stopped. Now he was twirling her locks around his fingers to hold her mouth in place. No need. She didn't intend to go anywhere.

At least she thought she wouldn't be. Suddenly, he pulled her up and tossed her down on the sofa. The moment her back hit the cushions he was there, lifting her T-shirt over her head and sliding her capris and panties down her legs, leaving her totally naked.

The heat of his gaze raked over her, and she felt it everywhere, especially in her feminine core. "No need to let a good erection go to waste, Micah," she said saucily.

He evidently agreed with her. Tugging his jeans and briefs down over his muscular hips, he didn't waste any time slipping out of the clothes before moving to take his place between her open legs.

She lifted her arms to receive him and whispered, "Just think of this as giving me a much-deserved treat."

Kalina would have laughed at his snort if he hadn't captured her mouth in his the moment he slid inside her, not stopping until he went all the way to the hilt. And then he began moving inside her, stroking her desire to the point of raging out of control. She lifted her hips off the sofa to receive every hard thrust. The wall of his chest touched hers, brushing against her breasts in a rhythm that sent sensations rushing through her bloodstream.

Then he pulled away from her mouth, looked down at her and asked in a guttural voice, "Why?"

She knew what he was asking. "Because it makes no sense to deny us this pleasure."

He didn't say whether he agreed with her or not. Instead, he placed his hands against her backside and lifted her hips so they would be ready to meet his downward plunge. She figured he probably wasn't happy with her. He wouldn't appreciate how she had tempted him and pushed him over the edge. She figured he would stew for a while, but that was fine. Eventually he would get over it.

But apparently not before he put one sensuous whipping on her, she thought, loving the feel of how he was moving inside her. It was as if he wanted to use his body to give her a message, but she wasn't sure just what point he was trying to make. She reached up and cupped his face in her hands, forcing him to look at her. "What?" she asked breathlessly.

He started to move his lips in reply, but then, instead, leaned down and captured her mouth in his, leaving her wondering what he had been about to say. Probably just another scolding. All thoughts left her mind when she got caught up in his kiss and the way he was stroking inside her body.

She dropped her hands to his shoulders and then wrapped her arms around his neck as every sensation intensified. Then her body exploded, and simultaneously, so did his. They cried out each other's names.

This, she concluded, as a rush swept over her, was pleasure beyond anything they'd shared before. This was worth his irritation once everything was over. For now, she was fueled by this. She was stroked, claimed and overpowered by the most sensuous lovemaking she had ever known. By Micah's hands and his body.

This had been better than any fantasy, and she couldn't think of a better way to be welcomed to Micah's Manor.

Nine

Okay, so she hadn't held a gun to his head or forced him to make love to her, but he was still pissed. Not only at her but at himself, Micah concluded the next morning as he walked out of the house toward the barn.

After they'd made love yesterday, Kalina had passed out. He had gathered her in his arms and taken her up the stairs to the guest room. After placing her naked body beneath the covers, he had left, closing the door behind him. He'd even thought about locking it. The woman was dangerous. She had not been so rebellious the last time.

Cursing and calling himself all kinds of names—including whipped, weakling and fickle—he had cleaned up the kitchen, unpacked his luggage and done some laundry. By the time he'd finished all his chores, it had gotten dark outside. He'd then gone into his office and made calls to his family to let them know he'd returned. Most had figured as much when they'd seen lights burning over at his place. He had again warned them that he didn't want to be disturbed. He'd assured them that he and his houseguest would make an appearance when they got good and ready. He ended up agreeing to bring her to dinner tomorrow night at the big house.

By the time he'd hung up the phone after talking to everyone, it was close to nine o'clock and he was surprised that he hadn't heard a peep out of Kalina. He checked on her and found her still sleeping. He had left her that way, figuring that when she'd caught up on her rest she would wake up. Still angry with himself for giving in to temptation and momentarily forgetting his plan, he'd gone to bed.

He'd awakened around midnight to the sound of footsteps coming down the stairs. He was very much aware when the footsteps paused in front of his closed bedroom door before finally progressing to the first floor. He had flipped onto his back and listened to the sound of Kalina moving around downstairs, knowing she was raiding his refrigerator—probably getting into those three flavors of ice cream.

When he had woken up this morning he had checked on her again. Sometime during the night she had changed into a pair of pajamas and was now sleeping on top of the covers. It had taken everything within him not to shed his own clothes and slide into that bed beside her.

Then he'd gotten mad at himself for thinking he should not have let her sleep alone. He should have made love to her all through the night. He should have let her go to sleep in his arms. He should have woken her up with his lovemaking this morning.

He had quickly forced those thoughts from his mind, considering them foolish, and had gone into the kitchen. He had prepared breakfast and kept it warming on the stove for her while he headed to the barn. He preferred not to be around when she woke up. The woman was pure temptation and making love to her every chance he got was not what he had in mind for this trip.

He had thought about getting into his truck and going to visit his family, but knew it wouldn't be a good idea to be off the property when Kalina finally woke up. He glanced at his watch. It was nine o'clock already. Was she planning to sleep until noon? His family probably figured he was keeping them away because he didn't want them to invade his private time with her. Boy, were they wrong.

"Good morning, Micah. I'm ready to go riding now."

He spun around and stared straight into Kalina's face. "Where did you come from?"

She smiled and looked at him as if he'd asked a silly question. "From inside the house. Where else would I have been?"

He frowned. "I didn't hear you approach."

She used her hand to wave off his words. "Whatever. You promised to take me riding yesterday, but we didn't get around to it since we were indulging in other things. I'm ready now."

His frown deepened, knowing just what those "other things" were. She was dressed in a pair of well-worn jeans, boots and a button-down shirt. He tried not to stare so hard at how the jeans fit her body, making him want to caress each of her curves. She looked good, and it took everything he had to keep his eyes from popping out of their sockets.

"Are we going riding or not?"

He glanced up at her face and saw her chin had raised a fraction. She expected a fight and was evidently ready for one. Just as she had been ready for them to make love yesterday. Well, he had news for her. Unlike yesterday, he wouldn't be accommodating her.

"Fine," he said, grabbing his Stetson off a rack on the barn wall. "Let's ride."

Kalina couldn't believe Micah was in a bad mood just because she had tempted him into making love to her. But here they were, riding side by side, and he was all but ignoring her.

She glanced over at him when he brought the horses to a stop along a ridge so she could look down over the valley. His Stetson was pulled low on his brow, and the shadow on his chin denoted he hadn't shaved that morning. He wore a dark brooding look, but, in her opinion, he appeared so sexy, so devastatingly handsome, that it was a total turn-on. It had taken all she could not to suggest they return to his place and make love. With his present mood, she knew better than to push her luck.

"Any reason you're staring at me, Kal?"

She inwardly smiled. So...he'd known she was looking. "No reason. I was just thinking."

He glanced over at her, tipped his hat back and those bedroom-brown eyes sent sensations floating around in her stomach. "Thinking about what?"

"Your mood. Are you typically a moody person?"

He frowned and looked back at the valley. "I'm not moody," he muttered.

"Yes, you are. Sex puts most men in a good mood. I see it does the opposite for you. I find that pretty interesting."

He glanced back at her. A tremor coursed through her with the look he was giving her. It was hot, regardless of the reason. "You just don't get it, do you?"

She shrugged. "Evidently not, so how about enlightening me on what I just don't get."

He inhaled deeply and then muttered, "Nothing."

"Evidently there is something, Micah."

He looked away again and moments later looked back at her. "There is nothing."

He then glanced at his watch. "I promised everyone I would bring you to dinner at the big house. They can hardly wait to meet you."

"And I'm looking forward to meeting them, too."

He watched her for a long moment. Too long. "What?" she asked, wondering why he kept staring at her.

He shook his head. "Nothing. I promised you a tour of the place. Come on. Let's go back home."

It was only moments later, as they rode side by side, that it dawned on her what he'd said.

"Let's go back home..."

Although she knew Micah hadn't meant it the way it had sounded, he'd said it as if they were a married couple and Micah's Manor was theirs. Something pricked inside her. Why was she suddenly feeling disappointed at the thought that Micah's home would never be hers?

* * *

"I like Kalina, Micah, and she's nothing like I expected."

Micah took a sip of his drink as he stood with Zane on the sidelines, watching how his female cousins and cousins-in-law had taken Kalina into their midst and were making her feel right at home. He could tell from the smile on Kalina's face that she was comfortable around them.

Micah glanced up at his cousin. "What were you expecting?"

Zane chuckled. "Another mad scientist like you. Someone who was going to bore us with all that scientific mumbo jumbo. I definitely wasn't expecting a sexy doctor. Hell, if she didn't belong to you, I would hit on her myself."

Micah couldn't help smiling. He, of all people, knew about his cousin's womanizing ways. "I'm sure you would, and I'm glad you're not. I appreciate the loyalty."

"No problem. But you might want to lay down the law to the twins when they arrive next week."

He thought about his twin cousins, Aidan and Adrian, and the trouble they used to get into—the trouble they could still get into at times although both were away at college and doing well. It was something about being in Westmoreland Country that made them want to revert to being hellions—especially when it came to women.

"You haven't brought a woman home for us to meet since Patrice. Does this mean anything?"

Micah took another sip of his drink before deciding to be completely honest. "I plan to marry Kalina one day."

A smooth smile touched Zane's features. "Figured as much. Does she know it?"

"Not yet. I'm trying to give her the chance to get to know me."

If Zane found that comment strange he didn't let on. Instead, he changed the subject and brought Micah up to date on how things were going in the community. Micah listened, knowing that if anyone knew what was going on it would be Zane.

Micah was well aware that Westmoreland Country would become a madhouse in a few weeks, when everyone began arriving for the christening of Gemma's baby. They were expecting all those other Westmorelands from Atlanta, Texas and Montana. And his brothers and cousins attending college had planned to return for the event, as well.

"I hadn't heard Dillon say whether Bane is coming home."

Zane shrugged. "Not sure since he might be in training someplace."

Micah nodded. Everyone knew of his baby brother's quest to become a Navy SEAL, as well as Bane's mission to one day find the woman he'd given up a few years ago. And knowing his brother as he did, Micah knew Brisbane would eventually succeed in doing both.

"I like Kalina, Micah."

Micah turned when his brother Jason walked up. The most recent member of the family to marry, Jason and his wife, Bella, were expecting twins. From the look of Bella, the babies would definitely arrive any day now.

"I'm glad you do since you might as well get used to seeing her around," Micah said.

"Does that mean you're thinking of retiring as the

Westmoreland mad scientist and returning home to start a family?" Jason asked.

Micah chuckled. "No, it doesn't mean any of that. I love my career, and Kalina loves hers. It just means we'll be working together more, and whenever I come home we'll come together."

He took a sip of his drink, thinking that what he'd just said sounded really good. Now all he had to do was convince Kalina. She had to get to know the real him, believe in him, trust him and then they could move on in their lives together.

He still wasn't happy about the stunt she'd pulled on him yesterday. He was determined to keep his distance until she realized the truth about him.

Kalina glanced across the room at Micah before turning her attention back to the women surrounding her. All of them had gone out of their way to make her feel at home. She hadn't known what to expect from this family dinner, but the one thing she hadn't expected was to find a group of women who were so warm and friendly.

Even Bailey, who Micah had said had been standoffish to Patrice, was more than friendly, and Kalina felt the warm hospitality was genuine. She readily accepted the women's invitation to go shopping with them later this week and to do other things like take in a couple of chick flicks, visit the spa and get their hair done. They wanted to have a "fun" week. Given Micah's present mood, she figured spending time away from him wouldn't be a bad idea.

After they'd returned to the ranch from riding, he had taken her on a quick tour of his home. Just like yesterday, she had been more than impressed with what she'd seen. His bedroom had left her speechless, and she couldn't imagine him sleeping in that huge bed alone. She planned to remedy that. It made no sense for them to be sleeping in separate beds. He wouldn't be happy about it, but he would just have to get over it.

"Um, I wonder what has Micah frowning," Pam Westmoreland, Dillon's wife, leaned over to whisper to her. "He keeps looking over this way, and I recognize that look. It's one of those Westmoreland 'you're not doing as I say' looks."

Kalina couldn't help smiling. The woman who was married to the oldest Westmoreland here had pegged her brother-in-law perfectly. "He's stewing over something I did, but he'll get over it."

Pam chuckled. "Yes, eventually he will. Once in a while they like to have their way but don't think we should have ours. There's nothing wrong with showing them that 'their way' isn't always the best way."

Hours later, while sitting beside Micah as he drove them back to Micah's Manor, Kalina recalled the conversation she'd had with Pam. Maybe continuing to defy his expectations—showing him that his way wasn't the best way—was how she should continue to handle Micah.

"Did you enjoy yourself, Kalina?"

She glanced over at him. He hadn't said much to her all evening, although the only time he'd left her side was when the women had come to claim her. If this was his way of letting her get to know him then he was way off the mark.

"Yes, I had a wonderful time. I enjoyed conversing

with the women in your family. They're all nice. I like them."

"They like you, too. I could tell."

"What about you, Micah? Do you like me?"

He seemed surprised by her question. "Yes, of course. Why do you ask?"

"Um, no reason."

She looked straight ahead at the scenery flying by the car's windshield, and felt a warm sensation ignite within her every time she was aware that he was looking at her.

She surprised him when she caught him staring one of those times. Just so he wouldn't know she was onto what he was doing, she smiled and asked, "Was your grandfather Raphel really married to all those women? Bailey told me the story of how he became the black sheep of the family after running off in the early 1900s with the preacher's wife and about all the other wives he supposedly collected along the way."

Micah made a turn into Micah's Manor. "That's what everyone wants to find out. We need to know if there are any more Westmorelands out there that we don't know about. That's how we found out about our cousins living in Atlanta, Montana and Texas. Until a few years ago, we were unaware that Raphel had a twin by the name of Reginald Westmoreland. He's the great-grandfather for those other Westmorelands. Megan is hiring a private detective to help solve the puzzle about Raphel's other wives. We've eliminated two as having given birth to heirs, and now we have two more to check out."

He paused a moment and said, "The investigator, a guy by the name of Rico Claiborne, was to start work on the case months ago, but his involvement in another case has delayed things for a while. We're hoping he can start the search soon. Megan is determined to see how many more Westmorelands she can dig up."

Kalina chuckled. "There are so many of you now. I can't imagine there being others."

Micah smiled. "Well, there are, trust me. You'll get to meet them in a few weeks when they arrive for Gemma and Callum's son's christening."

"Must be nice," she said softly.

He glanced over at her. "What must be?"

"To be part of a big family where everyone is close and looks out for each other. I like that. I've never experienced anything like that before. Other than my grandparents, there has only been me and Dad…and well, you know how my relationship with him is most of the time."

Micah didn't say anything, and maybe it was just as well. It didn't take much for Kalina to recall what had kept them apart for the past two years. Although he was probably hoping otherwise, by getting to know him better, all she'd seen so far was his moody side.

When he brought the car to a stop, she said, "You like having your way, don't you, Micah?"

He didn't say anything at first and then he pushed his Stetson back out of his face. "Is that what you think?"

"Yes. But maybe you should consider something?"

"What?"

"Whatever it is you're trying to prove to me, there's a possibility that your way isn't the best way to prove it. You brought me here so I could get to know you better. It's day two and already we're at odds with each other, and only because I tempted you into doing something that I knew we both wanted to do anyway. But if you prefer that it not happen again, then it won't. In other words, I will give you just what you want...which is practically nothing."

Without saying anything else, she opened the door, got out of the truck and walked toward the house.

Be careful what you ask for, Micah thought over his cup of coffee a few mornings later as he watched Kalina enter the kitchen. She'd been here for five days. Things between them weren't bad, but they could be better. It wasn't that they were mad at each other. In fact, they were always pleasant to each other. Too pleasant.

She had no idea that beneath all his pleasantry was a man who was horny as hell. A man whose body ached to make love to her, hold her at night. He wished she could sleep with him instead of sleeping alone in his guest bedroom. But his mind knew his decision that he and Kalina not make love for a while was the right one to make. It was his body wishing things could be different.

They would see each other in the mornings, and then usually, during the day, they went their separate ways. It wasn't uncommon for one of his female cousins or cousins-in-laws to come pick her up. On those days, he wouldn't see her till much later. So much for them spending time together.

"Good morning, Micah."

He put down his cup and pushed the newspaper aside. "Good morning, Kalina. Did you enjoy going shopping yesterday?"

She sat down at the table across from him and smiled. "I didn't go shopping yesterday. We did that two days ago. Yesterday, we went into town and watched a movie. One of those chick flicks."

He nodded. She could have asked him, and he would have taken her to the movies, chick flick or not. He got up to pour himself another cup of coffee, trying not to notice what she was wearing. Most days she would be wearing jeans and a top. Today she had put on a simple dress. Seeing her in it reminded him once again of what a nice pair of legs she owned.

"Are you and the ladies going someplace again today?" he decided to ask her.

She shook her head. "No. I plan to hang around here today. But I promise not to get in your way."

"You won't get in my way." He came back to the table and sat down. "Other than that day we went riding, I haven't shown you the rest of my property."

She lifted an eyebrow in surprise. "You mean there's more?"

He chuckled. "Yes, there's a part that I lease out to Ramsey for his sheep, and then another part I lease out to my brother Jason and my cousins Zane and Derringer for their horse-breeding business."

He took a sip of his coffee. "So how about us spending the day together?"

She smiled brightly. "I'd love to."

Hours later when Micah and Kalina returned to Micah's Manor, she dropped down in the first chair she came to, which was a leather recliner in the living room. When Micah had suggested they spend time together, she hadn't expected that they would be gone for most of the day.

First, after she had changed clothes, they had gone

riding and he'd shown her the rest of his property. Then he had come back so they could change clothes, and they had taken the truck into town. He had driven to the nursing home to visit a man by the name of Henry Ryan. Henry, Micah had explained, had been the town's doctor for years and had delivered every Westmoreland born in Denver, including his parents. The old man, who was in his late nineties, was suffering from a severe case of Alzheimer's.

It had been obvious to Kalina from the first that the old man had been glad to see Micah and vice versa. Today, Henry's mind appeared sharp, and he had shared a lot with her, including some stories from Micah's childhood years. On the drive home, Micah had explained that things weren't always that way. There would be days when he visited Henry and the old man hadn't known who he was. Micah had credited Henry with being the one to influence him to go into the medical field.

Today, Kalina had seen another side of Micah. She'd known he was a dedicated doctor, but she'd seen him interact with people on a personal level. Not only had he visited with Henry, but he had dropped by the rooms of others at the nursing home that he'd gotten to know over the years. He remembered them, and they remembered him. Before arriving at the home, he had stopped by a market and purchased fresh fruit for everyone, which they all seemed to enjoy.

Seeing them, especially the older men, made her realize that her father would one day get old and she would be his caretaker. He was in the best of health now, but he wasn't getting any younger. It also made her realize, more so than ever, just what a caring person Micah was.

She turned to Micah, who'd come to sit on the sofa across from her. "I'll prepare dinner tonight."

He raised an eyebrow. "You can cook?"

Kalina laughed. "Yes. I lived on my grandparents' farm in Alabama for a while, remember. They were big cooks and taught me my way around any kitchen. I just don't usually have a lot of time to do it when I'm working."

She glanced at her watch. "I think I'll cook a pot of spaghetti with a salad. Mind if I borrow the truck and go to that Walmart we passed on the way back to get some fresh ingredients?"

"No, I don't mind," he said, standing and pulling the truck keys from his pocket. His cousins had stocked his kitchen, but only with non-perishables. "Although you might want to check with Chloe or Pam. They probably have what you'll need since they like to cook."

"I'm sure they do, but I need to get a prescription filled anyway. I didn't think about it earlier while we were out."

"No problem. Do you want me to drive you?"

"No, I'll be fine." She stood. "And I won't be gone long."

"Glad to see that you're out of your foul mood, Micah," Derringer Westmoreland said with a grin as he fed one of the horses he kept in Micah's barn.

Micah shot him a dirty look, which any other man would have known meant he should zip it, but Derringer wasn't worried. He knew his cousin was not the hostile type. "I don't know what brought it on, but you need to chill. Save your frown for those contagious diseases."

Micah folded his arms across his chest. "And when did you become an expert on domestic matters, Derringer?"

Derringer chuckled. "On the day I married Lucia. I tell you, my life hasn't been the same since. Being married is good. You ought to try it."

Micah dropped his hands to his sides and shrugged. "I plan on it. I just have to get Kalina to trust me. She's got to get to know me better."

Derringer frowned, which didn't surprise Micah. Whereas Zane hadn't seen anything strange by that comment, Derringer would. "Doesn't she know you already?"

"Not the way I want her to. She thinks I betrayed her a couple of years ago, and I believe that once she gets to know me she'll see I'm not capable of doing anything like that."

Now it was Derringer who crossed his arms over his chest. "Wouldn't it be easier just to tell her that you didn't do it?"

"I tried that. It's her father's word against mine, and she chose to believe her father."

Derringer rubbed his chin in a thoughtful way. "You can always confront her old man and beat the truth out of him." He then glanced around. "And speaking of Kalina, where is she? I know the ladies decided not to do anything today since both Lucia and Chloe had to take the babies in for their regular pediatric visits."

"She's preparing dinner and needed to pick up a few items from the store." Micah checked his watch. "She's been gone longer than I figured she would be."

Concern touched Derringer's features. "You think she's gotten lost?"

"She shouldn't be lost since she was only going to that Walmart a few miles away. If she's not back in a few more minutes, I'll call her on her cell phone to make sure she's okay."

The two men had walked out of the barn when Micah's phone rang. He didn't recognize the number. "Yes?"

"Mr. Westmoreland, this is Nurse Nelson at Denver Memorial. There was a car accident involving Kalina Daniels, and she was brought into the emergency room. Your number was listed in her phone directory as one of those to call in case of an emergency. Since you're local we thought we would call you first."

Micah's heart stopped beating. "She was in an accident?"

"Yes."

"How is she?" he asked in a frantic tone.

"Not sure. The doctor is checking her out now."

Absently, Micah ended the call and looked at Derringer. "Kalina was in an accident, and she's been taken to Denver Memorial."

Derringer quickly tied the horse to the nearest post. "Come on. Let's go."

"Do you know an E.R. doctor's biggest nightmare?"

Kalina glanced over at the doctor who was checking out the bruise on her arm. "What?"

"Having to treat another doctor."

Kalina laughed. "Hey, I wasn't *that* bad, Dr. Parker."

"No." The older doctor nodded while grinning. "I understand you were worse. According to the paramedics, you wouldn't let them work on you until they'd checked out the person who was driving the other car. The one who ran the red light and caused the accident."

"Only because I knew I was fine. She's the one whose air bag deployed," Kalina said.

"Yes, but still, you deserved to be checked out as much as she did."

Kalina didn't say anything as she remembered the accident. She hadn't seen it coming. She had picked up all the things she needed from the store and was on her way back to Micah's Manor when out of nowhere, a car plowed into her from the side. She could only be thankful that she'd been driving Micah's heavy-duty truck and not a small car. Otherwise, her injuries would have been more severe.

"I don't like the look of this knot on your head. I should keep you overnight for observation."

Kalina shook her head. "Don't waste a bed. I'll be fine."

"Maybe. Maybe not. I don't have to tell you about head injuries, do I, Dr. Daniels?"

She rolled her eyes. "No, sir, you don't."

"Are you living alone?"

"No, I'm visiting someone in this area. I think your nurse has already called Micah."

The doctor looked at her. "Micah? Micah Westmoreland?"

Kalina smiled. "Yes. You know him?"

The doctor nodded. "Yes, I went to high school with his father. I know those Westmorelands well. It was tragic how they lost their parents, aunt and uncle in that plane crash."

"Yes, it was."

"The folks around here can't help admiring how they all stuck together in light of that devastation, and now all of them have made something of themselves, even Bane. God knows we'd almost given up on him, but now I understand that he's—"

Suddenly the privacy curtain was snatched aside, and Micah stood there with a terrified look on his face. "Kalina!"

And before she could draw her next breath, he had crossed the floor and pulled her into his arms.

Ten

Back at Micah's Manor, Kalina, who was sitting comfortably on the sofa, rolled her eyes. "If you ask me one more time if I'm okay, I'm going to scream. Read my lips, Micah. I'm fine."

Micah drew in a deep breath. He knew he was being anal, but he couldn't help it. When he'd received a call from that nurse about Kalina's accident, he'd lost it. It was a good thing Derringer had been there. There was probably no way he could have driven to the hospital without causing his own accident. He'd been that much of a basket case.

"Don't fall asleep, Kalina. If you do, I'm only going to wake you up," he warned.

She shook her head. "Micah, have you forgotten I'm a doctor, as well. I'm familiar with the dos and don'ts following a head injury. But, like I told Dr. Parker at the hospital, I'm fine."

"And I intend to make sure you stay that way." Micah crossed the room to her, leaned down and placed a kiss on her lips.

He straightened and glanced down at her. "I don't think you know how I felt when I received that call, Kal. It reminded me so much of the call I got that day from Dillon, telling me about Mom, Dad, Uncle Thomas and Aunt Susan. I was at the university, in between classes, and it seemed that everything went black."

She nodded slowly, hearing the pain in his voice. "I can imagine."

He shook his head. "No, honestly, you can't." He sat down beside her. "It was the kind of emotional pain and fear I'd hoped never to experience again. But I did today, when I got that call about you."

She stared at him for a few moments and then reached over and took his hand in hers. "Sorry. I didn't mean to do that to you."

He sighed deeply. "It wasn't your fault. Accidents happen. But if I didn't know before, I know now."

She lifted a brow. "You know what?"

"How much I care for you." He gently pulled her onto his lap. "I know you've been thinking that I've been acting moody and out of sorts for the past couple of days, but I wanted so much for you to believe I'm not the person you think I am."

She wrapped her arms around him, as well. "I know. And I also know that's why you didn't want to make love to me."

She twisted around in his arms to face him. "You

were wasting both our time by doing that, you know. I
realized even before leaving India that you hadn't lied
to me about our affair in Sydney."

He pulled back, surprised. "You had?"

"Yes. I had accepted what you said as the truth
before I agreed to come here to Denver with you."

She smiled. "I figured that you *had* to be telling the
truth, otherwise, you were taking a big risk in bringing me here to meet your family. But then I knew for
a fact that you had been telling the truth once you got
me here and wanted to put a hold on our lovemaking.
You were willing to do without something I knew you
really wanted just to prove yourself to me. You really
didn't have to."

He covered her hand with his. "I felt that I did have
to do it. Someone once told me that sacrifices today
will result in dividends tomorrow, and I wanted you
for my dividend. I love you, Kalina."

"And I love you, too. I realized that before coming
here, as well. That night you took me dancing and I felt
something in the way you held me, in the way you were
talking to me. That night, I knew the truth in what you
had been trying to tell me. And I knew the truth about
what my feelings were for you."

She quieted for a moment and then said, "Although
there's not an excuse for my father's actions, I believe
I know why he did what he did. He's always been controlling, but I never thought he would go that far. I was
wrong. And I was wrong for not believing you in the
first place."

He shook his head. "No, like I said, you didn't know
me. We had an affair that was purely sexual. The only
commitment we'd made was to share a bed. It didn't

take me long to figure out that I wanted more from you. That night you ended things was the night I had planned on telling you how I felt. Afterward, I was angry that you didn't believe in me, that you actually thought I didn't care, that I would go along with your father about something like that."

He paused. "When I came home, I told Dillon everything and he suggested that I straighten things out. But my pride wouldn't let me. I wasted two years being angry, but the night I saw you again I knew that no matter what, I would make you mine."

"No worries then," Kalina said, reaching up and cupping his chin. "I am yours."

He inhaled sharply when her fingers slid beneath his T-shirt to touch his naked skin over his heart. It seemed the moment she touched him that heat consumed him and spread to every part of his body. Although he tried playing it down, his desire for her was magnified to a level he hadn't thought possible.

All he could think about was that he'd almost lost her and the fear that had lodged in his throat had made it difficult to breathe. And now she was here, back at his manor, where she belonged. He knew then that he would always protect her. Not control her like her old man tended to do, but to protect her.

"Make love to me, Micah."

Her whispered request swept across his lips. "I need you inside me."

Micah studied her thoughtfully. He saw the heat in her eyes and felt the feverishness of her skin. Other than that one time on the sofa, he hadn't touched her since coming to Denver, wanting her to get to know the real him. Well, at that moment, the real him wanted her with a passion that he felt even in the tips of his fingers. She knew him, and she loved him, just as he loved her.

"What about your head?" he whispered, standing, sweeping her into his arms and moving toward the stairs.

She wrapped her arms around him and chuckled against his neck. "My head is fine, but there is another ache that's bothering me. To be quite honest with you, it was bothering me a long time before the accident. It's the way my body is aching to be touched by you. Loved by you. Needed by you."

Just how he made it up the stairs to his bedroom, he wasn't sure. All he knew was that he had placed her in the middle of his bed, stripped off her clothes and taken off his own clothes in no time at all. He stood at the foot of the bed, gazing at her. He let his eyes roam all over her and knew there was nothing subtle about how he was doing it.

This was the first time she had been in his bed, but he had fantasized about her being here plenty of times. Even during the last five days, when he'd known she was sleeping in the bedroom above his, he had wanted her here, with him. More than once, he had been tempted to get up during the night and go to her, to forget about the promise of not touching her until she had gotten to know him. It had been hard wanting her and vowing not to touch her.

And she hadn't made it easy. At times she had deliberately tried tempting him again. She would go shopping with his cousins and then parade around in some of the sexiest outfits a store could sell. But he had resisted temptation.

But not now. He didn't plan on resisting anything,

especially not the naked woman stretched out in the middle of his huge bed looking as if she belonged there. He intended to keep her there.

"I love you," he said in a low, gravelly voice filled with so much emotion he had to fight from getting choked. "I knew I did, but I didn't know just how much until I got that phone call, Kalina. You are my heart. My soul. My very reason for existing."

He slowly moved toward the bed. "I never knew how much I cherished this part of our relationship until it was gone. I can't go back and see it as 'just sex' anymore. Not when I can distinctively hear, in the back of my mind, all your moans of pleasure, the way you groan to let me know how much you want me. Not when I remember that little smile that lets me know just how much you are satisfied. No, we never had sex. We've always made love."

Kalina breathed in Micah's scent as he moved closer to her. Not wanting to wait any longer, she rose up in the bed and met him. When he placed his knee on the bed, they tumbled back into the bedcovers together. At that moment, everything ceased to exist except them.

As if she needed to make sure this moment was real, she reached out and touched his face, using her fingertips to caress the strong lines of his features. But she didn't stop there, she trailed her fingers down to his chest, feeling the hard muscles of his stomach. Her hands moved even lower, to the hardest part of him, cupping him. She thought, for someone to be so hard, there were certain parts of him that were smooth as a baby's behind.

"What are you doing to me?" he asked in a tortured groan when she continued to stroke him.

She met his gaze. "Staking my claim."

He chuckled softly. "Baby, trust me. You staked your claim two years ago. I haven't been able to make love to another woman since."

Micah knew the moment she realized the truth of what he'd said. The smile that touched her features warmed him all over, made him appreciate that he was a man, the man who had *this* woman.

Not being able to wait any longer, he leaned over and brushed a kiss against her lips. Then he moved his mouth lower to capture a nipple in his mouth and suck on it.

She arched against him, and he appreciated her doing so. He increased the suction of his mouth, relishing the taste of her while thinking of all the hours he'd lain in this bed awake and aroused, knowing she'd been only one floor away.

"Micah."

The tone of her voice alerted him that she needed him inside that part of her that was aching. Releasing her nipple, he eased her down in the bed. Before he moved in place between her legs, he had to taste her. He shifted his body to bury his head between her legs.

Kalina screamed the moment Micah's tongue swept inside her. The tip of it was hot and determined. And the way it swirled inside her had her senses swirling in unison. She was convinced that no other man could do things with their tongue the way he could. He was devouring her senseless, and she couldn't do anything but lie there and moan.

And then she felt it, an early sign that a quake was about to happen. The way her toes began tingling while her head crested with sensations that moved through every part of her.

She sucked in a deep breath, and it was then that she saw he had sensed what was about to happen and had moved in place over her. The hardness of him slid through her wetness, filling her and going beyond.

She was well aware of the moment when their bodies locked. He gazed down at her, and their eyes connected. He was about to give her the ride of her life, and she needed it. She wanted it.

He began moving, thrusting in and out of her while holding her gaze. She felt it. She felt him. There was nothing like the feeling of being made love to by the one man who had your heart. Your soul.

He kept moving, thrusting, pounding into her as if making up for lost time, for misunderstandings and disagreements. She wouldn't delude herself into thinking those things wouldn't happen again, but now they would have love to cushion the blows.

At that moment, he deliberately curved his body to hit her at an angle that made her G-spot weep. It triggered her scream, and she exploded at the same time as he did. They clung to each other, limbs entwined, bodies united. She sucked up air along with his scent. And moments later, when the last remnants of the blast flittered away from her, she collapsed against Micah, moaning his name and knowing she had finally christened his bed.

Their bed.

The next two weeks flowed smoothly, although they were busy ones for the Westmoreland family. Gemma and Callum were returning to christen their firstborn. Ramsey and Chloe had consented to be godparents.

All the out-of-towners were scheduled to arrive by Thursday. Most had made plans to stay at nearby hotels, but others were staying with family members. Jason and his wife, Bella, had turned what had been the home she'd inherited from her grandfather into a private inn just for family when they came to visit.

Pam had solicited Kalina's help in planning activities for everyone, and Kalina appreciated being included. Her days were kept busy, but her nights remained exclusively for Micah. They rode horses around the property every evening, cooked dinner together, took their shower, once in a while watched a movie. But every night they shared a bed. She thought there was nothing like waking up each morning in his arms.

Like this morning.

She glanced over at him and frowned. "Just look what you did to me. What if I wanted to wear a low-cut dress?"

Micah glanced over at the passion mark he'd left on Kalina. Right there on her breast. There was not even a hint of remorse in his voice when he said, "Then I guess you'd be changing outfits."

"Oh, you!" she said, snatching the pillow and throwing it at him. "You probably did it deliberately. You like branding me."

He couldn't deny her charge because it was true. But what he liked most of all was tasting her. Unfortunately, he had a tendency to leave a mark whenever he did. Hell, he couldn't help that she tasted so damn good.

He reached out and grabbed her before she could

toss another pillow his way. "Come here, sweetheart. Let me kiss it away."

"All you're going to do is make another mark. Stay away from me."

He rolled his eyes. "Yeah. Right."

When she tried scooting away, he grabbed her foot to bring her back. He then lowered his mouth to lick her calf. When she moaned, he said, "See, you know you like it."

"Yes, but we don't have the time. Everyone starts arriving today."

"Let them. They can wait."

When he released his hold on her to grab her around the waist, she used that opportunity to scoot away from him and quickly made a move to get out of bed. But she wasn't quick enough. He grabbed her arm and pulled her back. "Did you think you would get away, Dr. Daniels?"

She couldn't help laughing, and she threw herself into his arms. "It's not like I'm ready to get out of bed anyway," she said, before pressing her lips to his. He kissed her the way she liked, in a way that sent sensations escalating all through her.

When he released her lips she felt a tug on her left hand and looked down. She sucked in a deep breath at the beautiful diamond ring Micah had just slid on her finger. She threw her hand to her chest to stop the rapid beating of her heart. "Oh, my God!

Micah chuckled as he brought her ringed hand to his lips and kissed it. "Will you, Kalina Marie Daniels, marry me? Will you live here with me at Micah's Manor? Have my babies? Make me the happiest man on earth?"

Tears streamed down her face, and she tried swiping them away, but more kept coming. "Oh, Micah, yes! Yes! I'll marry you, live here and have your babies."

Micah laughed and pulled her into his arms, sealing her promise with another kiss.

It was much later when they left Micah's Manor to head over to Dillon's place. Dillon had called to say the Atlanta Westmorelands had begun arriving already. Micah had put his brother on the speakerphone and Kalina could hear the excitement in Dillon's voice. It didn't take long, when around the Westmorelands, to know that family meant everything to them. They enjoyed the times they were able to get together.

Micah had explained that all the Westmorelands were making up for the years they hadn't shared when they hadn't known about each other. Their dedication to family was the reason it was important to make sure there weren't any other Westmorelands out there they didn't know about.

Kalina walked into Dillon and Pam's house with Micah by her side and a ring on her finger. Several family members noticed her diamond and congratulated them and asked when the big day would be. She and Micah both wanted a June wedding, which was less than a couple of months away.

Once they walked into the living room, Kalina suddenly came to a stop. Several people were standing around talking. Micah's arm tightened around her shoulders and he glanced down at her. "What's wrong, baby?"

Instead of answering, she stared across the room and

he followed her gaze. Immediately, he knew what was bothering her.

"That woman is here," was all Kalina would say.

Micah couldn't help fighting back a smile as he gazed over at Olivia. "Yes, she's here, and I think it's time for you to meet her."

Kalina began backing up slowly. "I'd rather not do that."

"And if you don't, my cousin Senator Reggie Westmoreland will wonder why you're deliberately being rude to his wife."

Kalina jerked her head up and looked at Micah. "His wife?"

Micah couldn't hold back his smile any longer. "Yes, his wife. That's Olivia Jeffries Westmoreland."

"But you had me thinking that—"

Micah reached out and quickly kissed the words from Kalina's lips. "Don't place the blame on me, sweetheart. You assumed Olivia and I had something going on. I never told you that. In fact, I recall telling you that there was nothing going on with us. Olivia and Reggie had invited me to lunch while I was in D.C., but it was Olivia who came to pick me up that day. I couldn't help that you got jealous."

She glared. "I didn't get jealous."

"Didn't you?"

He stared at her, and she stared back. Then a slow smile spread across her face, and she shrugged her shoulders. "Okay, maybe I did. But just a little."

He raised a dubious eyebrow. "Um, just a little."

"Don't press it, Micah."

He laughed and tightened his hand on hers. "Okay, I won't. Come on and meet Reggie, Olivia and their twin sons, as well as the rest of my cousins. And I think we should announce our good news."

The christening for Callum Austell II was a beautiful ceremony, and Kalina got to meet Micah's cousin Gemma. She couldn't wait to tell her just how gifted she was as an interior designer, which prompted Gemma to share how her husband had whisked her off to Australia in the first place.

It was obvious to anyone around them that Gemma and her husband were in love and that they shared a happy marriage. But then, Kalina thought, the same thing could be said for all of Micah's cousins' marriages. All the men favored each other, and the women they'd selected as their mates complemented them.

After the church service, dinner was served at the big house with all the women pitching in and cooking. Kalina felt good knowing the games she had organized for everyone, especially the kids, had been a big hit.

It was late when she and Micah had finally made it back to Micah's Manor. After a full day of being around the Westmorelands, she should have been exhausted, ready to fall on her face, but she felt wired and had Micah telling her the story about Raphel all over again. She was even more fascinated with it the second time.

"That's how Dillon and Pam met," Micah said as they headed up the stairs. An hour or so later, he and Kalina had showered together and were settling down to watch a movie in bed, when the phone rang.

He glanced over at the clock. "I wonder who's calling this late," he said, reaching for the phone. "Probably Megan wanting to know if we still have any of that ice cream she bought."

He picked up the phone. "Hello."

"Are you watching television, Micah?"

He heard the urgency in Dillon's voice. "I just turned it on to watch a DVD, why?"

"I think you ought to switch to CNN. There's something going on in Oregon."

Micah raised a brow. "Oregon?"

"Yes. It's like people are falling dead in the streets for no reason."

Micah was out of the bed in a flash. He looked at Kalina, who had the remote in her hand. "Switch to CNN."

She did so, and Anderson Cooper's face flared to life on the screen as he said, "No one is sure what is happening here, but it's like a scene out of *Contagion*. So far, more than ten people have died. The Centers for Disease Control has…"

At that moment Micah's phone on his dresser, the one with a direct line to Washington, rang. He moved quickly to pick it up. "Yes?"

He looked over at Kalina and nodded. Her gaze held his, knowing whenever that particular phone rang it was urgent. "All right, we're on our way."

He clicked off. "They're calling the entire team in. We're needed in Oregon."

Eleven

Micah looked around the huge room. His team was reunited. Kalina, Theo and Beau. They had all read the report and knew what they were up against. The Centers for Disease Control had called in an international team and the three of them were just a part of it. But in his mind they were a major part. All the evidence collected pointed to a possible terrorist attack. If they didn't get a grip on what was happening and stop it, the effect could make 9/11 look small in comparison.

It didn't take long to see, from the tissue taken from some of the victims, that they were dealing with the same kind of virus that he, Kalina and Theo had investigated in India just weeks ago. How did it get to the States? And, more important, who was responsible for spreading it?

He felt his phone vibrating in his pocket and didn't

have to pull it out to see who was calling. It was the same person who'd been blowing up his phone for the past two days. General Daniels. He was demanding that Kalina be sent home, out of harm's way. Like two years ago, a part of Micah understood the man's concern for his daughter's safety. He, of all people, didn't want a single hair on Kalina's head hurt in any way. But as much as he loved Kalina and wanted to keep her safe, he also respected her profession and her choices in life. That's how he and the old man differed.

But still…

"That's all for now. I'll give everyone an update when I get one from Washington. Stay safe." Micah then glanced over at Kalina. "Dr. Daniels, can you remain a few moments, please? I'd like to talk to you."

He moved behind his desk as the others filed out. Beau, being the last one, closed the door behind him. But not before giving Micah the eye, communicating to him, for his own benefit and safety, to move the vase off the desk. Micah smiled. Beau knew of Kalina's need to throw things when she was angry. He had tried telling his best friend that the vase throwing had been limited to that one episode. It hadn't happened again.

"Yes, Micah? What is it?"

He pulled his still-vibrating phone out of his pocket and placed it in the middle of his desk. "Your father."

He then reached into his desk and pulled out a sealed, official-looking envelope and handed it to her. "Your father, as well."

She opened the envelope and began reading the documents. Moments later, she lifted her head and met his gaze. "Orders for me to be reassigned to another project?"

"Yes."

She held his gaze for a long time as she placed the documents back in the envelope. He saw the defeated shift of her shoulders. "So when do I leave?"

He leaned back in his chair. "I, of all people, don't want anything to happen to you, Kalina," he said in a low voice. "I love you more than life itself, and I know how dangerous it is for you to be here. The death toll has gone up to fifteen. Already a domestic terrorist group is claiming victory and vows more people will lose their lives here before it's over, before we can find a way to stop it. I don't want you in that number."

There was an intensity, a desperation, in his tone that even he heard. It was also one that he felt. He drew in a deep breath and continued, "You are the other half that makes me whole. The sunshine I wake up to each morning, and the rock I hold near me when I go to bed at night. I don't want to lose you. If anything happens to you, I die, as well."

He could see she was fighting the tears in her eyes, as if she already knew the verdict. She was getting used to it. She lifted her chin defiantly. "So, you're sending me away?"

He held his gaze as he shook his head. "No, I'm keeping you safe. Your father doesn't call the shots anymore in your personal or professional life. I'm denying his orders on the grounds that you're needed here. You worked on this virus just weeks ago. You're familiar with it. That alone should override his request at the CDC."

She released an appreciative sigh. "Thank you."

"Don't thank me. The next days are going to be rough. Whoever did this is out there and waiting around for their attack to be successful. There have been few survivors and those who have survived are quarantined and in critical condition."

She sat down on the edge of his desk. "We're working against time, Micah. People want to leave Portland, but everyone is being forced to stay because the virus is contagious."

Already the level of fear among citizens had been raised. People were naturally afraid of the unknown… and this was definitely an unknown. Each victim had presented the same symptoms they'd found in India.

"I wish the CDC hadn't just put that blood sample I sent to them on the shelf," she added. "It was the one thing I was able to get from the surviving—"

Micah sat up in his seat. "Hey, that might be it. We need someone to analyze the contents of those vials, immediately. I don't give a damn about how behind they are. This is urgent." He picked up the phone that was a direct line to Washington and the Department of Health and Human Services.

Four more people died over a two-day period, but Micah put the fire under the CDC to study the contents of those vials that Kalina had sent to them weeks ago. He had assembled his team in the lab to apprise them of what was going on.

"And you think we might be able to come up with a serum that can stop the virus?" Beau asked.

"We hope so," Micah said, rubbing a hand down his face. "It might be a shot in the dark, but it's the only one we have."

At that moment, the phone—his direct line to the

CDC—rang, and he quickly picked it up. "Dr. Westmoreland."

He nodded a few times and then he felt a relieved expression touch his features. "Great! You get it here, and we'll dispense it."

He looked over at his team. "Based on what they analyzed in those vials, they think they've come up with an antidote. They're flying it here via military aircraft. We are to work with the local teams and make sure every man, woman and child is inoculated immediately." He stood. "Let's go!"

Five days later, a military aircraft carrying Micah and his team arrived at Andrews Air Force Base. The antidote had worked, and millions of lives were saved. Homeland Security had arrested those involved.

Micah and every member of his team had worked nonstop to save lives and thanks to their hard work, and the work of all the others, there hadn't been anymore deaths.

He drew in a deep breath as he glanced over at Kalina. He knew how exhausted she was, though she didn't show it. All of them had kept long hours, and he was looking forward to a hotel room with a big bed... and his woman. They would rest up, and then they would ease into much-needed lovemaking.

They had barely departed the plane when an official government vehicle pulled up. They paused, and Micah really wasn't surprised when Kalina's father got out of the car. General Daniels frowned at them. All military personnel there saluted and stood at attention as he moved toward them.

As much as Micah wanted to hate the man, he

couldn't. After all, he was Kalina's father and without the man his daughter would not have been born. So Micah figured that he owed the older man something. That was all he could find to like about him. At the moment, he couldn't think of a single other thing.

General Daniels came to a stop in front of them. "Dr. Westmoreland. I need to congratulate you and your team for a job well done."

"Thank you, sir." Micah decided to give the man the respect he had earned. Considering the lie the man had told, whether he really deserved it was another matter.

The general's gaze shifted to Kalina, and Micah knew where she had gotten her stubbornness. She lifted her chin and glared at her father, general or not. Micah noticed something else, as well. It was there in the older man's eyes as he looked at Kalina. He loved his daughter and was scared to death of losing her. Kalina had told him how her mother had died when she was ten and how hard her father had taken her mother's death.

"Kalina Marie."

"General."

"You look well."

"Thank you."

The general spoke to all the others and then officially dismissed them to leave. He then said to Kalina when the three of them were alone. "I'm here to take you and Dr. Westmoreland to your hotel."

Kalina's glare deepened. "I'll walk first. Sir."

Micah saw the pain from Kalina's words settle in the old man's eyes. He decided to extend something to General Daniels that the old man would never extend to him: empathy.

He then turned to Kalina and said in a joking tone,

"No, you aren't walking to the hotel because that means I'll have to walk with you. We're a team, remember? And if I take another step, I'm going to drop. I think we should take your father up on his offer. Besides, there're a couple things we need to talk to him about, don't you think? Like our wedding plans."

The general blinked. "The two of you are back together? And getting married?"

Kalina turned on her father. "Yes, with no thanks to you."

The man did have the decency to look chagrined. Micah had a feeling the man truly felt regret for his actions two years ago. "And there's something else I think you should tell your father, Kalina."

She glanced up at Micah. "What?"

Micah smiled. "That he's going to be a grandfather."

Both Kalina and her father gasped in shock, but for different reasons. Kalina turned to Micah. "You knew?"

He nodded as his smile widened. "Yes, I'm a doctor, remember."

"And you still let me stay on the team? You didn't send me away, knowing my condition?"

He reached out and gently caressed her cheek. "You were under my love and protection, but not my control."

He then looked over at her father when he added, "There is a difference, General, and one day I'll be happy to sit down and explain it to you."

The old man nodded appreciatively and held Micah's gaze as a deep understanding and acceptance passed between them.

"But right now, I'd like to be taken to the nearest

hotel. I plan on sleeping for the next five days," Micah said, moving toward the government car.

"With me right beside you," Kalina added as she walked with him. She figured she'd gotten pregnant during the time the doctor had placed her on antibiotics after the auto accident. Even as a medical professional, it hadn't crossed her mind that the prescribed medicine would have a negative effect on her birth control pills. There had been too much going on for her emotionally at the time. Since she'd found out, she had been waiting for the perfect time to tell Micah that he would be a father. And to think, he'd suspected all the time.

Micah took Kalina's hand in his, immediately feeling the heat that always seemed to generate between them. This was his woman, soon to be his wife and the mother of his child. Life couldn't be better.

Epilogue

Two months later, on a hot June day, Micah and Kalina stood before a minister on the grounds of Micah's Manor and listened when a minister proclaimed, "I now pronounce you man and wife."

All the Westmorelands had returned to help celebrate on their beautiful day.

"You may now kiss your bride."

Micah pulled Kalina into his arms and gave her a kiss she had come to know, love and expect. He released her from the kiss only when a couple of his brothers and cousins began clearing their throats.

With the help of Pam, Lucia, Bella, Megan, Bailey and Chloe, Kalina had found the perfect wedding dress. She'd also formed relationships with the women she now considered sisters. Kalina and Micah's honeymoon to Paris was a nice wedding gift—compliments of her father.

And Bella had taken time to give birth to beautiful identical twin daughters. And Ramsey and Chloe now had a son who was the spitting image of his father. Already, the fathers, uncles and cousins were spoiling them rotten. Kalina had to admit she was in that number, and couldn't wait to hold her own baby in her arms.

A short while later, at the reception, Kalina glanced over at her husband. He was such a handsome man, dashing as ever in his tux. More than one person had said that they made a beautiful couple.

She had been pulled to the side and was talking to the ladies when suddenly the group got quiet. Everyone turned when an extremely handsome man got out of a car. The first thing Kalina thought, with his dashing good looks, was that perhaps he was some Hollywood celebrity who was a friend of one of Micah's cousins, especially since it seemed all the male Westmorelands knew who he was.

When Micah approached and touched her hand she glanced up at him and smiled. She hadn't been aware he had returned to her side. "Who's that?" she asked curiously.

He followed her gaze and chuckled. "That's Rico Claiborne. Savannah and Jessica's brother."

Kalina nodded. Savannah and Jessica were sisters who'd married the Westmoreland cousins Durango and Chase. "He's handsome," she couldn't help saying. Then she quickly looked up at her husband and added sheepishly, "But not as handsome as you, of course."

Micah laughed. "Of course. Here, I brought this for you," he said, placing a cold glass of ice water in her hand. "And although Megan is hiring Rico, they are meeting for the first time today," he added. "But from the expression on Megan's face, maybe she needs this cold drink of water instead of you."

Kalina understood exactly what Micah meant when she, like everyone else, watched as the man turned to stare over at Megan, who'd been pointed out to him by some of the Westmoreland cousins. If the look on Megan's face, and the look on the man's face when he saw Megan, was anything to go by, then everyone was feeling the heat.

Kalina took a sip of her seltzer water thinking that Micah was right. Megan should be the one drinking the cooling beverage instead of her.

"Are you ready for our honeymoon, sweetheart?"

Micah's question reclaimed her attention and she smiled up at him, Megan and the hottie private investigator forgotten already. "Yes, I'm ready."

And she was. She was more than ready to start sharing her life with the man she loved.

* * * * *

"This is about you and me, Rosebud.

This is about me liking you and you liking me, slow dances to fast songs and not going down without a fight. You promised me you wouldn't go down without a fight, and I'm going to hold you to that. Have dinner with me tonight."

"I can't."

Which was a hell of a lot different from "I won't."

"Someplace quiet," Dan continued. "That's all I want. Just you and me."

"What makes you think it would be any different the next time?" Her voice shook as she blinked rapidly and pulled away from him. "Or the time after that? Or any time? We can't hide forever. I can't, anyway."

Anger flashed through him. "I do *not* hide, Rosebud—and you don't, either."

Dear Reader,

This story began when an image popped into my head of an Indian Princess riding bareback out of the past and into the hero's present. Before the hero could figure out who she was, she took a shot at him and rode away. This image was so powerful that it stayed with me for months while the characters waited for me to figure out who they were, why she'd put a bullet through the hero's hat and, most important, how they could ever fall in love.

I like to think of this book as my Polaroid® book—the story took a long time to develop, but it was worth the wait. The hero turned out to be Dan Armstrong, the Chief Operating Officer of an energy company looking to build a hydroelectric dam. The heroine was Rosebud Donnelly, the tribal lawyer for the Red Creek Lakota, whose reservation will be flooded by Dan's dam. I imagined that having your whole world sunk to the bottom of an artificial lake was a good reason for a woman to be fighting-mad, and Rosebud agreed.

The surprise to Rosebud was how much Dan, an oil tycoon, turned out to be a man of principle and honesty. On top of all that integrity, he is one good-looking cowboy who knows his way around a horse—and a woman. He'll use all that charm to get to the bottom of who killed his hat. The question Dan has to answer is, what else is he willing to lose?

A Man of His Word is my first Mills & Boon® Desire™ book, and for that alone, it will always be one of my favorites. I hope you enjoy reading it as much as I enjoyed writing it! Be sure to stop by www.sarahmanderson.com and join me when I say, long live cowboys!

Sarah

A MAN
OF HIS WORD

BY
SARAH M. ANDERSON

MILLS
BOON

Published in Great Britain 2012
by Mills & Boon, an imprint of Harlequin (UK) Limited,
Eton House, 18-24 Paradise Road, Richmond, Surrey TW9 1SR

© Sarah M. Anderson 2011

ISBN: 978 0 263 89205 5
ebook ISBN: 978 1 408 97777 4

51-0812

Harlequin (UK) policy is to use papers that are natural, renewable and recyclable products and made from wood grown in sustainable forests. The logging and manufacturing processes conform to the legal environmental regulations of the country of origin.

Printed and bound in Spain
by Blackprint CPI, Barcelona

Award-winning author **Sarah M. Anderson** may live east of the Mississippi River, but her heart lies out west on the Great Plains. With a lifelong love of horses and two history teachers for parents, she had plenty of encouragement to learn everything she could about the tribes of the Great Plains.

When she started writing, it wasn't long before her characters found themselves out in South Dakota among the Lakota Sioux. She loves to put people from two different worlds into new situations and see how their backgrounds and cultures take them someplace they never thought they'd go.

When not helping out at school or walking her two rescue dogs, Sarah spends her days having conversations with imaginary cowboys and American Indians, all of which is surprisingly well-tolerated by her wonderful husband and son. Readers can find out more about Sarah's love of cowboys and Indians at www.sarahmanderson.com.

To Mom and Dad, two history teachers who planned family vacations around national monuments and Civil War battle sites instead of theme parks and beaches.

One

For today's ride, Dan Armstrong had brought along his custom-made six-shooter, but he couldn't believe he'd need it.

He didn't normally wear it, but his uncle had told him to take a gun if he went out alone. And since it had been years since the man had shown a whit of interest in Dan's well-being, he'd listened. Now he was glad he'd done so because his imagination was working overtime.

There was something about this forest that said Old West, South Dakota style. His sprawling estate outside of Fort Worth was a jewel, but north Texas didn't have stands of pines this pretty or the carved sandstone bluffs that ran along the Dakota River.

It was a damn shame the trees, the river and the land wouldn't be the same once his company got done with them. His uncle, Cecil Armstrong, who ran one half of Armstrong Holdings, wanted to clear-cut these hundreds of acres before building a dam on this river, about five hundred yards upstream. No sense in throwing away perfectly good logging rights, Cecil had said. Logically, Dan couldn't argue with that, but he'd hate to see this forest go.

He didn't doubt that this place looked the same today as it had hundreds of years ago, back when cowboys and Indians rode the range. If he closed his eyes, he could almost hear war whoops and the thunder of hooves.

He twisted in the saddle, squinting as he looked into the afternoon sun. He really did hear hoofbeats.

The sound stopped when he moved, and by the time he got his eyes shaded with the brim of his Stetson, all he could see was a dust cloud about a hundred yards back, down the well-worn deer path he'd come in on.

Instinctively, Dan dropped his hand to the butt of his pistol. Sure, the engraved nickel firearm was only good for six shots, but he'd wanted a piece that was specifically weighted to his grip.

His hand flexed around the gun and waited. The dust settled around a figure. The sunlight provided an almost sparkly air around her. He blinked. What he saw didn't change, so he shook his head. Still there.

A Native American princess sat astride a paint horse. Her hair hung loose behind her, blowing in a breeze that Dan couldn't feel. He couldn't feel much of anything but sheer shock. *What the hell?*

Her horse took a step closer. She wore nothing but an old-fashioned, unadorned buckskin dress that rode high up on lean thighs that clung to the sides of her paint horse with natural ease. It was clear this princess knew how to ride bareback. The length of her legs ended with simple moccasins. Her horse's face was coated in red. Was that war paint?

Could this be happening? She looked like she belonged to a different time, as pure and untouched as the land around her. He'd seen a few Lakota Indians in the three days since he'd arrived, but none of them looked like this.

None of them looked at him like she was looking at him.

One of her hands held the reins of her horse, the other was relaxed by her leg. She tilted her head, sending all that black hair off to one side. She was stunning. A princess of the high plains.

Dan's heartbeat picked up and he slid his hand away from his revolver. She was not what he expected. Cecil had warned him that the local Lakota Indians were a bunch of lazy drunks—but not this woman. The proud way she held her body as her clear eyes swept over him made it obvious that neither of those adjectives applied to her. He'd never seen a woman as stop-what-he's-doing-and-stare beautiful as she was. She leaned forward, and he caught the shape of her buckskin-clad chest. His pulse wasn't the only thing that picked up. What the hell was wrong with him?

The princess flashed him a smile, which didn't help. He had trouble reading her expression at this distance, but there was no mistaking the wide grin or the brightness of her teeth. Then, as quickly as she'd smiled, she was a blur of motion. Her horse shot forward in the same second her hand shot up. His hat went flying as an explosion rocked the valley.

His horse jumped and spun, and Dan lost track of the woman. His first instinct was to rein in Smokey; his second was to duck for cover. That explosion had sounded a hell of a lot like a gunshot.

By the time he got his stallion turned back around, she was gone. Dan didn't think, he just acted. He touched his spurs to the horse's side and took off for the deer trail. Fueled by adrenaline, he plunged into the shadowy woods. Beautiful or no, no one took a shot at him. No one.

He could hear the sound of a large body crashing through the underbrush, over to his left. Whoever she was, she was abandoning the deer path. Dan blinked hard, forcing his eyes to adjust to the dim light. He thought he caught a flash of white ahead.

The harder he rode, the madder he got. In the oil business, he'd dealt with plenty of shady characters—men with agendas or histories—but no one had ever taken an unprovoked shot at him. Hell, no one had ever taken a shot at him, period. He didn't have enemies because he didn't make them. That "man-against-the-world" crap might have been the way of things back in the old days, but Dan was no gunslinger. He was a businessman—a successful one. His word was his bond, and his lawyer rode herd when a deal went south.

He caught the flash of white again and froze.

A white-tailed deer was high-tailing it away from him.

Cursing, Dan pulled Smokey to a stop and tried to figure out what the hell had happened. Maybe it hadn't been real. People imagined sounds, right? But then he remembered his hat. It had come off in the confusion. No matter what had actually happened, he wasn't going to leave his hat. He loved that hat—it fit his head perfectly. Slowly, Dan worked his way back down to the tall grass until he saw the brown brim of his Stetson. He got down to fetch it.

His gut clenched in a terrifying rage. A hole pierced the front peak of the hat, less than an inch from where it had rested on his head.

She'd shot at him. That beautiful woman—bare legs, bareback—had shot at him.

Somebody owed him an explanation.

Dan was still plenty steamed by the time he got back to the ranch house. For some crack-brained reason, his uncle had decided to set up the hydro division of Armstrong Holdings in one of those grand old mansions some cattle baron had built back in the 1880s. As far as mansions went, it was a beautiful piece of work—three floors of hand-carved banisters and stained-glass windows on sixty acres—but corporate headquarters it wasn't. Why Cecil was camped out on the edge of the middle of nowhere, halfway between the state capital in Pierre and the Iowa border, instead of at the small staffed office he had in Sioux Falls was beyond him. It was almost like the old man was trying to hide.

As chief operating officer of Armstrong Holdings, the family business that Dan's father had started with his brother Cecil forty years ago, Dan owned half of this house. Technically, he owned half of the water rights on the Dakota River over which the Red Creek branch of the Lakota Indian tribe was suing Cecil. He owned half of that pretty little valley where his hat had met an untimely death. Technically, he was an equal partner in this whole damn enterprise, and had been since he'd assumed control of the petroleum division in Texas from his mother when he turned twenty-one.

He'd be damned if he let Cecil destroy the company he'd worked so hard to expand.

Cecil had never been one for technicalities, an opinion made abundantly clear last week when he'd ordered Dan to drop everything in Texas and come to South Dakota. Cecil had a problem with the dam he'd spent nearly five years trying to build and had threatened that Armstrong Holdings would lose billions of dollars and just about every government contract they had if Dan didn't get his ass on a plane within a week.

Dan hated to let anyone think he was at the old man's beck and call—least of all, the old man himself—but this problem with the dam gave Dan the perfect opportunity to come up here and figure out what those little—and not so little—blips in the company's financial reports were all about. He didn't know what exactly he was looking for, but he knew he wouldn't find it in Texas. He was going to have to suffer his uncle until he could force Cecil out of the role of chief executive officer.

Now that he thought about it, Dan remembered that it was Cecil who had warned him about the local Indians—that he was having trouble with negotiations with some of them. Dan just hadn't realized that the problem would require body armor and a helmet.

The gabled roof of the ranch house looked even more ominous as the late-afternoon sun cast deep shadows over the front yard. The cast-iron fence looked less like it wanted to keep Cecil's old coon dog in and more like it wanted to keep armed assailants out. Dan stormed through the front door, making the housekeeper jump.

"Is everything all right, Señor Armstrong?" Maria's thick Mexican accent was the closest thing to Texas in this whole house.

Dan slowed. From what he could tell, Cecil treated this poor woman like dirt, which made Dan go out of his way to be polite. Being friendly with the staff had always helped him in the past—especially when he needed information. Mom always said Dan could catch more flies with honey when he wanted to, and right now, he had a bunch of flies bothering him. "Maria," he said, his voice slipping down just a notch as he whipped off his hat. Her cheeks colored. "Do you all have trouble around here?"

The color deepened as she dropped her eyes to the ground. Dan guessed that maybe thirty years ago, Maria had been quite a looker. He didn't mean to make her blush, but sweet-talking a woman was second nature for him. "Trouble, *señor?*"

"Native American trouble?" Maria blinked in confusion, so Dan tried again. "Indian trouble?" Even saying the phrase felt wrong, like it was the 1880s and he was stuck in the middle of a range war. He cleared his throat. If it weren't for the bullet hole in his hat, he'd be certain he'd lost his mind. He held his hat out to her.

Maria went very still as she looked at the hole, and then at his head. *"Dios mi!* No, *señor,* we do not have that kind of trouble."

Damn. Dan was good at reading people, women in particular. Maria was telling the truth.

"You'll let me know if you hear of any, won't you?" He shot her his *please* smile.

Her head bobbed as she began to back toward the kitchen. *"Sí, señor."*

Satisfied, he continued on to his uncle's office. It had probably once been the formal dining room, capable of seating twenty, but no more. Now it was crammed full of everything a man needed to run a major energy corporation. In Texas, Cecil had been a ruthless businessman, squeezing out small-time operations and buying land for astonishing prices. By the time the SUV craze rolled around, he held a near monopoly on Texas oil.

Cecil was whip-smart. By the time the writing was on the fossil fuel wall, he'd already invested deeply in hydroelectric dams. That's what had brought him to South Dakota. The water rights were cheap up here, and the potential was huge. Armstrong Hydro was quickly becoming not just the major player in the field, but the only player.

Dan didn't like the man, never had. Not one bit. But family was family, and Cecil and Dan were tied by blood and by business. Dan couldn't get rid of the old man without hard evidence of malfeasance that he could present to the Board of Directors. Maybe on this trip, he'd find just what he needed to finally cut their connection. Without breaking stride, he burst into the room.

"Well?" Cecil demanded without bothering to look up from the report he was studying. The old man still had the same pompadour and trimmed mustache he'd worn since the 1950s. The only thing that had changed in five years were the jowls Cecil was now sporting. Those jowls, combined with the careful grooming, made Cecil look like the poster boy for the banality of evil. Emphasis on the *evil*. Those pictures of Cecil and his brother Lewis, Dan's father, with their first oil derrick were the only proof Dan had ever seen that his uncle smiled. He'd certainly never smiled at Dan—not once.

Dan gritted his teeth and threw his hat on the desk. The hole landed directly in front of Cecil's face. "Someone took a shot at me."

Cecil appeared to study the wounded hat for a moment. "Did you get them?" He didn't sound concerned or surprised.

"No. I lost her."

A sneer wrestled one corner of Cecil's mouth up. "You let a *girl* get off an unanswered shot?"

He didn't have to defend himself here. Cecil had told him to pack his revolver. "Thanks for the warnin'."

"Are you sure it was a girl?" The sneer didn't falter.

Dan thought back to the lean, bare thighs, the long hair and that smile. Girl, no. Woman? Hell, yes. "Positive."

"No one's seen...*her* before." Cecil hadn't known a woman was out there? He seemed to be struggling to digest the information. "If it's the same troublemaker, she's sabotaged the engineer's work site on more than one occasion."

He had heard about the trouble with the work site, but only third-hand from an engineer Cecil had sent packing. Cecil apparently didn't believe an ecoterrorist attack on an Armstrong project was worth reporting to the board—yet another thing he was hiding. How many other things were there?

Dan had dealt with ecoterrorists before. The Earth Liberation Front—ELF—had burned more than a few of his derricks before Dan had managed to negotiate a truce of sorts. But even ELF had never gone to all the trouble of disguises in broad daylight. They'd been strictly an under-cover-of-night group, more bent on the destruction of property than of people. He could handle ecoterrorists. What he couldn't handle were armed—and beautiful—Native American princesses.

Without missing a beat, Cecil threw Dan's hat back at him and picked up a sheaf of paper from the top of a neat pile. "I have a new assignment for you."

Dan's teeth ground together. An *assignment*. Cecil always tried to treat Dan like he was some two-bit underling instead of an equal partner. Like that little bit of self-delusion gave the old man sole control of the company. "Anyone going to be firing on me this time?"

Cecil let the comment slide. "I'm sending you to meet with the Indians. You're better at—" his hands waved like he could grab hold of a word out of thin air "—talking."

There's an understatement, Dan thought with a concealed snort. Cecil didn't talk. Cecil ordered. "Why them?"

"It's a bunch of bull. They think they're going to get an injunction against the dam construction over water rights—rights I already own."

"That *we* already own. Don't you have lawyers? Why the hell do you need me for this?"

"The tribal lawyer is a bearcat. Rosebud Donnelly. She's eaten three of my lawyers for lunch." Cecil spat the words out with true disgust.

Rosebud? Like the sled from that old movie Mom loved? Couldn't be. Whoever she was, Dan felt a small thread of admiration for her. Anyone who could successfully stonewall his uncle was a person to be taken seriously. "And?"

Cecil looked him over with mercenary eyes. "You are an attractive man, son. Good with women. Hell, you treat that maid like she's some damn queen."

Dan's jaw stiffened. *Son.* He hated it when Cecil called him that. Dan was many things to Cecil, but a son he wasn't.

"You handled those ELF nuts in Texas. This is no different. She's just a woman."

Dan managed to clear his throat. "You want me to do what—sweep her off her feet so she forgets about suing us?" It was Cecil's turn to stiffen. *That's right,* Dan thought. *Us. This is my company, too.*

"All I'm suggesting is you distract her. And if you happen to get access to some of her files…" He let the words trail off, but the meaning was clear. He thought he could use Dan as nothing more than a male bimbo.

Dan snatched the papers out of Cecil's hand. The sooner he got out of this room, the better life would be. Just breathing Cecil's air was toxic. "Where?"

"On the reservation. Tomorrow at ten." Cecil waved his hand in dismissal.

For the second time that day, Dan was so mad he couldn't see straight. Cecil had known someone was out there. If Dan didn't know any better, he might be tempted to think the old man was trying to get him killed.

He looked down at the papers, a Google map to the tribal headquarters and some names. On one hand, he detested letting his uncle think Dan would do his heavy-handed bidding. On the other hand, if Cecil was having "problems" with Indians, maybe they had something on him, something Dan could use. Besides, if a man was looking for a Native American princess packing a pistol, the reservation was the place to be.

He was going to start with one Rosebud Donnelly.

Two

Rosebud Donnelly looked over the rims of her glasses to see Judy, the receptionist, standing in the doorway with an unusual look of confusion on her face.

"He's here."

"Johnson came back for more?" Here, in the privacy of her office—even if it was just a modified broom closet—Rosebud allowed herself to smile at the thought of that twit Johnson breaking. A pitiful excuse for a lawyer, that one.

"No." Judy's eyes got wider.

"It's not *that man,* is it?" She couldn't imagine that Cecil Armstrong would actually show himself in public, in daylight. She'd never met him, but she imagined him to be some sort of vampire, except instead of sucking blood, he was hell-bent on draining her reservation dry—and then flooding it.

"He said his name was Dan Armstrong. He said he was Cecil's nephew."

The satisfaction was intense. She was getting to *that man.* Cecil Armstrong had run out of high-priced lawyers who wouldn't know tribal law from a hole in the ground. He'd been reduced to family—as if Rosebud could be swayed by emotional pleas. "A regular mini-me, huh?"

"No," Judy said again, her voice dropping. "He's…something else entirely. Be careful with this one, Rosebud."

Judy's befuddlement was worrisome. "I'm always careful." Which was true. She took no chances—she couldn't afford to. "He can sit. Make sure he's got coffee—plenty of coffee," she added with a nod. She preferred her sworn enemies to be as uncomfortable as possible. "And let me know when Joe and Emily get here."

After Judy left to go perk another pot of coffee, Rosebud took the time to break out her pitiful makeup bag. Her good looks were just one of her weapons, but she considered them her first best line of defense when meeting a new adversary.

After three years of representing the tribe in their dealings with Armstrong Holdings, she'd honed her game plan to perfection. Johnson was just the latest victim. Rosebud had played the bubble-headed babe for three weeks—long enough for Johnson to be sure he had the upper hand and, more importantly, long enough for Rosebud to secure some rather incriminating pictures of the man meeting with a supplier of prescription painkillers. Although he'd made bail, Johnson had recused himself from the case rather than tangle with Rosebud again.

Men, she thought with a snort. Especially *white* men. They all thought the rules applied to everyone else. She plaited her hair and wound the braid into a bun that projected both an old-fashioned innocence and an austere severity. To hold the bun in place, she inserted two sticks that would have looked like chopsticks, except for the bright green beaded tassels hanging from the ends. The sticks were the only things of her mother's she'd kept.

Her lipstick set, Rosebud gathered up her files. She held

no hope that this Dan Armstrong would be different from the others—after all, that rat-bastard Cecil had sent him—but there was always a small chance that he'd let something slip that could be connected back to her brother Tanner.

Judy knocked on the door. Rosebud glanced at the clock. Almost half an hour had passed. Perfect. "They're here."

"How do I look?" Rosebud batted her eyes.

"Be careful," Judy repeated, sounding awed.

Oh, Rosebud couldn't wait to see this guy, not if he was throwing Judy for such a loop. She met Joe White Thunder and Emily Mankiller outside the conference room. "Did Judy tell you it's a new guy?" she said as she kissed her aunt on the cheek.

Joe's eyes sparkled, and in that second, Rosebud saw the man who'd occupied Alcatraz back in the day. Some days, she longed to have known old Joe back when he raised a lot of hell, but she appreciated who he was now—a tribal elder whose vote carried a lot of weight. "I knew that last one was no match for you."

Rosebud blushed under the compliment as Aunt Emily shook her head at Joe in disapproval. Aunt Emily had never been one for disobedience, civil or otherwise. "You're making a dent, dear, but don't get overconfident."

Whatever, Rosebud thought as she nodded in deferential agreement. Cecil Armstrong had thrown the best lawyers money could buy at her, and she was not only holding them off, she was officially irritating *that man.* "I know. You guys remember what to do?"

Joe playfully socked her in the arm. *"How, kemo sabe."* And then his face went blank and Rosebud stood in front of the stereotypical Stoic Indian. Joe wouldn't say a single thing today. His job was intimidating silence. Rosebud knew he wouldn't even look at Dan Armstrong. If there was one thing self-important lawyers hated, it was being ignored. It drove them to distraction, and a distracted lawyer was a defeated lawyer.

Aunt Emily sighed. Rosebud knew she hated these meetings, hated all the haggling and hated it when Joe acted like a fake Indian. But she hated the idea of Armstrong Holdings flooding the rez more. "We're ready."

Here we go, Rosebud thought to herself as she opened the door. Her blood started to pump with excitement. Another adversary was another battle, and Rosebud was confident she could win the battles. She honestly didn't know if she could win the war with Cecil Armstrong, but she could slow him down for years.

The first thing she noticed was that Dan Armstrong was standing. His back was to the door and he was looking out the conference room's sliver of a window. The prick of irritation was small. She preferred her victim to be sitting in the chair that was two inches shorter than the others, with the bum wheel that gave the chair an unexpected wobble with every movement.

What she noticed next erased the irritation. Dan Armstrong was tall without being huge, his shoulders easily filling out the heathered brown sport coat. The brown leather yokes on his shoulders made his back seem even broader. She could see the curl in his close-cropped hair, the light from the window making it glow a golden-brown.

She caught her breath. Johnson he wasn't—in fact, she couldn't remember the last time she'd seen a real man in this building, a man who looked like he belonged out on the open range instead of in a dark little office. Hell, she couldn't remember the last time she'd seen a real man *outside* of this office.

And then he turned around.

Him. The breath she'd caught was crushed out of her chest. Suddenly she felt vulnerable, the kind of vulnerable that comes from making a mistake and then thinking she'd gotten away with it, only to be caught red-handed.

She was screwed.

He must have noticed her confusion, because he smiled the kind of smile a man wore when he knew exactly what effect he had on a woman. The implied arrogance—and not recognition—was enough to snap Rosebud out of her momentary terror. She might know who *he* was, but he didn't seem to recognize *her*. And if there were no witnesses, who was to say that a crime had occurred?

"Mr....Armstrong, is it?" she began, striding into the room like she couldn't be bothered to remember his name. That's right, she thought as she drew herself up to her full height in three-inch heels, there wasn't a single thing wrong with any of this. Except he had a good four inches on her. "I'm Rosebud Donnelly, the lawyer for the Red Creek Lakota Indian reservation."

"A pleasure, ma'am." Oh, he had a faint drawl, a way of stretching out his vowels that sounded like warm sunshine. *Ma'am* had never sounded as good as it did coming out of his mouth. Armstrong lifted a hand as if to tip his hat, but then appeared to realize that he wasn't wearing one. Instead, he swung his hand down and offered it out to her. Rosebud wondered if he'd gone back for the hat she'd seen fly off his head, or if it was still out there. She'd have to check tonight. No hat, no crime.

Rosebud thanked God she'd done this enough to go on autopilot, because her head was swimming. Not one of the last three lawyers had even sniffed at a polite introduction. She let the seconds stretch as his hand hung in the air. Normally, she let her hand loosely clasp the other person's—all the better to create an impression of weakness—but not this time. This time, she felt an intense need to be in control of this situation. She returned his grip, noting that his hand was warm, but not sweaty. He wasn't nervous at all. She was going to have to do better, so she gave him her best bone-crushing shake.

He tilted his head to one side as if he was questioning her. Eyes the color of the sky right before a twister measured her with something that looked a hell of a lot like respect. God only knew what his uncle had told him about her—it probably started with *ball-buster* and ended with *bitch.* As the heat from his hand did a slow crawl up her arm, she had the sudden urge to tell him that she really wasn't like that.

Which was ridiculous—the whole point of this little introduction was to demonstrate that she was *exactly* like that. No wonder Judy had warned her about this one.

She stepped away from him, pulling her hand with her. He tried to keep his grip for just a second, then the firm pressure was gone. She shivered, but forced herself to forge ahead. "This is Joseph White Thunder, a tribal elder, and Councilwoman Emily Mankiller." Yes. Formal introductions were the next step. She needed to get back on track here.

Emily must have sensed Rosebud's hesitation, because she stepped into the gap. "Mr. Armstrong," she began as she and Joe took their seats without shaking hands, "are you familiar with the Treaty of 1877 between the United States government and the Lakota, Dakota and Nakota Sioux tribes of South Dakota?"

"Ma'am," Armstrong replied with a polite half bow as he sat down. Rosebud smiled internally as the whole thing tilted off-kilter and he clawed at the table to keep his balance. Still, he managed to sound nonplussed as he said, "I can't say that I am."

Thank God for that. Aunt Emily was one of the few women on this reservation with a master's degree in American history, and her role in this little meeting was to wear the adversary down with a complete recounting of the wrongs the Lakota Indians had suffered back in the day at the hands of the American government, and now, thanks to corporations such as Armstrong Holdings. Rosebud had about forty minutes to get her head together.

Aunt Emily droned on while Joe stared at a spot on the wall just over Armstrong's head. Rosebud unpacked her files and began reviewing her notes from the last go-round with Johnson. There wasn't much new to go on. Unlike with Johnson, usable dirt on Cecil Armstrong was just plain hard to dig up. He was courting both political parties, visited a respectable divorced woman twice a month in Sioux Falls and had no personal secretary. As far as she could tell, he hadn't ever set foot in the Armstrong Hydro office in Sioux Falls, and what few staffers worked there didn't seem to know anything. That was all she had after three years. It was frustrating.

She snuck a glance at Armstrong. Not only was he paying attention to Aunt Emily, he was taking notes. What the hell? Rosebud thought when Armstrong interrupted the lecture to ask for the specific dates of the last treaty signed. He must not be a lawyer, she decided. Lawyers didn't give a hoot for history lectures. Why would *that man* send someone who wasn't a lawyer?

Aunt Emily began to wind down when she got to the reason they were all here today. Rosebud waited as Armstrong finished his notes before she began. "*Mister* Armstrong," she began, going right past condescending and straight on over to contemptuous, "are you aware that Armstrong Holdings is preparing to dam the Dakota River?"

"Yes, ma'am," he replied, trying to lean back in the chair without tipping. "Down in a valley about two miles from here, as the crow flies. Armstrong Holdings owns the water rights and has secured the government permits to begin construction this fall."

Oh, she knew where the valley was. "And are you also

aware that the reservoir created by that dam will flood thirty-six hundred acres of the Red Creek reservation?"

Armstrong regarded her with open curiosity. "I understood the reservoir will cover several hundred square miles. I was told that land was mostly unoccupied."

Her eyes narrowed. What the hell was *that man* doing, sending an unarmed nephew into battle? He might as well have sent an errand boy instead of this...male. There was just no way around it. Everything about Dan Armstrong said *male,* from the good—no, great—chin to the way he sat in that chair, legs spread wide like he was just itching to get back on his horse.

God, he'd looked so good on that horse. Looking had been her first mistake. Instead of just firing over his head from the shadows like she'd planned, she'd wanted to get a better view of the behind that had been sitting in that saddle, a better look at the forearms laid bare for the sun. She'd come out of the shadows, and he'd spotted her. She'd nearly shot his head off, all because he was a man who looked good in a saddle.

She had to remind herself that, at this exact moment in time, she was not a woman, no matter how much she might like to be one. Right now, she was a lawyer, damn it. Men and women didn't count in a courtroom, and she couldn't afford for them to count in this conference room. The only thing that mattered was the law. "Then this is just a waste of our time, isn't it?" She stood and began to shove paper back into the files. Aunt Emily and Joe scrambled to their feet.

"Ms. Donnelly, please." Armstrong rose to his feet, too, which didn't make Rosebud any happier, because nothing good could come from looking up into those green-gray eyes. The only other option was to look at his jaw, which was strong and square and freshly shaved. "Educate me."

Educate him? After that history lesson, he was coming back for more? Suddenly, Rosebud realized just how great a danger Dan Armstrong was. She knew how to fight against faceless corporate stool pigeons. She had no idea what to do with a real man who apparently had a grasp on compassion—and already had her at a disadvantage. The feeling of helplessness left her with only one other emotion to grab at—anger.

"Fine." She unpacked all the files again at a rate that struck even her as irritated. "Cecil Armstrong has been a blight upon this land since he came here five years ago. He's strong-armed local ranchers—many with whom we had unspoken agreements—out of their water rights and lands. He's filed frivolous lawsuits against the tribe and attempted to use eminent domain as legal justification for taking our land." Eminent domain was the biggest threat to her whole legal standing, the one she knew she'd lose. Who the hell cared about a few hundred Indians when they could get their electricity for pennies-on-the-kilowatt cheaper? No one, that's who. No one but the tribe.

Armstrong sat down and began scribbling furiously. If this was an act, it was a damn good one, she decided. This must be why *that man* had sent him. The new, caring face of Armstrong Holdings. When he paused, she continued.

"He has engaged in a campaign of intimidation against members of the tribe." And wouldn't it be lovely if she had some proof of that? But who else would be responsible for Aunt Emily's shot-out windows or Joe's missing spark plugs and punctured tires? Who else would have left another skinned raccoon spread-eagled on her front porch three days ago? No one, that's who. No one else hated her with the passion of Cecil Armstrong.

"That's a serious charge," Dan said without looking up. His voice held steady, with no trace of knee-jerk denial.

"Men have died." Too late, she realized her voice was cracking. Aunt Emily reached out and rested a calming hand on Rosebud's arm. Dang it, she was losing her cool in a meeting. She *never* lost her cool.

Armstrong raised his eyes to meet hers. "Do you have proof?" It didn't come out sneering. It was just a simple question.

With a complicated answer. "The FBI determined that both cases were suicides. The tribal police didn't agree. Nothing ever came of it." Because money talks. The tribe had no money. Cecil Armstrong, it seemed, had it all. Broken, drunk Indians shot their heads off all the time. What were another two? Who cared that Tanner had never had a drink before in his life? He was just another Indian—who'd realized the danger Armstrong Holdings posed to the tribe from the beginning. Who'd happened to be making a run at the tribal council. Who'd happened to be her brother. Just another Indian, that's all.

Armstrong looked at her, then at Aunt Emily's hand, then back to her. "I'm sorry for your loss." And the hell of it was, he really seemed to mean it. Rosebud felt the ground shifting under her feet. Suddenly, she wasn't sure where she stood. "As I said, those are serious charges. I'd like to review your documents before I do anything else."

Finally, something technical she could hold on to. "I'm sure you can understand that we can't let the originals leave this building." *That man* would have himself one hell of a bonfire, that much she knew.

"Of course," he agreed far too easily. "Can you have a copy made for me?"

Another unpleasant reality smacked Rosebud upside the head. Of course this Dan Armstrong was used to a world where copiers worked. That world had shiny new computers that connected to the internet, real office space and chairs that didn't try to eat a person alive.

That wasn't her world.

She held her head high. "Your predecessor in negotiating, Mr. Lon Johnson, had a copy of all my files." Or at least, that was what he *thought*.

"Actually, I looked into that last night." Armstrong's mouth bowed up into an appreciative smile. "It appears that all those files up and disappeared out of his car one day, about a week ago. In addition to his laptop, iPod and three candy bars."

Hmm. That sounded like Matt, who was trying to fashion himself as the ideological heir to Tanner but thus far had just succeeded in being a low-level criminal. She would have loved to have gotten her hands on Johnson's laptop, but there was no question that it had already been pawned off or sold outright. Dang it, she thought. Another missed opportunity. She tried to look surprised, but given how Dan's grin got bigger, she didn't think she'd made it. "That's unfortunate." Armstrong cleared his throat. Time to go to the lame-excuse file. "Our copier recently had an…incident, shall we say. We are awaiting the parts." Which was only a small lie. The copier had had an incident, all right. Two years ago.

Armstrong seemed to buy it. "I guess that leaves only one other option. I'd like your permission," he said, directing his statement to all three of them, "to come back and review the files myself and take notes. That way, they don't leave the building, and I still get what I need."

Rosebud deferred to Aunt Emily, who was weighing the offer. Finally, she nodded. "Of course, Mr. Armstrong, you understand that there'll be conditions."

"Of course," he agreed, leaning back in the chair. He seemed to be getting used to the wobble. He looked to Rosebud, and again she saw the arrogant smile. A man used to getting his way. "I imagine you won't want me to have unsupervised access to original documents."

The implication was clear. He had her cornered, and they both knew it. Nobody else on the rez grasped the full import of all the details Rosebud had meticulously collected over the last three years, not even Aunt Emily. Rosebud was the only one who could possibly make sure nothing original "walked off." She was going to have to sit in this small room for hours—days—on end with a handsome, charming man while he copied her life's work by hand. He was going to leverage all that compassionate charm against her under the auspices of a fact-finding mission.

Whoever the hell Dan Armstrong was, she had to give him credit. He was a worthy opponent.

Aunt Emily took up her cue again. She began to go on about how the tribe just wanted to be left in peace and get a little respect from the outside world. Rosebud tuned her out. Instead, she found herself studying Armstrong's hands. He had calluses that told her he'd earned them the hard way. As he leaned back, she saw an impressive buckle that didn't look store-bought. Actually, upon closer inspection, she didn't think that his shirt was store-bought, either. She glanced down at his boots. Top-of-the-line alligator. They probably cost more than she took home before taxes last year. He wasn't some office gopher, but a man who worked and made more than a nice living. Somehow, she knew he didn't send anyone out to do his bidding. If this Dan Armstrong needed something done, he either asked the right person or he went and did it himself.

If she wasn't careful, she was going to be caught staring. She wondered what he'd been doing in the valley, and immediately, the guilt began to build. God, what a mess. She'd assumed he was one of Cecil Armstrong's mercenary "security" guards. That had been her second mistake. She couldn't be sure it had been her last one.

Finally, as Aunt Emily began to wind up, she noticed that Armstrong was starting to fidget in his chair. All that coffee was finally getting to him. Normally, she'd take advantage of his discomfort to really rake him over the coals, but not today. She needed to get out of this room, far away from this unusual man, and figure out her next move.

On Dan's way out the door, Joe still didn't shake Armstrong's hand, but Aunt Emily did. Then Dan shook Rosebud's hand. "I look forward to working with you," he said as he put the slightest pressure on her fingers. The warmth was still there, but this time it moved up her arm with a greater urgency until she was afraid her face was going to flush.

Damn. Damn, damn, damn. She was afraid she was looking forward to it, too.

Three

Rosebud was sure she'd thrown the files in her office and locked the door, but that part was a little hazy. The next thing she was really conscious of was the soft breeze and the warm sun on her face as she stood in the parking lot, facing south. The breeze still had a touch of cold spring in it, which was just enough to let her mind clear a little.

The situation was far from out of control, she quickly decided. Dan Armstrong might be a different kind of danger to her, but he was still just a man, and a woman didn't make it through law school without figuring out how to handle a man. She just needed to remember who he represented, not what he looked like or how he addressed her with all that "respect" and "compassion."

"You okay, Rosie?" Joe's hand rested on her shoulder.

"Oh, fine." Not true, but she was a lawyer, after all. Never admit weakness, because weakness is defeat. She opened her eyes to see Aunt Emily standing before her, a serious look on her face. "What?"

Aunt Emily looked to Joe and then sighed. "That man…"
"I can handle him."

Aunt Emily regarded her for a painful second. Then she leaned forward and grasped the sticks holding Rosebud's braided bun into place. The whole thing unfurled like a sail. "He is different. He is a handsome man, dear. And you are a handsome woman."

Something about the way she said it hit Rosebud funny. "What are you saying?"

"Keep your friends close, but your enemies closer," Joe said, sounding surprisingly serious about it. The weight of his hand suddenly felt like a vise, pinning her in place.

"You want me to—what? Sleep with him?" When Aunt Emily didn't say anything, Rosebud tried to take a step back, but Joe held her in place. The breeze—colder now, so cold it chilled her to the bone—caught the straggling remains of her braid and unwound it for her. "You *want* me to sleep with him?" Shame ripped through her.

Of all the things asked of her—leaving home for so many years to get that damned law degree when she really wanted to study art; giving up any semblance of a normal life to eat, drink and breathe legal proceedings against Armstrong Holdings; having dead animals show up around her house; losing her brother—sleeping with the enemy was the worst. Even if the enemy was as attractive as Dan Armstrong. That was irrelevant. It didn't matter that she'd given her life to the tribe. Now it wanted her body, too.

"No, no," Joe finally protested, too late. "But a beautiful woman can muddle a man's thinking."

"This may be the chance we've been waiting for, dear," Emily added. Rosebud could hear how little her aunt really believed it, but she kept going. "He could let something… useful slip about his uncle. He might know something about Tanner."

The blow was low. For a second, Rosebud wanted to smack the woman for pouring salt in her wound, but it was a short second. Of course, they were right. Dan Armstrong was an opportunity to do a little domestic spying, that was all. And if she could link Tanner's death to an Armstrong—any Armstrong—she'd be able to sleep at night. Hell, she might even find a new way to stop that dam.

Aunt Emily gave her an artificial smile. "It's what Tanner would do." She pulled Rosebud's glasses off her face and gently tucked them into the pocket of her one-and-only suit jacket. "Do it for Tanner."

Tears that she normally kept out of sight until the middle of the night, when no one would know she cried them, threatened to spill. She squeezed her eyes shut to keep them in. "All right," she managed to get out.

Aunt Emily kissed her cheek in painful blessing. "Find out what you can. Give away nothing."

"Do your best," Joe added, finally removing his clamping hand from her shoulder.

Her best. She'd been doing her best, fending off that dam for three years, but it hadn't been good enough. She wondered if anything ever would be.

She heard both car doors shut, heard both of them drive away, but still she couldn't open her eyes. The breeze tickled her hair, and the sun tried to reassure her it would, in fact, be all right, but she couldn't move. When Tanner had died, she'd sworn to do anything to find out who put that gun in his hand and pulled the trigger. She'd never thought it would come to seducing Cecil Armstrong's nephew.

"Ms. Donnelly?"

Oh, hell.

"Mr. Armstrong," she said without turning around. How on God's green earth was she supposed to muddle his thinking when her own mind was exactly as clear as the Dakota

River during the spring floods? "Thank you for coming today."

He stood next to her. She didn't know how she felt it, but one moment, she was alone, and the next, his solid warmth was close enough that she thought he was touching her arm. Moving slowly, she turned to meet his gaze.

As she did, the breeze surged like a trickster, throwing her hair around. The look in his eyes went from curious regard to recognition—the wrong kind of recognition. His nostrils flared as his jaw clenched. She was no longer facing a compassionate man. Any fool could see that Dan Armstrong was fighting mad.

"Tell me, Ms. Donnelly," he said through gritted teeth. "Do you ride?"

He knew—or thought he knew. In a heartbeat, she realized she needed to play innocent. "Of course. Everyone out here does. Do you?"

She couldn't even see those lovely greenish eyes. They were narrowed into slits. He wasn't buying it. "Sure do. What kind of horse do you ride?"

"Scout is a paint." She wanted to cower before that hard look, but she refused to break that easily. With everything she had, she met his stare. "Yours?"

"Palomino." He stepped around her so quickly that she couldn't help but flinch. "In fact, I was riding him near the dam site in a pretty little valley the other day."

"Is that so?" That was the best she could do as he threw open the door of an enormous, shiny black truck and yanked out a brown cowboy hat.

With a bullet hole through it.

She'd gotten a lot closer than she meant to. She hadn't actually been trying to hit him. She'd been trying to go right over his head, just close enough that he could hear the bullet. But she'd missed. She'd come within an inch of killing a man.

For the first time in her life, she felt really and truly faint. The only thing that kept her on her feet was the knowledge that fainting was a confession of the body. No weakness. No confession.

No matter if she was guilty of attempted murder.

Armstrong was watching her with cold interest. "Someone took a shot at me in that valley."

She managed to swallow, hoping that her reaction would be interpreted as mere shock and not guilt. "That's awful!" Her voice sounded decidedly strangled, even to her own ears. "Did you see who did it?"

He took a step toward her, until he was close enough that she could see how much his pupils had dilated. The almost-green was gone, replaced by a black so inky that he looked more like a *sica,* a spirit, than a man. "It was a woman." His voice was low and quiet, which gave him an air of danger. "A beautiful Native American woman with long, black hair." With his free hand, he reached out and grabbed a hank of her hair, twisting it around his hand until she had no way to escape. He pulled her face up to his. "Wearing buckskins and moccasins. Riding a paint."

Beautiful. She swallowed again. He smelled vaguely of coffee and horse, with a hint of something more exotic— sandalwood, maybe. He smelled *good.* And he was less than a minute from committing assault.

"Buckskins, Mr. Armstrong?" She paused long enough to muster up a look of slight disbelief. "Most of us prefer T-shirts and jeans these days." His mouth opened to protest, but she cut him off. "I can ask a few questions, Mr. Armstrong." Oh, thank God her lawyer voice had returned. She pressed on. "While we do not approve of your uncle's actions, we certainly wouldn't resort to attempted murder."

"A few questions?" His lips—nice, full lips, with just a

hint of pink—twisted into a full sneer as he leaned in even closer. "I want answers."

Friends close, enemies closer. She swallowed, and saw his eyes dart down to her mouth. This was playing with fire, but what else was there? "Are you going to kiss me?" Her lawyer voice was gone again, and instead she sounded like a femme fatale from a '40s film. Where that came from, she didn't know. She could only hope it was the right thing to say.

It was. His jaw flexed again, answering the question for her. Then his other hand moved, brushing a flyaway hair from her face and stroking her cheekbone with the barest hint of pressure. A quiver went through Rosebud, one she couldn't do a thing to stop. The corner of his mouth curled up, just enough to let her know that he'd felt that betraying quiver, too.

He wanted to kiss her, which should have made her feel successful—Aunt Emily would be proud. But his mouth had something else to say about the matter. "Are you fixing to take another shot at me?"

"I don't have any idea what you're talking about." She couldn't even manage to pull off indignant. The best she could do was a throaty whisper better suited to that kiss that still hung in the air between them.

His hand tightened around her hair. Oh, no, he wasn't about to let her off easy. "I thought lawyers were better liars."

Now she was back on more familiar footing. "That's funny. I always heard that liars were better lawyers."

Her stomach turned in anticipation. She'd been kissed, of course, but she'd never been hit. She had no idea which way this would go.

Kiss me. The thought popped into her head from a deep, primitive part of her brain that had nothing to do with Aunt Emily or self-defense. How long had it been since she'd been properly kissed? How long had it been since she'd been this close to a man who looked this good, a man who *smelled* this good? That primitive part of her brain did a quick tally. Way too freaking long. That part didn't care that this was the enemy, didn't care that she'd perpetrated a crime upon his hat. It just cared that he was a man touching her hair, a man who seemed to see past all of her artificial "lawyer" constructs— a man less than three inches from her face.

Kiss me.

He didn't. With a jerk of his head, he let her hair slip through his fingers and took an all-important step away from her. A sense of irrational rejection immediately took up battle with relief.

She wasn't out of the woods yet, though. He was still watching her every movement, her every twitch. Her footing became more familiar. She could do this, whatever *this* was. "I do not take kindly to being a target," he finally said into the wind.

"I don't know of anyone who does." She watched his face as she flipped her hair back over her shoulder. His eyes followed the movement. Why hadn't he kissed her? "If I find out anything about it, I'll let you know."

He licked his lower lip. Yes, it did appear that a beautiful woman could muddle a man's thinking. He pulled his wallet out of his back pocket and fished out a business card. "If you find out anything," he said, the sarcasm dripping off every syllable, "give me a call. I'd like to press charges. That address is wrong, but the cell number is still good."

Armstrong Holdings, the card said. Wichita Falls, Texas. Daniel Armstrong, Chief Operating Officer. Damn. He wasn't just some errand boy, he operated the whole company. Did that include the part that wanted to build the dam? "Of course," she tried to say smoothly as she tucked the card into her pocket behind her glasses. She had the feeling that pressing charges was the least of her worries. But a cell phone number wasn't exactly an in. She needed something more. "Where are you staying now?"

The steel left his eyes a little. Yes, maybe they were both back on familiar footing now, because a smaller version of that arrogant smile was back. "At my uncle's house." He slouched back against the side of his truck, one thumb caught in a belt loop, the other holding the apparently forgotten hat. Now that the anger had left his face—or at least gone deeper under cover—he was right back into handsome territory. "You should come to dinner."

"Excuse me?" Of all the things she thought he might say at that exact moment, dinner wasn't even on the list.

"Look, I can appreciate you not—" he shrugged his shoulders in defeat "—*liking* my uncle very much. But he's not such a bad guy. You should see for yourself."

The spawn of Satan wasn't *such* a bad guy? Even Dan didn't sound like he believed it. With her last bit of self-control, she managed to keep her snort to herself. Besides, a dinner invitation was exactly the sort of in she'd been angling for. Aunt Emily would be thrilled that Rosebud had managed to get invited to that creepy ranch house. God only knew what sort of dirt she could dig up from the inside.

He was falling into her trap—or, she suddenly realized, she was falling into his. After all, two could play at this game.

He notched an eyebrow at her. Oh, yes, *play* was the operative word. She mustered up her best sly grin as she pretended to think about it. "Quite the peacemaker, aren't you, Mr. Armstrong?"

"Mr. Armstrong is my uncle." His smile broadened. "Please call me Dan, Ms. Donnelly."

Suddenly, she decided she might not mind playing this game. After all, she could string him along with a wink and maybe a kiss—okay, definitely a kiss—without giving away anything, including her body. Just so long as she was the one doing the stringing. "Rosebud," she corrected him as she batted her eyes and managed a faint blush.

His smile grew warmer—she thought. "Saturday night? Around seven?"

Two days? He wasted no time. She wouldn't have the chance to find out anything about him before then. She'd be walking into the devil's lair with nothing but her wits and her looks to keep her safe. Sometimes, she thought as she carefully considered his offer, that was all a girl needed. "All right. Saturday at seven."

If she wasn't careful, that smile was going to be her undoing. "Would you like me to pick you up?"

Chivalry had apparently not died. But there was no way in hell she wanted this man in this truck to be seen picking her up on the rez. The wrong people would get the wrong idea, and she had enough to deal with right now. "I know where it is."

He nodded his head in acknowledgment, and she felt the heat from three paces. Definitely a kiss. At least one. One kiss to hold her for the next three years—was that too much to ask? "Good. I'll see you then."

She couldn't tell if it was a threat or a promise.

Four

Dan sat in his truck, fighting the urge to head straight for the barn, saddle up Smokey and head for the valley. The expectation of bad days were the whole reason he'd driven himself and his horse up here from Texas. He wasn't going to leave Smokey, his champion palomino stallion, at home—being around Cecil practically guaranteed he'd need to ride.

A bad day at the office was always made better by taking Smokey out to check on the Armstrong oil derricks. Dan paid people to make sure the derricks ran properly, but there was something about getting his own hands dirty that made him feel like the company was all his. Usually, by the time he rode back in, whatever problem that had been bugging him had either ceased to be important or a solution had presented itself. Sometimes both.

He could sure use a solution to his long list of current problems, starting with who'd fired on him. He had a feeling that if he camped out in that valley long enough, his Lakota princess would come back to the scene of the crime. He'd rather take his chances there than go in and see his uncle. Going in would mean reporting back, and reporting back would mean having to say something about Rosebud Donnelly, and saying something about Rosebud was...tricky.

He couldn't be sure, but damned if that woman hadn't looked just like his Indian princess, minus the horse. She had the nerve to do it, too. The cold-eyed determination he'd seen when he called her on it told him she had nothing but ice water running through her veins. No doubt about it, that was the bearcat Cecil wanted dealt with. She was why Dan was here. Regular lawyers couldn't budge her. He was supposed to *woo* her, for God's sake, with all his "talking." He was supposed to talk his way into her panties, compromise her position and report back.

He was no lapdog.

His princess. Somehow, he knew there was more to her than just that. Underneath all that cold determination, he'd seen something in her eyes, something that had spoken of a deep sorrow, a deep regret. Something that made him think that if she had taken that shot, she hadn't shot to kill.

He couldn't be sure. But he had a hunch, and he hadn't had one lead him astray in a long time.

But what was he supposed to do with it? Make wild accusations—the kind Rosebud was making? What the hell was that about—"Men have died"? Cecil was an ass—that much he knew—but he wasn't a killer. He didn't need to be one—it was just a dam.

Most every person has a reason, his mother's voice whispered in his ear. If ever there was a situation where his mother's sensibilities would come in handy, this was it. He turned his phone over in his hand, debating whether or not he should check in with Mom. On one hand, her opinion on these sorts of matters was worth its weight in oil. On the other hand, he'd have to tell her about the gunshot, and once he did that, she'd go all Mom on him, and she was plenty busy keeping the day-to-day operations going while he was up here dealing with the Cecil "situation." She was the reason he had time to spend days taking notes with Rosebud. Nope. He couldn't bring Mom in on this yet. He needed her focused on the meetings and deals he'd lined up before he left.

Dan thought hard, trying to review the interview as his mother would. Rosebud Donnelly's voice had cracked and Emily Mankiller had touched her, like a mother comforting her child. His first instinct—she'd lost someone, maybe a husband—had been true. Maybe Rosebud had taken a shot at him to make up for a different shot, a better shot. That had to be it.

Did that even the score? Was she satisfied? No, he decided. A woman like that was never satisfied with *just* once. He smiled at the thought. But he didn't think she was going to take another shot at him. He'd looked her in the eyes. Her mouth may have been lying, but he didn't think her eyes were telling the same tale.

No, they'd been saying something…different. He adjusted his jeans. Damn it all. He shouldn't have gotten so close to her, so close to the way she smelled, to those beautiful eyes the shade of a doe's fur in the early spring. He never should have touched her hair, one long swath of silk. He never should have shaken her hand.

For that matter, he never should have come here.

And now, he thought in resignation, he had to go in *there*. *Time to get this over with.* Dan grabbed his dead hat off the dash. He needed a new one, pronto. A man didn't go without a hat where he was from.

"Well?" Dan hadn't even made it to the door of the dining room. He sighed. There was no avoiding his uncle. The whole house stunk of him.

Dan was so busy mulling over the best way to handle telling Cecil about the situation that he didn't see the man in the black leather jacket sitting in front of Cecil until he stood up. Another Lakota Indian? What was Cecil doing with someone who sure as hell looked like one of the very people suing Armstrong Holdings?

"Dan Armstrong," he said, making the first move. A fellow could tell a lot about a person by his handshake.

"Shane Thrasher," the stranger said. His grip started out rock-hard, but quickly went limp, like he was trying to hide something. Dan decided he didn't like the man, an opinion reinforced by his uncle's warm smile for Thrasher. Nope. Didn't like him at all.

"Thrasher is—what are you, again?" Cecil opened a lock-box Dan hadn't seen before and pulled out a thick file. The box looked old—like the house. Definitely not something Cecil normally had in his office.

"Half Crow," Thrasher replied as he sat back down. He acted like he'd sat in that chair a lot.

Hadn't Emily Mankiller said something about the Crow tribe? Something about Custer and Little Bighorn and Greasy Grass? What Dan needed was an eighth-grade history book, but if he was remembering correctly, according to Ms. Mankiller, the Crow were the ones who worked with the whites against the Lakota.

"That's right. I can't keep you all straight." Dan winced at Cecil's words, even though Thrasher didn't blink. "Thrasher is my head of security. An inside man, if you will."

Head of security? Dan looked him over. More like gun for hire. The bulge at his side wasn't hard to see. Maybe Rosebud Donnelly had taken a shot at Dan, maybe she hadn't. Dan had a hunch that he needed to be more worried about Shane Thrasher than a beautiful, conflicted lawyer. "Pleasure to make your acquaintance."

A muscle above Thrasher's left eye twitched in response. It appeared the insincere feeling was mutual.

Cecil was studying a thick file. "What did you think of that Donnelly woman?"

"She's trouble." An honest assessment—but he couldn't figure out if she was the good kind or the bad kind of trouble. More than likely, she was both.

Thrasher snorted in a way that struck Dan as too familiar. Wielding a red pen, Cecil made a note in the file. "Think you can handle her?"

For the first time in his life, Dan wasn't sure if he could handle a woman. In the space of one afternoon, he'd been impressed by, furious with and turned on by Rosebud Donnelly. The combination was dangerous. "I invited her to dinner Saturday night." Cecil's eyebrows shot up. "She accepted," he added. In the space of a second, he'd seen a crack in her ice-cold lawyer front. He had the feeling that keeping her on her toes was the only way to get through to her. That, and making sure she wasn't armed. But he'd be damned if he'd bring up any of that in front of Thrasher.

"That's my boy." Cecil's grin was wide. He looked downright happy, in an evil sort of way. "What did I tell you, Thrasher?"

"You were right," Thrasher replied, the butt-kissing tone of his voice at odds with the way his face kept twitching.

Dan had the sudden urge to punch that face. Instead, he dug his fingers into the chair's armrest. "I thought it would help if she could see you as a person, not just an adversary." Although, with that grin, Dan was having trouble seeing Cecil as more than an adversary right now, too.

Cecil gave him the same look he'd been giving Dan since the day after his father's funeral—the shut-up-and-be-an-Armstrong look. "I don't give a rat's ass how she sees me. I'm not running some feel-good love-in around here. I want you to find her weak spots. I want you to bring her *down*. Understood?"

Right then, Dan wished he'd never had to leave Texas. In Texas, he ran a tight ship. Armstrong Holdings was one of the twenty best places to work in Texas, or so some award hanging in the reception area said. But the South Dakota division of Armstrong Holdings seemed to be a different can of worms, and Dan was feeling particularly slimy today. He reminded himself that Cecil's lack of ethics was the exact reason he'd come—there was no place for slime in any part of Dan's company. "She won't make me any copies of her files, but she'll let me see them to take notes."

A look that was dangerously close to victory flashed over Cecil's face. "Well, then, that's something, isn't it? I underestimated you, son."

Son. The chair creaked. Dan was in serious danger of breaking off an armrest or two. Thrasher had the nerve to snort in amusement.

"I've got a fundraiser in Sioux Falls Saturday night. It'll be just the two of you," Cecil went on as he made another note with the red pen. "I expect results."

Dan would also like to see some results—but he wanted to believe his reasons were more noble. "Interested lust" was better than "cold-blooded scheming." Wasn't it? At least Thrasher hadn't gotten this assignment. But then, Dan didn't think Thrasher would get anywhere with Rosebud. She didn't seem like the kind of woman who went for jerks.

"What about him?" Dan didn't even look at Thrasher—he was too afraid he'd lose the last of his cool and punch him.

"Don't worry your pretty little head about me," Thrasher replied as he stood, conveniently moving out of range. "In fact, I doubt you'll ever see me again, Armstrong."

Dan shot to his feet. But by the time he got turned around, Thrasher was gone. Dan swung back around, his fists ready.

"We're all on the same side here," was all Cecil said as he locked the box back up.

No, Dan didn't think they were.

He didn't know whose side he was on.

Five

Her aged, dented Taurus made it to the Armstrong ranch house. That was a good thing. And the weather wasn't so hot that she was sweating in her suit, so that was also a good thing.

But beyond those two good things, Rosebud was grasping at straws. The whole situation had an air of unreality to it. Was she really about to have dinner—at his house—with the one-and-only Cecil Armstrong? With Dan Armstrong? Was she really this scared about it?

Oh, yeah, she was terrified. If she'd owned chain mail, she would have put it on under the jacket, but she didn't, so she'd settled for a lower-cut-than-normal tank top in a soft-and-flirty pink under her gray suit. That was as close as she got to pretty when she was about to do battle.

She could do this. She was a lawyer, damn it. She'd argued a case before the South Dakota Supreme Court, for God's sake—argued and won. She could handle the Armstrong men.

She grabbed her briefcase and put on her game face. But before she could get anywhere, the front door swung open and out stepped the cowboy of her dreams.

The white, button-up shirt was cuffed to the elbows, and the belt buckle sat just so on the narrow V of his waist. For a blinding second, she hoped he'd turn around and go right back inside, just so she could see what that backside looked like without a saddle or a sports coat to block the view. She thought she saw a loaded holster at his side, but she realized it was a cell phone. All that was missing was a white horse and a sunset to ride off into.

Just one kiss, she thought as she fought to keep a satisfied smile off her face. Kissing Dan Armstrong wouldn't be the worst thing in the world, would it?

"You're right on time," Dan said as he came down to greet her. When he shook her hand this time, he acted like he was one step away from kissing it.

Maybe two kisses. Darn it, this whole situation was driving her crazy. She fought the urge to swing her briefcase in between them like it was a guillotine. "I'm sure your uncle appreciates punctuality."

Dan still had her hand. Warm, again, and still not sweaty. He wasn't nervous. The realization made *her* even more nervous. "He probably does. But he's not here."

Relief flooded her system at the same time her heartbeat picked up another notch. "Oh?" Was it just the two of them?

The look in Dan's eyes said yes, it was just the two of them. The gentle pressure his fingers were exerting on her wrist seconded the motion. "He's at some fundraiser."

She was going to have to draw the line at three kisses, tops. Any more than that, and this man would have her in a compromising position behind enemy lines. "You understand that no matter what party he tries to buy off, I'm going to do everything in my power to make sure he doesn't get elected?"

"Completely." No, there was no mistaking Dan's feelings. He didn't like his own uncle. But if that was true, what was he doing here, with her? Finally, he let go of her hand and stepped back. As his eyes skimmed her body, she saw his brow wrinkle. "This isn't a business meeting, you know."

Just her luck—he really was that observant. He'd noticed her suit—what were the odds he remembered it was the same one she'd had on two days ago? She jutted out her chin in defiance of all known fashion laws and bluffed her way past the blush she was sure she was working on. "You didn't expect me to treat this as a social call, did you?"

"No, I guess I didn't." He offered her his arm. Chivalry was not only *not* dead, it was also apparently alive and well in his part of Texas. She ignored the flattered feeling that started to hum high in her chest. So what if it had been an awfully long time since any white man had done more than look down his nose at her? She was not going to let this "respect" thing go to her head. "Shall we?"

As they walked up the porch steps, Rosebud had the distinct feeling that she was walking into the jaws of hell, and the demon house would swallow her down in one big gulp. She fought the urge to cling to Dan's arm. She wasn't some weak female who needed a male protector. It wasn't her fault if her fingers wrapped around his bare skin.

"Have you ever been here?" he said as he held the door for her.

"Never *in*. Just *by*," she said as her eyes adjusted to the darkened interior of the foyer. Actually, it looked nothing like a dungeon. Everything was neat and clean—even the mounted buffalo head she could see in the parlor was dust-free. The rooms had a warm, almost feminine sensibility to them.

He nodded as he guided her down a long, dark hallway. "To hear Maria tell it, Cecil's never set foot in any rooms but the dining room and his bedroom. I guess the rest of this place is like a museum."

"Who's Maria?"

"The housekeeper. She made us dinner tonight." Dan pushed open a swinging door. "Oh, good. Maria, meet my guest, Rosebud Donnelly, the Lakota lawyer who's suing Cecil. Rosebud, this is Maria Villerreal. She basically runs the place." His tongue rolled the *R*s right. She flushed hot, thinking of his tongue rolling anything.

"Señor!" Maria was a small woman with a thick accent who was in the middle of putting on her coat. She ducked her head to Rosebud. "It is an honor to meet you, *señorita.*"

"The pleasure is mine." Again, this was not what she expected. A pristine mansion and kindly hired help? Maybe she had Cecil Armstrong all wrong.

"Dinner is in the oven, *señor.* Do you need anything else?"

Dan patted her arm, and Rosebud saw the girlish blush rise up. "No, Maria, it smells wonderful. You can head out—give my best to Eduardo and the boys, okay?"

"Sí, señor." Maria held out her hand to Rosebud. "Señor Daniel is a good man, *señorita.*"

As opposed to…his uncle? The statement opened the door to about twenty questions. Dan couldn't have been around that long, or she would have heard about his arrival *before* he showed up at her office. How long had Maria worked for Cecil? Clearly, Dan was working his charm on more people than her. That wasn't a bad thing, either, she decided. This wasn't any different than judging a date by how he treated the waiter—except, she reminded herself, this wasn't a date. Now that Maria was out of the house, Rosebud had to remember that.

Dan pulled out a stool at the huge kitchen island and motioned for her to sit. She felt a little silly about the formality, but she couldn't say no to that smile. "We're eating in the kitchen?"

"The dining room is Cecil's headquarters." Dan got busy with plates and forks before he opened the oven. The scent of Mexican—good Mexican—filled the air. "The kitchen is a much nicer place, trust me. I hope you like tamales."

Sounded like the dining room was the place she needed to be. Something occurred to her. "You call him Cecil?"

Dan paused, a sheepish smile on his face. "Yeah, I guess I do."

"You don't like him very much, do you?"

"Not many people do." He dug out some cheese and proceeded to garnish the tamales. *A good-looking man who knows how to garnish,* Rosebud thought in amazement. *No,* she caught herself. She would *not* be impressed. "You don't like him."

That was putting it mildly. "I've never actually met him. He's *your* uncle."

"And there's not a damn thing I can do about that." He sounded lighthearted, but the tension in his voice was unmistakable as he set her dinner before her. "I'd offer you a beer, but that suit says I'd be wasting my breath." Here, just the two of them in a kitchen that smelled of warmth and goodness, she allowed herself to smile. His eyes latched on to her smile, and she froze. Did he think he recognized her from the valley? Or was he just staring? "Lemonade?" he finally said into the silence.

Disaster averted, she thought with a mental sigh. "I'd love some."

"Tell me about your name." He set the lemonade down in front of her, but he didn't withdraw. Instead, he stood in the space between touching her shoulder and not touching her shoulder.

She looked up. No, there wasn't any of that wariness she

thought she'd caught a glimpse of. His eyes weren't so stormy, she decided. They were more like the palest jade with just a hint of gray. A precious stone. "Is that the nice way of asking if I'm named after a sled?"

Jade probably didn't sparkle as much as Dan's eyes. "My mother loves *Citizen Kane,*" he said and then headed back to the stove to scoop out Spanish rice. "I bet you get that question a lot."

Her mouth watered. Whatever else happened tonight, at least the food was going to be good. "Only from white people."

His shoulders shook with laughter. "Guilty as charged."

At least he had a sense of humor about it. That was a rare thing in and of itself, especially considering the past three years. She was used to dealing with *that man's* lawyers, who held her in obvious contempt. When she was in college, she'd become familiar with white people who had an overdeveloped sense of liberal guilt. And the locals? They mostly treated her—or any Indian, for that matter—like dirty, dumb Injuns. Dan didn't fit into any of those categories. "You don't have to be all politically correct, either—*Indian* is fine. I think of myself as a Lakota Indian."

He regarded her with a look that was between frank curiosity and open respect. "Duly noted. So are you named after a sled?"

She couldn't help but grin widely at him. "I'm named after a distant relative who moved to New York in the '40s, Rosebud Yellow Robe. Family legend is that Orson Welles named the sled after her—they both did radio shows for CBS back in the day."

"Interesting." His voice dropped a notch as he served dinner with a flourish. "And the Donnelly?"

She wasn't much of a cook, and this was, hands down, the most delicious meal she'd had in ages. She forced herself to focus. If she wasn't mistaken, that was a pretty slick way of asking if Donnelly was her maiden or married name. "A grandmother married a white man after the Civil War, and they had nothing but sons for a while."

"Until you."

She froze, the fork halfway to her mouth. Her appetite disappeared, leaving only uneasiness in her belly. Carefully, she lowered the fork back to the plate and cleared her throat. "I had a brother. He was one of the deaths deemed a suicide by the FBI."

Out of the corner of her eye, she saw his hand flex. *Way to go,* Rosebud scolded herself. Way to play the pity card. *Way to use Tanner's memory.* Suddenly, she felt dirty. This whole situation was wrong. There had to be better ways to get to Cecil Armstrong. If she thought real hard, she was sure she could come up with *something.* Anything would be better than this intimate dinner with his nephew.

He finally spoke into the silence. "I'm goin' to look into it."

"You said that." She tried to shrug this whole awkward conversation off but failed miserably.

He pivoted on his stool, put a hand on her shoulder and turned her to face him. "I mean it."

She wanted to believe him, but she'd had too many men—white and Indian—break too many promises. Still, something about the way he met her gaze made her think that maybe, just maybe, this time would be different.

She was getting warmer. Just like when he'd shaken her hand, she could feel the slow burn moving from where he was touching her shoulder down her arm and across her chest. Despite the confusion that swirled in her head, she still felt the pull of sexual tension. She tested out a small smile and got an honest one in return as his hand drifted down to her arm and gave it a little squeeze. That burn got a lot less slow.

Oh, boy. If she wasn't careful, all this promising and smiling and touching would pull her right under. She was already a mess right now. She couldn't afford something as distracting as sexual tension to further unscrew her head. "A man of his word?"

"Always." His fingers trailed down her arm, leaving scorch marks under her jacket. He motioned to the food. "It's goin' to get cold."

Luckily, dinner was still warm—and delicious. Eating it gave her a little time to get her thoughts organized, because the last thing she wanted to do was add the embarrassment of spewing half-chewed tamales across the kitchen island. Finally, the plates were nearly empty and she'd moved on to the lemonade. She decided to start with the least dangerous topic she could think of. "You'll have to tell Maria that I said this was wonderful."

"She'll like that."

"How long have you known her?"

"About a week."

Okay, that answered her question about how long he'd been here. No wonder she hadn't heard about his arrival. "Really? You seem like old friends."

Maybe that grin wasn't arrogant. Maybe that grin was just confident. "My mother raised me to be nice to everyone, regardless of whether they were the maid or the king of the world." Then the grin slid right on over into arrogant. "Plus, I gave Maria a—what do they call it these days? A retention bonus. My uncle was still paying her the same wage he hired her at five years ago."

That didn't surprise her. "Your mother sounds like a wise woman," she said, hoping she was using the right tense.

"She is. She's the executive vice president. We run the Texas division of the company as a team—before this thing with Cecil pulled me up here, that is." He began to rummage through the fridge. "I think Maria left a cake—interested?"

"Yes, please. Will your mother be visiting you here?" Because she'd kind of like to meet the woman who produced this charmer.

"She wouldn't be caught dead in the same state as Cecil."

It was interesting to watch him drift between hot and serious, chatty and silent. Dan didn't exactly wear his heart on his sleeve, but she got the feeling he didn't win a lot of poker games. "Sounds like a long story."

"It's not so much long as it is old. Mom picked Dad instead of Cecil. Cecil never forgave either of them. He didn't even come to Dad's funeral."

"And you work for him?" It was out of her mouth before she could stop it.

Dan set a piece of cake in front of her, pulled up his stool and sat down. Only then did he turn to her, his eyes going right past serious and straight on over into dangerous. She wondered if other people made him look this dangerous, or if it was just her. "Let's get something straight," he said, sounding very much like a man who would take all comers. "I don't work *for* Cecil. I inherited my father's stake in the family business. I own half of this house, the water rights and the dam project. This is my company just as much as it is his."

That nerve she'd hit was *huge*. She wondered if Cecil had the same interpretation of the situation. "But you're helping him."

He glared at her. All the charm was gone. "I'm *helping* my company."

She had pushed this just about as far as she could, but she couldn't quit. This was her in—Dan didn't like his uncle, and he didn't like the job the old man was doing. The chance that she could convince Dan to abandon the whole thing was small, but it was a chance she had to take. "Well, *your* company is going to flood *my* reservation."

He looked away, like she'd won and he'd lost. But then he said, "Eminent domain."

So he'd been doing his homework, and they both knew who the loser here was going to be. The government would give the reservation to Cecil because lower electricity rates were good for politicians and their reelections. It was a new twist on the old story—the white people needed the land more than the Indians did. And yet, she felt like she needed to comfort him. He actually looked miserable about the whole damn thing. Leaning over, she touched one of those forearms and said, "I won't go down without a fight."

Moving slowly, he set his fork down and took her fingers in his hand. Calluses rubbed against the length of her index finger, then moved on to her palm. If she hadn't been sitting, her knees would have buckled. "I'm counting on that." Oh, that wasn't a threat—that was a promise, pure and simple. "But the question is, what kind of fight?"

She couldn't help it. Three long years of loneliness threatened to swamp her altogether. She leaned into him, close enough that she could see a faint scar above his cheek, close enough that his short hair could tickle her nose. "You can check my briefcase. I don't have a gun."

He turned to her as he pulled her hand into his rock-solid chest. "Not here, anyway," he murmured as his lips brushed hers. "You're too smart for that."

Huh? *She* was smart? She was the one sitting in Cecil Armstrong's kitchen, kissing Cecil Armstrong's nephew— a man she barely knew, a man she'd shot at, for God's sake!

But how was he being any smarter? He knew—or thought he knew—that she'd put a hole in his hat, less than two inches from his skull! What kind of man came on to a woman he believed to be armed and dangerous? What kind of man worked for—with—Cecil Armstrong? What kind of man *was* Dan Armstrong?

Oh. My. God. The kissing kind, that's what.

His touch wasn't an act of aggression or domination, but more like he was asking for permission. Not the kiss of an enemy, but of something…different. Even though his fingers tightened around hers, he hung back, waiting for a sign. His other hand came up and stroked her cheek with the lightest of touches. Tension—the good sort—hit her like a small jolt of electricity, pushing her into him. That must have been what he was waiting for, because his tongue brushed her lips, and she forgot all about being smart. Instead, she remembered being a woman, remembered the feeling of desire as it surged from her mouth, flamed to her breasts and scorched down farther until she wanted nothing more than to see exactly how far this kiss could go.

Six

He really hadn't meant to kiss her—not before dessert, anyway. But she'd touched him, and promised that she'd fight him every single step of the way. The way she'd said it.... She'd said it not like she was about to serve him a subpoena, but like she was suggesting they continue their discussion in bed.

He was supposed to be getting to her, breaking down her defenses, finding her weak spots and exploiting them. But that wasn't what was happening.

What was happening was that she was getting to him.

He couldn't give less of a damn about whatever business pretense he'd used to get her here. What mattered was that she was here, now, kissing him. He wanted to taste more of her. Hell, he wanted to taste all of her. She had a honeyed sweetness that was tempered with a hint of tart lemonade. Her fingers tightened around his shirt, pulling him into her. She opened her lips for him, and he felt her jolt when his tongue touched hers. For a second, he knew he was about to get lucky. His body was aching for it, too.

Then, suddenly, he was puckering up to nothing but air. She jerked back, yanking her hand away from his chest so hard that she just about took his shirt with her—but not in the fun way.

What the hell? She went right past a pretty pink and straight on over to hit-with-a-tomato red, her eyes fastened on the forgotten cake in front of them. Just as much as her hands and her mouth had been telling him "yes" a second before, the rest of her was screaming "no," loud and clear. The buzzy hard-on he'd been working on slammed right back up into his gut. Gritting his teeth, he tried to get his eyes to focus. It didn't help. She looked more miserable than a woman he'd been kissing ought to.

And that cold shoulder she was giving him said nothing but *mistake* and *regret.* It left a bad taste in his mouth that had nothing to do with the lip-lock. "I shouldn't have done that," he offered. It sounded weak, even to his own ears.

She jumped at the words and was off the stool before he knew what was happening. "I should go." Her eyes cut back to him. The softness there was disappearing faster than a puddle in August. "Now."

No use arguing with that. She'd made up her mind, that much was clear. "I'll walk you to your car."

She didn't offer any resistance, but she made sure to keep her distance from him as she stomped down the hall, out the front door and into a deepening dusk. It was only when she got to the gate that she pulled up. "Thank you for dinner." She put both hands behind her back. "Please tell Maria I enjoyed the food."

Just the food? Ouch. The woman's claws were razor sharp. "I'm still coming by your office Monday at nine." Even though the dusk was settling, he could see the flash of anger in her eyes. But she'd said it herself—he was a man of his word, and he needed to know more about her brother before he started digging around. "If it's all right with you."

She let the question hang for a long moment without so much as a blink. No wonder Cecil had already gone through three lawyers. A pissed Rosebud Donnelly was an intimidating Rosebud Donnelly. His eyes darted back to her ugly little car, but thankfully he saw no gun propped up against the window or anything.

"Of course," she finally said, her chin jutting out in a way that said it was anything but okay with her. "You're just doing your job."

Once she was in her car, the rear tires spun out on the gravel before she got enough traction to peel out, but her words hung around. *Just doing his job.*

He felt lower than a rattler's belly in a wagon rut, all because he was *just doing his job.*

As he turned to go back into the house, an orange light caught his eyes. Just a small dot of bright color that had no business being about six feet off the ground behind some bushes. As quick as he'd seen it, it was gone. He couldn't see anything else amiss.

The hairs stood up on the back of his neck. *"In fact,"* Thrasher's voice sneered in his ear, *"I doubt you'll ever see me again."*

His uncle was having him watched. A deep rage threatened to break free, the same rage he'd felt shortly after Dad had died, when his uncle had showed up and informed Mom that if she didn't marry him, he'd take the company away from her. Dan had only been sixteen at the time. He hadn't let Cecil call the shots then—he and Mom had gotten enough stock to keep the board firmly on their side—and he sure as hell wasn't going to let Cecil call the shots now.

Screw it, Dan thought, forcing himself to walk calmly back into the house. No need to let Thrasher know Dan suspected anything. *Screw Cecil Armstrong. Screw this whole job.*

Except for the kiss.

Dan had just one thing he *could* do. He spent the rest of his Saturday night taking the kitchen apart, looking for hidden cameras and microphones.

He knew whose side he was on.

"Good morning, Mr. Armstrong."

Dan didn't even have one foot in the door, and already the receptionist was coming at him with a cup of coffee. Today, he was going to hold steady at two cups, max. "Ms. Donnelly is waiting for you."

"Thank you…Judy." Her friendly smile told him he'd gotten that right.

She led him back to the sorriest excuse for a conference room he'd ever been in. To his surprise, Rosebud was already settled in with a banker's box of files in front of her. "Good morning, Mr. Armstrong." She didn't even look up. "You're on time."

She sounded exactly like the receptionist and nothing like a woman he'd kissed two nights ago. "Rosebud." To heck with this *mister* and *miz* stuff. "I thought you would appreciate punctuality."

That got her to look up, and even earned him a small smile. Man, how did she manage to shine in a room this ugly? The walls were the color of overcooked oatmeal, and he thought he deserved a buckle for managing to make the eight seconds on that chair last time.

As quick as that smile had shown up, it disappeared again. He wondered if she had a gun in her briefcase. "Are these your files?"

"Not all of them." He leaned over to try and see what she was writing, but she caught him and flipped the top sheet back over the one she'd made notes on. "But this is more than enough to keep you busy for today."

Dan looked around and was surprised to see that the two extra chairs had disappeared. He'd have to sit in that craptastic chair again. He had to hand it to Rosebud. She didn't have a lot to work with, but she made the most of it. "Which files are these?"

"What do you mean?"

"Cecil files, dam files or police files?"

No reaction this time. He had his work cut out for him today. Right now, not only was Rosebud *not* a woman who invited a touch or a kiss, but she wasn't exactly leaving any of her weak spots out in the open. "Police files." She turned her attention back to her own notes. "You are a man of your word, after all."

"Yes, ma'am." Moving cautiously, he lowered himself into the evil chair. It promptly let out a muffled squeak, like he'd sat on a squirrel—or worse. He glanced up to see the amusement on her face. "Enjoyin' yourself?"

"Immensely."

So she was laughing at him. The difference between Rosebud scowling and Rosebud smiling was worth sounding like he'd eaten nothing but chili for the last month. He pulled the top file and started reading the first police report.

Tanner Donnelly, male, age twenty-eight when he was found by his aunt, Emily Mankiller, with a .22 in his hand and the matching slug in his temple four years ago. Survived by his aunt and his sister, Rosebud. The file noted that the women claimed Donnelly's dog tags were missing, but the investigators could find no trace of them.

The FBI agent in charge had been Thomas Yellow Bird. Rosebud had a separate file on Yellow Bird—seemed he was an acquaintance of Tanner Donnelly and had pushed the investigation as far as his supervisors would let him. There was also a log of emails and phone calls with a James Carlson, who was a federal prosecutor in D.C.

Something didn't add up, Dan thought as he wrote the name down. A guy named Yellow Bird he could understand, but Rosebud had D.C. contacts? Well, maybe not. The last date she'd written down was over ten months ago. She must have hit a brick wall—which was why she was asking *him* for help, of all people.

In addition to police and FBI files, there was a thick file of notes and interviews, some typed and some handwritten in a delicate script. Handwritten? This whole thing just got odder and odder, but he pressed on, copying down every possibly relevant piece of information. His hand began to cramp. He didn't normally like those little computers—too easy to drop—but he was thinking maybe he'd pick one up the next time he was in town.

By the time he finished, Dan was pretty sure he knew everything about Tanner Donnelly, from what kind of cereal he ate for breakfast to the name of the first girl he'd ever kissed. Seemed like a decent guy. If Rosebud's notes were accurate—and he had no reason to doubt that—then he could see how she refused to accept the suicide ruling.

But he'd seen no red flags, nothing that said Cecil or even Thrasher. Not even a casual connection to Armstrong Holdings.

He had nothing.

When he leaned back to rub his eyes, he found Rosebud watching him. "Well?"

"You're nothing if not thorough."

She cocked her head to one side and bounced the end of her pen on the table. Dan had the distinct feeling he was about to be cross-examined. "Is that what you told your uncle?"

"Beg pardon?"

"When you reported back about our evening. I'm sure he was…curious, shall we say, to know if you accomplished your assignment."

He might be mistaken, but he thought he saw a little bit of that pink come back into her cheeks. "Are you asking me if I told him I kissed you?"

He wasn't mistaken. The pink got prettier as her eyes cut to the doorway, but it was empty. "That was your assignment, wasn't it? I'm not stupid, Mr. Armstrong."

She had him dead to rights. He really hoped she didn't have a gun in that briefcase. "Only a fool would assume you were." Because it sure would be nice to know she didn't think him a total idiot—or worse, Cecil's lapdog.

She smirked at the compliment, but didn't return the favor. "You're avoiding the question."

He couldn't tell which part of her was doing damage control, the lawyer or the woman. "You act like my company kissed your tribe."

For a second, he saw a little bit of doubt on her face. "Wasn't that the point?"

He knew the chair might kill him, but he took the chance and leaned forward—not close enough to touch her, but close enough that he could tell she was biting the inside of her lip. The chair whined pitifully, but at least it held. "Did it ever occur to you that *I* was kissin' *you?*"

Oh, she was tough. Aside from that lovely blush she was working on, she didn't react at all—not even to lean away from him. "Does your uncle see such a distinction?"

Which was a nice, polite way of saying "answer the damn question." He shook his head, hoping his amusement didn't further piss her off. "You want to know what I told him?"

"Please." She sat up a little straighter.

Dan looked at her for a few more seconds before he hazarded leaning back in his chair. If Cecil heard what he was about to say, he'd draw and quarter Dan for treason. But the search for bugs in the kitchen had turned up nothing, as had the search of his room. He was going on a hope and a prayer that this room wasn't bugged. "I told him that you were tougher than I thought. I told him you couldn't be wined and dined. I told him I'd need more time."

She was silent. Her pretty blush drained away, but that was the only sign she'd heard him. "I see. Did you give him an idea of how much time you'd need?"

Hell, he was in this far. "He told me the next court date is in five weeks." Besides, she'd said so herself. She wasn't stupid.

"Let me guess. He wants me out of the picture before then." Her voice had a new, pinched tone to it.

"That's what *he* wants."

A stillness came over her. Her pen didn't bounce, her eyes didn't blink and he couldn't tell without staring, but he was reasonably confident that her chest didn't even rise. When she did speak, it came out as a whisper. A pained whisper. "What do *you* want?"

Which was a hell of a good question. But he wasn't going to come up with an answer sitting in this demon chair. He got up as smoothly as he could and went to the window. She needed a moment to get herself together, he rationalized. "You know Google? The company motto is 'Don't be evil.'"

She snorted behind his back. "That's noble, but naive."

"No, dinner was noble but naive," he shot back.

"I'm *not* naive."

"Not you. Me." Because thinking he could walk the line between "interested lust" and "cold-blooded scheming" was obviously one of his dumber ideas. And to expect her to believe him? He turned back to her. "It was naive of me to think that me kissin' you could be a separate…thing from your tribe suing my company." So much for being good at talking.

Even sitting in judgment of him, she was beautiful. What he wanted was to ask her out on a real date, to take her someplace far away from this crappy conference room and Cecil's ranch house, someplace where it wasn't Armstrong Holdings talking to the Red Creek Tribe, but just Dan and Rosebud. He'd love to get her hair out of that braid, get her out of that… For the first time, he noticed her suit. It looked like the same one she'd worn to dinner—and the same one she'd had on last week.

She only had one suit?

He must have been staring, because she began gathering up files. The movement did little to hide the embarrassment on her face.

"What happened to your copier?" The question was out before he knew where it came from. Somehow, he knew the answer was connected to a lawyer that only owned one suit.

He could see the tension ripple along her shoulders. "It's broken." She hefted the banker's box and made a break for the door. "Good day, Mr. Armstrong."

The door shut behind her.

As Dan's eyes adjusted to the bright sunlight in the parking lot, he noticed the man immediately. The black Crown Victoria, the full-wrap sunglasses and the black suit were hard to miss in this heat. Some kind of law was trying mighty hard to look casual in the middle of the parking lot at four in the afternoon.

The guy looked a little like a Lakota Indian—right color, but wrong everything else. His hair was short and that suit probably set him back a cool grand. Not the local police. And the man was watching him behind those glasses. Dan could tell by the way his chin moved.

This place must be throwing him for a loop because right now, Dan felt like he was walking into a trap and he wished with all his might he had his gun.

"Dan Armstrong?"

"Depends. Who's askin'?" Yep. Old-timey talk was just pouring out of him.

"Tom Yellow Bird." He stuck out his hand, his jacket flashing open to reveal a Glock.

Good grip, Dan thought. Not a grip of dominance, but there wasn't an ounce of weakness in the man. "What can I do for you, Mr. Yellow Bird?"

Yellow Bird gave him the once-over. "Depends on what you're doing here. Heard you were looking into the Donnelly suicide."

"Word gets around."

"It's a small rez. Going to get a lot smaller if Cecil Armstrong gets his way." Yellow Bird waited, but Dan was in no hurry to set the man's mind at ease. Yellow Bird broke first. "You've met Rosebud?"

"I have. You know her?"

"Knew her brother." The way he said it made it sound like he considered Rosebud to be the pesky little sister—always had, always would. For some reason, that made Dan want to smile—but he didn't. "We lost a good one in him."

The *we* said Indian first, FBI second. "You don't buy the suicide ruling?"

Yellow Bird scratched his throat. "Officially, that's what happened. The case has been closed for two years."

"Unofficially?"

Yellow Bird smirked, which gave his face a hard edge. Not a man to be taken lightly, that much was certain. "You know that by this time next year, where we're standing will be under about ten feet of water?"

Unofficially, Yellow Bird was still on the case. "I'm aware that that's the current plan."

"Things can always change." Yellow Bird pulled a card out of his jacket. "Unofficially."

Dan watched as the Crown Victoria pulled away, then did a slow circle to see if anyone else had witnessed the meeting. The lot was still empty, and he didn't see any faces at the narrow windows.

What the hell had that been about? For some reason, the conversation had struck Dan as being less about Tanner Donnelly and more about Armstrong Holdings. If he didn't know any better, he would have sworn that, unofficially, Yellow Bird was leaving a door open, just in case.

Damn hunches. Dan had no idea if this one was right.

As far as Rosebud was concerned, the rest of the week was simultaneously better and worse than that first meeting with Dan. He showed up at nine each morning, sat in the wobbly chair and took notes while Rosebud reviewed her case for the upcoming hearing on the preliminary injunction against the dam construction. It should have been boring, dry work, but it wasn't.

On Tuesday, Dan brought homemade chocolate-chip cookies. Wednesday was brownies and Thursday was cupcakes for the whole office. By Friday, he knew the names of everyone in the building and brought in extra cinnamon rolls for Rosebud to take to Aunt Emily. She couldn't tell if he was just buttering them—her—up or if he'd been doing his homework and knew that bringing gifts was a Lakota custom, but either way, it seemed to be working.

Judy was officially crushing on the man, and Rosebud couldn't blame her. He was easy on the eyes, smart as a whip, quite possibly richer than sin and just all around thoughtful. Add in the fact that not only did he not wear a ring, but he didn't even have the telltale faint tan lines. And one thing was certain: Dan Armstrong was eminently crushable.

Rosebud kept her defenses up, but she got the feeling that was a waste of energy. Dan was nothing if not a gentleman. He didn't make another attempt to touch her, much less kiss her. He didn't even bring up that kiss again. Instead, he did a reasonably good job of acting like the whole thing had never even happened. Conversation was kept strictly to the facts of the matter, and the fact was, he seemed to believe her about Tanner.

She decided that he'd been telling the truth—or something close to it—about keeping that kiss from his uncle. That should have made her happy. As much as she'd enjoyed it, she just couldn't bring herself to throw her body at the man, and it was clear he wasn't asking her to. He was a gentleman of the highest order.

Except that she was having dreams about that kiss—and more. In the dreams, the kiss was just the beginning. One night, they went riding and wound up a tangled mess of naked arms and legs on the banks of the Dakota. The next, an old-fashioned tepee hid them from the world. She was waking up hot and all kinds of bothered, only to have to ignore everything she actually liked about Dan to go to work. By Friday, she was officially irritated with the whole situation.

At least she wouldn't have to see him this weekend. Assuming her car could get her there in one piece, she was going to drive to her alma mater, the University of South Dakota. She needed to find out a hell of a lot more about Dan Armstrong, and she needed a computer with internet access to do it.

She only had four weeks left.

Seven

Dan stood over the huge architectural drawing, comparing the plans on the blue sheet to the engineering report. Virgil Naylor, the chief of Naylor Engineering, hovered behind him, pointing out the details. Naylor was a slight, nervous man, no doubt made all the more nervous by Dan's silence.

Something about the engineering report didn't add up, but he was having a hell of a time nailing Naylor down. He flipped to a footnote in the middle of the report. "But you say here that a run-of-river dam would generate almost as many megawatts."

"Given optimum conditions." Naylor's hands fluttered as he waved the suggestion away.

"Yes, given. So why aren't we doing a run-of-river dam?" Because that would make the most sense. A run-of-river dam wouldn't flood that pretty little valley or any significant part of the Red Creek reservation.

Naylor's mouth puckered like he was sucking on a lemon.

"Because run-of-river dams cannot store any electricity for slow times."

"And the cost benefit of that storage is?"

Naylor seemed to get a shade pinker. The effect was not a pretty one. "Over the life of the dam, it averages out to a .019 cent gain per kilowatt."

Dan stared at the man in surprise. "With a peak operating capacity of 150 megawatts?"

"Yes." Naylor snapped the word off.

Dan did the math. "That's a difference of less than three thousand dollars a year."

"Mr. Armstrong, I'm sure you can understand the advantages of long-term hydroelectric storage…" Naylor launched into all the reasons why it was best, for the third time in the last two hours.

Hell of a way to spend a Saturday, Dan thought in increasing frustration. He wondered if he could get Jim Evans, his engineer down in Amarillo, up here to look over this mess. Just then, his phone buzzed. *Thank God,* he thought as he unsnapped it from the holster. He didn't recognize the number, but it was a South Dakota area code. "Hello?"

"Dan? This is Rosebud. Donnelly," she added, like he knew tons of Rosebuds.

She was calling him. All those cookies must have worked. Dan ordered his face not to smile as he excused himself and hurried outside, away from any prying ears. "Hey. What's up?" Sheesh, what was he—thirteen again?

"Um, well, I'm…well, I'm stuck." She sounded thoroughly miserable about it. "My car died, and no one else can come get me. I need help."

A damsel in distress. And she was calling him. She was either really desperate or…well, no use getting ahead of himself. "I'm just finishing up a meeting. Where are you?"

He thought the call had been dropped, but finally she said, "Do you know where the University of South Dakota is?"

"No. Why are you at a university?"

"Um…research. Can you pick me up or not?"

The damsel was really desperate, it seemed. "Give me fifteen minutes to finish this meeting."

"I'm in parking lot D, behind the library. You should get here in an hour."

"Then I'll be seein' you in an hour." He ended the call and stared at the phone. Research? Did the university even have a law library?

"Mr. Armstrong?" Naylor hovered his way out onto the porch. "It's getting late. Do you have any other questions?"

"Just one." It took a second to get his brain off Rosebud waiting for him and back onto engineering reports. "Who else have you told about the run-of-river option?"

The man turned positively red, which was an ugly shade on his sallow skin. "I assure you that all the work at Naylor Engineering remains completely confidential at all times. We take client privileges—"

Dan cut him off with a wave of his hand. "You haven't told any of the members of the Red Creek tribe?"

"Certainly not." Naylor actually stamped his foot on the porch, looking for all the world like an indignant parakeet. "And those—those—those *savages* destroyed several thousands of dollars' worth of equipment. I wouldn't be caught dead anywhere near the lot of them."

The little man sounded just like his uncle. Dan hadn't gotten out much around here—just making the rounds between the rez, the ranch house and the dam site. Did everyone here talk like that? Was that why Rosebud had shut down that kiss so quickly—she was afraid he'd call her a savage?

He knew better. Compared to this wart with an engineering degree? Dan had no doubt that Rosebud could fit in anywhere from a honky-tonk to the boardroom to one of those garden parties Mom was fond of having in the summer. As he watched the little man get into his sedan, he knew who the real savage was—and it wasn't the pretty lawyer.

By the time he found parking lot D, it had taken him almost an hour and a half. *Damn GPS,* he grumbled to himself as he kept an eye out for an old car and a young woman. He could track the value of the euro versus the yen from up in the saddle, no wires required, but with this GPS, left versus right turns seemed to be beyond the stupid thing. It was almost five o'clock on a Saturday night, and the campus was nearly deserted. There was Rosebud's old car, parked at the far end of the lot. He didn't see her—until he pulled into the parking space.

She was sitting in the driver's seat, a white-knuckle grip on the steering wheel. Her hair was long and loose, and she was wearing a pale green T-shirt that was wonderfully snug. She almost looked like a college student instead of a top-notch legal eagle.

When she saw him, she hopped out of the car, her eyes darting around. What was she so afraid of? But that thought was arrested by the sight of Rosebud stretching herself out. Dan decided that, no matter what came out of this evening, it was all worth seeing her in that particular pair of jeans, held tight to her hips with a respectable-looking buckle.

He took it back. College girls never looked as good as she did.

"Hi," she said with a careful smile. Her eyes darted up, and her grin grew. "Nice hat."

Dan tipped the new beaver-fur felt at her. "Thanks. I'm hoping to keep this one hole-free for at least a few days."

She tilted her head to one side, and all that black silk she called hair tipped over her shoulder. His mind immediately pulled up a memory from that first ride in the valley.

It had to have been her. Sure, he'd heard some clueless idiots in the town outside the reservation claiming that all Indians looked alike, but no one else looked at him like she did. Again, he wondered what the hell her reason was. Most everybody had a reason, after all. His eyes darted down to the passenger seat. He didn't see any gun-shaped lumps—but there was a lot of glove-box room. "I'm still asking around." She was less than convincing, almost like she was tired of the lie.

Dan let it slide. It was Saturday night in what passed as a big town in this state, and he was officially in the company of a beautiful, if slightly dangerous, woman. "You didn't have to wait in the car. It's a nice night out."

She gave him a look he couldn't read. "Safer that way. The library's already closed." Before he could ask her what that was supposed to mean, she visibly shook herself and favored him with a sweet, almost shy smile. "Thanks for coming."

"What's the problem with your car?"

The weariness he thought he'd heard in her voice spread to her eyes. "It refused to start. It sounded a little funny on the drive down, but I thought it might at least get me home."

After she popped the hood, Dan poked around. He'd taken an engine or two apart in his time, but this thing was a dinosaur. The verdict wasn't good. He could see one belt in pieces and another that looked like it could go at any time. When he had Rosebud try to turn over the engine, the whole thing clicked. The starter sounded deader than a doornail and he was pretty sure the battery was corroded to the car. "When was the last time you had this thing checked out?"

She shrugged, but he noticed that she bit her lip. That was her tell. "A few years ago."

"Years?" He shook his head at her, and she managed to look sheepish. "You're probably lucky you got here."

She stuck out her chin, a move he recognized as defiance now. But she also stuck her hands into her back pockets, which emphasized her chest. "I'm lucky you were able to come get me."

Dan had long prided himself on reading the signals from the opposite sex, and he'd be damned if that particular signal didn't say "Saturday night on the town." "I guess we're both lucky, aren't we?"

Her gaze took its time working over him. By the time she got back to his face, he was working with a whole different definition of *lucky*. "That remains to be seen." He swore she purred it.

He might never figure this woman out, but he was going to have a fine time trying. "Did you call a tow truck yet?"

That was the wrong thing to say. All that goodness she'd been telegraphing his way died. "No."

"Why not?"

She was right back to looking embarrassed, and he hadn't even kissed her. Yet. "Joe can tow it home for me."

"When?" She didn't answer, which was answer enough. This hunk of steel might be here for days before someone towed it—and chances were it would be towed to the impound lot. He got his cell phone out and punched up an entry. "I've got Triple A."

"No!" She moved lightning-fast. Before he could react, her hand was on his wrist. "I mean...please."

Her touch was light, but she had a hell of a grip. That was not a bad thing. "Give me one good reason."

He prayed she couldn't feel his blood pumping as he looked down into her eyes. Then she batted her eyelashes, and he stopped caring about his pulse. "I haven't allocated the funds for a situation such as this."

Allocated the funds? It took a second for him to translate that statement to English. "You don't have the money to fix your car?"

She dropped his wrist like it was a hot potato and backed away from him, looking for all the world like a cornered animal. "No, okay? I don't have the money."

A broken copier. One suit. Handwritten notes. Driving an hour south to do "research."

She had no money. Period. A true damsel in distress.

To hell with this. It only took a second before he knew what he had to do. He began to dial. "Actually, you do." She spun on her heels, looking all sorts of angry. He held up a hand before she could let loose on him. "I've been taking up a lot of your time. My lawyer in Texas charges a hundred and twenty-five dollars an hour for consulting. Figure, what? Six hours a day for five days? That's about four thousand."

Her jaw dropped. "Dollars?"

"Yup."

"I can't—"

A voice crackled over the phone. "Yeah, I need a tow to a repair shop."

By the time he got off the phone, Rosebud was sitting on the curb, her knees tucked up under her chin. She didn't look happy about being rescued. Instead, she looked nervous. Trapped.

Dan sat down next to her. "Will you believe me if I tell you that no one knows I'm here?"

She shrugged, making sure to keep a solid eight inches between them. "Should I?"

"You might consider the option, as it happens to be the truth."

He caught the corner of her smile in his peripheral vision. Took a lot of work not to stare. "I'm a lawyer, Dan. The truth is highly relative."

"I'm more of a black-and-white guy, myself. My mom always said to be up front about the black and white because it makes lyin' about the gray a hell of a lot easier." She snorted in what he hoped was appreciation. "The fact of the matter is that I told no one about the kiss. After you left, I checked the kitchen for bugs and came up empty. Today, I took your call outside where no one could hear me, and told no one—not even Maria—who called or where I was going."

Her head nodded as she thought about it. Thinking was progress. "So what's the gray area here?"

Dan looked out. The summer sun was just scooting behind some of the taller buildings, throwing cozy shadows over the parking lot. "I'm going to be hungry by the time we get out of here. We're going to stop somewhere and get dinner, and I'm buying."

She was on her feet, backing away from him. Cornered, he thought again. "I can't—"

He climbed to his feet and took a chance by taking her hand. She didn't pull away—yet—but her hand was like a bar of steel. "You can, and you will. The gray area is that I'd like to call it a date—a date between you and me," he hurried to add when she tried to yank her hand away. This was not going as well as he wanted it to. "I'd like it to stay between you and me. No uncles, no aunts, no corporations, no tribes."

"What if I say no?"

"You wouldn't be the first." It had been close to a year since he'd parted ways with his last lady friend. There wasn't anyone left in Wichita Falls who was interested in him instead of his money. He was usually too busy to try to make the Fort Worth social scene anymore. But he still managed to have a few dates every now and then. She wouldn't be the first, and she wouldn't be the last.

She was chewing on the inside of her lip again. Thinking was definitely progress. "You've only got four weeks left. You might get desperate and tell someone."

"I might get desperate." He went for broke. Keeping a tight hold on her hand, he stepped in real close and ran a thumb over her cheek. Her eyes fluttered and, ever so slightly, she leaned into his hand. "But not *that* kind of desperate."

She let him kiss her, let him entwine his fingers with hers, let him pull her into his chest close enough that he could feel her nipples harden under her shirt. He'd give anything to get her out of that shirt so he could see those nipples for himself. God help him, her body was saying yes to a date and maybe a whole lot more. He had no idea what her mouth would say, though, so he hung back. Just a simple kiss, that's all.

If only the rest of their situation could be this simple.

A horn blared behind them, nearly sending them both out of their shoes. "Hey, buddy, you call for a tow?" the driver sneered out the window.

"Think about the date," he whispered to her as he let go of her hand.

"Okay."

Eight

A girl could tell a lot about a man by his vehicle. And according to the license plate, this seemed to be Dan's actual truck, not some rental. He'd driven all the way up from Texas.

Rosebud ran her hands over the premium leather of the passenger seat, trying to snoop without it looking like she was snooping. Dan had given her his keys after the tow-truck driver had called her "honey." It felt weird to just let a man take over for her, but frankly, she'd rather sit in the truck and try to figure out Dan Armstrong than stand next to that driver and wish she had some mace.

Dan had satellite radio. Of course he did. A man like Dan wouldn't want to listen to stations with commercial interruptions. She flipped through his preprogrammed channels. Willie's Place, Outlaw Country—those she expected. Dan probably hired those famous country singers to perform at company picnics or something ludicrous like that. But what came next surprised her—Alt Nation? Lithium? A Phish song filled the cab. She blinked hard in the dim light, but the name on the receiver stayed the same. Unreal. Not the standard cowboy tunes.

She went back on the dial until she found a Miranda Lambert song, then she looked around. The truck's interior was spotless—no crumpled-up wrappers or crushed cans underfoot, not even a layer of dust on the burled walnut dash. A shotgun hung on a rack on the rear window, but a quick look told her it either wasn't loaded or only had one round in the chamber. Did he always have that gun there, or was it just because of her "little" misfire?

She looked again. Man, it was a piece of work. The walnut stock was polished to a warm gleam, and the silver was inlaid with hunting dogs done in what looked like gold. The trigger looked like real gold, too. She didn't know much about high-end weapons, but she was willing to bet she could buy a house with the money that gun cost.

She began to feel a little out of place. Okay, a lot out of place. She'd caught glimpses of this kind of wealth during law school in D.C., but not even her boyfriend James had been this casually comfortable with the finest that money could buy. She was one step above dirt-poor. What the heck did an oil tycoon—because she was starting to realize that's what Dan was—want with the likes of her?

She was getting antsy. What was taking so long? She searched for Dan and the tow-truck driver in the rearview mirror. Dang. Dan had a heck of a rear view, all right. He was bent over the front end of her car, looking at the engine. Dan was doing a lot of pointing and the driver was doing a lot of head shaking. She didn't take all the gesturing as a positive development, which made the pit in her stomach grow a little wider. She had no idea if the hunk of steel was worth fixing, but it was the only car she had—and there was no way in hell she could afford a new one.

Lord, this seemed like a bad idea. Letting him pay for her

tow—and then letting him take her to dinner? On a date? Was Dan one of those guys who thought that dinner and car repairs guaranteed getting lucky?

She shuddered. She knew he was charming, handsome and under orders to trap her. But even given all that, she still couldn't help but feel—not think, but really and truly *feel*—that he was being totally up front with her. She thought back to their phone conversation. He hadn't said her name, or anything that would point to her. *He* wanted to ask *her* out.

She wanted to go out with *him*. If only his last name wasn't Armstrong.

Oh, what a mess she'd gotten herself into.

Well, she knew how to test his mettle. She dug out her notes as he got back in the cab.

"He's going to give you a call when it's ready." He set his hat on the dash and cocked his head to one side, listening to the song "Gunpowder and Lead." "You tryin' to tell me something?" he said with a grin as he fired up the truck.

The engine purred. A slight twinge of jealousy, so small she barely noticed it at all, flittered across Rosebud's mind. Wouldn't it be lovely to have a car that just *started* whenever she wanted it to? "Purely coincidental. And I'm also not a crazy ex-girlfriend."

Dan gave her a long look—long enough that Rosebud suddenly felt like she was on the witness stand. "I never did figure you for one." Then he shot her that confident smile again and began backing up. "I'll bring you back down, if you want, but it's going to be a few weeks."

"You really don't have to do that, but I appreciate it." A few weeks was a long time to be carless, but as long as she didn't have to leave the rez, she could ride her paint, Scout.

He shot her a snarky look out of the corner of his eye. "Besides, that'll give you the chance to do some more research. Where to?"

Would a date be such a bad thing? Two consenting adults having dinner and maybe another kiss? She had one left—and heaven help her, she hoped it was a good one. She scrambled to think of a place where Dan would be comfortable, but she was coming up blank. She'd hardly been able to afford fine dining when she'd gone to school here, and that had been almost seven years ago.

"Doesn't have to be anywhere fancy," Dan said, doing a pretty good job of interpreting her silence. "Anyplace with steak is fine by me."

She remembered Tanner had mentioned Bob's Road-house—he and Tom Yellow Bird used to hang out there back in the day. It must have been good—they'd gone back several times. "I know a place that's supposed to be good. Take a left here and head for the highway. And actually, I think I found everything I needed this time."

"Yeah? Digging up dirt on Cecil?"

"Nope." He didn't see this coming? She couldn't help but enjoy springing this on him. "You."

The truck lurched to a stop at an intersection. Even better than the wobbly chair, she decided. "Me?"

"You. This was the first chance I've had." The question was, would he own up to any of the stuff she'd found? Or was it all part of that undefined gray area? "You've got quite a public record, you know."

He sighed in resignation, slouching against his window. "You found the poster, didn't you?"

"This poster?" She slid the grainy grayscale poster out of the folder. The crummy printer had made it all but impossible to see what had been as plain as day on the computer screen—a young boy with a head full of blondish curls smiling up at an oil derrick. "You were literally the face of Armstrong Oil?"

"Cut me some slack. I was seven, and Dad bought me

ice cream for smiling." His fingers drummed on the steering wheel. "Mint chocolate chip, if I remember correctly. That damn poster floated around for almost ten years. I think every girl I went to high school with had a copy in her locker." He glanced over at her, the embarrassment making him look even more like the little boy in the picture. "*Not* worth the ice cream."

"*Cute* wasn't what you were going for in high school?"

He was in serious danger of pouting. But instead of looking childish, it illustrated what *cute* would look like on the man. "I hated it. That's why I did all the un-cute stuff."

"I'll give you *un-cute* for being on the honor roll for four years, but the rodeo team?" She clucked at him. Rodeo might not be cute, but she had a feeling that hadn't mattered to high-school girls. "No football?"

"Mom wouldn't let me play football. She was too worried about me getting hurt."

"Rodeo was safer than football? Now I've heard everything." The stats from the county fairs had been quite impressive. Dan made the time on broncos, won the steer wrestling and was unbeatable in calf roping. At least he'd earned that buckle the hard way. "Why didn't you go pro?"

"I said it was safer. Not safe. Mom rode barrels," he added by way of explanation. "Besides, didn't you ever do something a little wild, a little crazy?" His head swiveled to look her full in the eye.

"Does this count?" she asked, gesturing to the truck.

"Not yet, it doesn't." Even in the dim light of a summer night, she could still see the twinkle in his eye. "Why did you come all the way down here just to dig up that stuff? I would have told you if you'd asked."

That was the sort of statement that was easy to say after the fact. "Yeah?" She flipped to the more interesting stuff—the mug shot. "Tell me about college, then."

"Man," he groaned. "Remind me to avoid you in a court-room."

"Don't think of it as the Red Creek tribe asking about why you got arrested your sophomore year." She scooted around in her seat and tucked one leg under the other. "I'm asking. Just me."

"We haven't even had a date yet, and you want to know about that? That's third date stuff, at least."

"Maybe this is a date."

He glanced at her, a wide smile on his face. "Yeah?"

She had no right to feel so giddy about the smile he was wearing, but she couldn't help it. "*Maybe*. Now spill it. De-struction of college property? That doesn't seem like you, Dan."

He sighed again, but it seemed heavier this time. "When you went to college, what did you do?"

Not a good sign, if he was going to start turning the tables on her this early in the "date." "Well, I studied—"

"No, I mean, what did you *do?* Because when I went to college, I was tired of being Lewis Armstrong's boy, tired of eating steak, tired of being the poster boy for an oil com-pany." He shook his head at the memory. "I missed my dad, but I didn't want to have to live up to him anymore."

Suddenly, this seemed like it was about a lot more than a drunken prank. "Like how?"

"You've heard of the metaphorical preacher's daughter?"

"Sure. The more religious the preacher, the more rebel-lious the daughter."

"I'm the son of a cattle-raising, oil-drilling, shotgun-owning, good old boy."

So that's why his hair had been past his shoulders and he'd been wearing those round glasses like John Lennon always wore. "You were a hippie?"

She liked him embarrassed—it was both cute and a little

bit sexy at the same time. "I tried. Did you know vegetarians don't eat *any* steak?"

"Shocking," she said in mock surprise. That explained the alternative channels. "How long did you last?"

"Almost two years at school, but the moment I came home, I was dying for a good hamburger." He chuckled at the memory. "I tried it all out. Smoked a little weed, burned a little incense, carried a few protest signs."

Normal hippies weren't known for their destructive tendencies. However…she put two and two together. "Hung out with a few ecoterrorists?"

"Proto-ecoterrorists," he corrected. "I made friends with some people."

"I've noticed you make friends with everyone."

"Not everyone," he corrected her with more force than she expected. He didn't like *someone,* that much was clear. "But most any reasonable person. That one time was the first and last time I ever did anything I truly regretted."

Despite the deep confession going on, Rosebud couldn't help but think that he didn't regret kissing her—either time. Her giddiness level rose. "What happened?"

He rubbed his seven-o'clock shadow. "When campus security showed up, I was the one holdin' the matches in front of a burning Dumpster. Oddly enough, no one believed that I was just trying to draw attention to the amount of garbage the school produced."

"You burned Dumpsters?" That wasn't *proto*-ecoterrorist in her book. "What did your mother do?"

"Well, first she cried, then she threatened to let the judge lock me up and throw away the key before I dragged my father's good name into the mud, then she cried some more." He shrugged in that embarrassed way again. "If I recall correctly, there was a lot of crying."

"I think I like your mother."

He chuckled, like maybe he agreed with her. "Between all the cryin' and the community service—I scrubbed a lot of garbage cans—I saw the light. A man doesn't like to upset his mama, you know."

"Not a good one, anyway." He shot an appreciative look at her.

This whole conversation had an air of the unreal to it. Rosebud should be holding on to this info, saving it for when she needed the leverage against Dan during negotiations, but instead, they were *just* talking. "So?"

"So, I grew up and joined the family business. Some of my old friends grew up and joined ELF."

She flipped through her notes. "The same ELF that targeted seven Armstrong Holdings derricks?"

"The very same. After the second time, when the police were still coming up empty, I started doing a little digging and all the signs pointed to my old buddies." He shook his head. "They knew it was my company—just punishing a traitor, I guess. I busted them red-handed one night. Oil derricks are a long way from Dumpsters, but they couldn't argue with a shotgun. They chose to negotiate instead of the alternative."

"Duly noted." She couldn't tell if that meant he had been willing to shoot, or if he'd have just turned them in to the authorities. She shivered. Her mind flashed back to that day in the valley—she'd never been sure if he'd had a gun on him or not. The *what-if* loomed *huge* in her mind. "So what was the truce? Take this exit, by the way."

He was silent as he took the exit that led to Bob's Roadhouse Bar and Grill. A bright red neon T-bone blinked above the sign advertising Rapid City Rollers Live Tonite. A line of motorcycles took up half the parking lot in front of a long, low building that looked like it was slouching to the left; a line of trucks filled the other half. Two people she hoped were only kissing backed up against a pickup truck, and another group was standing in a circle. Were they cheering? A flash of movement caught her eye, and she realized that a fight was going on in the middle. She shuddered.

Suddenly, Rosebud remembered why she'd never been here before. It was one thing for Tanner and Tom to go into a place like this—rough and gritty and full of people who were happy to throw a punch or three, all in the name of a good time. Tanner had always liked a game of pool and a loud band, and Tom—well, he'd never been afraid of anything, including what might happen to a couple of Lakota Indians in a white man's bar. The two of them wouldn't have had any trouble attracting plenty of feminine attention—or holding their own during the inevitable fights. Because the fights *were* inevitable.

She hated the way Tanner would come home with his face a bloody mess, telling her all about how he and Tom had shown those "racist *wasicu*," those white devils, what a true Lakota warrior could do. Tanner may have lived clean and sober, but he had still itched for the fight and lived to count coup on his enemy.

As if his face wasn't warning enough, Tanner had always lectured her on staying away from places like Bob's. *"Promise me,"* he'd say, his eyes serious as she patched up his cuts. *"Promise me you won't go to a place like that. It's too dangerous for you."*

He'd made her so mad back then. Always trying to tell her what she could and could not do. He'd been the one who'd sent all the cute boys packing because no one was good enough for his sister. He had been the one who'd told her she had to go to law school. And every time he told her to make that promise, she'd wanted to strangle him. *"Oh, you're the only one allowed to do stupid things?"*

But every time, Tanner would only shake his head. *"Just promise, little sister."*

At the time, she hadn't thought Tanner would ever run into something that was too dangerous for him. She'd always thought he'd be able to take whatever came his way. Until that night... *"Promise."*

The neon sign seemed less bright, and more like blood spilling into the night. This place was dangerous. The promise was old and Tanner was dead, but that didn't change what she'd promised.

She looked over at Dan, the words *Let's go somewhere else* right on her lips.

But then she saw the look on his face—a broad smile, fingers tapping on the steering wheel. "Now this is my kind of joint!" he said, checking out the row of bikes.

"Are you sure you don't want something else? Something nicer?"

He only shook his head. "There's a lot to be said for a good old-fashioned honky-tonk on a Saturday night." He turned a blinding smile to her. "Almost feels like home."

Shoot. Well, she'd gotten herself into this mess. Unless she wanted to admit—out loud—that she was scared *and* had no clue about dining options of any sort, she had no choice but to tough it out. And if she stayed close to Dan, no one would give her any trouble, right?

Swallowing down her hesitation, she turned to Dan. It took a second for her to remember what they had been talking about. Oh, yeah. Ecoterrorists staring down the business end of a shotgun. "So, about that truce?" She'd just focus on Dan—which was also dangerous, but in a totally different way.

"Bribery," he said as he unbuckled his seat belt. "Once, they were my friends. I couldn't forget that. So certain people who shall remain nameless are on the company payroll."

Not what she'd expected. "Seriously? That's the truce?"

"That and the fact that if anything else happens to my

pumps, the FBI will be all over them like white on rice. I'm literally the only outsider to know who some of these people are."

She was silent for a moment. He really could keep a secret—did that include car repairs and dates? "Is that what this is? A bribe? My car magically gets fixed and I'm supposed to shut up and go away?"

His hand was on the door, seconds from opening it, but he froze. Moving at glacier speed, he turned, his face hard to read in the flashing red light. And then his thumb brushed against her cheek before he wrapped his hand around the back of her neck, pulling her to him until their foreheads were touching. She flinched. He was going to kiss her—the third kiss. Three and she was out.

"I don't want you to shut up," he said in a whisper that made his drawl sound like it belonged in a bedroom. "And I most definitely do not want you to go away, darlin'." His other hand traced the hollow in her neck before it drifted down to her shoulders, leaving a trail of fire in its wake.

But he didn't kiss her. He didn't even cop a feel. She wasn't out yet.

"What *do* you want, Dan?" Her heart pounded away in her chest as her hands found their way to his cheeks. The stubble scratched at her palms, small pricks of irritation that did nothing but turn her on. Kind of like Dan himself. *Tell me the truth,* she thought. *A truth I can believe.*

"I want to buy you dinner, and if the band is halfway decent, I want to dance you around."

"Is that all?"

"Nope." He touched his lips to her forehead, leaving a scorch mark on her skin. Not a kiss, she quickly justified. Didn't count if it wasn't on the lips, which conveniently meant she wasn't out yet. *Anything* to still be in—even Bob's Roadhouse Bar and Grill. "But that's all I'm asking for right now."

Nine

His "please" smile got them a quiet table in the back of the restaurant—quiet, that is, by bar standards. They only had to shout a little over something that sounded like Charlie Daniels locked in a closet with KISS and an angry cat. "Halfway decent" was pushing it, but the dance floor was packed with every shade of hick, good old boy and white trash possible. The Rapid City Rollers were apparently quite a draw, Dan mused as they looked over the menus. He hadn't been honky-tonkin' for a good long time, and not with a pretty lady by his side for even longer. He was glad she'd picked this place. He wanted to show her that he wasn't all thousand-dollar hats and million-dollar oil wells—he was perfectly happy being a regular guy, if that's what she wanted to see. The night was shaping up real nice.

"Four-drink minimum," a skinny waitress with unreal blond hair yelled as she bounced her pen on the pad. She pointed her chin toward a handwritten sign over the bar. "4 Drinks, No Execptions. $4 Longnecks Friday and Saterday," it announced. *Exceptions* and *Saturday* were misspelled. "What'll ya'll have?"

"Bud—in the bottle—and the T-bone, bloody," Dan shouted back. Then he looked at Rosebud.

Her sweet mouth was twisted off to one side. She looked like she was five seconds from wrapping all her hair back up in a business braid and grilling him under oath. Great. Now what had he done? "I'll have the New York strip, medium, and a Coke."

"Four-drink minimum," the waitress repeated, slamming the tip of the pen for each drawn-out word, like she was talking to a little kid. "Four, understand?"

"I can count," Rosebud shot back, slapping her menu on the table.

Both women bristled, and Dan had that weird out-of-time feeling again, like he'd waltzed into a saloon in 1886 instead of into a bar in the twenty-first century. What next—armed bandits holding up a stagecoach? "We're here for the band," he said with his best smile as he dug out two twenties and a ten and placed them on top of the menus he handed back to the waitress. Pre-tipping never hurt anyone. "Four drinks shouldn't be a problem."

He couldn't hear over the wailing music, but he thought Rosebud hissed. For her part, the waitress broke into an ugly grin and winked at Dan. "No, I guess not. Two steaks, coming right up, *sugar.*" So much for the night being real nice. This was starting to look like a bad idea.

This time, Rosebud definitely hissed. He looked at her. She was hunched defensively, her eyes darting around the room. Anything good he'd started in the truck was long gone. "I take it you've never been in here," Dan said, hoping to keep the conversation as light as possible while still screaming over the music.

She shot him a smile that looked ferocious, but Dan

watched as she got herself back under control. Her mouth untwisted as she leaned back in her chair, one arm slung over the back. At least she was trying. "No, I've never attempted this before." The way she said it made it clear that she ranked honky-tonking right up there with skydiving without a parachute.

If she'd never been here, why had she picked this place? There had to be other restaurants in this town. But rather than put her on the spot, he tried to keep things positive. "There's a first for everything, huh?"

For a second, Dan wished they were back in the truck. Not that he loved getting grilled about his past, but Rosebud was way too on edge in this place, and he had no idea why.

He glanced around. Seemed like a run-of-the-mill honky-tonk to him. On second glance, he noticed everyone was looking at her, and not like he looked at her. No, just about every female in the joint was glaring at Rosebud out the corner of their eyes like she was wearing a huge scarlet *A*—and no pants. Most of the men had taken notice, too, but Dan decided he didn't like those looks anymore.

Dan couldn't figure out where the attitude came from until it hit him like a bolt out of the blue. Rosebud was the only Indian in a sea of white faces. Over the din of the band, he remembered that weasel Naylor sputtering out *savages* and the way his uncle talked down to that slime Thrasher. No doubt about it, Dan thought as he mentally smacked his head. This attempt at a date *was* a bad idea.

They should go. Dan started to stand, but he caught the defiant way Rosebud crossed her arms and lifted her chin. She may not be comfortable here, but she showed no sign of bolting. Of course she wouldn't. She wouldn't turn tail when Cecil wanted her gone, and she wouldn't bail now. Somehow, he knew she would never give anyone the satisfaction of defeating her.

He settled back into his chair, positioning himself between her and the crowd. If she wasn't about to run and hide, he wasn't, either.

The waitress flitted past, setting down their drinks. Dan caught the way Rosebud stared at his beer. "Is this okay?" he asked, taking a cautious swig.

She shrugged and scooted her chair next to his. It was only natural to put his arm around her shoulders and make sure she knew she was safe with him.

"How much do you know about me, Dan?" The way she leaned up to speak in his ear, using a nearly normal tone, was more than enough to make him forget about all the dirty looks they were getting.

"I've done my research." A little bit of the internet went a long way.

"So you know about my parents?"

Parents? Who the hell wanted to talk about parents at a time like this? But she was resting her head on his shoulder. She fit there real nice. He sighed and dredged through his memory. "They died in a car wreck, didn't they?"

"Dad was drunk—they both were. Drove into a tree. The official report blames the road conditions, but I know what really happened."

Midswig, Dan paused. "Tanner didn't drink." He remembered now—that was one of Rosebud's main arguments against the suicide ruling. Tanner Donnelly didn't drink; therefore, he couldn't have been drunk enough to shoot his head off.

She sighed, a sound of sheer weariness. "No."

"You don't drink."

"No."

He swallowed and nearly choked on his beer. Suddenly, that four-drink minimum looked like a mountain because, as much as he wanted a few beers, having more than one and then climbing behind the wheel wasn't an option. "I'll just have the one, and we won't leave until I'm stone-cold sober, okay?"

"But the waitress—"

Speak of the devil. The waitress leaned over his shoulder, grazing him with her boobs. "Get you another one, sugar?"

Next time he managed to talk Rosebud into anything resembling a date, it was going to be someplace quiet and secluded. He'd thought the tribal members had given him the cold shoulder at that first meeting—but if this was how they were treated by white folks off the reservation, he couldn't blame them.

Rosebud had never treated him coldly, though—all of her chill seemed to be an occupational hazard. When she wasn't being a lawyer, she looked at him with a gaze that was much warmer. Although he had no idea if he was going to get any warmth in this bar. He sighed in frustration. What they needed was some neutral territory. "You know, I'd like to buy the band a round." He dug out two more twenties. "That's…" he leaned forward and counted. "Four beers. Keep the change." If that's what it cost to buy them a little breathing room in this place, then that's what it cost.

The waitress snatched the bills out of his hand and shoved one into her back pocket. "Anything you want, sugar."

"If she calls you that again, I'm going to rip her lips off," Rosebud whispered as the waitress finally left them alone. She sounded serious, too.

The note of jealousy had him grinning. "I wouldn't want you to get your hands dirty."

"Do you do this often? Go out to the dives and pay too much for beer?"

"Naw." He leaned in—so she could hear him better, not so he could catch a hint of her scent. "And before you ask, I don't spend all my time in an exclusive club sipping martinis, either. I don't have the time for that, and I don't often have anyone I want to go out with, either."

Rosebud took a long sip of her Coke before she settled back into his arm. "What about Tiffany?"

What was he going to do with—to—this woman? "I suppose I should have seen that one coming."

"Probably," she agreed. He couldn't see her face, but her shoulders sort of moved, like she was giggling at him.

"If I tell you about Tiffany, will you be done researching me?"

Unexpectedly, her hand wrapped around his waist and she hooked a finger through a belt loop as she molded herself to his chest. The full-body contact—oh, sweet Jesus, the weight of her breasts pressed against him—made his erection try to stand up and salute. "Well, done with the secondhand research, anyway."

Which left firsthand possibilities wide-open. He shifted his hips until he was certain that the table was covering them both from the waist down. "Deal. What do you want to know?" Talking about his oldest lady friend didn't seem like foreplay, but if it worked for Rosebud, then it worked for him.

"I counted about thirty or so mentions of you two in the society pages of the Dallas papers—none of which involved places like this. That seems like a lot for not having anyone you want to go out with."

He knew what this was. This was Rosebud trying to figure out if he was a love-'em-and-leave-'em kind of guy or not. Full disclosure was the only way to go. "Tiffany's a wonderful girl. I haven't seen her since I danced with her at her wedding, though. She thought that was for the best. She still sends me Christmas cards. Got a couple of cute babies now. Her husband's a real nice fellow."

"Why didn't you marry her?"

He went stiff, and not in the fun way. Just when he thought he'd gone and figured this woman out, she went and asked him something like that. Hands down, this was the weirdest date he'd ever been on. "I didn't want a wife."

She stilled against him. "What *do* you want, Dan?"

That was the second time she'd asked him that question tonight. If they were going to get all deep, he sure wished he could have another beer. "Tiffany was what I needed in Texas—someone to go to charity balls with, someone who understood that my company comes first."

"Men have married for less than that."

"I don't want a wife," he repeated with more force. "I want a partner. I don't want someone to cook my dinner and make my bed. I don't want a maid. I want an equal. I want someone I can talk to, someone I can respect."

Someone like Rosebud.

The thought popped into his head like a prairie dog popping out of the ground.

Dan had thought once—only once—about actually marrying Tiffany, but aside from the sex and the next corporate dinner party, he didn't actually have a single interesting thing to say to her, and vice versa.

Despite his little outburst, he realized he was stroking her hair. And that she was still holding on to him. She didn't say anything, but she hadn't run screaming, either.

The waitress shot Rosebud a look when she came back with the steaks, but when Dan pleased and thanked her for a Coke to go with his meal, he got the kind of smile a waitress gives a big tipper. Man, he'd forgotten how hungry he was, and the steak was bleeding red. Perfect.

"What about you?" he said between bites of meat.

She was digging in herself, which he found refreshing. Too many times he'd taken a woman out to dinner only to have her pick at a sad little salad. "What do you want to know?"

Well, now, that was a change of pace. "I found some stuff. I'm honored to be in the presence of the Indian Days Powwow Princess."

She rolled her eyes, but still gave him a royal wave. "I bet there was a picture with that one."

"Yup." In fact, she'd looked exactly like an old-fashioned Indian princess—her hair in two tight braids, her dress covered with those little jingly cone things—but not a whole lot like *his* Indian princess, the one in the simple buckskin dress with loose hair. Except for the smile—Rosebud's smile of victory. "But there were huge holes." In fact, all he'd found were the honor rolls. Top of her high school class, summa cum laude all four years at the university, top twenty-five percent in law school. That, and the ongoing legal battle with Armstrong Holdings. That was it.

She grinned at him, fork hovering in the air. "Some of us have the good sense to stay out of the society pages."

"Trust me, I'm all for keeping a low profile these days."

Her eyes shot over his shoulder. He followed her gaze and saw their waitress standing with several other barmaids, doing everything but pointing. "You need more practice." At least she sounded amused. He hoped.

"Tell me about the holes. Do you like being a lawyer?"

Her face hardened a little, but not so much that she stopped chewing. "I'm good at it."

"Now, ain't that jest like a lawyer," he said in his heaviest drawl. "Answerin' the question she wants to answer, not the question I *asked*."

She notched an eyebrow at him that said, *Oh, come on*. "Well, I am. But I wanted to study art—fiber arts. I…" Her eyes dipped down, and he swore she was blushing. "I like to quilt."

Quilting? At first, that surprised him, but then he thought

about it. One tiny stitch at a time, over and over, until the big picture was finished. Methodical. "I bet you're good at it."

Even in the dim light of the bar, the blush deepened. Now he was getting somewhere. "I don't get the chance to do it very much. Something *else* takes up all my time."

"I don't want to talk about *that*," he said, finishing his beer. No way was Cecil invited to any part of this party.

"Agreed." He watched her finish her steak fries. She caught him looking. "What?"

"I'm just curious."

She sort of smiled, in that grimacing kind of way. "About?"

"What else you did while you were staying out of the society pages."

"That's not a proper question."

"Technicalities. You know all about Tiffany. Did you ever have a boyfriend?"

"Ever?" She snorted at him, but at the same time, she pushed her plate away and leaned back into him. "You make it sound like I'm either a nun or a leper."

"You're a beautiful woman," he replied, settling his arm back around her. It just felt so easy, so right. "I bet you've had a lot of men chasing you."

"You have no idea."

"Why don't you give me one?"

She giggled—yeah, he was sure that's what the gentle shaking meant. "I worked at a coffee bar to help pay for college. It didn't take long to figure out that more lipstick meant better tips."

"That's just guys hitting on you—most any red-blooded American male would do that. That's not what I'm askin' about."

Her hand looped back around his waist. Maybe she felt

safer there—or maybe she liked it. Either way, he wasn't about to shoo her away. "I had one, once. In law school."

"A boyfriend?"

"Was Tiffany your girlfriend?"

"Not really. She was just…convenient." Which sounded bad, but happened to be the truth. Convenient for both of them, really, until it wasn't anymore. That's when it had ended with a smile and a handshake.

"Friends with benefits," she agreed. "That's what James was."

Lucky bastard. The name rang a faint bell, but he couldn't place it. Dan could only hope this James had known how lucky he was. "A James doesn't sound like your type."

"He wasn't. He was from this real blue blood D.C. family." She sighed. Her free hand was resting on his thigh now, and he thought she might be swaying to the beat of the music a little. Dancing was about to occur. Whether or not they made it to the dance floor remained to be seen. "No one knew. He wouldn't have ever taken me home to meet his parents, and there was no way in hell he would have made it one day on the rez. Just one of those things."

He pulled her to her feet and led her out onto the dance floor. Whatever this thing between them was, it would be different from what she'd had with James, from what he'd had with Tiffany, he decided as the band began to butcher some Toby Keith song. Because Rosebud was different.

With one hand on her waist, the other wrapped around her fingers, he led her into the crowd of two-steppers. Space was tight, so he was forced to hold her real close as they moved in small circles around the floor.

His mouth found her ear. It took just about everything he had not to wrap his tongue around her earlobe. "What about this?"

"This what?" She tilted her head into his until they were

dancing cheek-to-cheek, which sure as hell seemed like an invitation to him.

"Is this 'just one of those things'?" He actually felt a little nervous about the question, mostly because he had no idea what she'd say.

She didn't answer for a few beats, but then she pulled away, just far enough that she could look him in the eyes. "No," she said, and her soft voice found his ears despite the thumping bass beat. "This isn't."

She kissed him. *She* kissed *him,* and not one of those slow-building, wait-and-see kisses like the ones he'd been giving her. She bit his lower lip as her fingers dug into his shoulder. *She's hungry,* he thought as she devoured his mouth.

He went hard in a second. Given that there was no space between them, she knew it immediately, and answered by grinding her hips into his. She was going to bring him to his knees, right in the middle of the dance floor. He fought back the only way he could, by kissing her with a vengeance. Yeah, they were supposed to be two-stepping around the floor, but he pulled her hand in close enough to their bodies that he was able to graze her breast with his thumb. She shuddered into him with a moan he felt more than heard.

They had to get out of here, pronto.

Finally, she saved him from himself by pulling back, just enough that he could catch his breath. "Three," she breathed, her eyes closed as she licked her lips at a painfully slow speed.

"Three?" His brain wasn't working, but he wasn't sure he cared, just so long as she kept kissing him like that. "You wanna get out of here?"

Starving, he thought as she looked at him, the need in her eyes naked for the world to see. "Yeah. Let's go."

The bar was more crowded and the band was louder, but finally they made it back to their table, hands locked together. "Just give me a second," she said, pointing at the rest-rooms sign.

"Okay." Hell, she could have a whole minute if she wanted, as long as they got out of here and went...where?

Damn, he thought as she disappeared down the hall. They probably couldn't go back to her place, and Cecil's house was out of the question. Once they'd left the university area, he didn't remember seeing a single hotel that had a room for the night, and, damn it all, he didn't want to make love to her in the front seat of his truck. He may be hard up, but that was crass. She deserved silk sheets and whirlpool tubs big enough for two.

Neutral territory. For some reason, the blueprints he'd been looking at this afternoon—a lifetime ago, it seemed—popped into his mind. No, not the blueprints. The map of Armstrong land and the Dakota River underneath them.

A small building, he remembered seeing now. Just a dinky square next to a little creek that fed into the Dakota, about seven miles from the dam site and a long way away from anything else. No roads went there, no power lines, either. At the time, he hadn't thought much of it, but now, in his desperation, he wondered what that building was. If it was a cabin, territory didn't get much more neutral than that. Probably didn't have silk sheets or room service, but if it was quiet...

They couldn't get there tonight. But this wasn't just about tonight. This was about—

"Hey!" A shrill shout broke above the ending chord of a song. "I said— Dan! *Help!*"

Ten

Rosebud pushed her way down the crowded hall to the ladies' room, her head swimming. Someone shoved her, but she barely noticed. Three kisses, and she was *supposed* to be out, but she was in deeper than she'd ever thought possible. They were leaving and she didn't know where they were going, but she'd officially stopped caring the moment he'd touched her. That clear moment of sheer heat made thinking an unnecessary, unwelcome action. Instead, the only action she wanted was to peel his jeans right off him and see exactly what she'd been missing.

Three kisses, three years. How could she have forgotten what she was missing? Maybe it was because James had never made her feel quite this hot, and certainly never this weak. Unlike the other white men she'd known before college, James had never treated her like The Indian, which had been a relief. But he'd never really treated her like a lover, either. She'd just been a girl he knew, just as he'd always been a boy she knew. Just some guy she occasionally went to bed with.

To Dan, she was a woman, pure and simple. Not merely a lawyer or an Indian, but all of those things and more. In his arms, she felt alive. To hell with dams and lawsuits, family members long gone and still here. Right now, she was really living.

Which was why she chose to ignore all the drunk and disorderly people around her. It didn't matter how evil their glances were. The only eyes she was concerned with were Dan's.

She pushed her way into the ladies' room. The bathroom wasn't big, but it was packed. The air was thick with hairspray, cheap perfume and industrial-strength air freshener as women crowded around each sink and mirror, a sea of bottled blond, exposed bra straps and short skirts.

By the time the door shut behind her, the whole bathroom had come to a silent halt. Mascara wands froze in midair, cigarettes dangled from lipsticked mouths and every eye was on her.

Damn. Her euphoric high dissipated in a heartbeat. That waitress was in the corner, giving Rosebud a look she'd seen before, too many times to count.

She'd seen it the first day of junior high, when her aunt had arranged for Rosebud to go to a successful white school off the rez. She still remembered the way the girls had acted like she was a blatant threat. No one had talked to her for months, but the rumors had reached her ears anyway. She stole purses, did drugs, screwed the teachers, ate garbage, had the IQ of a dog and on and on.

What was she to do then? She'd only been twelve. She wasn't the fighter Tanner had been, so she did what Aunt Emily told her. She said nothing. She looked at no one. She'd done the best work she could do. The first time she'd said something in social studies—in February—the teacher was shocked that Rosebud actually knew how to speak English.

After that, Rosebud had found her own way. She didn't brawl like Tanner, but she refused to be silent. The next time she'd heard the whispers, she went on the offensive. Her mouth was her gift, so she used it. But that was then, in the relative safety of a public school. The worst that had happened was the fat lip she'd gotten for pointing out that one of her tormenters wasn't smart enough to know that her boyfriend was cheating on her with her so-called best friend.

This was now, in the middle of a dive bar in a state with concealed carry laws on the books. She was not welcome. She swallowed, torn between a flash of panic and her always intense need to be in control of the situation. Control? Please. This was fast becoming one of the more dangerous situations she'd been in.

No fear, she decided as she strode to the only open stall, her head up and her shoulders back.

Just as she sat down, the stall door shuddered under the weight of a sudden, silent kick, quickly followed by a second. Rosebud managed not to scream, but she clutched her purse to her chest. The third hit was higher, like someone using the palm of her hand, but the fourth one was another kick. Rosebud braced a leg against the door as it bowed, and each succeeding kick felt like a sledgehammer driving into her hip socket.

Peeing while every single woman smacked or kicked the door on their way out was nothing if not challenging, but finally, the room was silent. Rosebud managed to finish. Before she opened the stall door, she listened, but she couldn't hear the sound of breathing over the reverberations of the band.

Just to be sure, she dug in her purse until she came up with a ballpoint pen. Her gun would have been better, but guns and university libraries didn't mix. A ballpoint would have to do.

She slung her sack over her shoulder and slowly opened the door. Empty, thank God. Even that waitress was gone. Rosebud washed quickly, reviewing her exit strategy. She had twenty-five feet of hallway to get through, and then another fifteen feet to get to Dan. She assumed he was still at their table, waiting for her. If she went low and fast, she might be able to snake through the crowd without anyone noticing her.

Hell, who was she kidding? Almost half the place knew she was in here.

I am not afraid, she thought, as if thinking it would make it so. Taking a few deep breaths, she clutched the pen like a knife. She'd stab anyone who tried to stop her. Sometimes, self-defense was the only defense. Forty feet. She could do it. She barreled out the door.

She only made the first twenty feet before she ran into a wall of bikers. Actually, it was just one biker, but he made a wall all by himself, completely blocking the last few feet of the hallway. "Well, now," the man said, leering down at her.

The overwhelming smell of onions and whiskey smacked her upside the face. She couldn't see past the do-rag embroidered with flames on his head—where the hell was Dan? Before she could sidestep him, he grabbed the arm that had the pen. "My buddy bet me twenty bucks I couldn't get you to dance with me, Pocahontas."

That was her least favorite racist nickname, the one that irritated her like lemon juice in a paper cut. She tried to twist out of his grip, but the jerk held tight as he pulled her toward the dance floor. At least they weren't in the hall anymore. Her eyes shot around the bar, but she didn't see Dan. Where the hell was he?

"Sorry," she said, forcing herself to smile while she tried to peel his fingers off her biceps. Why were bikers always so burly? "I'm afraid you're going to lose that bet."

"One dance, little squaw. I saw you out there dancing with that cowboy. I want some of that sugar."

Squaw. She took it back. *That* was her least favorite nickname. "Let me go," she said with more force, hoping she sounded serious instead of just terrified.

It didn't work. "You think you're too good for me? Is that it? You're just some damn Injun!" He hauled her up, closer to his face.

"Hey!" That did it. Screw this scared thing. She wasn't going down without a fight. She kicked toward his groin as hard as she could, ever thankful she'd worn her boots today. "I said—"

The biker snarled a curse at her. He didn't let go, but he did bend double. Confident that she'd connected with his nuts the first time, Rosebud tried for two.

Suddenly, her head whipped back with enough force that she lost her footing. Between the hold the biker had on her arm and whoever had a death grip on her hair, she was suddenly, completely helpless. Fight or no, she was going down. "Dan! *Help!*"

The biker staggered to his knees, pulling her down with him, but she couldn't go far. "You little slut," a female voice screeched behind her as her head jerked back again. Rosebud saw stars. "What did you do to my man?"

"Dan!" Rosebud screamed at the top of her lungs. Pain and fear were duking it out, and the fear was winning.

Her head jerked again. A sharp pain on her forehead blinded her to everything else. That waitress wouldn't scalp her, would she? "Savage," the woman's voice said, close to her ear, as calm and as clear as the noon sun. "I'll teach you to show your red face around here."

Oh, hell, she would. She *was*.

Rosebud heard bones crunch, but instead of feeling the searing pain that should have gone with it, she only heard the biker's howl.

"Let her go." Dan. Even better, he sounded furious—worse than when he'd realized she'd shot at him.

Her arm was free. In the next second, her head was free and she fell. But instead of hitting the floor, she fell into familiar arms and was up on her feet before she knew what was going on. Blinking the tears out of her eyes, she saw that Dan was standing on the biker's hand. He had one arm looped under both of hers to hold her up, and in the other he had a knife. A knife? Rosebud's eyes narrowed in on the flash of metal, but it still took a few seconds for her to realize it was a steak knife from dinner.

"She kicked my balls!" The biker wailed from the floor. Dan responded by grinding his heel in a little harder. "My hand!"

"I don't want any trouble," Dan said, his voice low—but she heard him loud and clear. He swung around, blade out, pulling Rosebud with him. The music, she realized. The band had stopped playing. The entire bar was silent. Off to her left, the unmistakable sound of a pump-action shotgun filled the air. "No trouble," he repeated.

They were going to die, all because Dan asked her out on a date and she'd had the nerve to say yes.

"Walk," Dan said under his breath. His hand was clamped around her ribs, so when he took a step forward, he practically carried her with him.

Rosebud was too afraid to look in the direction of the shotgun, too afraid to look at anyone but Dan in case they took that as an act of aggression. She kept her eyes focused on his hand and the blade. A steak knife was a hell of a lot better than a pen. He held it like he wasn't afraid to use it, but it still didn't beat a shotgun. She didn't want to die in this bar. The steak hadn't even been that good.

Dan spun around again, careful to make sure she followed. They were backing toward the door, she realized. Freedom.

"She started it!" That had to be the waitress, screeching at the top of her lungs.

Rosebud tensed, afraid that was the straw and she was about to become the camel's back. She couldn't even protest her innocence. Her throat was clogged with terror—if anything came out, it would be a scream.

"I don't care who started it. I'll finish it." How in the hell could Dan manage to sound so calm? They were outnumbered two hundred to two, and he sounded like he was negotiating a business deal!

Rosebud heard the sound of chairs scraping over the floor, but they kept moving backward. "Get ready," he whispered to her. A rush of night air hit her in the back of the neck, and then suddenly they were outside while all those angry faces were still inside. Dan let go of the knife and the tip stuck into a wood slat of the porch at the same time his fingers unglued themselves from her ribs. "The truck," he said. "Now!"

They ran so fast that Rosebud couldn't hear anything but her own sounds—her breathing, her heartbeat—so she couldn't tell if anyone was behind her. She sure as hell wasn't going to stop and check. Dan had a hold of her arm now, pulling her along with him in the mad dash to his truck. They made it in seconds. "Get down," he ordered as he cranked the engine.

"Your shotgun?" she asked. Adrenaline flooded her system. Part of her wanted to fire that bad boy off. They wanted a savage? By God, she'd give them savage.

"No," he replied, still pulling off calm even as the truck peeled out of the parking lot. He adjusted the mirror and zigged the truck left. "Just stay down for a minute. We're almost clear."

A huge boom exploded behind them, and Rosebud screamed as the truck lurched hard right. Dan floored it.

"They just fired over us," he said, like this whole assault was no big deal. "We're on the highway, darlin'. We're okay now."

Rosebud tried to nod, tried to do something, but the last ten minutes flashed through her mind again—the bathroom door shuddering, the guy's repulsive breath as he manhandled her, the way her neck snapped when her hair had been yanked. She touched her forehead and her fingers came away with a smear of blood. Her stomach rolled. "I'm going to be sick," she gasped.

"Hold on." The truck picked up speed, and then took another hard right before coming to a screeching halt.

She flung the door open and stumbled out of the truck, landing on her knees on a gravelly patch of scrub grass. Her stomach gave up the fight.

Suddenly, her hair was pulled up and away from her face, and a warm hand rubbed between her shoulder blades. Oh, just wonderful. Here she was, throwing up her guts and a bad steak in front of Dan. She supposed it beat the hell out of gunshot wounds, but at this exact moment in time, things couldn't get any worse. The sickening embarrassment brought on another round of heaving.

When she was finished, she sat back on her heels. Dan crouched down next to her, still holding her hair. "Better?"

"Um…um…" No. But even in her weakest moment, with the undeniable evidence all over the shoulder of the road, she couldn't admit it.

Dan's eyes searched her all over. She couldn't meet his gaze—she didn't know if she'd ever be able to again. "I'll be right back."

Rosebud sat there in a state of shock, and all she could co-herently think was, *You knew it was three and you were out, girl. And this is* out.

Dan's footsteps crunched on the gravel behind her, and then he held out a bottle of water and a damp cloth. She rinsed out her mouth, which helped tremendously. "Hold still," he said, and he wiped her face for her.

The cut stung, but the pain told her it was small. "It's not bad," he said, his voice doing its level best to be calm. He cupped her chin in his palm and tilted her head toward the truck's headlights.

Suddenly the terror that had been clogging her throat dis-solved into hysterical cries. Clamping her eyes shut, she tried to bite them back.

"I'm sorry. It was all my fault."

This time, the tears wouldn't be bitten back, choked down or hidden until she was alone. "I'm going to cry now," she managed to say as the sobs broke free. "But I don't want this to negatively impact your opinion of me in the courtroom."

Dan gave her a look that made it quite clear Rosebud had officially lost it. "It won't."

"And this in no way reflects on our date—before the attack," she sobbed. She sounded hysterical. The fear and pain and relief all melted into one major circuit overload, one that apparently tripped several wires in her head, because suddenly she couldn't stop babbling. "It was a nice date. I actually like you a whole lot. If only your name wasn't Arm-strong. If only you weren't *that* Armstrong, Dan."

The next thing she knew, the gravel wasn't digging into her knees anymore. Dan was clutching her to his chest and carry-ing her back to the truck, but he didn't set her down. Instead, he slid into the seat and held her on his lap, her feet dangling out the door. He rocked her back and forth as he stroked her hair and whispered, "I know, darlin'. I know," over and over, which Rosebud took as a sign that she was still talking.

She had no idea what she was saying.

Eleven

Slow and easy, Dan said to himself as he tried to walk calmly into the Red Creek tribal headquarters Monday morning.

So what if the last time he'd seen Rosebud had been at about three in the morning on Sunday? So what if she hadn't let him walk her to her door? So what if she hadn't returned either of his calls yesterday? So what if he was nigh on to frantic with worry about her? As far as he knew, no one else was aware of the busted car, the dinner date or the near scalping, and he wasn't about to give anything away by running around like some fool chicken with its head cut off.

"Good morning, Mr. Armstrong," Judy said, cup of coffee ever at the ready. "Ms. Donnelly is running a few minutes late. She'll be with you shortly."

He couldn't help it. He looked past Judy, past the conference room door, down the long hall. Somewhere down there, Rosebud had an office. He prayed she was in it. "But she's here, right?"

"Of course." Judy blocked the hall and motioned Dan to the depressing conference room.

Resigned to his fate, Dan handed over the cookie bars Maria had made and took to doing laps around the conference table. If Rosebud didn't get her behind in here in five minutes, he was going looking for her.

He was reaching for the doorknob when it turned and Judy appeared, carrying a different box of files. Behind her, Rosebud stood by the door, her eyes focused on something Dan couldn't see. It reminded Dan of that first day he'd come to the reservation, when Joe White Thunder had acted like Dan didn't exist. Bad sign. She had a small bandage over the cut, but she otherwise looked normal. Hair in that braid-bun thing, the suit over a light blue shirt, glasses settled firmly on her nose.

Rosebud stood stock-still until the receptionist was gone, and then she silently shut the door. Dan fought the urge to rush to her and pull her into his arms. He tried to tell himself that she was just upset, which was a far cry better than hysterical. Her behavior seemed like more than upset, though. She was acting like they were strangers.

Finally, he broke the tense silence. "Are you okay?"

"Fine." That was a lie. He could see her biting the inside of her lip. "I knocked my head against a kitchen cabinet."

"Oh. Of course." As good a story as any. "I was worried about you." He felt obliged to drop his voice down to a whisper. "I called. Twice."

She flinched, but finally, she looked *at* him, instead of *through* him. "My aunt was home."

"I'm really sorry," he blurted out, desperate to get some sort of reaction out of her. "I should have waited to take you to a better restaurant. I should have put that waitress in her place. I should have waited for you outside the bathroom."

Those were the top three things he'd done wrong, but he was hard-pressed to tell which one would have kept her safe.

She moved slowly, like she had a raging headache. "It wasn't your fault," she said as she settled into her chair. "I should have known better than to—"

"Wait—what happened Saturday night wasn't your fault."

"Of course it was," she continued, selecting a file from the top of the box and opening it up as if they were just reviewing the facts for the upcoming court date. She didn't even sound angry. "I…" Finally, Dan saw a crack in her professional demeanor. She closed her eyes and took a deep breath. "I appreciate your offer to pay me for my time, but that won't be necessary."

"What about your car?"

"Aunt Emily has a car I can use if I need to leave the reservation."

"So you're just going to stay on the rez for the rest of your life?"

"This is where I belong."

She was pissing him off, plain and simple. "You're going to let a bunch of dumb hicks at one bar scare you off like that? If you want, I'll buy the damn place and raze it to the ground."

Her hand smacked the table. The sudden pop made him jump. "You don't get it, do you? It's not just one bar. Believe it or not, that's just how people around here treat me. Us. Ignorant savages and slutty squaws—the only good Indian is a dead one."

Dan's jaw dropped. "That's not how I treat you, and you know it."

For a second, she looked away, but then she came right back at him, both barrels blazing. "No? Get back to me in three and a half weeks, Dan. Then we'll see how you treat me."

Damn his uncle. Dan had thought it before, lots of times,

but he'd never meant it as much as he did right now. Just as Rosebud had said that night, if only he wasn't that Armstrong—an Armstrong like Cecil. "I don't give a damn about that dam. That is *not* what this is about."

"Then what?"

He grabbed that crappy chair and pulled it up next to her so that he could look her in the eye. "This is about you and me, Rosebud. This is about me liking you and you liking me, slow dances to fast songs and not going down without a fight. You promised me you wouldn't go down without a fight, and I'm going to hold you to that."

As hard as she was biting it, she had to be putting a hole in that lip. A blotchy red blush broke over her face, and for a second, she didn't look that different from when he'd driven her home—just miserable.

"Have dinner with me tonight." It wasn't much, but he had to do something to get her to stop being so mule-stubborn. And he owed her a better ending—if she'd let him give her one.

"Or?"

He gaped at her. The way she said it made it sound like he was holding something over her head. "Or I'll eat alone?"

She forcibly swiveled her chair away from his and picked up her pen again. He waited. He'd pushed this just about as far as it was going to go, and whatever she said next was going to have to stand—for the time being, anyway.

"I can't."

Which was a hell of a lot different from an *I won't.* "What if I found some neutral territory?"

Her eyebrows jumped and she winced. "Neutral?"

"You can't come to my place, I know. You don't want me at your place. Obviously, local bars are a no-go...." He reached out and traced a finger along her bandage. She scrunched her eyes shut, and he thought she might be on the verge of

crying. "Someplace quiet." His finger trailed down the rest
of her face until he was running his thumb over her cheeks.
He wanted to kiss her, but this wasn't the time or the place.
"That's all I want. Just you and me."

"What makes you think it would be any different the next
time?" Her voice shook as she blinked rapidly and pulled
away from him. "Or the time after that? Or anytime? We
can't hide forever. I can't, anyway."

Anger flashed through him. "I do *not* hide, Rosebud—and
you shouldn't, either."

"You'd tell your uncle about this?" She pointed to her forehead, her eyes swimming. "About me?"

"No. I'm not stupid." He leaned back, frustrated with how
lousy a job he was doing of convincing her. "Look. It's nobody's business when we see each other or what we do, and I
want to keep it that way. I don't want to have to worry about
what your aunt or my uncle or some moron on the street
thinks about me or you or us." He'd like to kiss that lip she
was hell-bent on chewing, but he didn't want to corner her.
"It's like you said," he added, trying to back off a little, but
not succeeding. He stroked her cheek again. "I'm just trying
to stay out of the society pages. That's all."

Her whole face tensed, but then quickly relaxed as she
leaned into his hand. Her eyelids fluttered. "Where?"

"Do you know where Bonneau Creek is?" At least, he
thought that was what the map said. She nodded, so he must
have said it right. "I think there's a cabin near there. No roads,
no wires. Nothing else around for miles."

"That's almost ten miles away. I can't ride there tonight."

"What about this weekend? Will you spend it with me?"

The words hung in the air, and he realized exactly what
he'd asked. Not dinner, not dancing, but the whole weekend—
nights included.

Say yes, he thought.

Her hand covered his. She was shaking, just a little. "You won't tell anyone?"

His heart jumped. "Not even on my dying day."

She turned her head and kissed his palm. "Don't make me hold you to that," she said as she shot him a sly look and then pushed his chair away. Her meaning was clear—*Yes. Now get back to work.*

A yes was a yes. Despite the world's worst date, she'd still said yes. He was probably grinning like an idiot, but he didn't care. Even though he was an Armstrong, she actually liked him a whole lot—enough to come away for a weekend. "Don't worry. I won't."

Except for when her aunt Emily came in to check on her and to thank Dan for all the cookies, they worked in near silence for the rest of the day. Rosebud kept a safe distance from him above the table, but underneath, she rested one bare foot on his thigh.

Friday seemed a hell of a long way off.

Five days later, as he rode Smokey toward Bonneau Creek, the first thing Dan noticed was the way the world hushed around him. The silence wasn't something that came down like a hammer, but instead seemed to sneak up on him until he couldn't hear anything but the sound of Smokey's legs cutting through the tall grass. No birds. No bugs. Not even the wind blew.

A twig snapped. Dan zeroed in on the noise. About a hundred yards over his right shoulder, on the same deer path he'd heard it the first time. He grinned. She'd come. Keeping his ear focused on the spot, he carefully turned Smokey.

He blinked. Instead of his Indian princess, Rosebud sat astride her paint, buried within the shadows of the wood. Her horse took one more step out of the woods and into the sunlight. Her hair hung in a long, loose braid draped over her shoulder underneath a straw cowboy hat. She had on a plain white tank top, jeans and boots this time.

Same smile, though. She trotted down to him, and he took the time to appreciate the way her body moved. "Hi."

He leaned over as far as he could in the saddle and kissed her. Honey sweet—he wondered if the rest of her tasted the same. "I thought you were beautiful the first time, but I think I like you even better like this. More modern."

Her mouth opened and shut while she gave him a hell of a look. Yup—she was biting her inner lip again. He was getting a little tired of his former hat coming between them. Dan wished she'd just tell him the truth—and *why* would be nice, while she was at it. Giving her time to get herself organized, he turned Smokey north. At a walk, it would take them an hour and a half to get to the cabin.

"Here's what I don't understand," she said as her paint came parallel with him. "*If* you think that I took that shot, why are you here with me now?"

"I don't *think*." The horses fell into an easy stride, and he gave Smokey his head. They'd made this journey every night this week in preparation—although sometimes Dan took a different route, just in case. Smokey knew where they were going. "I *know*."

"If I took that shot," she repeated with more force.

Stubborn to the very end, he thought with a smile. He'd sort of thought that saving her at the bar might have gotten him a little more in the trust department, but he wasn't really surprised. "My mother always says, 'Most every person has a reason.'"

"And you think *that person* who took the shot had a reason?"

Dan's eyes swept along the valley and over the woman at his side. Her hips swiveled with every step her horse took, and her chest was a thing of beauty in slow motion. She held the tail end of the reins in her free hand, against her thigh. The sun glittered off her bare arms, but his eyes kept coming back to her face. No forced smiles, no dangerous stares. Just Rosebud, as nature intended. She belonged here, by the river, on horseback—not in some stuffy suit in an ugly office.

Most every person had a reason. He'd made it through all the police reports for vandalism on the rez in the past seven months. What had she said, back at the beginning? "What if *that person* had reason to believe they were shooting at someone who had 'engaged in a campaign of intimidation against members of the tribe'—that's what you said, right?" He knew now that was lawyer-speak for someone had been slashing tires and leaving bloody animal parts on her doorstep. She'd given him the files, but he hadn't asked her about the dead animals yet.

She was silent. He forced himself not to look at her. She'd spook easy right now, and that wasn't what led to a good weekend. But he wanted to know—he had to know—before they took this date to the next level. "That would be…a reason, but I'm sure *that person* wasn't trying to hit you. I'm sure *that person* was just trying to scare you off. I'm sure it was a mistake—*just* a mistake."

Lawyers, he thought with a snort. Still, this was progress. At least they were talking about it—without blanket denials. "*That person* needs to work on her aim. Scared the hell out of me—and Smokey." Smokey bobbed his head in agreement.

In the distance, he could see the river bend. After that, it was less than a mile until Bonneau Creek fed into the Dakota. They were halfway there.

Part of him—the part that needed to keep her safe—wanted to ask her if she knew who Shane Thrasher was, if that was who she'd thought she'd shot. But the part of him that was going to spend the weekend hidden away from the world with his Indian princess—that part held him back.

They couldn't do anything about Thrasher right now anyway. No need to ruin the moment.

"I'm sorry," she said unexpectedly. Her voice was soft and shaky, he thought, like she was making a confession. "I'll pay for your new hat. It's a nice one."

Now he did look at her. She was holding the reins so tight that her knuckles were white, and she was blinking at an unnaturally fast clip. It wasn't much of a confession, but it was something more than she'd given him before. "It won't happen again, will it?"

"No."

That was the truth, he could tell. Finally, there wasn't anything else between them. He reached over and rubbed her arm. He had her word, and that was good enough for him. "It's all right." She gave him a hesitant smile. Maybe she didn't believe him? "It really is. It was just a hat." It was nice of her to offer to pay for his new one, but she probably didn't have an extra thousand bucks lying around.

"It was almost your head." Her eyes were wet as she looked at him.

He held up a hand to cut her off. "It's done and over, and dwelling doesn't do anyone any good. I know you now. I know you're not some cold-blooded killer." He stood up in the stirrups to get closer to her. Smokey came to a confused halt, and Rosebud's paint followed suit. Dan was planning on hauling Rosebud over to him, but he didn't have to. She met him halfway, grabbing a handful of his shirt to brace him. "I trust you, Rosebud."

He was semibalanced about a foot away from her face. He wanted to kiss her, but he was afraid he might head-butt her at this angle. Her cheeks prettied up, but she held his gaze—and his shirt. "I shouldn't trust you," she said, looking coy and embarrassed at the same time.

"But?"

"But I do." She shot forward, and he felt her lips graze his cheek before she let go. He sat back down in the saddle hard, but he couldn't tear his eyes away from her. "I can't seem to help myself when it comes to you," she said.

Now *that* sounded like a good weekend in the making. "Good. Now, I want to see you ride that horse." He touched his heels to Smokey's side and picked up speed. "Come on, darlin'," he called over his shoulder. "Let's get gone!"

She let out a "Yeah!" and came thundering up behind him. The weekend had officially begun.

Twelve

Feeling lighter than she had in a long time, Rosebud watched as Dan built the campfire with his bare hands as the sun set lazily behind the woods. She'd apologized—without actually admitting any wrongdoing—and he'd forgiven her. She was on a vacation of sorts. She hadn't had a true day off since last Christmas, and she felt giddy about spending it with—whoa. He took his T-shirt off and used it to fan the fire.

Holy cow, Dan shirtless was about a thousand times better than Dan clothed—and he was pretty damn fine with his shirt on. She must have whistled, because his head popped up and he shot her a grin that walked a fine line between snarky and sultry. Was she really doing this? Running away for the weekend with a white man—an Armstrong, no less? It was one thing to get swept away while dancing at a bar—but this? This was a certain kind of crazy. Rationally, she knew she shouldn't trust him. But *rational* had nothing to do with anything anymore.

For a second, she felt horrible that she'd missed out on this last week. She rubbed the small Band-Aid on her forehead. Nope. Not thinking about it. She had too much else to think about right now—like Dan hauling a bucket of water up from the creek for the horses. Wow. Muscles in action.

She was staring. Again. Dan brushed the horses, a true cowboy to the core. His hands moved the brush over each muscle with due diligence. Logically, she knew the horses had to be cooled down before they could get on with their evening, but she didn't know how much longer she could wait for him.

The weight between her legs was heavy, and the tension of holding in sheer, unadulterated desire was wearing her out. The ride out here had gotten her blood pumping, and Dan doing chores kept it pumping. She tore her eyes away from his bare torso and dug her condoms out of her bag.

No nightstand. Hmm. The bed was one of those old-fashioned foldable things on metal springs, but the sheets were fresh and surprisingly soft. Much softer than the ones she had at home. God, how much would that thing squeak? Finally, she decided to put the condoms just under the bed—within reach, but not exactly in line of sight. She might only have another three weeks with Dan—she had to make it count. After the court date, she had no idea what would happen. She found herself hoping he would stay, but she was afraid he was itching to get back to Texas.

Condoms tucked away, she straightened up as she heard him kick off his boots at the door. If she turned around, she might just throw herself at him, so she stayed put. "You've been busy."

Dan wrapped his arms around her waist and pulled her back into his chest. He smelled of horse and wood smoke, with just a little of that sandalwood. He whipped off his hat and threw it onto the only other piece of furniture in the room, a rickety table. She officially didn't care how much the bed would squeak. "Not the penthouse or anything, but how do you like it?" His voice was low and close to her ear. Then he kissed her neck.

Which *it* was that—the cabin, the man in it or what she wanted to do to that man? Didn't matter. "I love it."

"I brought dinner." His stubble scratched over her ear as his arms tightened around her waist. One hand splayed out just below her breast, the other found her hip, and they were dancing again, slow and sweet. The heat from his chest made her shirt stick to her back. "If you're hungry."

Keeping time with the silent rhythm of their bodies, she turned in his arms. His eyes locked on to hers. The scent of sex seemed to pour off his skin, filling the room. "I didn't come here for dinner."

"Me neither." This time, he didn't wait for permission, and he didn't hold back. His lips fastened onto hers with a driving need that must have tripped another wire in her brain, because all of a sudden she was yanking his belt free and he was peeling her shirt off and the next thing she knew, the bed was squeaking. Loudly.

She couldn't help but giggle at the horrific noise. Anyplace else, and she'd be mortified that someone somewhere would hear them. But not here. She lifted her hips as he worked her jeans and panties off. She had no idea where her bra had gone, but in less than a minute, she was nude before him.

A lone finger traced down between her aching breasts to just below her belly. *"Damn."* The moment her legs were free of all unnecessary fabric, she sat up and began unbuttoning his jeans. The bed wailed in protest of all this movement, which set off another round of giggling, but then she froze. She hoped he didn't think she was giggling at *him*.

"It's okay." His voice was thick with strain as he grabbed at his back pocket before she could shuck his pants entirely. He pulled out a condom and tore it open with his teeth. He'd planned ahead, too. Could this man get any more perfect? "I kind of like it a little loud."

"Yeah?" Briefs. Not that they stayed on for long.

He was—well, not *huge* per se, but firmly into the *well-endowed* category. Very firmly. He rolled the condom on and then knelt on the bed between her legs. The whole thing shuddered, and Dan paused to grip both sides of the mattress. The anticipation was going to kill her if the bed didn't do her in first. "Maybe we should—"

Nope. Not waiting another minute. She grabbed his face and hauled him down to her as she wrapped her legs around his waist. She wanted to lick every inch of him until the taste of his musk was burned into her memory. She wanted to feel every inch of him until her hands had memorized every muscle. *Make it count,* she prayed.

He pulled away, his chest heaving as he tested out the bed. It held. "Easy."

"I don't want it easy." Her fingers scraped over his chest and around to his backside. She pulled him toward her, toward the heaviness that was driving her mad. The slickness of the condom touched her, but having that dull weight on the outside wasn't doing her any favors. "I want you. Now."

Moving slow enough not to flip the bed, he reached down between her legs and touched her center. His fingers spread her wide. He was against her, then in her. Her body convulsed. "Is this what you want?"

"Yes," she moaned, shimmying around his width. He pulled back—almost out—and a whimper escaped her lips.

"This?" He drove all the way in, his head bowing over hers until their foreheads were touching. Panting, his breath surrounded her. He surrounded her, filled her. She was safe, here in his arms. Nothing and no one could hurt her.

He was everything she'd hoped, but nothing like she'd imagined. Better. So much better. *"Dan."*

He pulled back again and paused. What was he waiting for? "Tell me what you want." His voice was stretched thin, like he was just barely holding on to the edge of a steep cliff.

Her hips shimmied again, hoping to draw him back in. "Loud?" Because what he wanted was what she wanted.

"Yeah." He moved in small circles, just inside her. He was toying with her, damn it.

"Harder." He buried himself with more force, and her cry broke free. "Oh!"

He made a noise in the back of his throat, an instinctive growl that was pleasure and hunger and satisfaction all rolled into one. But again, he pulled back, slow and steady.

Her orgasm was so close, but it was stuck behind a wall of three years of waiting for this exact moment. Dan had to break through that wall, he just *had* to. Slow and steady wasn't the way. "Faster," she demanded, smacking the flat of her hand on his behind. "Harder. Faster."

He grunted, his body picking up wonderful speed. Each thrust did make her louder. He was driving into her with a passion—a force—that she'd never felt before. All the wires in her brain tripped, and before she knew it, she was shouting his name in time with each meeting of their bodies.

"Can't...hold on...long," he got out through clenched teeth.

He drove in again, but this time his lips found hers. The final, intimate touch shattered the wall around her. *Dan!* But the word didn't come. All that came was a scream that he seemed to swallow whole. He exploded in a flurry of hurried thrusts before his head flew back and he made a noise closer to a mountain lion roaring than a man coming. He shivered through a final half thrust and fell on top of her.

The bed was silent while she tried to catch her breath with his weight on top of her. Sated, she ran the pads of her fingers over his back more slowly now, taking her time to really feel him.

"Oh, Rosebud." His voice was muffled against her neck—and then he started kissing her skin. "I—you—"

She was afraid to open her mouth, because her head was buzzing with all the circuits he'd not only tripped, but blown completely. However, when his lips moved over her collarbone and began to make their way to her bare breasts, she started to giggle.

His head popped up, and the bed creaked. "Rosebud?"

"Oh, no, not you—I just— Oh, my God—you were amazing. I've been wanting—since that first time—on the horse—I mean—just, you know, that was amazing. Not that—*you*—you were—*are*—amazing." Yup. Circuits blown. She was babbling.

He propped himself up on one hand and grinned at her. "Interesting." He sounded amused, which was probably the best she could hope for. "So, what you're sayin' is, you liked it."

"Uh-huh." She couldn't even get that out without another round of giggles as he swung his legs over the bed. She rolled over and traced the shape of his shoulder blades. No, she decided, he couldn't get any more perfect.

"And you wouldn't mind doin' it again a little later?"

"Not *too* much later."

That made him laugh, and despite the bed's protests, he reached around, picked her up—actually picked her up—and sat her on his lap. He kissed her forehead, her cheeks, her eyelids. "Can you wait half an hour?"

Finally, she felt a little bit of sanity returning to her brain. "I suppose I don't have much choice, do I?" She needed to get cleaned up. Some recovery time would probably be good for both of them.

At that moment, Rosebud realized there was no bathroom in the cabin.

Dan laughed again, a satisfied sound rounded out by happiness. "You've got your choice of the tree to the left, or the bush to the right."

She stretched out on his lap, and his hands slid over her bare flesh. "Bush." She'd peed behind both trees and bushes, and the bush held the promise of slightly more coverage.

By the time she got her clothes back on, Dan was crouched before the fire. A plush blanket was spread out on the ground and over some old stumps, giving them someplace to sit. Dinner was the best cold fried chicken and biscuits she'd ever eaten. Then he broke out the marshmallows and chocolate wrapped in gold foil. "S'mores?" That chocolate looked far too expensive to waste on graham crackers.

"We're camping," he replied, stripping a stick and handing it to her. By now, the sun had set, and the only light for miles around was a crescent moon and the fire. "I think there's a law that says if you've got a campfire, you've got to make s'mores." Stripping his own stick, he sat down next to her.

With the light flickering over his face, he looked a whole lot more like the little boy in the poster than the man who ran Armstrong Holdings. "Far be it from me to argue with the law. Or chocolate. Pass the marshmallows."

By the time she'd set three marshmallows on fire, he was snickering like a boy, too. "What am I going to do with you?" he asked as he blew out another victim.

"That's sort of a good question." One she'd love to know the answer to.

He paused in the middle of squeezing his perfectly melted marshmallow between the chocolate and graham crackers, and then handed her the finished product. "You got all serious on me there."

She tried to laugh it off. "Sorry. I haven't had a day off in a long time. It's hard to shut off my brain."

He skewered another marshmallow, but he didn't roast it. He stared at the fire in silence for such a long time that she was sure she'd pushed him too far—although she didn't see how. Finally, he pivoted on his heels and stared at her.

"Rosebud," he said in such a serious voice that for a second, she was afraid he was going to do something completely irrational and ask for her hand in marriage. Her heart started to thud. "What if there was no reservoir?"

Thirteen

"What?" she gasped, scooting away from Dan. "What do you mean, no reservoir?"

Mistake, he thought. He shouldn't have tried to mix business with what had been an unabashed pleasure up to that point. "I'm going to bring my engineer up here in a few weeks." She stopped scooting, her eyes trained on him with a laserlike focus. At least he had her undivided attention. "I've been studying the plans. We could do a run-of-river dam."

She sucked in air like it was going out of style. Then she sprang to her feet, hovering between backing up some more and maybe grabbing him by his lapels and shaking him senseless. "*We* could do a *what?*"

"A run-of-river couldn't store electricity for when the river's low, but it wouldn't require a reservoir. The difference is only a few thousand—way less than Cecil's spent on lawyers the last few years." He stood, but slowly. He didn't want to spook her—any more than he'd already spooked her.

"You—the dam—no?" She spun around, stalked off into the darkness, and was back in the circle of light in a heartbeat. "We?"

As the firelight danced over the flustered planes of her face, his mind flashed back to the sex. She'd lost all control—he'd seen her do it twice now. Her mouth ran a mile a minute when it happened, good or bad. This? This was good. She had one hand over her heart, the other waving in his general direction. Way more than half an hour had passed, and he couldn't wait to get her good and flustered all over again.

"I'm not makin' any promises—I've got to get Jimmy up here to look it over—but it's *possible*. That's all." He took her hand and pulled her into his arms. Man, she just *fit*, all warm and soft and sweet.

"No flooding?" He could feel her heart racing against his chest.

He shook his head. "I don't trust Cecil's engineering firm any more than I trust Cecil. They've got to have an ulterior motive for pushing the reservoir, but I don't know what it is."

"Dan—you mean it? No dam?"

"I didn't say that. I said *maybe* no reservoir. Look," he said, taking her face in his hands. "This is Cecil's deal—but it's still my company, and the *company* has sunk a lot of money into this. I can't afford to walk away from the deal."

He could see the wheels in her mind spinning. His own wheels were picking up speed. A lot of things had to go right—like wrestling control of this project, and eventually the company, away from Cecil, for starters—but he'd spent his every waking moment for the past few weeks either being near Rosebud or thinking about being near her. She didn't make it easy on him, but somehow, being with her was the kind of difficult that a man could get used to.

She opened her mouth to say something, but nothing came out. The only sound she made was a small squeak.

Not just any woman would consider run-of-river dams foreplay. But if he'd learned anything, it was that Rosebud wasn't just any woman. He tightened his arms around her, enjoying the way she rubbed against him as he leaned down to kiss her. "Yeah, I thought that's what you'd say."

Her honey sweetness was tempered with chocolate this time, and it only made him want to kiss her more. She ran her hands over his five o'clock shadow as she licked his lips. Oh, yeah, the half hour was up, and so was he. He growled in satisfaction as she ground her hips against him. Already he had her shirt half-off, but he couldn't make the move toward the bed. That damned thing was just too loud.

"I've been dreaming about this," she said as she whipped his shirt over his head and pushed him back down toward the blanket. The cool night air just made him want to get warm the old-fashioned way.

He dug another condom out of his back pocket before he lost his pants again. Man, but she was fast with those buttons. "Yeah?" Her mouth was running. This was going to be good.

"After that first kiss—you and me—by the river—*dreaming,*" she repeated.

She pushed him down to the ground, and with an agonizingly slow pace, undid her jeans. In the firelight, the peaks of her nipples gleamed like rubbed copper. Her hips swiveled as she worked them free of her jeans, and then she undid her braid. Her hair fell free around her in loose waves. She jutted out that chin and squared her shoulders, showing none of that typical self-consciousness that always had women turning out lights or wrapping up in robes. No, she was a proud Indian princess, and she'd brought the cowboy to his knees.

"Damn, darlin'." Her mouth might be going, but his was freezing up. All he could do was stare and wait for her.

As she lowered herself onto him, her wetness surrounding

everything he had to offer her, she scraped her breasts over his stubble and groaned.

The sound of her making love to him was enough to send him right over the edge all by itself. The first time he'd been with a woman who liked it loud had been like his very first time all over again. Something about a woman who didn't hold back drove him wild. "You like that?" Because if she was driving him wild, he wanted to make damn sure she came driving with him.

"Oh, yeah." She arched her back, thrusting those all-natural beauties into his face. Her hair pooled down behind her, covering them both in a blanket of black silk. "So good. So— *Oh!*"

His mouth fastened to her nipple, Dan couldn't help but smile as she bucked so hard he had to grab her around the waist to keep her from falling off him. Holding her to him with one hand, he sucked as hard as he could on one breast and let his fingers do the tugging on the other.

Her hands grabbed his hair and held on. Her nipples were rock hard in his mouth, and each pass of his tongue or his teeth or his stubble—especially his stubble—upped her volume. Finally, Dan couldn't take it anymore. He had to come, and he had to come right now. He grabbed her hips and pumped in as hard and as fast as he could, the sounds of her screaming his name into the wide-open night putting him in a place he'd only just glimpsed before. Her noise—her pleasure—blotted out everything else, even the coppery glow of her skin. All he could see and feel, taste and touch, was the sound of what he was doing to her.

He couldn't remember ever coming as hard as she made him come.

By the time the rest of his senses caught up with him, she had her head buried into the crook of his neck. She was sort of moaning, sort of whimpering, but the meaning was the same.

"Yeah." Which was not some of his better pillow talk, but it was all he had left. "Me, too."

He didn't want to let her go, but the night air came down hard on them now that they weren't actively keeping it away. Moving wasn't easy. He was six kinds of tired, and at least that many kinds of satisfied. By the time he got the fire out, she'd pulled the mattress to the floor and curled up in the bed.

"A woman after my own heart." Exhaustion clawed at him as he crawled in next to her. Tiffany had never stayed the night—her choice. Staying meant a more permanent thing, she'd told him once, and Dan could never do permanent. She'd been right—then.

Now?

Rosebud snuggled up against his side—she didn't have much of a choice, the bed wasn't that big—and draped a leg over his. Now, this close tangle of legs and arms and skin seemed more permanent than anything he'd ever felt for a woman.

"You never answered the question." Her voice managed to beat back the sleepy darkness, but just barely.

"What question?"

"What *are* you going to do with me?"

More permanent, he thought, finding her fingers and lacing them with his. Sleep could not be denied much longer, but he didn't want to leave her hanging. "I'm thinking about keeping you."

By the time Sunday rolled around, Dan was doing a lot more thinking. Sure, he'd gone camping plenty of times—but he couldn't remember ever liking it as much as he did with Rosebud around. Maybe it was because he hadn't gone camping since he'd taken control of the petroleum division

ten years ago—it was hard to pitch a tent in a tie. Maybe it
was because she liked the stuff he liked—riding the horses
after breakfast, taking a skinny dip in the afternoon and cud-
dling by the campfire at night. Maybe it was because they
made sweet, sleepy love in the morning and had screaming
hot sex by moonlight. Maybe it was because she couldn't
roast a marshmallow if her life depended on it. Whatever it
was, by the time they packed up and headed out, he was already figuring out the plans for next weekend.

"We should take a different route," he said when they got
back to where the Bonneau Creek fed into the Dakota.

"Why?" She kept close to him—not close enough to crowd
the horses, but close enough that he could still reach out and
touch her arm.

"Because—" His brain bit back the words *I might be followed* before they got all the way out.

"Dan," she said, and he knew by the tone of her voice that
he hadn't been fast enough. "*Why* do we need to take a different route?"

At least the weekend had already been great. He wouldn't
ruin the whole thing now. "Do you know who Shane Thrasher
is?"

"No." He swore that, even though they were still riding,
she froze. "Should I?"

Damn his big mouth. She'd gotten him all relaxed and
comfortable, and this was what popped out. "He's Cecil's
'head of security,'" he said, using air quotes. "And he's half
Crow."

She sucked in air hard, but managed to keep her game face
on. He didn't like her game face. He liked her real face. "And
he's tailing—you? Me? Us?"

"I'm not sure, but it's possible he's tailing me. I haven't
seen any other tracks, so I'm sure he hasn't found our cabin."
Given the way she was getting all splotchy on him over there,

he'd better be damn sure, but he'd checked around the campsite every time they left and every time they came back, and had seen no signs of anyone or thing. No cigarette butts. Not even a questionable hoofprint. "Better safe than sorry, though. I don't want him to find our place."

They rode north for a little bit before they came to a wide spot in the river. When he turned Smokey into the water, Rosebud finally spoke up. "You're scaring me."

He shot her a confused look. "It's real shallow here. I've come this way twice. Won't even get your boots wet."

"That's not what I mean." She looked over her shoulder, and he saw the fear. "What if…"

"No one saw us. No one will see us," he promised, suddenly wishing he'd checked a little more thoroughly. All that screaming… "And I won't let anyone scare you. That's a promise, Rosebud." She gave him a worried smile, one that said she wasn't really convinced. "I mean it. Anyone messes with you, and I'll shoot them myself."

She took another long look around, but the river valley was the same wild, untouched place it had been before he'd been dumb enough to bring up Thrasher. "That won't be necessary," she finally said as they crossed the river. "I can take care of myself."

That all-business tone of voice was what worried him the most. "Will you still come away with me next weekend?"

She looked to the heavens, as if that was where the answer lay. "I shouldn't." His heart dropped a pained notch or two, but then she sighed and added, "If we leave real early Saturday morning, no one will know where we went."

"Darlin,' I'll go anywhere, anytime, as long as I'm with you."

She twisted in the saddle and shot him a look that was a

whole lot of knowing and a little bit of longing. He waited for her to say something, but she didn't.

She just rode away from him. He had to hurry to catch up.

Fourteen

"Where were you this weekend?" Cecil didn't look like he'd moved from his desk since last Thursday, the last time Dan had seen him.

Dan bristled. For a split second, he felt like a hormonal teenager busted for being out past curfew. "Out." He didn't owe Cecil anything more than that, but the monosyllabic response caused the man to look up.

"Who with?"

"My horse. I rode down south to check out a few things on the map." As far as he could tell, there wasn't much down south except scrub grass and a lonely, forgotten cell phone tower. South would be a good direction for Shane Thrasher to go to get lost. Maybe he'd be eaten by a coyote.

Something about Cecil changed. He went from his normal pissed look to something that was supposed to be warm and inviting—if one liked eels. "So," he said, his tone suddenly all buddy-buddy. "How are things going with that Donnelly woman?"

Dan would rather chew off his own arm in a bear trap than give away anything about his Indian princess. "I don't know what you think I can do with her. She's real easy on the eyes, but she doesn't take anything from anyone—me included. I can't even get her to dinner again. She caught wind of my scheme that first time and won't even look at me. It's like I'm not even there."

"No progress, huh." Dan took the mild look of disappointment as a compliment. Cecil was actually buying that load of bull crap. The old man flipped to a calendar and thought. "We've got less than three weeks until that court date. Keep at her, son. Even the toughest nuts can be cracked."

So help him, the only thing Dan could think of cracking was Cecil, right across the mouth. "Why are we pushing the reservoir? Why aren't we doing a run-of-river?"

"Do you have any idea how much money we've sunk into this?" Cecil slapped his hand on the desk in an unnecessary show of force.

Dan didn't flinch. "*We* didn't." He kept his voice calm and level—his COO voice, Mom always said. His cut-the-crap voice was how he thought of it. "*You* did."

For the blink of an eye, Cecil actually looked surprised. But the contempt washed away everything else real quick. "Don't tell me you're listening to that woman. For Christ's sake, she's a lunatic! A raving lunatic who's cost this company millions of dollars!"

"Seems to me you may be the one costing this company millions. I'm going to be bringing some of my people in— *my* engineer, *my* audit team. We're going to need to review *your* books, Cecil."

Surprise flashed over his face again, but this time he looked more cornered. "I should have known bringing you up here was a mistake. You're too soft for this business. Just like your mother." The words weren't even sharp enough to cut, not with the way his voice wavered.

Dan had the old man trapped, and they both knew it. "I'll be sure to mention you to her. She does enjoy hearing what you're up to, being as her vote carries such weight with the board."

Cecil blanched. "You can audit your ass off, but we're breaking ground in three weeks."

Nothing but bluster. Chances were decent that Rosebud was going to get her injunction, and Dan needed the stay to get his team organized. He wanted his top guys and gals up here, but they were all hip-deep in various other projects. Three weeks out was the earliest he could pull everyone out of Texas without compromising the other jobs.

And he needed that time to figure out what Cecil was up to. If he couldn't prove that Cecil was doing anything illegal, then the board would have no reason to force the old man out. Dan turned on his heels and headed for his room.

How was he going to get Cecil out of the picture? He needed hard evidence. But what?

Dan was emptying his bag out and rounding up the dirty laundry when it hit him.

Maria.

She was in the kitchen, humming as she rolled tamales. He hadn't checked for bugs since he'd had dinner here with Rosebud, so he made up some lame excuse about wanting to check her tire pressure to get her out of the house.

"Maria," he asked as he bent over her tires, "who do you work for? Me, or Cecil?"

"Señor Cecil," she replied after a long minute. "But I would like to work for you." Her voice was so quiet that he almost couldn't hear it over the faint rush of air that escaped the tire gauge. "You are a better man, *señor.*"

"Well, I'm hiring." Going through the motions, they moved

around to the other tire. "I'm looking for something. A lock-box that Cecil keeps separate from his other files."

"I'm not allowed in his office, *señor*." They moved to the back tires. "What does it look like?"

Dan hid his grin. He was definitely hiring. "It's made of wood—oak, I think—and it looks real old. He had a key with it—small. Silver, I think." One more tire to go. "It had a file in it that he marked up with a red pen."

"I have not seen such a thing before." The tires were done. Maria straightened. "Thank you for checking." Then, under her breath, she added, "I will look."

"Yeah, just tell Eduardo to keep an eye on that front one," he said a little louder than he meant to as they walked back into the house.

The number of Armstrong Holdings employees in South Dakota had just gone up by one.

"Rosebud?" Aunt Emily was sitting in her chair, the quilt square spread out before her. "Honey, where have you been?"

"Out." Which was the lamest of all possible excuses. She'd lived with Aunt Emily for so long that they really didn't have secrets. "I just needed a weekend off. I've been so busy with the dam...."

Aunt Emily looked at her, at her backpack, then back at her before she turned her eyes back to her work. She wasn't buying it, but Rosebud wasn't about to crack. Maybe when she'd been a teenager, she could be intimidated by the know-ing silence, but not anymore. She didn't have to explain her-self to anyone—one of the fringe benefits of being an adult.

Rosebud set her bag down and began to make a peanut butter sandwich. Food had been secondary this weekend, and even the rumble in her belly was enough to make her smile in contentment. *Dan*. Just thinking his name was enough to make her shiver. Still, the sandwich hit the spot.

Rosebud was rummaging in the fridge to see if they had any apples when Aunt Emily's voice cut through her hazy happiness. "Have you gotten anything out of that Dan Armstrong yet?"

The hackles on the back of her neck shot up. All her training kicked in, and Rosebud went on the offensive before she knew what she was doing. "I don't know what you think I'm going to 'get' out of him," she snapped as she slammed the fridge door. "He doesn't know anything about dams, and from what I can tell, Cecil keeps him clueless." All statements that were true three weeks ago. Now? Everything was different. Which made it official. She was lying to her aunt. Something she had never done before.

And to make things worse, they both knew it. Aunt Emily looked at her with a sense of confused wonder on her face. "He doesn't know anything."

It should have been a question, but it wasn't. Aunt Emily was just repeating the bald-faced lie as a matter of statement.

Guilt smacked Rosebud upside the head, and for a second, she wanted to tell Aunt Emily about the run-of-river option. Rosebud had done what she was supposed to, after all. She'd gotten into Dan's head, muddled his thinking and made him see her side. Aunt Emily would be proud of her. Except that wasn't why Rosebud was doing it. At this point, the dam was almost secondary. Almost.

Rosebud looked Aunt Emily in the eye. "No." The lie came easier this time. Part of it was self-preservation. Maybe this thing with Dan was only a weekend thing. Maybe he'd go back to Texas in three weeks. Maybe he'd stay around long enough to see her rez at the bottom of a lake. She didn't want people thinking she'd lost her head and sunk the tribe over a man, over an Armstrong.

Or maybe it would all work out. The chances were slim, but the element of surprise was key. If Cecil got wind of what

Dan and Rosebud were up to, the run-of-river option might
fall apart. She'd be lucky if *just* the rez went under. It would
all be on her head.

Aunt Emily held her gaze for a year-long moment before
the older woman sighed and turned back to her quilting. "Be
careful, Rosebud."

If her hackles stood up any more, they'd rip themselves
right off her neck. "What's that supposed to mean? When am
I not careful?" Her mind flashed back to the look on Dan's
face when he'd told her they should take a different route to
the cabin next time. The peanut butter sandwich felt like a
lead weight in her belly.

Aunt Emily clucked at her. At least she wasn't staring
Rosebud down anymore. "You can't forget who he is. Who
you are. Who you represent." Rosebud thought for a second
that Aunt Emily was about to launch into the history of the
tribe, just like she did when Rosebud wanted her to wear
down an opponent.

For one wonderful weekend, Rosebud had managed to
forget exactly who she represented. For two days, there had
been no Armstrong Holdings and no Red Creek tribe. For two
days, she hadn't felt like she had the weight of the world on
her shoulders. For two wonderful, freeing days, she'd been
happy for the first time in so long…since before Tanner died.
She couldn't help it—even now, she wanted nothing more
than to go back to where it was just Dan and Rosebud.

And that alone was enough to make her one of "them" instead of one of "us."

"I know what I'm doing," she managed to get out. Which
was not the same as knowing what she was *supposed* to be
doing. But she was damn tired of living her life for someone—everyone—else. Was it too much to ask to do what she
wanted for once?

Aunt Emily shook her head in what looked a hell of a lot like disappointment.

Rosebud focused all of her energy on not slamming the door to her room. She knew what she was doing.

Next weekend, she was going to the cabin with Dan.

Fifteen

Rosebud sat across the table, staring at Dan. She could tell he knew she was staring, because he kept grinning as he handed over sheet after sheet of official company biography. "And Jim Evans—he's my chief engineer. They'll all be coming up together in two weeks—the day after the hearing, actually. If Jim gets done with his current project, he might make it in earlier, but I can't guarantee that."

A small part of her was immensely relieved that he really was flying up his own team. She had been worried silly that Dan had just been whispering sweet nothings in her ear because he wanted to get her into a compromising position. But he was nothing if not serious about it—and he had the itineraries to prove it. "They aren't going to be staying with you, are they?"

"I don't think Cecil is open to that option," he replied, answering the correct question. But then his face got dark—the same look he'd gotten when he'd asked her about Thrasher. He flipped a piece of paper over and began scribbling.

He doesn't like you. Dan's handwriting was borderline atrocious, but she could still make it out.

Big shock there. *Aunt Emily's not a big fan of you, either,* she wrote back.

Dan sighed, like he'd been hoping for a better outcome. *I kind of hate this sneaking around thing,* he wrote back.

Me, too. But I don't know how to get around it.

He looked at her, and she saw something in his eyes that wasn't like and wasn't even lust. She'd never seen that look before—on anyone—and the intensity of it gave her goose bumps. "What?"

I'm working on it, he wrote. *Be careful.*

I will, she promised.

Careful was harder than it sounded. For one thing, Rosebud and Aunt Emily weren't exactly on speaking terms, which made dinner every night awkward. All that awkwardness spilled over to the office. Judy could tell something was wrong, and began acting like it was her job on the line.

For another thing, every day Rosebud saw Dan made it that much harder to keep her hands off him. They both knew that there could be no touching and certainly no kissing anywhere they might get caught. No temptation allowed, period.

But Dan had the nerve to let his stubble get a little closer to a full beard, until just the sight of his face made her ache in good ways. She had wild fantasies about stripping for him at the office and doing all sorts of crazy things on the conference table—even on the wobbly chair. All the unresolved tension nearly gave her a tummy ache.

Careful also required that they take long and winding routes to the cabin both weekends—so long that, by the time they got there, it took everything she had not to rip his shirt off.

But once they were at the cabin, *careful* was the last thing on their minds. She had been afraid that there was no way the sex could top the excitement of that first weekend, but Dan took great pleasure in proving her wrong. The first time he went down on her, scraping his near-beard over her breasts, down her belly and between her thighs, she screamed so loudly that she lost her voice.

The first time he took her from behind and reached down between her legs from the front until he found her throbbing little spot, she came so hard that she accidentally knocked him off the mattress and onto the floor. But instead of being mad at her, he just rolled her onto her back and promised she wouldn't get away the next time.

The first time he gathered her into his arms after another explosive orgasm and said, "I think I'm falling for you, Rosebud," he brought her to tears—tears he kissed away.

"I think I'm falling for you, too." Which was, of course, a gross understatement of the situation. Rosebud didn't think—she knew she was falling in love with Dan. She was already in love with him.

"Just Dan and Rosebud," he said, sounding happy and solemn at the same time as the crickets chirped away outside. The world—their world—was calm and peaceful. "That's what I want. Just Dan and Rosebud."

Her breath caught in her throat. "That's what I want, too." But they both knew it wasn't that simple.

"Dan coming in today?" Judy asked as the coffee perked.

Rosebud worked at keeping her face still, although she knew it was pointless. Dan—and her relationship with him—was sort of an open secret by now. No one could prove anything, but lots of people had noticed how much time the two of them had spent in the conference room in the past two and a half weeks. "I'm not sure," she said, trying to be convincing. "I don't know if I'll have time for him. The court date is tomorrow, after all." Judy was not convinced, to say the least. Rosebud sighed. "Let me know if he shows up, okay?"

"Of course," Judy replied with a wink.

Great, Rosebud thought. *So much for being careful.*

Tomorrow was the big day, although it was just another battle in the war. She was doing the final check on all her ducks. Each row had to be perfect. Dan had told her that if she got the preliminary injunction, the odds were decent that he could get control of the project by the time the order expired. Rosebud was itching to tell someone about their plan, but unfortunately, the plan included telling no one. Neither she nor Dan could afford to have their positions compromised. Things had to go off smoothly or they wouldn't go off at all.

She dove into her briefs, only vaguely aware that it was well past Dan's normal arrival time. He'd said he might have things to do—after all, his team was coming in this weekend—so she refused to spend much time thinking about it.

It wasn't until Judy knocked on her door that she realized it was half past ten. "Is he here?" she asked as she dug for her lipstick.

"No." The sheer terror in Judy's voice snapped Rosebud's head up. Judy was as pale as was physically possible. If Rosebud wasn't mistaken, the woman was on the verge of passing out.

"Who is it?" Her voice rang tinny in her own ears. Something was wrong.

"It's Cecil Armstrong."

Rosebud's blood ran middle-of-January cold. After all this time, *that man* had the nerve to show up? What the hell was he doing here? Where was Dan? *Snap out of it,* she ordered herself. Now was not the time to panic. "What does he want?"

"He wants to talk to you. And he's got another man with him. Not Dan."

"Did you get a name?"

"I think he said Shane Thrasher, but…" Judy waved her hands, which only seemed to spread a sense of panic around the room like an aerosol can. "He's got a gun. I can tell—I've seen those cop shows. Under his jacket."

"Oh, hell." Shane Thrasher. "Okay. Don't panic." Like that was even an option right now. Rosebud wasn't even sure her heart was still pumping. "Can you get them some coffee?"

Judy looked like she wanted to cry.

"Don't worry about it," Rosebud said before the water-works started. "Just get Joe. I don't care if you have to drag his butt out of bed—I want him to get that gun out of this building, okay?"

"Okay," Judy said and all but sprinted to her phone.

Rosebud wasn't much better. She grabbed her phone so fast she dropped it. "Come on," she said as Dan's number rang in her ear. "Pick up."

He didn't. The call went straight to voice mail. The panic in her belly ratcheted up a notch. Where the hell *was* he?

"Dan? It's Rosebud. Your uncle and Shane Thrasher are sitting in my conference room, and I don't know where you are. If you could…" Could what? Get the cavalry and ride to the rescue? Bust in here with both barrels blazing? "If you could just let me know if you know what's going on, I'd really appreciate it. I—" Her mouth snapped shut, biting the *love you* in half. No weakness. No confession. "Uh, I'll talk to you later, right? Bye."

She forced herself to go through her normal pre-meeting routine. Braided hair—check. Lipstick—check. Files in order—check. But there was no convincing herself. Nothing about this unscheduled meeting was normal, and that unavoidable fact had her stomach churning so fast she was nauseous.

After all this time, Cecil Armstrong had come to see her.

There was always a chance he'd come in peace, she thought as she buttoned up her suit jacket. Or maybe he was here to give up. Surrender would be nice.

Her pep talk failed to make her peppy.

"Rosie?" Joe White Thunder popped his head in the door. She jumped so hard that she almost knocked her chair over. "What's going on?"

"Oh, thank God." Joe was here. The whole world hadn't gone completely mad. "Cecil Armstrong is in the conference room with his head of security, a man named Shane Thrasher. Judy said she saw Thrasher's gun. I need you to make sure he gets it the hell out of here."

Joe stared at her for a long second in what could only be shock before he squared his shoulders. "I'll take care of him," he said, looking twenty years younger in an instant and sounding every inch the Lakota warrior.

Rosebud's heart was pounding so hard she was sure her whole body was visibly shaking. She did *not* want to go in that room before she knew where Dan was, but the longer she put it off, the more nervous she would become. She had to get this over with quick.

She stood with her hand on the doorknob, trying to get her body to respond to her orders. Joe put his hand on her shoulder and gave her a strong squeeze. "You can do this, Rosie," he whispered.

"Right." She still wasn't sure what *this* was, but she could do it. Taking a last breath of Cecil-free air, she opened the door to the conference room. *Into the abyss,* she thought.

Cecil Armstrong stood over the wobbly chair with a man who had to be Shane Thrasher on his hands and knees, looking at the undercarriage of the wounded seat. A small sense of victory calmed her nerves. She still had the upper hand.

Armstrong looked much like he did in the photos she'd found of him, but in person he seemed more shriveled, more…yellow. Sallow, she thought, remembering the name for it, like he never saw the sun. In her mind's eye, she had always thought of him as this huge mountain of an obstacle she had to conquer, but in person he was a good eight inches shorter than Dan. Just an old, shriveled-up man, she thought. The realization gave her strength. He had no power over her, none at all. She was not afraid, and she was not going down without a fight. It didn't matter that Dan wasn't here. She was confident that he had a good reason for not answering the phone. He probably didn't even know Cecil was here. She and Dan had a plan, and she was going to stick with that plan, come hell or high water.

"Mr. Armstrong, what a surprise." At least her voice was listening to her orders. It came out strong and confident. She turned to Thrasher, who was now standing. "And Mr.… Thrasher, is it?"

Thrasher's eyes slid over her with cold familiarity. He smirked without saying anything, and Rosebud saw a muscle above his eye twitch. Forget middle-of-January cold. Her blood was running Arctic-circle icy.

"Miss Donnelly, at last we meet." Armstrong's smile was wide—and dangerous, like a shark circling. He looked at Joe with utter contempt. "I assure you, Miss Donnelly, this is strictly a business call. I only have business with *you*."

He could bring his muscle, but she couldn't have Joe in the room? To hell with that. But Rosebud refused to get even one feather ruffled by this man. "Mr. Thrasher, we have a strict policy on firearms in the building. Mr. White Thunder will be happy to escort you to your vehicle, where you can lock your firearm in your trunk."

Thrasher did that mercenary smirk again, but he held up his hands in a motion of surrender. "Sure thing." He turned to Armstrong. "You don't need me here for this part, do you?"

Armstrong gave the wobbly chair a little shake. The chair

wailed in protest, which made Armstrong smile. Rosebud swore she saw a few extra rows of teeth in there. "I think I can manage this just fine."

Manage what? Rosebud would give her left foot to know what the hell this little visit was about. Still, she held her position until Joe and Thrasher were out of the room. "How can I help you today, Mr. Armstrong?"

Still standing, Armstrong opened his briefcase and took out a large manila envelope. "Miss Donnelly, I'm sure you can appreciate that your little legal maneuvers have cost my company a rather large sum of money."

She immediately felt a little better. This territory was more familiar. "Mr. Armstrong, I'm sure you can appreciate that your little dam will cost my entire tribe a place to live."

"That's unfortunate," he said in the same tone of voice one might use to describe three-day-old roadkill. On the one hand, he was creeping her out. On the other hand, she was glad to see her impression of the man had not been wrong. He was a blight upon the land.

He tapped the envelope on the table. "All the same, I'd like to formally ask you, for the last time, to drop all your lawsuits against *my* company."

Rosebud's attention zeroed in on that envelope. If her blood got any colder, it would freeze solid. Where the hell was Dan? "I'm afraid I can't do that, Mr. Armstrong."

Armstrong tilted his head to one side and appraised her. She was not afraid, she repeated to herself.

"Dan mentioned you were a real looker, but I don't think that does you justice."

The clap of fear she felt might as well have been thunder. But she could handle this. She *had* to. "I'm flattered."

Armstrong gave her another dangerous smile. "I have something I want you to see." He slid the envelope over the table.

Instinctively, she knew she didn't want to know what was in there, because whatever it was, it was the end of the world as she knew it. She refused. She wouldn't take it.

Some circuit in her brain must have tripped in the thunderclap, because unexpectedly, she saw her hands reach down and pick up the envelope. *No!* her brain screamed. *Don't open it!*

But her body wasn't listening. Mentally frozen in a state of horror, she saw her hands undo the clasp on the envelope and slide out a short stack of photos.

Of her.

Naked.

With Dan.

A searing pain cut across her forehead, for a second, and all she could think was that she was back in the bar with someone ready to scalp her. Her hand moved up to her forehead and then down to her eyes, but she saw no blood.

"I should think you'd be very flattered," Armstrong was saying. "Some of those are quite good shots. You photograph well. Have you considered a career in modeling?"

The pain got sharper, but her hands kept flipping the pages over and over. Her, stripping off Dan's pants in front of the fire. Her, wiggling out of her jeans. Her, straddling Dan.

Dan, pulling her legs wide apart. Dan, sucking on her nipple. Dan, clearly sliding into her.

"Oh, that's my favorite." Armstrong was still talking, but his voice seemed farther away. "Enough to make me wish I was a younger man. Would have *loved* to have had a run at you in my prime."

She wanted to throw up. She wanted to scream, to fight back, to show this man what a true Lakota woman could do. But she was frozen solid, her body operating mechanically without her express permission.

All she could do was count. Thirteen in all. Thirteen photos of her having sex with Dan.

"There's a jump drive in there, as well." Armstrong's voice seemed to float to her from somewhere in another state. "With the video version on it."

Operating on automatic, her hands tipped the envelope up, and out spilled a small black stick drive. Her, naked, having sex with Dan—screaming. Crying. Being reduced to a babbling idiot, because that's what she'd been—the world's biggest idiot to ever trust a white man. To trust an Armstrong.

And Cecil Armstrong had the pictures to prove just how much of an idiot she'd been. She'd believed Dan when he said he would protect her, when he told her they were safely hidden at the cabin. Lies. All lies. He wasn't even answering her calls now. For all she knew, he was already back in Texas. Maybe he'd already called that Tiffany. Maybe Rosebud had never meant anything to him beyond a means to an end—the end of everything.

"What do you want?" Somehow, she was able to talk.

His voice still seemed far away, but that shark smile was close enough to bite her. "What I want is very simple, Miss Donnelly. I want all past, current and future legal proceedings against Armstrong Holdings dropped. And I'll tell you what else—I'll tell you what I don't want. I don't want to see you in court tomorrow. In fact," he went on, like this whole conversation was the most natural thing in the world, "if you show up, a website named RosebudDonnellyHasSex.com will go live from a remote location. Someone already had the domain name RosebudDoesDan.com," he said with a chuckle.

Scalped alive, that's what this felt like, but instead of taking her hair, he was taking her soul. She'd let herself get conned into falling in love and conned right out of her home, her life.

Her hands were flipping through the photos again, and her

eyes couldn't look away. Dan's face was hard to make out because his head was buried in her breasts in most of the shots, but Armstrong was right. She photographed well. Everybody would see. Everybody would know about her betrayal.

"You've got until tomorrow to think about it. And you can keep those for your scrapbook. I have others." She heard the briefcase shut. "Miss Donnelly, it's been a pleasure." She felt a hand stroke her arm. "A *real* pleasure."

From the other side of the ocean, the door shut. And Rosebud lost the world.

Sixteen

"Maria?" Dan stuck his head into the kitchen. She was where she always was, making something for lunch that promised to be good. A pan of muffins sat cooling next to her, ready to take to Rosebud today. "Cecil's not here. Do you know where he went?"

Maria's head popped up and she looked around like she was worried about something. "No. He left *muy* early today."

"Huh." It was Thursday. If Cecil left the office at all, he did it on Saturday. Something wasn't right. "Thanks," Dan said, digging out his cell phone as he turned to go. He needed to check in with Rosebud.

"Señor Armstrong? I…"

The way Maria said it—all nervouslike—pulled him up short. He turned back around and saw her twisting her hands in her apron. She was always a timid woman, but right now she looked like she was on the verge of disappearing entirely. "What is it?" he asked in his calmest voice.

"I found…*something.*"

The hair on the back of his neck shot to attention. She'd found the *box*. He shut his phone off. "Where is it?" Maria scanned the room again, but no one else was in the house. "Is it here?"

"*Sí.* Come." She led him down into the basement—a place Dan had not been before—and over to a small metal door fastened to the wall. Without speaking, she opened the door and pulled out a garbage bag, which was covered with a thin layer of black dust.

Coal—a coal chute. He'd had no idea it existed. Dan peeled back the bag and there it was. The *box*. Twelve inches wide, three inches deep and almost two feet long, like a safety deposit box from an old, old bank. His pulse picked up the pace. He wasn't sure what was in here, but he had a hunch that it was enough to get Cecil out of the picture and save Rosebud's reservation. "When did you find it?"

"Two days ago." She was still whispering, even though they were in the basement. The whole place reeked of old onions and rotten potatoes.

"And it was here?" Maria might not realize it just yet, but she had the mother of all retention bonuses coming her way. "*How* did you find it?"

At that, she managed to look proud. "It was not in any place I clean. So I started looking in all the places I do not clean."

Dan fought the urge to hug the woman. "The key?" Although the key was secondary. If he had to, he'd bust this damn box open with a sledgehammer—although a busted box was harder to hide from Cecil, if he needed to keep it hidden.

"*Sí.*" The basement was dark, but he was sure he saw her wide smile. "Come."

They went back upstairs, Dan clutching the box to his chest. In the sitting room, she stood on tiptoe and reached up behind the mounted buffalo head hanging on the wall. She pulled out a small silver key on an Armstrong Holdings key chain. "I checked. It works."

"Maria, I love you." Which, of course, made her blush like a prairie fire, but he couldn't help it. "You will always have a job with me, okay? But no one knows about this. *No one,* got it?"

"Sí, señor."

Dan all but ran to his room. When he got there, he shoved the old dresser up against the door, just to be safe. Then he sat down on the bed and opened the box.

The first file was filled with detailed schematics for a lakeside resort. Dan stared at the plans in dumb shock. Over four hundred and twenty acres of golf, horseback riding and luxury hotel accommodations—all situated on the edge of the soon-to-be-constructed Dakota Lake. There was even a casino, because part of the resort was located on what was left of the Red Creek reservation.

So that was it. Dan was stunned. He hadn't come close to guessing Cecil's intent, branching out into real estate. The old man was financing construction with Armstrong Holdings money, but the resort would be all his.

He wasn't pushing the dam—he was pushing the reservoir. He was pushing beachfront property in South Dakota.

Finally, Dan set the resort plans aside, confident they would be enough to get Cecil permanently removed from Armstrong Holdings. He picked up the next file. At first, it was just lists of names, some with dates written next to them. He couldn't make heads or tails out of any of it. None of the names rang the slightest of bells. But then the lists began to include dollar figures in the hundreds of thousands next to the dates. The third list had job titles. *Royce Maynard, Chief Judge—$250,000; 4/12/10.*

Holy hell. Cecil had been bribing government officials.

His hands now shaking, Dan kept flipping until he got to a file marked *Indians*. A jump drive fell out when Dan opened the file folder. He grabbed the drive, but didn't get much further into the file before he got to names he recognized.

Rosebud Donnelly. It was circled, with a date written next to it that Dan recognized as his first meeting written above today's date—but no dollar amount. Joe White Thunder was there, as was Emily Mankiller. No money, just circles and dates. Near the back of the file, he found an envelope labeled Tanner Donnelly and dated over three years ago. He opened it and pulled out a set of dog tags.

He closed his eyes, not wanting to see any more. Not that he'd ever doubted Rosebud's murder theory, but there had always been the possibility that his uncle, his family—his *business*—wasn't involved. Not for a dam and not for a resort. But he held the proof in his hands.

Damn his hunches. Always proving themselves right.

There was more—much more—in the box, but Dan made the snap decision that ignorance was not only bliss, but also a matter of self-preservation.

He had to tell someone about this. His first inclination was to call Rosebud, but God only knew what that woman would do with hard evidence. She'd promised not to take another shot at him, but Cecil? Fair game.

He needed the authorities. What had that guy's name been? Tom…Yellow something? Dan dug into his wallet and found the card. Yellow Bird.

He turned his phone back on. One missed call from Rosebud, probably wondering where he was. He glanced at the clock. Man, he was late. Hell, it would take almost as much time to call her as it would to get there, and he needed some serious backup on this issue. Dan dialed Yellow Bird's number and then began putting the files back into the box.

"Yellow Bird," the gruff voice answered.

"This is Armstrong. Dan Armstrong." He locked the box. He couldn't afford to lose any of this, and he couldn't afford to give Cecil the chance to destroy the evidence.

"Officially or unofficially?" Yellow Bird asked after a long pause.

"I found something you've been looking for. I need to get it to the right person." What was that guy's name? Dan raced to his desk and flipped through his files. "Do you know who James Carlson is?"

"Don't jerk my chain, Armstrong." Yellow Bird's voice was sharp, but quieter, like he was trying not to be heard.

Dan bristled. "I can forget the whole damn thing if you'd like, Yellow Bird."

He heard Yellow Bird sniff. "I know Carlson. What do you have?"

"I'm not at liberty to say at this moment." All those weeks with Rosebud were wearing off on him. "Enough," he added.

"I'm going to hold you to that. Give me twenty." The line went dead.

That went well, Dan thought as he shoved his phone in his pocket and wrapped up the box in his pillowcase. If he floored it, he could be at Rosebud's office in twenty. He didn't even stop to grab the muffins.

He held all the winning cards, and he wanted to show her the hand.

The first thing that tipped him off was Judy—more specifically, the fact that she was crying. The second thing was when she looked up and saw him and physically recoiled in horror. The third thing was when she said, "What are you doing here?" like he'd just come back from clubbing baby seals.

If the hair on the back of his neck stood up any more, he'd be halfway to bald. "Is Rosebud here?"

"She left." The hatred in Judy's voice was unmistakable as she scooted back from her desk. If Dan didn't know any better, he'd think the woman was actually afraid of him.

He tried again, hoping to calm her down. "What happened?"

"What happened?" Judy gaped at him like he'd gone stupid. "What *happened* was that you didn't warn us that your uncle and some scary man named Shane Thrasher were going to show up an hour ago. What *happened* was that Joe had to escort that Shane guy out to his car because he had a gun under his coat. What *happened* was that your uncle left five minutes later, smiling like he'd won the freaking lottery, and what *happened* was that ten minutes after that, Rosebud walked out of here like she'd been zombified while you were nowhere to be seen. That's what *happened*."

"My uncle and Thrasher were here?" For a second, he didn't want to believe it. It was just not possible that Cecil would come here—with Thrasher, for God's sake—one day before the court date. The man never got his hands dirty.

"I'm sure you knew all about Cecil's visit, didn't you? Why else weren't you here? Oh, I should have warned Rosebud. I *did*. I told her to be careful with you—but did she listen to me?" Judy was a full five seconds from bolting down the hall, screaming bloody murder. "No. Instead, we let you in here, we let you bring us cookies and brownies, and we let you do..." Here she faltered, but the pause didn't last long enough for Dan to get a word in edgewise. "*Something* to her. And now it's all on *your* head."

She was talking like he'd set up Rosebud. Like he was already guilty just because of his last name. "Judy. You know me. You know I wouldn't do anything to hurt you—any of you." She didn't have a gun, but that hadn't stopped Dan's hands from going up. "Where did she go?"

"I'm not telling you anything. Get out!" Judy picked up the only weapon she had—the coffeepot—and threw it.

He was gone before it smashed behind him.

He'd start with Rosebud's house, he decided as he peeled out of the parking lot. Dan had only been there once—after the bar fight—and everything looked a little different in broad daylight. He tried calling her, but it went straight to voice mail, and he didn't think he could even get close to explaining himself in thirty seconds, so he kept trying.

As the phone rang and rang, he wavered between trying to figure out what Cecil had pulled and not wanting to know. Whatever it was, it was going to be bad. After all, the man had not only bought off public officials, but had even had at least one person killed. If Dan ever saw Thrasher again... Dan checked the glove box. He had enough shotgun shells to do the job right, law be damned.

Finally, he thought he recognized a dirt road. Another half mile down was a house that looked a hell of a lot more like a run-down shack than he remembered. The windows were spider-webbed with tape—more tape than glass, he guessed. No wonder she wouldn't let him visit her. This was what a top-flight lawyer could afford around here?

He was going to make this—all of it—up to her. He had to.

Dan was out the door, hauling the pillow-cased box with him. He was going to need all the backup he could get.

The first thing he noticed was the way a hard silence had come down on the world like a hammer. Nothing made a noise. Not even the wind managed to shush through the weeds.

"Rosebud, please!"

A woman's cry snapped through the silence like a pistol shot. Behind the house. Dan ran around the side just in time to see his Indian princess shake off Emily Mankiller like she was a fly. The older woman landed with a thud on her backside.

Emily saw him, too. During the one awful second when she looked up at him, he saw a world of hurt in her eyes. "No."

It was a warning—but not for Rosebud. For him.

Rosebud froze. She was wearing the buckskin dress with the moccasins. Her hair hung long and loose behind her, the ends blowing in a breeze he couldn't feel. She stood next to her paint horse, the reins in one hand. Her bag was slung over her shoulders.

He couldn't see her other hand.

The whole thing happened in slow motion. She turned around and locked eyes with him. It was like part of her wasn't even there—her eyes were dead. Zombified, Judy had said, and that wasn't far off.

She dropped the reins as her other hand came up, and Dan found himself staring down the barrel of a too-familiar pistol. Instinct kicked in. He let go of the box and stuck his hands up in the air. The box bounced off the tip of his boot, but not hard enough to make him break his stance.

"I should have known better." Her voice was mechanical, and despite how damn quiet the world had gotten, he could barely hear her over the rush of blood in his ears. "I *did* know better, but I..." She blinked at glacial speed, but the pistol didn't waver. "I have no excuse."

"Rosebud, don't!" Emily pleaded again.

"I don't know why you're so surprised. You're the one who told me to get close to him. You're the one who told me to muddle his thinking, to see what I could get out of him. I was just doing what I was told. Like I always do." Rosebud's voice cracked at the end. "I didn't want to. I didn't want to give anything up to you. I thought I could lead you on with a wink and a kiss and not lose who I was. I knew you were trouble, but I couldn't help myself." She laughed, a rote sound that held no pleasure. "I guess that makes me the naive one, doesn't it?"

A small sting quickly blossomed into a gut-clenching pain—not unlike the one time he'd tangled with a scorpion. She had been leading him on—the possibility had never occurred to him. He'd been too caught up in the chase, in the catch, to even realize that she was trying to catch him, too.

"I'm sorry!" Emily's cry was bordering on hysteria. "I didn't want it to be like this!" She turned to Dan. "She never told me anything nothing about you, I swear!"

The pain dulled, but only a little. He had no idea if he'd been double-crossed. But whether or not Rosebud had set him up was immaterial right now. He might be holding all the cards, but she was the one holding the gun.

He cleared his throat. He might be weaponless but he could still negotiate—although he'd never tried to close a deal when a gun was pointed at him. But he had no choice. "What happened?" Such a simple question. He could only hope it wouldn't get him shot.

Her lips curled up into a feral smile. "How nice of you to ask, but how unnecessary. You've seen the pictures. You helped Cecil set them up. Made sure that Thrasher got a good shot of my face and my…" Her eyes scrunched shut, like she was trying not to see something. He thought he saw her bite her inner lip.

Pictures? Oh, damn. He'd screwed up. He hadn't set her up, but that was immaterial. He'd promised Rosebud he wouldn't let anyone scare her. But he hadn't been able to protect her from his uncle and Thrasher. He'd let her down and, given the drop she had on him, he might not get the chance to apologize, much less make it right.

He made sure to keep his voice level, hoping that some

part of his calm would get through to her. "I didn't set up anything."

"You made me think I could trust you—that you cared about me." She sniffed then. He had no idea if she was crying for herself, or for what she was about to do to him.

"I love you."

"Words," she spat out. The gun jumped an inch, and he fought the urge to take cover. "Lies."

"The truth." She hadn't shot him yet, so he had that going for him. "When the dust settled and we got this dam thing figured out, I was thinking about asking you to marry me." It struck him as funny that it was the truth, but it was.

"You don't want a wife." He could see the tears that were just starting to spill over the edge. "You said so yourself."

"You would never be *just* my wife, darlin'. You will always be my equal."

She softened, and the gun barrel dipped a good half foot. "Dan…"

Keep talking, he prayed. The more she talked, the better chance he stood.

"Whatever he did—whatever pictures he took—I'll make him pay. Believe me, he'll get what's comin' to him."

She trained the gun back on his face. "Fool me once, shame on me. Fool me twice…" She cocked the hammer.

Dan's cell phone rang from deep in his pocket. The unexpected noise made them both jump, and she eased the hammer back down.

"This is important," he said as he slowly dug the phone out of his pocket. She barked out a harsh laugh, but didn't stop him. Yeah, he agreed. What could be more important than being held at gunpoint? But he thought he knew who was calling him. "Armstrong."

"Dan Armstrong?"

"Yeah."

"Carlson here."

"James Carlson?" At the mention of his name, Rosebud jolted with enough force that her horse skittered a step away from her.

"Special counsel for the Department of Justice. Thomas Yellow Bird said you might have something I want."

"Depends on what it is you're looking for."

"Do you know Rosebud Donnelly?"

Dan looked at the woman who was currently not acting in the capacity of a lawyer. "She's here with me now." Rosebud jumped again, the confusion plain on her face. "She contacted you some time ago about her brother's death and a possible connection to my uncle, Cecil Armstrong."

"You sound like a man up-to-date on the situation. Do you have something I can use?"

"Use for what?"

"You tell me what you've got, and I'll let you know if I can use it."

What the hell was this—a game? The arm he was still holding over his head was beginning to tingle. Time to lay his cards on the table. "I found a box of my uncle's. It's got plans for a waterfront resort, as well as lists of names, dates and dollar amounts. I think Tanner Donnelly's dog tags are there, too."

Both women gasped, and Emily broke into tears.

"Dollar amounts?" At least Carlson no longer sounded like he was playing a game of chess.

"I think he bought off some judges to make sure things went his way. I didn't recognize any of the names."

"Mr. Armstrong, you should know that we at the DOJ are pursuing an indictment of Cecil Armstrong and Armstrong Hydro on RICO charges. Your information will be invaluable."

Wait—Armstrong Hydro? It was hard to think straight,

what with the gun and the phone and the sobbing aunt and the zombified Indian princess. "What do I get in return?"

Carlson didn't say anything at first. "What do you want?"

"Leave my company out of this. Cecil left Texas five years ago and has been operating independently ever since."

"I'm not sure I can do that."

"Then I burn the box."

"That's uncalled for, Mr. Armstrong."

His hand was completely asleep now, but Rosebud still had the gun trained on him. "I'll give you all the evidence I have if you leave my company out of it. And you have to leave Rosebud out of it, too."

Another pause, this time longer. Dan wondered if the call was being recorded or traced. "Now why would I *have* to do that?"

"I think Cecil's trying to blackmail her." She jabbed the gun in his direction again, but this time he saw past it. Her face—blotchy and red and furious and hurt—told him he was spot-on. "I think he's got photos of her—compromising photos. I want them destroyed. No one else sees them. No one."

"Who else is in them?"

Dan swallowed the last shred of his pride. "Me."

Carlson said nothing for a painful minute. "You said she's there?"

"Yes."

"What's she doing?"

"Well, right now, she's got a gun pointed at me."

Carlson whistled. "Those must be some photos. Let me talk to her."

"James Carlson wants to talk to you," Dan told Rosebud. Moving as slowly as he could, he held out the phone.

Maybe her hand was getting tired, too, because the gun

was anything but steady. In one quick motion, she reached out and snatched the phone from him. "It's me."

Me? Something about the way she said it hit Dan as more than just two lawyers talking, but he was in no position to get his nose bent out of shape about it.

"No, I—yes." She scrunched her eyes shut tight, and for some reason, Dan was reminded of the first time he'd recognized her in the parking lot. She looked miserable, but her voice didn't waver at all—just like when she'd lost it after the bar fight and told him she hoped crying didn't affect his opinion of her in the courtroom. "They're awful, James. Everything. *Everything.*"

Thrasher must have found the cabin. That was the only logical explanation. He must have found the cabin, and them in it.

One box of shotgun shells wasn't going to be enough.

"He said—" Here she hiccuped, but had herself back under control in a second. "Cecil said that if I showed up in court tomorrow, he had a website that was going to go live. He has…he has video." She managed to get the last bit out, but finally the sobs had started.

Hot rage filled him. It was one thing to have pictures of him—but what Cecil was doing to Rosebud was beyond the pale. He had to pay—him and Thrasher.

"But I—yeah. Yeah. Do I have your word?" In no great hurry, she lowered her weapon. "I know. I understand. I will. No, I won't. Promise." Gun finally pointing at the ground, she held the phone out to him. "He wants to talk to you again."

Dan's first instinct was to get the gun, but sudden movement seemed like a bad idea right now, considering the fingers on one hand had completely fallen asleep. "Carlson?"

"Here's the deal, Armstrong. You give me Cecil, and you can keep your company. The company will plead no contest to bribing public officials and will be fined for an amount equal to, but not greater than, the amount of money paid in bribes."

"And Rosebud?"

"I can't destroy the photos—yet. I explained to her that blackmail is a serious charge. But I'll hold them under lock and key, and I promise they will never be made public."

"How do I know I can trust you?"

"Didn't she tell you about me?"

The lightbulb went off. "James—from law school?"

Rosebud nodded.

"I promise you—I won't let this out. But we need the site to go live, at least for a few minutes. She's got to go to court tomorrow."

"No."

"Five minutes, that's all I'm asking. Five minutes, and we'll have enough to put him away on blackmail alone. She's already agreed."

"Is that what you want?" he asked Rosebud.

"I made a mistake," she said. Her voice was as flat as three-day-old soda. "This is the price I've got to pay."

"Oh, and I told her not to shoot you," Carlson added as an afterthought. "You're a material witness now."

"Thanks. What about Cecil?"

"Yellow Bird is on his way to get the evidence. The moment the site goes live, we'll arrest Cecil. Yellow Bird thinks a man named Thrasher is our hit man, so we'll pick him up then, too."

Damn it. He wouldn't get the chance to make Thrasher beg for his life. He could only hope Yellow Bird would do it for him. "What do you want me to do?"

"Humor the old man—and don't kill him, okay? This is bigger than just your uncle. Yellow Bird has the details."

Chief Judge, that one entry had said. "You're going to roll him?"

Carlson exhaled into the phone, a man tired by a long fight. "I'm going to try. Either way, I need him alive. Can you do that, or do I need to send Yellow Bird to pick you up, too?"

Not killing Cecil was asking a lot of a man, but Rosebud was staring at him. "I get the company, Rosebud stays out of it and you get Cecil. That's the deal?"

"That's the deal."

"Done."

"I'll be in touch."

"What happened?" Emily had managed to right herself. She edged toward Rosebud. "Dear?"

"I…" Rosebud looked down at her hand and seemed to notice she was holding a gun. "Oh. I'm—I said I wouldn't do that again."

Considering the circumstances, he wasn't sure if an incoherent Rosebud was such a good thing or not. "It's all right."

"It's not! I— Oh, my God. I messed up. I messed up everything." Unexpectedly, she whirled, leaping onto her paint's back with surprising agility, considering the horse wasn't even wearing a saddle. The horse reared back, just enough that Dan could see she still had the gun in her hand. Then the two of them took off down the road before cutting through some tall grass and disappearing behind a low hill.

Something clamped down on his arm. It was only then that he realized he'd tried to run after her. He looked down to see Emily's strong hand gripping him. "No," she said again. "It's not safe for you."

"Not safe for me?" As if the last ten minutes had been a picnic? He shook her off—but not so hard that she lost her footing. "You tried to set me up."

Her eyes went wide in alarm. "We didn't know—"

His phone rang. Giving Emily a final glare, he walked away and did the only thing he could.

He answered it.

Seventeen

Cecil's yahoo lawyer said something and the old man laughed. It took every last bit of Dan's self-control not to crack those two heads together, and he was running low in the self-control department right now. He was operating on less than two hours of broken sleep. Every time his eyes had closed last night, he'd seen Rosebud's face, flitting between dangerously blank and shattered. He'd started awake, and then lain there, wondering where she was and if she was okay. She wasn't answering her phone, and he'd stopped checking with Emily at midnight.

He was having a hard time figuring out where to look in the courtroom. If he looked straight ahead, he'd be staring at Cecil, and he couldn't look at Cecil without the world getting red around the edges. He was real proud of the fact that, when Cecil had asked him yesterday evening how his meeting with "that Donnelly woman" had gone with a sick smile on his face, Dan had come up with some load of bull about her not feeling well. Thomas Yellow Bird had said to be clueless, so Dan was doing clueless. So far, Cecil was buying it.

If Dan looked to his left, he'd be forced to look at Thrasher, making a whole hell of a lot more than just the edges of the world go red. Dan wanted to reach across the divider and rip that slime-filled smile right off his face. Slowly.

If Dan looked to his right, he'd see the spot where Rosebud was supposed to be preparing for her court case today. The table was empty. No one from the tribe was here. Not even Councilwoman Emily Mankiller.

He'd desperately wanted to go after Rosebud, but Yellow Bird had called. Dan had to hand over the box and be convinced not to go all vigilante on the assholes sitting less than two feet in front of him. He wasn't supposed to alarm Cecil, so he'd been forced to have dinner with the man, forced to fake mild confusion at Rosebud's sudden "illness" right before the big day and forced not to sneak out and go looking for her. Hell, it had been hard enough answering his cell phone without spooking Cecil.

Cecil and Thrasher would be taken care of by the justice system. His company was in the clear and the tribe would keep their land. This was supposed to be the big victory. It didn't feel like it, though. Not yet. How was he supposed to fix the mess still between him and Rosebud when he couldn't even find out where she'd gone? He got that she was upset. Hell, he was furious about the whole thing. She'd taken a big risk by trusting him, and it had blown up on her. But she *had* to know it wasn't his fault. He had to prove to her that he was the man she'd fallen in love with, the man she could still trust.

He wanted them to leave here, get away from the memories they were both desperate to forget and make some new ones, untainted ones. They could go back to his estate in Texas. He'd introduce her to his mother, and Rosebud would see then that Dan wasn't an Armstrong like Cecil, but one like his father and his mother, someone better. Someone who would honor her as long as they both lived.

But he couldn't apologize, much less propose, if he couldn't find her.

Aside from a few local reporters, Yellow Bird was the only other person in the courtroom. He was sprawled out on a bench three rows behind Dan. Yellow Bird had found the one spot in the courtroom that streamed sunlight, so he had on his shades. Dan couldn't tell if Yellow Bird was watching him or Cecil, but he was pretty sure Yellow Bird had orders to shoot either of them if the setup went south.

"All rise," the bailiff intoned. "The Honorable Royce Maynard, presiding."

Dan did a double-take as he stood. Royce Maynard? Damn it all. Dan should have immediately realized that the judge on Cecil's list was the one presiding over the trial today. That meant that Rosebud would have lost her case today, no matter what. They wouldn't have been able to stop Cecil if Maria hadn't found the lockbox of evidence.

Dan had no idea what to think about Rosebud's disappearance. On the one hand, if Rosebud made it, the site would go live. He didn't want her to have to go through that, but he wanted to see her again. He needed one more chance to convince her that he'd do anything for her.

On the other, if she didn't show, they'd lose the blackmail charge, what Carlson had called the kind of insurance money couldn't buy. There was a small chance Cecil would go free without the blackmail charge as backup. If that happened, Dan would have a very hard time stopping the construction that was ready to begin. But at least Rosebud's public humiliation level would be a hell of a lot lower.

"Court is now in session," the bailiff said as Judge Maynard settled his considerable girth onto the bench.

"Be seated." Maynard glared at the lopsided courtroom. "Where is the attorney for the Red Creek tribe?"

Dan kept his face as benign as possible. On the take, but putting on a hell of a show. This country didn't need crooks ruling on matters of life and death, because that's what this was. A matter of life and death for her tribe. If she didn't show up…

"Here," a thin voice called out from the back of the courtroom. "I'm here, Your Honor."

Dan spun in his seat. Rosebud stood in the doorway, wearing her one-and-only suit. She had a white-knuckle grip on her briefcase, but her face was unreadable, betraying no emotion of any kind. She had her game face on, that much was clear as she walked into the room with the same confidence he'd been confronted with when he'd first accused her of shooting his hat. She could do this, he realized. Pride swelled in his chest as he watched her walk down the aisle.

She was the most amazing woman he'd ever met.

As she passed him, however, he got a better look at her. Her confidence didn't reach her eyes. In fact, her eyes didn't move. They didn't see him, Cecil or even the judge. Dan wasn't sure she was even *in* there. It might not be obvious to anyone except him, but she was operating on autopilot.

He saw blood red again as his gaze swung back to Cecil. At least he didn't have a gun—and he was sure Rosebud didn't, either. She couldn't have gotten one past the metal detector—he hoped.

Cecil snorted as Rosebud sat down at her table. He leaned over and whispered something to Thrasher that made him laugh out loud before Cecil pulled out his cell phone and made the all-important call.

"You're late, Ms. Donnelly." Judge Maynard's voice boomed into the room.

"My apologies to the court," Rosebud said. Her voice was

strong and confident. Despite it all, she was still one hell of a lawyer.

"Mr. Armstrong, court is in session," Maynard boomed even louder. "Whatever it is, it can wait."

"Of course, Your Honor." Cecil snapped his phone shut and sat there looking smug.

Dan wasn't going to make it without punching someone. That phone call was obviously related to the site going live, just like Cecil had promised. Everything was going according to plan, but Dan wasn't sure how much more of this plan he could take. He wanted Rosebud back. He wanted to show her that he hadn't set her up. He wanted Cecil and Thrasher to pay.

He wanted blood.

The judge asked if either side had a statement. To Dan's surprise, Rosebud said, "Yes." She stood. "Your Honor, the Lakota have survived smallpox, the iron horse and the United States Army. We survived the Black Hills gold rush, the death of the buffalo and the reservation. We have survived the white man's schools, his treaties and his greed."

She was doing it, he marveled, defending her case while Cecil ground her dignity into the dust. Whatever happened between them after this was over, he'd do his damndest to make sure she knew how proud he was of her.

"We have survived…" Her eyes scrunched shut, but her voice remained strong. "Intimidation, murder and blackmail."

Someone snorted. Dan thought it was Thrasher. Rosebud didn't appear to hear it. "We, the people of the Red Creek Lakota, have endured in the face of tragedy and horror. But if you allow the Dakota River to be dammed and the land flooded, you will sentence us to a fate worse than personal…" she paused long enough to clear her throat "…embarrassment, a fate worse than death. You will be accomplishing what all white men before you have failed to do—you will be condemning us to oblivion. You will erase the Red Creek tribe."

A swell of pride surged up in Dan's chest and managed to block out his simmering rage. Cecil hadn't beaten her. How could he have ever thought the old man could? She was stronger than that. He ached in ways he hadn't thought possible. She had to know he loved her, right?

The lawyer representing Dan's company got up and began to talk in bold, sweeping terms about "progress" and "action." Dan sat, not moving a muscle, because if he moved, he would lunge, and if he lunged, Yellow Bird would probably shoot him in the butt.

The lawyer droned on and on. All the while, Dan wondered what the hell Carlson was waiting for. Where was he? The website had to have gone live by now—what else did he need?

"I've reviewed the case," Maynard said after the yahoo lawyer finally sat down. "I find that the grounds for a preliminary injunction against Armstrong Hydro are baseless. Judgment for the defendant."

Time seemed to slow down as the gavel swung. Dan had just enough time to think, *this is it,* before the courtroom doors slammed open behind him. Suddenly, the number of people in the courtroom jumped as uniformed officers rushed in.

About time, Dan thought, as he shot out of his seat. He had to get to Rosebud. Now.

"What is going on here? Order! *Order!*" Maynard howled as he banged the gavel.

Dan jumped the barrier, dodging an officer and hoping he wasn't about to get shot. "Rosebud," he said as he knelt before her.

Her eyes closed as her head tilted away from him. Nope—she wasn't going to pull that stoic crap on him, not after everything they'd been through. He hadn't done anything wrong, damn it. He *loved* her.

"*Look* at me," he ordered. He managed to keep his voice gentle, but only just.

A tall man wearing an expensive suit strode into the room. "Your Honor, James Carlson, special counsel for the Department of Justice. I have a warrant of arrest for Cecil Armstrong." He handed the warrant to Cecil, who dropped it like it was radioactive.

"A warrant? On what charges?" Wasn't that just like Cecil, Dan thought. Ballsy to the very end.

Suddenly, shouts of "Get down, get down!" filled the room. A shot rang out. Without thinking, Dan threw his body over Rosebud's, knocking her off her chair and onto the floor. She grunted as he landed on top of her.

"Are you okay?" he asked, even as he realized it was a dumb question. So he tried again, searching her face. "Are you hurt?"

Her body was stiff under his, and her eyes scrunched shut tight. Maybe her confidence had been more bravado than he'd thought, because she looked like she was about to pass out. Then she said, "Just…tell me when it's over."

The pain that racked her voice cut through all Dan's redness, through the shouting and the sound of furniture scraping and breaking. At that moment, nothing in the world mattered as much as Rosebud. Screw everything—Cecil, the company, the dam—all of it. The only thing he cared about was this woman. His woman.

"I will. I won't let them hurt you anymore."

Nodding, she swallowed—and turned her face into Dan's neck. Her whole body curled into his, and suddenly she was right back where she belonged.

For what felt like the first time today, he took a deep breath. "It's okay," he murmured as he wrapped his arms around her. She clutched his jacket, pulling him closer. Relief flooded his system. "I'm here. You're here. You were amazing. Ferocious in the courtroom."

"I had to," she whispered, her breath warm against his skin. "I had to do it for the tribe. For Tanner." A piece of wood snapped and someone groaned. She shuddered. "Don't leave me."

She still needed him. She still trusted him. He pulled her as far into his arms as he could without crushing her. He didn't know if the gunfire was over or not, but he'd take whatever came his way—anything to keep her safe. "I won't."

Shouting was followed by the splintering of more wood giving up the fight, and then there was a moment of awkward calm. Dan hazarded a look over his shoulder.

Yellow Bird had Thrasher on the ground, a knee against his neck. One of them was bleeding, but no one acted like it was fatal. "I've been waiting three years to say this, you dog. You're under arrest for the murder of Tanner Donnelly," Yellow Bird said through gritted teeth.

Rosebud's chest heaved against his. "Is it over yet?"

"Almost, babe. Almost." For her sake, he prayed it was true.

"Bailiff, holster your weapon and clear this courtroom!" Maynard roared. "Now!"

Carlson stepped up to the bench and handed Maynard his own piece of paper. "Your Honor, with all due respect, he can't do that. You're under arrest for accepting bribes."

"Get your hands off me!" It was wrong to find so much satisfaction in the note of terror in Cecil's voice. But Dan found it anyway. "Dan, do something!"

"I'm not going anywhere," Dan whispered. He gave Rosebud a final squeeze before he rose and pivoted on the balls of his feet. Keeping one hand on her arm, he made sure his body was between her and his uncle. She remained curled

against his back as he surveyed the room. The place was in
shambles—more like a raid in a drug den than a house of law.

"Dan." Cecil still sounded defiant.

Dan glanced at his uncle. Cecil's arms were cuffed behind
him. Yellow Bird was just hauling Thrasher to his feet. The
bailiff, who had a bloody nose, had his gun trained on that
slime-bag. Thrasher must have tried to get the bailiff's
weapon. Even Maynard had his hands up, the sleeves of his
robe pooling in his armpits as an officer read him his rights.

"Dan?" Cecil said again. The defiance was fading fast,
replaced with stark terror. "Dan, please—I'm your uncle!
We're kin!"

Go on, Dan thought. *I want you to beg.* But he didn't say it,
because that wasn't what Rosebud needed to hear. He turned
his attention back to her. "It's safe now," he said, keeping his
voice as calm as he could. "He can't hurt you anymore."

A stream of curse words burst out of the old man's chest,
but Dan didn't pay him any mind. He waited for Rosebud.

It was her move.

Even though Rosebud was behind Dan, he kept his hands
on her arms, making sure she was protected. She didn't want
to look. She didn't want to see if someone had been killed,
didn't want to see Cecil Armstrong or Shane Thrasher. She
didn't want to see any guns, and she didn't want to see if one
was pointed at her or Dan.

For a fleeting, incomprehensible second, she had a powerful urge to click her heels together and say, "There's no place
like home," as if that would magically make this whole awful
week disappear into thin air.

"Ms. Donnelly?" James asked, sounding very much like
the lawyer he was now, not the lover he'd once been. "Are
you unhurt?"

Right. James was here. Dan was here. Cecil was here, for

God's sake—unless someone had shot him. No amount of
ruby-red slippers would whisk her away from this, so she'd
better snap out of it. She let herself breathe in Dan's scent
before she pushed herself away from his back. His hands
dropped to his sides.

"Mr. Carlson," she said.

On one hand, the formality was ridiculous. James had seen
her naked, after all, and had probably looked at those photos
to boot. On the other hand, the only other person in the world
who knew that James had seen her naked was Dan. As far
as the rest of the world was concerned, James Carlson and
Rosebud Donnelly had gone to law school together—nothing more than that—and she was damn sure going to keep it
that way.

She took a second to straighten her skirt and dust off her
jacket before she stepped around Dan. That one second gave
her a chance to compose herself and put on her game face,
something that now felt foreign and stiff. She didn't feel like
the lawyer she used to be. She didn't want to be a ball-buster
anymore. Her life wasn't her case—the case was over, but
she was still standing. Problem was, she didn't know what
else she could do.

Well, first things first, and the first thing was to get the
hell out of this courtroom. She squared her shoulders and
stuck out her chin as she opened her eyes. The extent of the
damage immediately made her wish she hadn't. The courtroom looked like downtown Baghdad. The barrier was crum-
pled against the first row of spectator seats. The defendant's
table was in about forty pieces. And, of course, there were a
few deputies aiming guns with the safeties off.

In the middle stood James. He looked older, his hair already picking up some salt at the temples. He seemed more
like a politician now, and with this sort of coup, he'd be in a
position to run for office. He'd be good at that, she thought.

He smiled at her—not that anyone else could tell, but she knew that when his lips thinned like that, he was pleased. And looking around at three years of his hard work in handcuffs, Rosebud knew he was very pleased.

"Ms. Donnelly, your government thanks you for your patience in this matter," he said, extending his hand for a formal handshake. "I want to personally thank you for your cooperation."

"I expect justice to be served," she said, feeling the barest hint of warmth spread from his hand to hers. He'd never loved her, that she knew. But he'd cared for her. And as he patted the top of her hand, she knew that he still cared for her. "I held up my end of the deal. May I safely assume you held up yours?"

He gave her hand a squeeze, which had the same effect as a comforting hug. "The site was live for one minute before I took it down personally," he replied. "No one saw."

Rosebud felt herself breathe for the first time in what felt like days. "I expect it to stay that way."

"Absolutely." He glanced toward Dan, the look on his face somewhere between jealous and all business as he gave her hand one last squeeze.

Rosebud got the hint. She turned to Dan and held out her hand. Without hesitation, he laced his fingers with hers and stepped up until he was standing hip-to-hip with her. Immediately, she felt his warmth surround her. She felt safe with him beside her—like nothing bad could happen. He rubbed his thumb over her knuckles as she said, "Have you met Dan Armstrong?"

"Not in person. Mr. Armstrong," James said as the two men shook hands. "The Department of Justice owes you a debt of gratitude for everything you've done here."

Rosebud couldn't help but notice that the grip went on a little too long—and that both men were clenching their jaws.

Men, she thought with an inner snort of disgust. Even so, she felt a little flattered, in a primeval sort of way.

A strange noise drew her attention away from Dan and James. It sounded like someone was strangling a cat.

"You did this?" Ah. Cecil Armstrong was all but blue in the face as he sputtered. *"You?"*

In a flash, Rosebud didn't so much *see* as *feel* the victory. After three long years, justice was served. A sense of righteous power flowed through her. She'd won. All it had cost her was…everything. Her brother, her life for all those years, her dignity…

The righteousness was short-lived. So she'd won.

Now what?

Then Dan settled his hand around her waist and pulled her in close. "We had a deal, Carlson."

"So we did." James's eyes cut from Dan back to Rosebud. "You have my word."

Dan shook his hand again as Cecil went from bluish to a bruised purple. Not that Dan noticed. He was focused on James. "Do you need either of us for anything else?"

"I think we're good. We've got the box."

"You!" Cecil was stuck on the one word, apparently. Good, Rosebud thought. He could just be stuck—for the rest of his life. He went well past conniption fit and into hysterics.

Dan had been working *with* James. He'd been working *against* Cecil. Somehow, in the midst of her embarrassment and turmoil, she'd gotten things wrong. Dan hadn't set her up—far from it. He'd been with her the whole time. He'd stuck to the plan, just like he'd said he would. After all, he was a man of his word. The back of her neck flushed hot.

"Where can I reach you?" James asked, also ignoring the impotent old man in shackles. Because that's what Cecil was now. Dan was right. Cecil Armstrong couldn't hurt her anymore, not as long as Dan was by her side.

Dan let go of her waist long enough to fish out his card. Two, actually. "That's my cell, and the other one is Betty Armstrong's home number. She's my mother. You can reach me and Rosebud there."

"Wait, what?" His mother was in Texas. Suddenly, Rosebud didn't know what was happening again.

Dan looked down at her and grinned. His hand wrapped around hers. Rosebud felt the flush spread all the way down her back. "I promised her I wouldn't marry you before she met you, so I thought we'd better get that out of the way, real quicklike." He turned his attention back to James. "We can go to Texas, right?"

Dan was going take her to meet his mother. He was going to marry her—real quicklike. "If you want to go to Texas," he added, his voice dropping several notches as his fingers tightened around her hand. "Do you want to go with me?"

James regarded them both with a stern eye. "Ms. Donnelly, we will not be pressing charges against Dan Armstrong. We believe he had no knowledge in *any* of Cecil Armstrong's illicit activities."

Somewhere in the next world, Tanner was nodding with approval.

Dan hadn't known about the photos. Dan had nothing to do with that awful website. Dan, she knew now, deep in her soul, hadn't set her up.

Dan wanted to marry her.

James cleared his throat. "Ms. Donnelly, do you want to go to Texas with Mr. Armstrong?" Nothing like a little cross-examination during the most important moment of her life.

Everyone in what remained of the courtroom stood silent. Even Cecil Armstrong was quiet, his mouth wordlessly opening and shutting as the world waited on her answer.

"Come with me," Dan whispered. "Just you and me. Dan and Rosebud. That's all I want. That's all I've ever wanted."

She opened her mouth, but nothing came out.

She closed her eyes and breathed. Sandalwood and musk—Dan's scent—filled her nose. Her hand found his chest and she felt his heart pounding. She knew if she leaned forward just a little, she'd be able to taste his breath with a kiss.

She leaned against Dan's chest, letting a flush steal over her body.

Just Dan and Rosebud.

Right now, that was all she wanted, too.

"Mr. Carlson, if you need me, I'll be in Texas."

Epilogue

In December, Shane Thrasher pled guilty to first-degree manslaughter, among other charges, and was sentenced to twenty-five years in jail, with the possibility of parole. In exchange for his plea, he testified about the work he'd done for Cecil Armstrong for four years. He was on the stand for six days.

Almost a year later, Cecil Armstrong was convicted of racketeering, bribing officials and conspiracy to commit murder, among other charges. He was sentenced to thirty-five years in prison without the possibility of parole, which, given the fact that he was seventy-three at the time, amounted to a life sentence. An audit of his books had revealed he'd misappropriated millions of Armstrong Holdings' funds in his pursuit of beachfront property in the middle of South Dakota. However, he never offered up any justification for his actions.

The only member of the Armstrong family in court that day was Betty Armstrong. She held hands with Emily

Mankiller as the sentence was handed down. Both women were escorted from the courtroom by Thomas Yellow Bird and offered no comment to the throngs of reporters waiting outside.

The sensationalist nationwide coverage of the trial led to a measurable uptick of visitors to the Historic Bonneau Homestead and Museum, former headquarters of Armstrong Hydro. The museum's curator and caretaker, Maria Villerreal, reported that, on average, a hundred visitors a day were coming to listen to her tours. Her sons made pocket money selling homemade cookies and lemonade. On the day her former boss was sentenced, no fewer than thirty reporters crowded the house. Maria gave them all brownies, but not a comment on the trial or her current employers.

Dan Armstrong was too busy to attend the trial, except on days when he was called to testify. He divided his time between Armstrong Petroleum in Witchita Falls, Texas, and Armstrong Hydro in Sioux Falls, South Dakota. At the time of the sentencing, he was busy supervising construction of the Red Creek dam, a run-of-river dam on the Dakota ten miles south of the Red Creek Indian reservation. The Red Creek tribe owned half the dam, and more than half of the workers were members of the tribe. Joe White Thunder was out there with them, swinging a hammer in time like he was beating a drum.

Rosebud Armstrong chose to avoid the lengthy trial entirely. Instead, she focused her efforts on joining an ongoing multitribal lawsuit against the Bureau of Indian Affairs for mismanagement of tribal funds. The case had already made it through the U.S. Court of Appeals on its way to the Supreme Court, where Rosebud became the first woman from her tribe to argue—and win—a case before the High Court. She discovered a renewed passion for the law, now that her life no longer depended on the outcome. She began to enjoy herself again.

After that sweeping victory, she took some doctor-ordered time off. On the day they led Cecil away in shackles, she sat in the nursery of the new ranch house that overlooked the Dakota River and finished Tanner's baby quilt. Lewis's was already on the crib. The twins were due in two weeks, but given how much they kicked, she hadn't been sure she'd make it. At first, the bed rest had driven her nuts. But she'd taken up her needle and thread again, rediscovering a part of her that she'd thought she'd lost.

She was happy here in this new home built on neutral territory, just Dan and Rosebud. Her family was close by, and they made frequent trips to Texas. It had become all she'd ever wanted.

Soon enough, though, it would be Dan and Rosebud and Tanner and Lewis.

She was more than happy here.

She was home.

* * * * *

A sneaky peek at next month...

Desire™

PASSIONATE AND DRAMATIC LOVE STORIES

2 stories in each book - only £5.49!

My wish list for next month's titles...

In stores from 17th August 2012:

☐ The Temporary Mrs King — Maureen Child

& The Paternity Proposition — Merline Lovelace

☐ A Perfect Husband — Fiona Brand

& A Scandal So Sweet — Ann Major

☐ Relentless Pursuit — Sara Orwig

& Ready for Her Close-up — Katherine Garbera

☐ Unfinished Business — Cat Schield

& The Ties that Bind — Emilie Rose

Available at WHSmith, Tesco, Asda, Eason, Amazon and Apple

Just can't wait?

Visit us Online

You can buy our books online a month before they hit the shops! **www.millsandboon.co.uk**

0812/51

Or fill in the form below and post it back to us

THE MILLS & BOON® BOOK CLUB™—HERE'S HOW IT WORKS: Accepting your free stories places you under no obligation to buy anything. You may keep the stories and return the despatch note marked 'Cancel'. If we do not hear from you, about a month later we'll send you 2 Desire™ 2-in-1 books priced at £5.49* each. There is no extra charge for post and packaging. You may cancel at any time, otherwise we will send you 4 stories a month which you may purchase or return to us—the choice is yours. *Terms and prices subject to change without notice. Offer valid in UK only. Applicants must be 18 or over. Offer expires 31st January 2013. **For full terms and conditions, please go to www.millsandboon.co.uk/freebookoffer**

Mrs/Miss/Ms/Mr (please circle)

First Name

Surname

Address

Postcode

E-mail

Send this completed page to: Mills & Boon Book Club, Free Book Offer, FREEPOST NAT 10298, Richmond, Surrey, TW9 1BR

Find out more at
www.millsandboon.co.uk/freebookoffer

Visit us Online

0712/D2YEA

The World of Mills & Boon®

There's a Mills & Boon® series that's perfect for you. We publish ten series and, with new titles every month, you never have to wait long for your favourite to come along.

Blaze®
Scorching hot, sexy reads
4 new stories every month

By Request
Relive the romance with the best of the best
9 new stories every month

Cherish™
Romance to melt the heart every time
12 new stories every month

Desire™
Passionate and dramatic love stories
8 new stories every month

Visit us Online

Try something new with our Book Club offer
www.millsandboon.co.uk/freebookoffer

M&B/WORLD2